BANE'S CHOICE

BANE'S CHOICE

ALYSSA

DAY

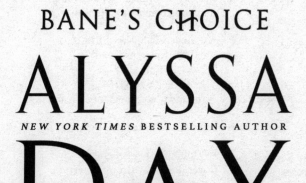

Entangled Publishing, LLC
10940 S Parker Road
Suite 327
Parker, CO 80134
Visit our website at www.entangledpublishing.com.

Amara is an imprint of Entangled Publishing, LLC.

Edited by Liz Pelletier
Cover design by Bree Archer
Cover art by Photographer Wander Aguiar,
DenisTangneyJr/GettyImages,
RuDVi/GettyImages and
draco77vector/Shutterstock
Interior design by Toni Kerr

Print ISBN 978-1-68281-475-8
ebook ISBN 978-1-68281-476-5

Manufactured in the United States of America

First Edition November 2020

AMARA

ALSO BY ALYSSA DAY

*To Liz Pelletier, whose enthusiasm and
grace are an inspiration.*

CHAPTER ONE

Bane raced through the night at the head of a band of thirty riders, the fury of a fierce territoriality burning through him.

Bent over his Harley, he hit a speed that would have been impossible for human reflexes and was almost too fast for most of the vampires on bikes behind him. He'd already heard the catastrophic sound of one of his club members smashing into the guardrail on that last hairpin turn. Maybe he or she would survive, not that Bane gave a fuck.

Club members were expendable.

Vampires were expendable.

Everybody was expendable.

Almost everybody, he remembered, just barely, to amend his thought. All but those he protected—those he could trust. He glanced to his right and then to his left and saw Luke and Meara keeping pace. Tonight's ride was not a recreational ride, done like so many, for an attempt to recreate the memory of the joy of being alive. The joy of charging down the road on a bike on a beautiful night in Georgia's sultry autumn.

Joy, like everything else in his life, had also apparently become expendable. He couldn't remember the last time he'd felt any emotion but rage—and he was currently experiencing a metric ass-ton of that.

Tonight, the Vampire Motorcycle Club was on a

mission—Bane's primary mission.

Death.

Three warlocks had entered his territory, and he'd be damned to the most fiery level of Hell before he'd let them establish a foothold anywhere near Savannah. His intel had reported that they'd set up a base in the Savannah National Wildlife Refuge, just over the border into South Carolina, as if arbitrary state borders set up by humans meant anything to his kind.

The warlocks had already bound more than a dozen people to them with blood magic, and they'd killed over a dozen more in their rituals.

Not that he gave a shit about protecting any humans who were not his allies. No, this was about something far more important. Protecting what was *his*. His people. His land. He'd laid claim to territory that included Savannah long, long ago, when he'd burned out the warlocks who'd come to town. They'd fought back and destroyed most of the city doing it, but ultimately, he'd prevailed.

And he'd be damned if he'd let the evil blood-magic-wielding fuckers get a foothold now. What he didn't understand was *why* it was happening. This was the third group in as many years to try to move in on him. After the way he'd destroyed the first two, he'd have thought everybody would get a fucking clue. Especially the Chamber, after he'd destroyed the last three delegations of "ambassadors"—read: conquerors—that they'd sent over the course of the past fifty or so years.

No Euro-trash group of dark magic practitioners was going to gain a foothold in his territory, no matter how powerful it was.

Edge, the club's director of intelligence, had pinpointed the warlocks' location to a shack bordering a freshwater marsh, all but hidden by the cypress trees surrounding it. Unluckily for them, nothing could hide from Edge for long. The man was lethal on two fronts—deadly as a vampire and equally dangerous as a brilliant computer hacker.

A little more than five miles out, Bane pulled into the parking lot of the Visitor Center and turned off his bike, breathing deeply of the clean night air, his senses honed to battle-readiness. Edge had cleared the space so the guards would be off duty—they'd find themselves with mysterious car breakdowns—and, when they did manage to make it to work, they'd find that the security cameras had malfunctioned.

Bane almost smiled at the memory of Edge's glee when he'd shown Bane the two-minute clip of baby otters playing with a ball that would loop continuously on the camera feed. In spite of everything he'd endured, the hacker still had a sense of humor about some things.

The rest of the group roared in behind him, until twenty-seven Harleys, parked in a rough circle, surrounded him.

"Samson's crash turned to fire. He's dead," one of the club members called out, anger harsh in his voice. "Maybe you could have slowed on some of those turns."

Bane pinned him with an icy stare. "Are you challenging me?"

The vampire immediately bent his head in submission. The rest of them froze in place, knowing what that look on their leader's face could portend.

All but Meara, who'd never been afraid of him once in

the centuries since they'd become brother and sister. And why would she? She was the daughter of the man who'd saved Bane's life—Bane's sister-in-blood, who'd been Turned at the same time as Bane, by the same vampire. He'd always protected her—she'd always protected him. Nothing was more important than family, even to a man who'd forgotten how to feel.

"We will compensate his people," she said, a flicker of something crossing her eyes. Regret, perhaps? He didn't know. Any softer emotions had long since been lost to him.

Bane focused on the mission and addressed the group. "The warlocks are mine. Luke and Meara will assist me, but they'll also help you. The people camped there are all under the influence of blood magic, so they'll be dangerous and very difficult to stop. They will also be completely unable to respond to reason." Warlocks possessed powerful magic of the darkest, most evil kind. Humans in thrall to it were as close to invulnerable as humans ever got.

"The warlocks will know we're coming when we're about a mile out, so go hell for leather after that," Luke, officially the club's Sergeant-at-Arms, told the group.

"Warlocks? Guy witches? That doesn't sound so bad," said a vampire who'd only been Turned within the past year and had evidently been useless when he was human, too.

"Warlocks can be male or female," Luke said. "Witches can also be male or female. The difference is that witches use benign, or earth, magic. Warlocks like to play with blood and death and worse things."

"Blood magic," Meara said. "It can be deadly to our kind. Let us handle the warlocks. We have experience at it."

Normally, Bane would never bring so many untested fighters on a job like this, but he needed them to keep the humans who'd been bloodthralled by the warlocks out of his way.

Unless he just killed them all.

In the old days, he would have. These days, with technology, disappearing humans caused more problems than he wanted to deal with, so he tried to leave fewer bodies in his wake.

The warlocks, though—they had to die. And when they were dead, he'd burn their bodies and salt the ashes. It was the only way to be sure that they wouldn't come back.

They were always worse when they came back.

"There's still time to change your minds and get out of here. The warlocks might have spelled the humans to use fire," Meara told them, looking around the circle. Somehow, shockingly, she still cared what happened to others.

Bane didn't. All he cared about right now was the hunt. He could feel the muscles in his body tense, readying for the fight, and his innate magic swirled to life inside him, eager to be unleashed.

"Come or not. If you don't show up, don't come back to the club. Ever," he growled. Then he raised one hand in the air and slashed it down, and every single one of them revved up their bikes and followed him to what very well might be their true deaths.

There were no cowards in the Vampire Motorcycle Club. A few were lunatics and sadists, maybe, but no cowards.

A flicker of something like satisfaction almost broke through his rage. The warlocks were in for a major surprise.

. . .

At the designated distance, Bane ditched the bike behind a tree and launched himself into the air. He couldn't use any magic of his own—not this close—their wards would detect and nullify it. But flight was natural to him, and they certainly wouldn't have warded against birds.

They'd just think he was a really big owl.

He soared over the canopy of trees, a rush of pre-battle adrenaline intensifying the fierce sensation of triumph that flying gave him. Turning vampire may have stolen the sun from him, but it had gifted him the sky. The sight of the more than twenty enthralled humans milling around didn't even slow him down. His people would take care of the humans.

The warlocks were his.

He was still smiling when he smashed through the roof of the shack.

All three were there—two men and a woman, robed in scarlet velvet that matched the blood of the human woman dying slowly and painfully in the center of an enormous, glowing pentagram carved into the wooden floor. The warlocks had been chanting and dancing before the fire; he'd seen it through the cracks in the rotting roof.

They weren't dancing now.

He saw in a glance that the human was beyond saving. They'd tortured her, of course, and undoubtedly eaten some of her internal organs while she lived, because their magic drew power from pain as well as from blood. Her death might end the spell, or it might make things worse by increasing its power.

The woman's agony broke the tie, because torture pissed him off. Kill if you must, but inflicting pain for its own sake was an offense against the laws of nature.

"Not in my territory, you nasty fucks," he snarled at the warlocks, who were still scrambling back and away from him. And then he snapped the dying human's neck.

Instantly, the reek of putrefaction and despair began to lessen. Their spells had been tied to her agony, then. The magic must have had an element of sound dampening, as well, because now the shouts and screams of the battle raging outside the cabin broke through.

"Marta, Otto, to me," one of the men—the tall, cadaverously thin one—shouted, holding out his hands. The other man and the woman rushed over to him and clasped his hands in theirs and began to chant. Tendrils of foul-smelling magic slithered up from the floor and started to coalesce in the corners and curl around the warlocks' feet.

Nausea swarmed up from Bane's gut to his throat, almost choking him—his body's automatic reaction to the blood magic.

But the fire of his rage burned through the nausea— burned through everything but the driving need to see their blood splashed on the ground.

To *end* them.

"No doubt casting a spell that will do truly horrible things to me," Bane said, his lips pulled back, fangs fully descended, not that he'd drink the blood of abominations like these. "You must be more powerful when you join hands. I can fix that."

With that, he blurred through the air and grabbed each

man by an arm, and then he ripped them off at the shoulder, ignoring the black blood that spattered in dual arcs across the room. He threw the arms into the old stone fireplace, where they immediately caught fire.

It was barely enough to slow them down.

Marta screamed out her hate and threw a spell at him that probably would have eviscerated him if he hadn't warded himself, Luke, and Meara before they came. His protection spells would have persisted even in the face of wards that blocked his battle magic, but depriving the warlocks of their victim had destroyed their wards.

Which would make the next few minutes a lot more fun for Bane and a lot less fun for the warlocks.

He grinned and flicked a stasis spell at Marta that knocked her back and pinned her against the wall of the shack. Just then, Luke and Meara burst in from windows on opposite sides of the room, blood dripping from a scrape on Meara's forehead.

"Starting all the fun without me," Meara said, leaping to his side and then whipping her daggers out of their sheaths and hurling them into Marta's throat. The warlock's spilled blood broke Bane's stasis spell, and she fell, but then she started crawling toward the dead woman in the pentagram. Horribly, she gurgled out laughter with the knives still in her throat, black blood bubbling out around the edges of the blade.

Luke, meanwhile, grabbed the tall man, who must have been the leader, by the back of the robe when he tried to flee. "Not this time."

A stinking, sulfurous wave of dark magic more powerful than any Bane had felt in three hundred years of existence hammered into him from behind, smashing him across the room and into the wall next to the fireplace so hard the entire cabin shook from the blow. He managed to turn in midair, though, and landed on his feet, immediately falling into battle readiness, his gut twisting in rebellion to the unnatural forces swirling through the air.

He'd known this would be bad.

He hadn't realized it would be something far, far worse than *bad*.

His skin tried to crawl off his body in reaction to the power stabbing into him—an unholy tidal wave of magic so foul that it could only come from a necromancer.

Luke was down, unconscious or dead, and Meara lay sprawled on the floor, eyes staring, unseeing, at the ceiling. Whatever the warlock had done, it had decimated Bane's wards, leaving Meara and Luke, who had no natural immunity to magic, at risk.

If the bastard had harmed them, he would die.

If he'd killed them, he would wish for death.

Bane started toward Meara, but an invisible force ripped a chunk of stone from the fireplace and hurled it at him, forcing him to dodge aside.

"Move again, and the next one crushes her head." The cold, dead voice that spoke the words preceded the speaker into the room. Unlike the three in the room, this warlock emanated power from his physical presence as well as his magic. He was tall and heavily muscled, with a gleaming bald head and a jutting nose. His thin lips were pulled away from his teeth in a sneer. "The Chamber sends its regards, bloodsucker. And our demand that you vacate the territory to your betters."

"If I had any betters, I might consider it," Bane said, stilling his rage to an icy calm. He could feel Meara and Luke now—they were alive. Unconscious, but alive.

He needed to use his brain—strength and magic would not be enough against this foe.

When the necromancer laughed, the three warlocks in the room started to convulse, pounding their heads against the floor, over and over. "Master," the male without a knife in his throat crooned. "Master Constantin, you will protect us."

"Clearly, I need to get better help," Constantin said, glancing down at them before returning his attention to Bane. "The Chamber warned me that you had magic, vampire, but they didn't know how strong you were. Seems that our intelligence was out of date. But you're still no match for me."

"Haven't seen one of your kind in more than a hundred years, necromancer," Bane said, his voice dangerously even. "After I kill you, I hope not to see another for at least as long."

"There are no others like me," Constantin boasted. "I am more powerful, more versed in the dark arts, more—"

But, by the third *more*, Bane had heard enough. He pulled on his own magic—fueled by the elements of Air and Water, fueled by the gravitational pull of the moon, fueled by starlight itself—and *shifted* through time and space.

But the necromancer was ready for him and blurred across the room in a magical shift of his own. Otto and the other male warlock, somehow still alive in spite of the blood pumping from the holes where their arms used to be, cried out to their master, beseeching.

Pleading.

Constantin made a downward slicing motion with both hands toward the men's heads, and Bane watched in disbelief as the tops of their skulls slid cleanly off, as if a razor-edged sword had sheared through bone and brain.

"If that's how you treat your own, it's a wonder the Chamber manages to recruit any new people at all," Bane said, shifting the currents of his magic to shield Luke and Meara.

"There are always fools," the necromancer replied, almost casually, pointing to Marta, who—in spite of what Constantin had just done—still crawled toward him, crooning, "Master, Master," again and again.

Luke and Meara now safe, Bane refocused his magic, channeling it into a single, deadly spear of invisible power, and then unleashed it, hurling it across the room at Constantin. The necromancer's head jerked up, his face contorting into a grimace. Then the necromancer flung both hands into the air, and two things happened at once: the wall behind Bane imploded, slamming into his back and knocking him to his knees, and the female—Marta—levitated into the air, Constantin using her as a human shield.

Bane's magic ripped her in two.

Bane leapt to his feet, gathering his power for another attack, but the necromancer's hands were already busy, flashing through the pattern of a complicated spell, fueled no doubt by Marta's death, that pushed waves of darkness and the stink of dread into the space around himself. Creating a portal to Hell, for all Bane knew.

"Another time, then, vampire," Constantin said. "Consider this a parting gift."

He stepped into the portal, and the shack exploded, raining wood, stone, and debris down on Bane, Luke, Meara, and the corpses of the three warlocks.

"No!" Bane shouted, smashing through the rubble, fighting his way to his family, pain searing through his chest. If his miscalculation had cost Luke and Meara their lives…

But Meara was already shoving splintered wood and rubble away from herself and standing. "What the hell kind of magic was that? I could hear and see what was happening, but it was like I was trapped in my body. I couldn't move… Luke? Where's Luke?"

Bane hurled stone and wood out of his way, digging for Luke, who suddenly started to moan and then sat up, pushing debris off his body.

"Ouch. What the fuck was that? Did you kill them? I hope you killed them all."

"Actually, no," Bane told him, holding out a hand to help him out. "The necromancer killed his own. This may be a much bigger problem than we thought."

"Chamber," Meara said grimly.

"Chamber," he agreed.

"We're going to have to kill that son of a bitch Constantin and ship him back to England in a box. A *small* box," she continued, wiping blood off her face. "Send a message."

"A very, very small box," Luke agreed, scowling. He had wounds of his own. His scalp was bleeding, and the explosion had driven a foot-long shard of wood into his shoulder. He yanked this out now with barely a grimace.

"For now, we need to deal with the humans and then

regroup," Bane said, wiping the blood from his own head wound out of his eyes. "Are you both okay?"

"We're fine," Meara said, dismissing his concern with a flick of her fingers. "But we need a new plan."

"A *better* plan," Bane said grimly, staring at the destruction around them. "Fucking necromancer. Next time, he may bring the dead against us, too."

The thought of Savannah's dead being reanimated and used as pawns in the Chamber's twisted schemes felt like a punch to Bane's throat.

"A *much* better plan."

· · ·

In the end, five of the formerly bloodthralled humans lay dead, but no more of Bane's people had fallen since the accident on the road. The rest of the humans had collapsed into confused huddles when the warlocks died and the necromancer disappeared.

"*You were lost in the swamp and ran into drug dealers who imprisoned you. Now, you'll go home and tell everyone the details are too traumatic to share,*" Bane ordered the thralls.

It was easy enough. Humans were always ready to believe an explanation that didn't involve magic, the supernatural, or anything that stalked the dark. And it made sense to them; it was the reality of movies and television and therefore carried more truth than the reality of vampires, warlocks, or necromancers. In dark times, a palatable fiction reassured those unwilling or unable to believe a terrifying truth.

Sirens ripped through the air, the response to Luke's call to 911. The authorities were near, and Bane wanted to be gone before they arrived. Meara and Luke flanked him at the edge of the bonfire they'd made of the cabin with the warlocks' bodies within.

"We did not win this fight." Bane stared at the fire. "Not even close. He was laughing at us."

"That's a problem for another night," Meara said, her voice ice. "My saddlebags are filled with salt. These three, at least, will never regenerate."

"And this park will recover from the stench of rot and decay, now that they're gone," Luke said. "Can you tell if there are more nearby?"

It wasn't an unexpected question.

"I've already tried but found nothing." But he tried again, sending his senses out to the surrounding area in search of life. He recoiled again at the wrongness of what he found. There were no living creatures within at least two square miles, beyond the former thralls, a few birds in flight, and some aquatic creatures in the waters around them. But then, just as he started to speak, a sign of hope soared through the clearing.

"A Golden Eagle," Meara said, her voice reverent. "This is his home, and he's back to reclaim it."

"Just as Savannah is *our* home, and we'll do the same," Bane said.

Meara nodded. "Good always prevails over evil, in the end."

"In the end," Luke repeated bitterly. "That's the problem, isn't it? All the shit that happens *before* the end. I need a drink." With that, he stalked off toward his bike, where he'd almost certainly stashed a bottle of tequila with the bags of salt.

"They'd think *we* were the evil, if they knew," Meara said, staring at the humans. "And yet we protect them, again and again. What is the point, really?"

It wasn't about the humans. He didn't give a flying fuck about humans he didn't even know. It was about protecting his territory. Keeping his club safe.

But when he turned to answer her, she was already gone.

• • •

Constantin, high in the trees and cloaked in shadows and power, stared at the final remaining vampire for several long moments before silently turning away.

Bane, indeed.

The vampire would learn the true meaning of the word when he died screaming.

CHAPTER TWO

Three days later...

Luke Calhoun shoved open the door marked CLUB MEMBERS ONLY: THIS MEANS <u>YOU</u>, SHITHEAD and walked into the ominously dark hallway behind the public front of the club. The next door he came to didn't have a sign, but it had a state-of-the-art retinal scanner. Luke shoved his hair out of his face with the hand not holding his helmet and stared into the unblinking lens.

"Calhoun, Lucas. Welcome back to Vampire Motorcycle Club headquarters," came the familiar, faintly British tones of the computerized female voice. "Access granted."

Vampire Motorcycle Club. He'd thought Bane was out of his damn mind. But the man everyone now thought of as their club president had been right—the best place to hide the truth was right out in the open.

"Now entering: Calhoun, Lucas," the top-secret, highly classified, no-way-could-a-civilian-get-his-hands-on-it technology announced. The AI was basically Siri plus Google but on steroids. It had access to almost every database in the world and combined that access with a facial recognition database that would have scared the shit out of any civil liberties group.

"Locate Bane," Lucas said.

"Bane is currently in the vault."

He closed the door behind him, tossed his leather jacket on a desk, and blew out a breath that he could almost see in the frigidly air-conditioned room that they called an office but looked more tech-heavy than the deck of the Starship *Enterprise*.

The man seated in front of a bank of state-of-the-art computers never even looked up. "I'm running every search I can think of but finding nothing about the Chamber at all. We need to know what they're up to, and none of our usual sources are returning my calls or email."

"Maybe they have a better computer guy than you," Luke muttered, not giving a damn about the subject at this particular time.

"There *is* no better computer guy than me."

When Luke didn't respond, the man shoved his prematurely pure white hair out of his face and turned his icy silver gaze on Luke. "What."

It wasn't a question. Edge rarely bothered with questions. It was more of a command.

On another night, Luke might have jumped down the scientist's damn throat for it, but this wasn't another night.

This was going to be bad.

Very fucking bad.

"Bane's in the vault?"

Edge said nothing. He'd clearly heard the AI tell Luke Bane's location, and he didn't bother answering inane questions any more than he'd ever ask one. Although, with an IQ way past two hundred, probably everything anybody ever asked sounded inane to him.

"*What*," Edge repeated, standing.

Luke closed his eyes and took a deep breath to keep the rage burning in his gut from escaping into a wave of searing heat that would fry the computers.

Again.

"That human. Hunter," he finally managed to rasp out past the boulder in his throat. "The one who saved Meara when she was caught out past sunrise a few years back."

"Dead?"

"Dying. Soon."

Something almost like compassion stirred in Edge's eyes, but then he shook his head. "He's the closest thing Bane has to a friend, not counting those of us in the family, so to speak. I'm out of here. Tell Bane—"

"I know," Luke said. There was nothing to say. When Bane found out that Evans was dying, there would *be* no words worth saying—no place safe to hide from their leader's fury.

In fact, the rest of them would be lucky to survive it.

Luke waited to feel sad…afraid…*anything*…about his impending death.

Waited.

Nothing.

He just didn't give a shit.

He'd already died once, after all. And now he was going to give bad fucking news to the man who'd brought him back.

"I'm headed to the vault."

He shoved past Edge and pushed open the steel door that led to the stairs and walked down into the darkness.

At the bottom of two flights of stairs, he only hesitated a fraction of a second before pushing open another door and walking into the heart of the club. The Boss's "Born in the USA" played at maximum decibel level, and the smell of Japanese Camellia seed oil told him that Bane was oiling his swords and daggers and brooding—never a good combination.

And Luke was the lucky son of a bitch who got to give Bane terrible fucking news while the warrior had his hands on a few dozen of his favorite weapons.

Not that Bane wasn't a weapon all by himself.

Three-hundred-plus-year-old vampires tended to get that way.

Bane took one look at him and was on his feet, dagger and bottle of oil crashing to the polished concrete floor, six feet, four inches of danger coming off the leash he held so tightly over his own immense power.

"Who?"

"Bane—"

"*Who*?" Bane roared the word, and the centuries-old stone walls vibrated with his fury.

"Hunter Evans. A fire."

Before he could get the next word out, Bane was on him, and Luke saw his own death in a pair of empty black eyes.

• • •

Bane wrapped one hand around Luke's throat and lifted the man several inches into the air, slamming him back against the metal door.

"Did. You. Do. It," he snarled, every atom in his body straining to kill, rend, destroy. "*Did you kill him?*"

Never mind that Luke was one of a very few that Bane

allowed near him.

That Bane had brought Luke over into this new life.

That Luke had proven himself over and over again.

And Luke was suffocating to death in Bane's grasp. He loosened his grip.

"Did you—"

"*No*! No, damn you, no, I would never do anything—" Luke stopped, choking and wheezing, bleak memory stark in his eyes. No doubt remembering the times that he'd nearly burned innocents to death when he first Turned.

First came into his fire-starter powers. Bane and Meara had been shocked when it happened. All vampires gained some small forms of magic when they Turned; it came with the gig. But they'd never heard of any vampire who could start fires with his *mind*.

It was a fucked-up power to have, for a creature who was even more vulnerable to fire than a human, that was for sure. But there you go: Luke's life had been a disaster when he was a human. Why would Bane have imagined it would be any different when he became a vampire?

Remembering the ones he *had* killed, before Bane had been able to stop him.

More innocent deaths on Bane's blackened soul.

Bane released Luke and flew back and away from the man before he killed him.

"He's not dead," Luke gasped. "Not yet. He saved a little girl—I happened to see the fire, but I was a mile away at a bar. By the time I got there, he'd already gone into the house. He wasn't on duty, just happened to be passing by. Her bedroom was on the second floor, and he was holding her out the window for a couple of neighbors who were trying to find a ladder." A coughing fit took him, and then he cleared this throat. "I got them both out. The kid's going to be okay—he reached her in time, but—"

He stopped. Shook his head. "I cleared memories at the scene, don't worry, but you need to get to Savannah General. Fast, if you want to see him before…before…"

By the second *before*, Luke was talking to an empty room. Bane pulled Shadows around himself and stepped into the Between.

Seconds later, he was on the roof of the hospital.

The two women standing at the edge of the roof, smoking and talking in the spring moonlight, never saw him. There could have been fifty humans on the roof— *hundreds*—and they never would have seen him.

He followed the smell of burned flesh to the room where what was left of Hunter Evans lay hooked up to wires and tubes and machines. The human's skin—what was left of his skin—was charred through to bone.

And he was screaming.

Burns—burns were always the worst. Bane had seen far too many fires and far too many victims of fire in his lifetime, especially back in the days when buildings were built of wood. He had to clench his teeth against the urge to retch at the rich, greasy stink of burned flesh; had to clench his fists against the urge to look away from the ruin of his friend's burned body.

The medical personnel in the room were moving with speed and purpose, but Bane needed none of them. Had no time for them. He knew the Reaper, and she was present in the room, already whispering her seductive call into Hunter's ear.

Bane was almost out of time.

"*Leave*," Bane told the humans, forcing so much compulsion into his words that they all scrambled to obey, not knowing why. One of them even thought as she passed him that she would go home immediately, lock her doors, and hide in her closet.

Even humans could sense the threat of an apex predator.

The Reaper, her outline only a faint shadow in the brilliant light of the hospital room, raised her head to pin her shining gaze on Bane.

"He's not for you," he ground out. "Not yet."

She stared at him for a long moment and then acquiesced, fading to a mere shimmer and then disappearing, until a faintly whispered, "Soon," was all that remained.

The room smelled of antiseptic and Hunter's seared body, and Bane was at the bed before the firefighter—his *friend*—could draw another shallow, faltering breath.

"Look at me," Bane commanded, and Hunter's screams cut off instantly.

Bane stared into eyes drowning with agony beyond human endurance and sent a mental *push*.

You don't feel the pain.

Hunter's charred and blackened face relaxed by a fraction of a degree, but his eyes remained unchanged.

He knew he was dying.

They always knew.

Bane lifted a hand but then let it drop. There wasn't an inch of unburned skin he could touch in comfort or solace.

My friend, you're beyond human *help.*

Hunter blinked slowly.

But I am not human, as you well know.

A question flared in smoke-damaged, blood-red eyes, but then resignation returned. Hunter's eyelids slowly closed. Disbelief or hopelessness, perhaps.

Simple acceptance of his impending end.

Well, fuck *that*.

NO! Bane roared through their mental connection, rage and grief searing through him. *I DO NOT ACCEPT IT.*

Hunter's eyelids flew open, and he tried to move his mouth, but his lips were burned away, showing the skull beneath.

Think your response. I'll hear.

Hunter blinked again, and then, after such a long moment Bane thought the human had given up, Hunter's voice sounded in Bane's mind.

I must be fucking dead already, but if this is Heaven, I want a do-over. I expected sexy, half-naked angels at the very damn least.

Bane blew out a breath, relief relaxing muscles he hadn't realized were clenched. Hunter was still sane, then, which hadn't been a given, considering the sheer agony he'd endured.

You can argue with Luke about angels later. Now, you must decide. You know what I am. I can make you like me, and you will survive. But you will be changed. Forever.

The hideous clanging of an alarm sounded in the hall, and running footsteps—probably of the humans who'd finally broken free of the compulsion and figured out they should be in Hunter's room—came toward them.

Decide. Now. *Live or die.*

Shockingly, unbefuckinglievably, the edges of Hunter's ruined mouth twitched.

If you promise I'll turn out to be as charming as your arrogant ass, then hey. Sure.

Bane was nodding when the woman he hadn't even known he'd been waiting three hundred years for ran into the room and started shouting at him.

"Who the hell are you, and where is my staff? My God, you're not even sterile, and 90 percent of his body is open to compromise!" She ran across the room, put herself between Hunter and Bane, and shoved Bane away from the bed, putting her entire body weight into it.

Bane blinked and actually fell back a step, not from her ineffectual shove, but from the fact that she'd actually done it.

Grown men feared him.

Vampires feared him.

Things that were far worse than even vampires feared him.

And this small human—with a face that was all furious, ocean-blue eyes and pale, creamy, glowing skin—was still pushing him.

And shouting in his face.

Every predatory instinct in his body woke up, shocking his nerve endings into an almost-electric state of heightened awareness, and his mind started shouting a warning at him—*threat, threat, threat.*

He looked into her eyes, and those same instincts

seared a demand into his brain—*mine, mine, mine.*

Who the fuck knew courage would be his aphrodisiac? And wait...*glowing* skin? Literally glowing? It had to be something that only a vampire's heightened vision could pick up. Bane couldn't imagine the people she worked with not noticing if their colleague lit up like a lantern.

She shoved him again, disrupting that train of thought, and he narrowed his eyes. The only threat this human could pose was to his equilibrium, regardless of his bizarre reaction to her.

"Get out of here before I have to hurt you," she shouted at him. "Security!"

He couldn't help it.

He smiled.

She froze, her hands still on his chest, poised to push again. "Are you out of your damn mind? Get out of my patient's room! You're a danger to him. Security!"

"Security is not coming," he told her, just for the pleasure of watching her react. Every emotion she felt showed on her face, and he suddenly wanted nothing more than to watch her experience them. For hours.

Days.

He flinched at the reaction, his shoulders tightening and his breath slowing. There was no logic in it. The sudden *wanting* came from a place far deeper than logic, far more primal than reason. A red haze of instinct started screaming at him to *take* her.

Keep her.

His *mind* was telling him to back away, fast.

She slammed her fists on his chest and leaned forward, still pushing, but all he could think was that her hair carried the scent of one of his most cherished memories: masses of wildflowers near a stream in a sun-drenched mountain glen.

"Are you…did you just *smell* me? What is *happening* here?"

On the bed, Hunter made a tiny sound, and Bane's focus snapped back to his friend, whose agony was beginning to break through the hypnotic command Bane had given him. What the fuck had just happened? How had he allowed himself to be distracted by this woman when Hunter needed him? A wave of self-disgust roiled through him like acid in his gut.

"Sleep. *Now*," he commanded her, and he reached out to catch her when she fell.

Froze in shock when she didn't.

"Who—"

But he didn't have time for her questions or for his own questions about how she could resist his command or for the soul-searing wonder that threatened to overwhelm him about how she could possibly *exist*.

Instead, he reached out and touched her. "*Sleep. Now.*"

Strong mind or no, a human couldn't resist compulsion combined with touch. She'd be out for hours. When she fell into his arms, the feel of her warmth and curves set off a tsunami of shock waves inside him—emotions he had long since lost any familiarity with: desire, protectiveness, an almost-feral need to possess—that rocked him back a step, still holding her.

But there was no time. Hunter was failing, and more humans would be coming.

He put her in the chair against the wall and read the

name embroidered in script lettering on her white coat. "I'll be back, Dr. St. Cloud."

He thought he caught a glimpse of something that absolutely should not be looking in the window and almost absently threw a blast of power at it, just in case. Then he yanked the life-saving lines out of Hunter's body, lifted the man into his arms, and stepped into the Between.

Before the Shadows had even fully formed around him, though, she was already opening those blue, blue eyes and leaping out of the chair, and his mouth fell open in shock.

Not possible.

It was utterly and completely impossible that any human could come out of such a powerful compulsion that quickly. Something was very wrong here...or else something was very wrong with *her*. He hadn't sensed or smelled any hint of magic, but no ordinary human could just snap out of the compulsion like that.

And yet, she was almost across the room.

"I'm coming for you," Bane repeated before the Shadows swallowed him, and not even he knew if it were a promise or a threat. He only knew that he wanted this woman with every fiber of his being—which made no sense at all. She was human, or maybe not. Whatever she was, her resistance to his magic and her glowing skin added up to a mystery. And he had no time for mysteries with the Chamber coming for him.

Sure, she was brave. And, clearly, she was smart. But... Oh. *Right.*

He was horny. It had been a while. He'd come back

when he had time and take her, fuck her, and get her out of his system. He ignored the way his mouth dried out and his body hardened at the mere thought of it. *No*.

Dr. St. Cloud would be no problem for him.

No problem at all.

Her ability to resist his compulsion, however—that was a big fucking problem.

CHAPTER THREE

The surplus waves of the vampire's portal magic blasted the Watcher off the side of the building, and he barely caught a tiny decorative ledge with one hand, but it was enough to save him from splattering on the ground far below.

He couldn't track Bane through the Between, but he knew where the vampire called home.

They all did.

He scrabbled around until he was facing the ground and scuttled down the side of the hospital, and then he raced off into the night. First, he'd confirm, and then he'd report. And then, his master would reward him.

He flinched and then picked up his speed, not even realizing he was whimpering and grimacing. Too intent on his mission.

Hell-bent on returning to his lord.

Maybe the Watcher would be the first to survive delivering bad news. His ears flicked up at the thought but then drooped again.

Hope died early in Minor demons.

If it ever really existed at all.

CHAPTER FOUR

Ryan leapt for the man carrying her patient—actually jumped into the air, her body stretched out, to grab for him—and got two hands full of nothing.

Her leap had been aimed at stopping him, so when she encountered nothing, a body in motion stayed in motion, and she slammed into the wall, shoulder first.

"Ow!"

She put a hand up to rub her shoulder and whirled around, just in case...

In case what? In case the magically disappearing man suddenly winked back into existence?

In case her clearly fractured sanity duct-taped itself back together, and she was once again alone in a room with her almost-certainly dying patient, instead of watching in disbelief as the hottest yet most terrifying man she'd ever seen in her life somehow hypnotized her and stuffed her in the beige visitor's chair?

Sure.

Great.

That little detail was going to go over great with the hospital review board. She could see it now:

"And then, sirs and ma'ams, the tall, blond hunk of muscle and sex turned invisible and disappeared. Yes, with my patient. No, I was too busy being whammied by his glowing blue eyes at the time to be able to stop him."

"I'm totally fucked."

"Would you like to be?"

She jumped and whirled around to face the doorway, where yet another decidedly non-hospital employee leaned against the wall, hands in the pockets of his jeans, staring at her with glowing eyes.

Glowing *green* eyes this time.

What the hell? Had she hit her head, too, and not just her shoulder?

This one was tall, dark, and definitely dangerous, with a sinful grin quirking up sensual lips. He probably had to fight off women wherever he went.

Oddly, though, her mind flashed back to the other one. The one who'd stolen her patient. He'd scared her, but she'd been drawn to him...

She shook her head once, sharply. What was *wrong* with her?

"Usually I get a quicker yes to that question," the jerk at the door drawled.

Question?

Oh. Right.

"Look, asshole, whoever you are, get out of this room. Now." She strode over to the wall by the bed and punched a button to call security. "I don't have time for you."

"Seems like you'd be more courteous to the public," he observed, his smile fading and something that looked like shock widening his eyes. "Also, what *are* you?"

"I'm a doctor. And it seems to me that you'd have heard of the Me-Too movement and realized that leading with a question about whether I'd like to be fucked is grounds to get a punch in the face."

"What? Look, I know humans may not be able to see it,

but your skin is decidedly luminescent. What are you?"

She stared at him in disbelief. "I said, I'm a doctor. And I don't have time for you now. Visiting hours are long over, anyway."

She took a deep breath and turned and scanned the room again, realizing the futility of it even as her brain refused to accept the truth: her patient—burned so badly he almost certainly wouldn't survive, even with the help of every resource she had in the state-of-the-art Burn Unit—was gone.

And she'd let it happen.

She heard the sound of masculine throat clearing and glanced back at the doorway. To add to her fantastic evening, the pervert wasn't leaving, either.

She sighed and put a hand on the wall phone. "I'll just call security, and they can help you find your way out, okay?"

"Fine," the man at the door snapped. "Let's do it the hard way."

He stalked into the room toward her, but she was too freaked out to be afraid, even though he was well over six feet tall, only a few inches short of the first man, who'd been enormous. This one was all muscle and cheekbones, too, though. Was there a gladiator movie filming somewhere nearby missing a few actors?

She held up a hand to stop him. "Look—"

He stopped but then, in a movement so fast she nearly didn't see it, he grabbed her wrist and leaned close. "*You saw nothing.*"

"I saw nothing?" She was too dumbfounded to even yank her arm away from him.

"Exactly." This time his smile spread across his entire

face. "Perfect."

With that, he turned and walked out the door, and she heard his footsteps as he headed down the hallway.

Apparently, he'd taken her question as agreement.

He'd been very, very wrong.

She'd seen *everything,* and she wasn't talking about this guy, either. She'd seen the man who'd somehow—some insane way how—stolen her patient. And she was going to find Mr. Evans if it was the last thing she did.

• • •

Three hours later, Ryan collapsed in a haze of boneless exhaustion onto the couch in the living room of her late grandmother's ridiculously luxurious townhome on Lafayette Square, in one of Savannah's wealthiest neighborhoods. Thirty-six hours on call, and that was all before the supernatural-patient-snatching incident. Now she'd spent three hours, first at work and then at home on the phone and computer, trying to figure out what the hell had happened.

She'd found nothing.

Nobody she'd talked to had admitted to seeing either one of the intruders.

None of the staff had admitted to seeing or treating Hunter Evans.

The paperwork had disappeared.

If she didn't know better, she'd believe she'd fallen into an episode of the *X-Files*, except the truth was damned well *not* out there.

Finally, at the hospital, she'd gotten to the point where

people were giving her concerned "Dr. Ryan must be overworked and possibly in danger of needing a psych consult" looks, and she'd been forced to give up.

Maybe she was? Overworked, sure.

Exhausted, yes.

But having a mental breakdown?

She put a hand to her stomach to quell the flash of nausea. Was she seeing things?

No. Definitely not.

She'd seen that man take Hunter, and she'd be damned if she'd doubt herself. It didn't matter how tired she was; she hadn't been hallucinating.

She'd been wide awake and had only stepped out of Evans' room for long enough to head over to the nurses' station when the resident, medical student, and nurses who'd been in his room had all come running out like they were being chased by monsters.

And when they hadn't answered her questions—had in fact run right past her like she didn't exist—she'd raced to the firefighter's ICU room only to find the monster in question was still there.

Only he hadn't looked at all like a monster. Or sounded like one.

No, he'd had a husky, whiskey-velvet voice to go with those dangerously sexy eyes—had they been glowing?

She drank more wine and stared unseeingly at her grandmother's piano.

Sure. Glowing eyes, why not? She'd seen a beautiful, terrifying man with glowing eyes who'd kidnapped a dying burn patient and disappeared into a magic portal. Happened every day, right?

Sure. On my Netflix queue of sci-fi movies, maybe...

Maybe she needed to accept a harsh truth.

Maybe it wasn't everyone *else* who'd been wrong—maybe it was her.

No. Not her. Not Rational Ryan. There was no way.

She drained the wineglass and started to pour another but then stopped. She'd only find another headache at the bottom of the bottle, not answers.

Not her patient.

The patient everyone claimed didn't exist.

The patient that *wasn't in the hospital computers.*

She paused again and rubbed her forehead, the doubt resurfacing. Because, in fact, he *hadn't* been in the computer.

And everybody was in the computer.

Everybody.

The second you stepped on hospital property, your ass was logged into a computer, because the great twin gods named Insurance and Medical Bills must receive their due. There was no way that a firefighter didn't have health insurance, and there was no way that Hunter Evans, who'd been there for at least an hour, hadn't been logged into the system.

If he'd existed.

If he even...

Firefighter.

She caught her breath. Of course! Maybe a gas leak or something was causing memory loss in the hospital personnel, but Evans had managed to tell somebody that he was a firefighter, right?

She grabbed her phone and did a quick search. There it

was. Contact information for Savannah Fire Rescue.

Nobody answered the phone, of course, because it was almost freaking midnight, and nobody in admin offices answered phones at midnight. So she'd call the stations. There were probably a few different...

There were sixteen. They were called Engine companies, according to Google. Sixteen of them. She grabbed a pad of paper and a pen off her desk and started calling.

An hour and sixteen frustrating conversations later, she threw the pen across the room.

Hunter Evans didn't exist.

And Ryan had to face the fact that maybe overwork and loneliness had caused her mind to play tricks on her.

She drained another glass of wine after all, finishing the bottle, because what the hell? Tomorrow, she'd call the hospital and get a little long-overdue vacation time to sort herself out. Tonight, she'd watch another of her Top 100 Movies of All Time.

"Hey, Alexa. What's the best movie to watch after you hallucinate a nonexistent hot guy who disappears with your nonexistent burn patient into a magic portal?"

The machine's light flashed for a moment, and then the familiar computer voice replied: "I'm sorry, I don't have that information."

Ryan started laughing. "Yeah. Me, neither, Alexa. Me, neither."

CHAPTER FIVE

Three hours earlier…

Bane walked out of the Between and into the vast room that Meara insisted was a ballroom and shouted for help. When four vampires and two humans all lived in the same mansion, someone was usually within hearing distance.

Luke was the first one to burst into the room, but he stumbled to a stop when he saw what—who—Bane carried. "Oh, shit. If you…is he? *Fuck*…I have to head to the hospital and fix this before we have hordes of peasants ready to shove flaming torches up our asses."

Edge floated in through the third-floor window and strode toward them. "Join this century. Flaming iPhones, maybe."

Luke rolled his eyes. "iPhones, my ass. We're talking flamethrowers, at a minimum. Bane, unless you need—"

"Go," Bane told him, carefully lowering Hunter's unconscious body to the center of a two or three-hundred-year-old teak table. The mansion and some of its furnishings were almost as old as he was. "There was a doctor…no. Just go."

Luke went.

Edge rolled up his sleeves and shoved his long, white hair out of his face. The scientist's hair had been black before his own government had imprisoned and tortured him and—far worse—tortured his brother to gain enough leverage to make Edge talk. If he hadn't killed six of them—Edge had been lethal even as a human—and escaped with his dying brother then raced straight to Bane, he might have ended up like the man on the table.

Or worse.

"What do you need?"

"I'm going to Turn him," Bane said, ready for a fight. Edge wasn't always happy to be a vampire; maybe he'd try to stop Bane from Turning another human. He'd nearly gone insane when he'd woken up and learned that his brother was now a vampire, too.

Even though it had been Edge's dying request that Bane Turn them both.

Death wishes and reality seldom meshed.

But something—some memory of humanity, an echo of a feeling from centuries ago—was pushing him to save this honorable man, who stood for others in a selfish world.

Edge's silver eyes gleamed hot, and he slowly raised his gaze to meet Bane's. "Did you give him a choice?"

"I did. He made it. Now, either help me or get out of the room. Where's Meara?"

"She's hunting," Mrs. Cassidy, their housekeeper, said disapprovingly, bustling into the room.

Meara liked to hunt the kind of human criminal who wandered around Savannah, preying on the weak. Meara taught *them* about weakness before she drank from them. Bane wasn't crazy about his sister's nocturnal habits, although they echoed his own, but he'd learned decades ago to shut the fuck up about it.

When Mrs. C caught sight of the man on the table, she caught her breath in an audible gasp. "Oh, the poor love.

What…is he…oh, Bane. Shouldn't he be in a hospital?"

"He's beyond hospitals. I need blankets and heat. Start the fire, bring space heaters, crank up the furnace, whatever it takes. It needs to be at least ninety degrees in this room for every minute of the next three days," Bane ordered.

When Mrs. Cassidy turned to race out of the room, not bothering to waste time on a reply, he turned to Edge. "You're still here, so you're helping?"

"I'm helping." Edge yanked the hospital blanket off Hunter's blackened body and muttered a curse. "This is bad. This is fucking awful. Is it—is it even possible, when his body is this damaged?"

Bane spared him a glance. "You were worse."

Edge hissed, lips pulling back from his teeth, fangs descending. "I still owe some payback for that," he snarled, his silver eyes shading to red.

"Later," Bane said, scanning Hunter for a spot undamaged enough to use.

"Here." Edge pointed. "Brachial artery. The inside of his upper right arm. He must have held the child with that arm, protecting her from the fire. There's a patch of unburned skin here." His jaw tightened. "Do you want me to do it?"

Bane appreciated the courage it must have taken for Edge to offer. The process of Turning could kill both participants. He shook his head, though.

"No. This is on me. Help Mrs. C get the heat going and find Meara. When Lucas gets back, I need him. I'll need all three of you to help me get through this."

"Do you want me to bring in extra…provisions? There's surely someone in Savannah who deserves to die tonight."

"No. Maybe later, if we must. Now, go. We need that heat. He's running out of time."

Edge nodded and raced out of the room, almost too fast for even Bane's eyes to see, and Bane looked down at Hunter.

"Say good-bye to your old life."

He stared at the dying man for a single moment, and then he lifted Hunter's arm and plunged his fangs into the artery.

It took less than five minutes to drain him dry.

. . .

"Bane! *Bane*!" Mrs. Cassidy shouted. "Bane, you get your behind down from there, or I'll…I'll…I'll get Tommy's shotgun and shoot you!"

The red haze of Bane's vision slowly cleared, and he realized he was floating up against the ceiling of the room, spinning in lazy circles, his arms and legs thrown wide, in the throes of a very vivid daydream about fucking the delicious Dr. St. Cloud until she screamed his name.

Blood drunk. He was blood drunk, and Hunter was dying.

Or already dead.

He arrowed down to the floor, viciously biting his wrist as he flew, and then he immediately put the open wound over Hunter's mouth. The man was gasping out his last breath, his body shaking in his final death throes, and Bane had been wallowing in the hedonistic joy of having consumed nearly a gallon of fresh blood.

He *was* a monster. A monster, he realized, who'd killed

the human he'd wanted to Turn.

Because Hunter wasn't drinking.

"I'll be damned if I'll let you die because of me," Bane growled, and he *pushed* a command into the dying human's brain.

Drink, damn you. Drink!

Suddenly, shockingly, Hunter's throat moved as he convulsively swallowed, first once, and then again, and then again and again and again. Ten, then twenty, and then thirty long seconds went by, and then Hunter found the strength to raise his hands and grab Bane's arm, clutching it to him as if afraid the blood might be taken away.

Mrs. Cassidy fluttered around them, not knowing what to do or how to do it. She'd only seen the process once, and she'd fainted that time, but only for a few minutes. She and her husband were made of sterner stuff than to run away at the sight of a little blood, she'd declared when she'd roused, and then she'd immediately gone off to make soup.

Soup was his housekeeper's secret weapon, her cure-all for every situation. Love was flavored with chicken and homemade noodles in this house.

"That's it, my friend. Drink now and survive to fight another day." Bane sank down into a chair someone had placed near the table and only then realized that there was a fire blazing in the stone hearth and space heaters were glowing hot at every electrical outlet in the room.

"Thank you, Mrs. C."

She nodded, biting her lip, and then she burst into tears. "Oh, you know I wouldn't have shot you, don't you? I'd never hurt one of you boys, or Meara, either. I just—I just

didn't know what to do, and you weren't hearing me, and
I...I..."

He forced himself to smile, although the blood draining
out of him was beginning to have an effect. "Don't worry
about it. You probably saved Hunter's life by snapping me
out of my delirium. But you know what we could really
use? Some hot soup. Do you think—"

She wiped her eyes with the backs of her hands and gave
him a shaky smile. "You know it, sir. I'll go do that right now.
Tommy should be home soon, and I'll send him to the store,
and I'll need chicken and..." She headed for the door, still
verbally composing her shopping list, and then she turned
and ran back to him.

"You be careful. With him *and* with yourself," she said.
Then she leaned down and kissed his forehead, blushed a
rosy pink, and ran back out of the room.

A wave of dizziness washed over him, and he realized
that Hunter had taken too much blood, and so far, there
was nobody back to help replenish Bane's.

So be it.

If he had to die, what better reason? He'd ruined so
many lives, caused so many deaths—would it deliver an
ounce of redemption to a blackened soul to save a single
life at the end of his miserable existence?

Worse, did he even care?

Blackness encroached on his vision, and then he heard a
voice which sure as hell wasn't one of Hunter's scantily clad
angels welcoming him to Heaven.

"You'd better not die on me, you fool."

Meara was back.

CHAPTER SIX

"Well, when a mommy demon and a daddy warlock love each other very much…"

Constantin Durance let the sarcasm in his voice finish the sentence for him.

The Minor demon he had by the neck choked and hissed but knew better than to try to fight back.

"The little creep knows how baby Minor demons are made, Con," Sylvie said mildly, her narrowed eyes giving the lie to her calm voice. She circled the human corpse on the floor of the abandoned warehouse on the outskirts of Savannah, tapping her chin thoughtfully. She nudged the side of the dead woman's head with one high-heeled boot. "Still dead. Hmm. And that's not what I was asking, as you very well know. 'How were you *made*' is human vernacular for how were you *caught*?"

The demon, its tail now drooping between its legs, tried to talk but could only make choking noises.

There was *spittle*.

Constantin grimaced and dropped the creature, who lay gasping on the floor, its claw-tipped hands and feet limp, its scaly red chest heaving for breath. Constantin observed this with a slight feeling of distaste and pulled a handkerchief out of his pocket and wiped his hands.

"Wasn't caught. Er, wasn't made," the demon rasped. "Saw him talk to a lady doctor. He couldn't glamour her. Disappeared with the human."

Sylvie glared at the demon. The creature howled and scuttled away to hunch against the corpse, as if in some hope of protection from a dead human who'd had none of her own.

Constantin sighed. Minor demons were almost as stupid as humans. And Sylvie wasn't helping.

"I don't care!" Sylvie snapped. "Where is Bane?"

"At his house. I think," the demon moaned, curling in on itself.

"You *think*? Since when did you learn how to think?" She advanced on the creature, but Constantin raised a hand.

"No. We need to know everything he saw, and he may yet be of use. You can kill him later."

The demon's ears, which had flickered a little, drooped down again.

Constantin pointed at him. "*Why* aren't you sure?"

"The house is warded. Strong wards. Very strong," the demon whimpered.

Sylvie sneered. "I'll take care of that. How strong can his wards be to the likes of us?"

Constantin held in a sigh. New warlocks were so arrogant, often unjustifiably so. And the female warlocks were always the most vicious.

"If we smash his wards now, he'll know we're here, before we're ready to announce our presence. We need to be ready to take them all out if we're going to claim this territory without massive casualties among our own people," he pointed out.

"Then what?"

He smiled at her, and her expression faded from

arrogance to something very much like fear. He found he liked that.

He liked it very much.

"Did you know he has a sister? Other vampires he protects? A human staff? All potential leverage, if he cares anything about them."

"Leverage," Sylvie repeated, and she began to smile. "I can work with that."

CHAPTER SEVEN

Bane's sister by blood and circumstance, Meara Delacourt had been a vampire exactly as long as Bane had. Count Delacourt, a minor French noble whose wife had died in childbirth, had Turned his only child—a daughter—and three other humans, including Bane, into vampires on that same night. And then, caught in a frenzy of blood drunkenness the likes of which Bane had never heard of, either before or since, the count had flown directly into a bonfire at the harvest festival, burst into flames, and died spectacularly.

Or so Bane had heard, he himself having been unconscious and at the beginning of the three-day-long coma that accompanied the Turn at the time of the conflagration. Neither Meara nor Bane knew how her father had become a vampire. It was another fact long lost to time and distance, like the names of the other two who'd been turned and, indeed, Bane's own name. The name his mother had given him at birth had gradually disappeared from his mind after Meara had started calling him Bane.

"You're the bane of everyone around us," she'd teased, when he'd been a human boy, and then repeated, more seriously, after they'd been Turned and were struggling to survive.

Back then, he'd been the bane of many.

Luckily for Bane and Meara, Pierre Delacourt had tucked them all away in a secret underground chamber

and left a roaring fire with plenty of wood and a thoroughly entranced servant to tend it before turning himself into
the centerpiece of the most memorable harvest festival in
Yorkshire, England's history.

Meara had been Bane's sister ever since. A golden-
haired, golden-eyed beauty who was smarter than anyone
he'd ever known, more stubborn than a herd of mules, and
the dirtiest fighter he'd ever met. Also, since then, she'd
had his back just as he'd had hers, in trouble on both sides
of the Atlantic.

When he scented her blood, he lunged for the wrist she
held over his mouth.

"If you die for this…this…*human*, I'm going to chase
you into Hell and drag your ass home," she snarled, just
before she smacked him on the side of the head.

Hard.

If he'd been human, she'd have given him a concussion.
For him, though, the blow didn't hurt nearly as much as the
knowledge that he'd caused the warm tears that dropped
on his forehead.

Partially revitalized from her blood but unwilling to
take more, he took one final swallow, swept his tongue
across his bite marks to heal them, and then pulled away
before taking a deep breath. "Don't cry for me, Meara.
Never for me."

He then turned to Hunter, and a faint feeling of satisfaction whispered through him at the sight of the man's
healing body. The blackened, burned skin was flaking away,
leaving only pink, new skin in its place. That doctor would
have lost her mind to see what she'd only be able to comprehend as a miracle—no science or medicine could have

healed these injuries.

When science and technology were gone, only miracles and magic remained.

Meara glared at him and turned away, her hands going to her cheeks. When she faced him again, the tears were gone, but the fury remained. "You promised me, after the last time. You said, 'Meara, I promise, I won't do it again.' Do you have any memory of that, you lying piece of crap?"

Edge walked into the room, carrying an armload of firewood, just in time to catch the end of Meara's angry question. He dumped the wood in the wrought-iron log holder next to the fireplace and then brushed off his hands and turned to face them, bleakness stamped on the lines and angles of his face. "I know. I'm sorry. Bane never should have risked his life to save mine."

She whirled on him. "No. He should not have. And don't try to make me feel guilty for saying what we all know is true. The Turning is far too dangerous. My father *died*. Bane, I won't lose the only family I have left for some ridiculous notion of…what? *Nobility?* Leave saving the humans to the doctors."

With that, she pulled invisibility around herself and vanished but deliberately didn't bother to mask the sound of her boots stomping across the gleaming wooden floor as she left the room.

"Hey! What did I do?" Luke walked into the room rubbing his jaw. "Why did Meara just punch me in the face?"

"Because she still can't bring herself to hit me," Edge said, sadness and something else Bane didn't want to think about darkening his silver eyes to storm cloud gray.

"What?"

"Never mind that," Bane said. "I need more blood. And what happened at the hospital?"

Luke casually bit open his wrist as he crossed the floor to where Bane sat next to Hunter. "Take what you need. I found a willing nurse who remembers only a few kisses and cuddles on the roof with a handsome visiting doctor, so I'm good to go."

Lucas used his much-bragged-about charm to feed, leaving his prey feeling sensual and satiated. Bane, when he did feed, didn't bother with any such niceties. He simply found the worst scum in town, took what he needed, and then—when he could be bothered—ripped the memories of the night from their minds.

He'd heard rumors of more than a few wild-eyed criminals turning themselves in to the police with tales of "coming clean to escape the monster." He and Meara were invariably the monsters. Mr. and Mrs. Cassidy, who were bound to them by family loyalty and an enthrallment that was more for ceremony than out of necessity, chided them for it, but what did he care?

Savannah was the most haunted city in the country, right? A crazy report of monsters would be laughed at or ignored.

This was how the monsters thrived in the age of cell phones with video cameras: when anything and everything was fodder for televised entertainment, even the monsters were nothing to fear.

Until they ripped your throat out.

Bane fed from Luke for just a minute or so, and then he was fine. "Thank you."

Luke nodded. "Whatever you need, whenever you need it, brother."

"And," Bane forced the words out, "about earlier. I should have known you wouldn't have hurt him."

Luke laughed, but it was a harsh, rasping sound with no humor in it. "Why would you apologize?"

Bane bared his teeth. "You'll notice I didn't."

"We both know I've hurt humans before. If I'm not careful, I'll do it again. I should have flown into that house and pulled them both out. If only I'd gotten there sooner…"

"All three of you would have died if you'd gone into that fire," Edge said flatly. "Don't be a fool. Even fire you didn't create can hurt you, fire starter or not, as far as we know."

"As far as we know," Luke repeated, his eyes going blank and far away.

The image of ocean-blue eyes flashed into Bane's mind. The woman whose image had seared itself into his brain. "The hospital? Did you remove any trace?"

Luke's lips quirked. "Naturally. And Edge accessed their computers from here to fix the records. There was a curvy little doctor in his room that I would have loved to get to know better, but…" He paused, and his eyes narrowed. "It was the weirdest thing. She didn't seem to be affected at all by my deliciously charming ways. In fact, her skin looked like it was glowing. I asked her what she was, but—"

Bane was up out of the chair before he knew he'd moved. "A doctor? What was her name? *What was her name?*"

Luke held up his hands and shook his head. "Whoa.

Calm down. I don't know her name. We didn't get to the point of exchanging names. I tried to flirt, she called me an asshole—which, let's admit it, I totally can be, but humans don't usually call me on it—and then I told her she remembered nothing, and she agreed, and I left."

Bane's mind felt like it was splitting apart. Rage and lust and something…something *else*…all swirled around inside him in a tornado of emotion so intense he wanted to put his fist through a wall.

"What did she look like?"

Luke blinked. "What? Oh, I don't know; I was in a hurry."

"*Think.*"

"Why? I don't—wait. She was ordinary. Dark hair pulled back from her face. You wouldn't look twice at her unless you caught sight of those intensely blue eyes. Except like I said, and I know this sounds stupid as hell, but her skin was this weird glowy gold. Like that sparkly lotion Meara likes. Why would a doctor wear that to work?"

Bane glared at him, and Luke blinked.

"Right. Sorry. One of those white coats. Oh, right. Her name was on her coat." He closed his eyes. "St. Cloud. Or St. John. No. Definitely St. Cloud." His eyes opened. "That was it. Dr. St. Cloud."

Bane's vision shaded to red, and he knew he was a hair's breadth away from sinking into a berserker's rage. What he didn't know was *why*. It almost felt like… *jealousy*?

It was *definitely* territorial.

"Your compulsion worked on her?"

Luke shrugged. "Yeah, of course. I told her she

remembered nothing, she agreed, and I left. Why wouldn't it work?"

Bane's hands clenched into fists at his side, and he had to fight to contain the unexpected wave of fury rising inside him. What was happening to him? Why was he having the powerful urge to smash Luke's head into the nearest wall?

An epiphany slammed into him with the force of a bulldozer. He felt about Dr. St. Cloud the way he felt about Savannah: she was his to *protect*.

She was *his*.

What the fuck?

He'd finally lost it. Three centuries of relative calm and a single human female had driven him out of his damned mind.

He took refuge in barking out orders. "Watch Hunter. You know the drill. Three days, constant heat, blood when he needs it. Mrs. C will try to come in and clean him up. Don't let her. If he wakes up early and smells her…"

Edge nodded. "You don't need to finish that sentence. We know. But where will you be?"

Bane shook his head. "Honestly? I have no fucking clue."

Before they could answer, he was already gone.

He had a doctor to find.

CHAPTER EIGHT

Ryan changed into her comfiest PJs, because why not, and took some time to ponder the question of what else she'd been hallucinating about lately while she decided on a movie to watch. She was definitely tipsy, working her way toward drunk, but who cared? What did a little wine matter when she was already able to see little pink elephants—and big, hot guys—while stone-cold sober? She shook her head at horror, wrinkled her nose at science fiction, and then considered and discarded the entire genre of romantic comedies, because who the hell wanted to watch other people find true love and happily ever after when she'd never had anything close herself?

Damn. No self-pity tonight. No, Dr. Ryan St. Cloud was going to tie one on.

Heh. *Tie one on.* Why were there so many euphemisms for drunk? She'd wasted a lot of brain cells on that particular question, even while she'd been pickling those brain cells with far too much drinking over the past few years. It was even a kind of joke in the ER, where drunk tourists provided a steady feed of patients.

Three sheets to the wind.
Bombed.
Crocked.
Pickled.
Wasted.
Wrecked.

Feeling no pain.

Well. That last was a joke, wasn't it? *Pain* was probably the reason most people drank too much in the first place. Pain. Loneliness. Despair.

There was far too much pain, and far too little celebration, in life overall, she'd discovered. At least in her life.

"And the winner of the award for Whiniest Self-Pity is…" She shook her head to shake off the mood. Enough, already. Better to think about movies than her boring, solitary life.

She had her best friend Annie, after all. She wasn't entirely alone.

She opened her second bottle of the night, fully aware that she was drunk off her ass. "But who cares?" she asked the portrait of her grandmother. "Tonight I drink, and tomorrow I'll go on a spur-of-the-moment and much-needed vacation."

She finally settled on the best, most awesome choice for a drunken movie fest and settled in to watch it, saluting the TV with the bottle, having quit bothering with the glass a while back.

"Yippee ki-yay, motherfucker!"

But before John McClane could get off the plane with that enormous teddy bear, things started to get weird.

She laughed. No, that was a ridiculous thought after the night she'd had.

Correction: things got *even weirder*.

Because that's when the magical kidnapper from the hospital appeared on her second-floor balcony.

The balcony that had no stairs, ladder, or fire escape.

"I'm more the Hans Gruber type," he said. "Hello, Dr. St. Cloud."

She blinked and then took another swig of wine, still staring at him. "Hey, call me Ryan. I've decided I should be on first-name basis with all my hallucinations. And damn, but you're just beautiful, aren't you? At least my brain dreamed up a hottie when it decided to go ballistic."

"I don't… You…" He shook his head and then raised a single eyebrow and pinned his glowing gaze to her, decidedly non-glowing, own. "I assure you, I am quite real."

"Right. And so, Mr. Quite Real, what did you do with my patient? You know, the one who was *dying*? The one I had no chance in hell to save, even before you picked him up and disappeared with him?" She was on her feet and shouting at him by the end but didn't remember standing. Also, unpleasantly, the rage smashing through her was, to borrow one of Annie's expressions, *harshing her mellow.*

"How do you remember that?" His eyes narrowed. "Luke said he'd compelled you to forget."

"I'd like to forget so much about tonight," she muttered. "And who the hell is Luke?"

"I'd like to explain, Doctor… *Ryan,* if you'd invite me in," her magical mystery guest said.

Ryan pointed her bottle at him. "No. Nuh-uh. No way. You keep your glowy-eyed magical ass away from me. And how did you climb up to my balcony? How did you even find me, more to the point?"

"*Invite me in, and I'll tell you,*" he said, but his voice had a weird, buzzy resonance that tickled the inside of her mind somehow.

It made her laugh. "Nope."

His eyes widened. "So it was true."

"What was true? And why are you here?"

He folded his arms and said nothing, which infuriated her.

"Where is my patient?"

"Invite me in, and I'll tell you," he said again, shrugging.

She blew out a breath. "Fine. Whatever. Come on in, Mr. Drunken Hallucination. And then you damn well better tell me where my patient is."

He smiled and took a step forward, into the room, and she started toward him but tripped over the coffee table and fell.

Into his arms. Damn, he smelled good. She rested her overheated cheek against his chest for a moment and inhaled.

Wait.

"You were clear across the room," she muttered, struggling to back up while pushing him away at the same time. *Trying* to push him away, rather, because he had chest muscles like iron boulders. Was that a thing? Iron boulders? Rock-hard steel?

Some kind of metaphor for hard, for sure.

Yummy. Hard.

Also, damn. Maybe opening that second bottle of wine had been a mistake.

"You seem to have been having a party," he said, and there was amusement mixed with something darker in his rich, deep voice.

God. He was the most gorgeous man she'd ever seen— imagined? Dreamed?—and his voice sounded like silken sin. A tingle of heat and electricity raced through her, and she could actually feel her nipples harden. Now she was *really* losing it, because her hallucination was making her hot.

No different from fantasizing about a movie star in the bathtub, she tried to tell herself. Except bath-time fantasies never came to life and walked into her living room.

She'd never felt one hold her in his arms before, either.

A tiny shiver of real fear managed to break through the haze of wine-induced fog, and she stumbled back and away from him. Then she glanced up to see that his eyes held the same confusing mix of emotions that she'd heard in his voice, or at least as much as she could actually read emotion from glowing blue eyes.

Maybe he really was thinking about pulling out his axe and murdering her.

"Do you have an axe?"

This time, he blinked. "A what?"

"An axe. Are you an axe murderer, here to kill me to shut me up, so I don't tell anybody about your magical patient kidnapping? Not like anybody would ever believe me, but what the hell. Go ahead." She swung around, looking for…what?

"I won't kill you unless I have to," he said in a reasonable voice that almost deceived her into not hearing that he would kill her *if he had to.*

She turned to face him. "I don't know what to say to that. I really have to give up drinking."

His gaze, inexplicably, lowered to her neck. "I don't think I'll ever give up drinking," he drawled, and even his voice was sexier than hell.

Whew.

"You need to listen to me, Doctor."

She glanced up at him. "I don't think so. And quit talking to me with that weird, buzzing voice. It tickles my brain."

His eyes widened. "What did you say?"

"I said, the voice thing. And I don't even know your name or how you're here or why an axe murderer stole my patient and then stalked me at home, so I think you should go. Now."

He started to speak, but then, before she could react or run or even think about running, he was somehow right in front of her, hands on her arms.

"How did you do that? Nobody can move that fast."

He stared down at her, and his eyes weren't just glowing anymore; they were burning balls of blue flame, and his lips twitched as if he were fighting a grin.

"Are you drunk?

"Well, duh." She rolled her eyes in case he'd missed the sarcasm.

He muttered an impressive string of swear words under his breath. *"Why can you resist my Voice?"*

"Dude. You may be freaking gorgeous, but you're not irresistible. And get your hands off me."

He released her so abruptly she swayed a little, or maybe that was the wine. She couldn't help it, then—she started laughing. An expression of wide-eyed shock spread across his face.

"Are you…are you *laughing* at me?"

"You don't get to tell me what to do, Buster. I don't even know your name. And anyway, you're not even real."

"My name is Bane, and I certainly am real," he ground out. "I don't know why the compulsion isn't working on you, but it did, at least briefly, when I touched you at the hospital, so—"

She laughed even harder. "Oh, sure. The old 'the compulsion isn't working, so let me feel you up' line. Hey, does that ever work for you? Also, *Bane*? What kind of name is that? What are you, a superhero?"

He shoved his hair out of his face with both hands. Or maybe he was clutching his head.

Maybe both.

"You're the most infuriating woman I have ever met in three hundred years of existence."

She rolled her eyes. "Please. Exaggerate much? You're the most infuriating man I've ever met in twenty-nine years of existence, and I know *surgeons*. From *Harvard*. Pretty hard to top, in other words."

She looked him up and down, and suddenly annoyance turned to something else. Something darker. Dirtier.

Delicious.

She wanted another bottle of wine or two.

Or hot sex.

With him.

Yeah, *definitely* that last one.

Because if her hallucination had developed to the point of appearing with lights, action, and surround sound, she might as well get something out of the deal before she checked out, right?

"I don't think I like the look on your face," he said, his eyes narrowing. "What are you thinking?"

She could feel the slow, wicked smile as it spread across her face. "I'm thinking you're the most beautiful man I've ever seen in my life, which is empirical proof that you don't exist."

It was the strangest thing, but she could have sworn her hallucination blushed. There was definitely a hint of dark red at his cheekbones that hadn't been there before.

"But—"

She laughed. "No. No *buts* in my fantasies. Enough talking. Take off your clothes."

CHAPTER NINE

This was not how things were supposed to go.

On the other hand, Bane was willing to adapt to changing circumstances.

"Now you're talking," he said. Then he yanked his shirt off and threw it on the floor.

Ryan gasped. "You…oh. You can't possibly look that good. I don't know where I'd even get a frame of reference for a hallucination like you. I'd have to have seen some astonishingly high-class porn." She whistled. "Or Brazilian soccer players. Yep, that's probably it. I watched that soccer game with Annie in the doctors' lounge, and my brain knows I like blue-eyed blonds, and here you are, with those muscles, and that six-pack—eight-pack? Oh dear heavens— and here you are, like sex on a stick, and—"

"You're babbling," he said, a feeling of smug, male triumph spreading through him like a river of warm honey. "Also, sex on a stick? I don't know what that means, but I find that I like it. A lot."

He took a step closer, unbuttoning his jeans as he moved. "Shouldn't you be taking your clothes off, too?"

By all the gods, she was gorgeous, although she also… wasn't. He blinked. In fact, her face was almost ordinary, as Luke had said.

What was happening to him? He, who'd seen and touched and tasted beauties from a dozen generations?

But then she smiled, and her face lit up like the sun.

As did her skin. He'd almost put her glowing skin out of his mind. She'd presented as completely normal—plain, ordinary human—when he'd entered her home. Until now. When she smiled, her skin had lit up, too. And the glow remained, making every inch of her uncovered skin luminous.

And any thought of *ordinary* disappeared. She was far more than the sum of her parts, this woman. The sheer intensity in her eyes had caught him—claimed him—and wouldn't let him go. But maybe it was merely illusion that her skin was gleaming in the soft light in the room?

She'd let down her hair since he'd seen her at the hospital, and it was a gleaming dark fall of chestnut brown that reached halfway down her back. He couldn't wait to see it spread across his pillow. And the curves that the lab coat had hidden were on full display in her silky nightclothes, which consisted of shorts and a cropped top that hugged her breasts. Were he a poet, he'd write odes to those breasts. They were so round and ripe, with nipples begging for his mouth.

The tiny pair of shorts, too, which revealed the most delicious, curvy legs he'd ever hoped to have wrapped around his waist.

Or thrown over his shoulders.

He swallowed, hard, when he realized his fangs were in danger of descending, and not from *blood* lust, either. His body had hardened, too, to the point of making his pants uncomfortably tight.

He also felt something…wrong.

Which made no sense.

A beautiful, okay and possibly glowing, woman wanted

him to take off his clothes.

He wanted to fuck her.

There was nothing wrong, and everything right, about this situation.

He took another step toward her, but something in his gut twisted.

What the hell?

It had been his way of life for three centuries—to take what was freely offered.

No.

This—this somehow felt wrong.

Ryan, who'd started unbuttoning her shirt, glanced up at him from beneath her lashes, and the gesture was so incredibly sexy that his cock hardened to the point of pain.

"Why are you stopping?" She bit her lips, suddenly looking more nervous than seductive. "I get to call the shots, right? This is *my* hallucination, after all. Keep taking your clothes off."

Oh, *hell* no.

"*I am not a hallucination,*" he ground out from between clenched teeth. "*Quit calling me that.*"

She stopped unbuttoning and put her hands on her hips, because, of course, compulsion didn't work on her. Why would anything be normal and reasonable about this enchanting, infuriating, fascinating woman?

"You don't get a say, buddy. You aren't even real. I'm actually standing here arguing with my own frontal lobe. Although I have to admit you're a lot sexier than the last frontal lobe I saw. I'm just saying. Which is lucky for you, since I dissected that sucker."

Bane started to feel like he was out of his depth, again,

which he'd felt a lot since first encountering Dr. Ryan
Gorgeous-But-Possibly-Nuts-and-Definitely-Drunk St.
Cloud.

"And you smell like flowers and sunshine, not guano," he
muttered. "Odd, for someone who's clearly bat-shit crazy."

She grinned and then leapt up and threw her arms
around his neck. His hands automatically lifted to catch
her, and he found himself groaning at the warmth and
weight of her deliciously round ass. Her hair was like silk,
touching his cheek, and she was warm and soft and lovely
and everything he had never known he'd always wanted.

Then she wrapped her legs around his waist, and the
torrent of electricity that shot through his body made his
brain quit working.

"Maybe, before we get naked, we should stop talking
and start kissing," she whispered. "Because if you're a lousy
kisser, the deal is off. I can't put up with another lousy
kisser, after—"

Having no desire at all to hear about whoever the soon-
to-be-dead man was who'd been a lousy kisser, Bane
simply decided to shut her up.

With his mouth.

He'd show her that...

　　Show her the...

　　　　Show her how...

Hell. He didn't know what he was trying to show her.

It was hard to show anybody anything when his entire
world was exploding.

So, instead, he just kissed her. He kissed her, and light
and sound and color disappeared into a maelstrom of
touch and feeling and pure, primal sensation.

He kissed her, and she made soft little moaning noises, and his body hardened beyond want, beyond need, beyond desire, to a place he'd never been before and never wanted to leave.

He kissed her, and suddenly he could hear and see and smell the blood, the sweet, intoxicating blood rushing through her veins, and he wanted her, needed her, *must have her in all possible ways, blood and sex and possession and belonging and forever and ever and...*

BANE! BANE, WHERE ARE YOU? WE NEED YOU NOW! THE HUMAN IS WAKING UP AND FIGHTING THE TURN!

When Meara's voice blasted into his mind, it snapped Bane back out of the blood frenzy, but it was too late, too late, *far too late*, because the first thing he realized was that his fangs were already in Ryan's neck.

The second thing he realized was that her blood was already in his mouth, and the taste of it sparkled inside him like the finest champagne. Like dreams made liquid and distilled into ambrosia. Like...like even her *blood* glowed.

But—

The final thing he realized was that she was dead.

And he was the one who'd killed her.

He fell to his knees, still holding her body to him, and he roared out his anguish and despair. "No, *no*, not now, not her, please, no."

And then she stuttered out a breath.

No, it was...a snore.

She was *snoring*.

He hadn't killed her at all.

He'd put her to sleep.

Literally to sleep.

He started to laugh.

BANE! WE NEED YOU NOW!

He stood, still holding Ryan, but so carefully, as if she were so fragile—so vulnerable.

As if she were the most important person in his world.

And then, pushing the thought aside to analyze and deny later, he called again to the Shadows and stepped back into the Between, this time carrying a sleeping human.

Only to arrive back at the mansion just in time to see Hunter, who was somehow—impossibly—awake, slam Meara into a wall.

And then, from clear across the room, Bane heard the sound of his sister's spine breaking.

CHAPTER TEN

Luckily for Hunter, a broken neck didn't kill a vampire, so Bane wouldn't have to destroy him for it.

Unluckily for Hunter, Edge wasn't feeling anywhere near as generous.

"Take her," Bane shouted, tossing Ryan over to where Luke stood, six feet away.

Luke caught her and shot Bane a look. "What the fuck is going on?"

But Bane didn't have time to chat, because he had to stop one of his brothers from killing another. He raced across the room in time to punch Hunter in the head, knocking him out, and then he caught Edge's arm and twisted it up and behind his back before Edge could strike a killing blow on Hunter.

"He doesn't know what he's doing," Bane told him. "And Meara's fine. Look, she's already healing."

Edge whirled to face Bane, his eyes wild with pain and fury. "He hurt her, and I'll destroy him," he snarled. "It is my *right*."

Behind Edge's back, a *popping* noise signaled them both that Meara had healed her spine.

"I think," she rasped out, "that if it's anybody's right, it's mine."

Edge leapt away from Bane and landed next to Meara in a crouching position that looked very far from human. "Did you just make a *joke*?" His voice was a harsh rasp.

"He could have *killed* you."

"But he didn't, did he?" She put a hand on Edge's arm, but he flinched away from her.

This time, Bane would have sworn that a flash of hurt crossed behind Meara's eyes, but it was gone so fast he'd probably been mistaken.

"Nobody's destroying anyone," Bane said, putting his shirt, which had been draped around his neck, back on. "Help me get him back to the table, and this time we'll tie him down. I've never seen anybody react like this, but I've heard about it. It's rare but not unknown."

Edge shot him a silver glare filled with contempt. "Get him back to the table yourself. But be warned: if he ever lays a hand on Meara again, I'll kill him."

Meara slowly pushed herself up off the ground, ignoring the hand Edge held out to her. Her golden eyes sparked with rage. "If you think for one minute that I'm going to tolerate—"

Edge threw back his head and roared out a sound filled with so much frustration and anger that Bane snapped into a fighting stance, prepared to defend Meara and everyone else in the room.

But Edge clamped his lips together, cutting off that horrible sound, and then stood and shook his head once, then again. "No. You tolerate nothing. I'm done. I had to watch my brother die. I won't go through that again with you."

With that, the scientist-turned-vampire flicked his fingers toward the window, which shattered into a thousand pieces exploding out into the dark, and then he flew out after them, disappearing into the night.

"Well, that's one way to make an exit," Luke drawled. "Now, are you ready to tell me why I'm holding an armful of warm, sleeping human? And what's wrong with her?"

Bane snarled at Luke and then carried Hunter over to the table, tied him down more securely, and gave him enough blood to allow him to lapse back into the deep sleep of the Turn. Then he retrieved his human and carried her over to a couch and sat down, holding her in his lap, before looking at Meara and Luke.

"Tell me. Now."

Meara shot him a narrow-eyed look of disbelief. "Really? Maybe you should go first, big brother, and explain to us why there's a random *human* in our *home*."

Bane opened his mouth and then shut it, realizing he had no fucking idea how to answer her.

"Well?" Meara tapped her foot. "I can't wait to hear this."

He glanced down at Ryan's sleeping face, still tasting the sweetness of her blood in his mouth. "I think...I think this human is mine. And maybe...maybe she's not entirely human."

A stupid grin spread across Luke's face, and then he started to laugh. "Oh, good. Now we're fucked."

Just then, a quick knock sounded on the closed door, and then Mr. Cassidy opened the door and his wife followed him in, carrying a tray. Her eyes went immediately to the broken window, but when she realized they were all alive and—as far as she knew—unharmed, she smiled.

"Soup?"

• • •

Ryan woke up to the quiet sounds of people carrying on a conversation and to the smell of chicken soup. She opened her eyes and discovered that she was wrapped in a very warm blanket in a very hot room and was possibly in danger of suffocating or suffering heat stroke at any minute.

She also had the headache and upset stomach from Hell, not to mention vague memories of hallucinating a hot guy in her living room who kissed her and...*bit her neck?*

She sat up, flinging blankets and pillows to the floor, and then jumped to her feet, whirling around to scan the little alcove, which held only the couch and a small table. She needed to figure out where the hell she was, because this was definitely not her place or the hospital, and she didn't think Heaven's waiting room looked like a portrait gallery in a museum. But she wouldn't be in Heaven, or even Hell, from a damn hangover. She hadn't crossed the line from drunk to alcohol poisoning.

She shook her head, which hurt like hell, and, suddenly, it all rushed back.

The hallucination at the hospital. The man in her house.

"You're awake."

She shrieked and jumped back, turning at the same time, and almost stumbled, which made both her head and her stomach very unhappy.

"It's *you*."

He stood there—*Bane*—his shirt back on, thankfully, but otherwise looking exactly the same as he had before. Unfairly gorgeous, and not at all like his mouth tasted like something had crawled in it and died, unlike hers.

"Yes," he agreed. "It's me."

He made no move to touch her; in fact, he put his hands

in his pockets when he caught her looking at them.

"So." She cleared her throat. "I'm not drunk, just hideously hungover now, so I'm guessing you're not a hallucination."

"Ha! If only," a female voice called out. A moment later, the woman who belonged to the voice walked around the corner and swept a bemused glance over Ryan's pajama-clad, wild-haired self.

"This is not at all your usual human," the woman said to Bane. And then, to Ryan, "Meara Delacourt. I'm pleased to meet you. If you'd like to borrow, ah, anything? My bathroom is down the stairs on the right. Maybe soap. Or mouthwash."

A hot wave of shame washed over Ryan at the snide comment, but she'd been belittled by far worse than the human fashion doll standing in front of her, so she simply smiled and gave Meara a Southernism. "Bless your heart. I'd be delighted to take you up on that, about half-past never. Now who the hell are you people, where am I, and which one of you is going to call me a car or taxi, since I don't appear to have my phone with me?"

Unexpectedly, Meara started laughing. "Well, the little human has a spine, does she? And look, Dr. St. Cloud, I know perfectly well that *bless your heart* means *kiss my ass* in Savannah, so don't think you're getting away with anything."

The woman was unbelievably beautiful—a tall, blond, goddess, everything Ryan was not—and jealousy mixed with envy for a nasty minute in Ryan's pathetic, hungover brain, but then she remembered that she was standing in her pajamas in a strange place with people she didn't know, and there were therefore more important things to worry about.

Speaking of things to worry about...

"Why do you keep calling me a 'little human'? Is that opposed to a supermodel-tall human, like yourself? Are you making short-people jokes? Who the hell *are* you people?"

Meara's astonishing golden eyes widened, and she turned to Bane. "She doesn't know who you are? I mean, it's not unusual for you not to tell them that you're a vampire, but they usually at least know your name."

Ryan started slow clapping. "Very funny. And for your next trick, we'll all go out to Bonaventure Cemetery and leave presents for the ghost of Little Gracie."

Bane took a step toward her but stopped when she held up a hand. "No. Stay away, or I'll call the police. Clearly, you kidnapped me when I was passed out drunk, but I seem to be okay, so we'll just call it even if you call me a taxi or car. Now. And stay away from me—far away from me—while I wait *outside on the porch* for it to arrive."

"She doesn't believe we're vampires, Bane. I mean, we always have to remove their memories after, but it's at least fun to watch them get all scared and run around screaming," Meara said in a voice filled with glee to match the huge smile on her face.

"Don't scare the human, Meara," Bane growled. "Ryan, I'm sorry. This isn't how I wanted this to go. I had to get back here, to help Hunter, but first I kissed you, and then your blood—Damn it. This is not how I wanted to explain."

Ryan tried to speak, but her throat had suddenly quit working. In fact, her legs quit working, too, and she stumbled back and fell onto the couch. "You had to help *Hunter*. Would that be Hunter Evans?"

"Yes."

"The firefighter?"

Bane blew out a sigh but then nodded. "Yes."

Ryan stood on legs that were no longer shaky at all. Because she was no longer a hungover woman caught in a situation she didn't understand.

Now she was a doctor, and she had a patient to protect.

"Take me to him."

"Good job explaining this," Meara said sweetly.

Bane shook his head. "No. You don't understand. I—"

Ryan clenched her hands into fists. "Take me to him. Right. Fucking. Now."

"I can't."

"Why? Is he dead? Did you kill him?" Ryan realized she'd started shouting, but she couldn't help it.

Meara rolled her eyes and reached out and grabbed Ryan by the arm in an unbreakable grip. "No, he's not dead. Bane saved him, much to my dismay. But he's soon to be a vampire, like the rest of us. See?"

With that, the woman smiled widely, and Ryan watched in shock as perfectly realistic-looking fangs snapped down and into place where Meara's canine teeth should have been.

"I don't—are those—so, big deal." She took a deep, steadying breath. "You can probably buy those at six different shops on Broughton Street."

Meara threw her head back and laughed.

Bane pointed to the door across the room. "Out."

"But—"

His eyes started glowing that hot blue again, and Meara sighed. "Fine. But can I play with her when you're done with her?"

"Out!"

She left, but she laughed all the way across the room.

Ryan folded her arms and waited until Meara was gone, and then she repeated her demand. "Take me to see my patient. Now. And enough of this vampire bullshit."

"Ryan. *Dr. St. Cloud.* You need to listen to me before I take you anywhere," Bane said, subtly moving to block her way when she tried to storm past him.

"I don't need to listen to anything. I need to see—"

"You need to see this," he snarled, grabbing her arms and yanking her against his chest. "You need to know. Now."

She shoved against him, but his grip was like steel. Finally, she decided she'd go along until she could escape and call the police, so she took a long, slow breath and nodded. "Fine. I need to know. What is it I need to know?"

He put a finger under her chin and tilted her face up to look into her eyes.

"The vampire thing. It isn't bullshit."

And then he opened his mouth and showed her his fangs.

Up close and personal.

Still, she might have believed they were fakes, too, except for the part where he lifted her into his arms and floated up into the air.

Levitated up in the air. Holy crap!

She clutched his shoulders and a vicious rush of vertigo swept through her. She closed her eyes and fought to keep from being sick.

Suddenly, still floating in the air, a horrible realization smashed into her terrified, alcohol-fogged brain. "You really are a vampire, aren't you? And you killed him, didn't you? You killed Hunter Evans, and now you're going to kill me?"

Bane closed his eyes and bent his head to rest his forehead against hers for a moment while she tried to come to grips with her new reality and probable impending murder.

"I didn't even get to finish watching *Die Hard*," she muttered.

"I told you. I won't kill you unless it's absolutely necessary," Bane growled.

"Well, *that's* reassuring," she snapped, because if she was going to die anyway, what the hell.

Bane scowled at her. "You are a very rude woman. But if it's the only way to allay your concerns, let's go see Hunter. He's asleep. Well, you'd probably consider it a coma, actually. And he'll be out for almost three days, if all goes well."

He slowly floated them back down to the ground, and her heart quit trying quite so hard to pound its way out of her chest. It was Savannah, after all. So, there were vampires. There were also pirate ghosts, or so people claimed. She could handle this.

She could *handle* this, she told her weak knees.

Bane caught her hand in his and led her out of the alcove and around the corner into another huge room, which was filled with a whole lot of nothing, except for a large table in the center of the room, with a man lying on top of it, sleeping. There was also a chair next to the table, in which another man was also asleep, and a small table next to the door they'd just entered, which held a tray with bowls, spoons, a basket of bread, and a soup tureen.

A faint rumble of appetite caught Ryan off guard for a moment, but then she forgot her stomach, the food, and the fact that she was standing in what appeared to be a ballroom in her pajamas.

Because the man on the table turned his head toward her, and his eyes snapped open.

His *red* eyes.

And flakes of burned skin fell off his body as he fought against the ropes she only just now saw were holding him down.

"Hunter," Bane called out, releasing her hand and racing over to the man, who—impossibly—must be Hunter Evans. "No!"

The man in the chair startled awake and then lunged up and caught Hunter's legs, helping Bane hold him down, and then Bane...

He...

Ryan's mind tried to shut down. Her logical, scientific, always-rational mind decided that she'd had quite enough and tried to force Ryan to turn and walk out of the room, down the stairs, and out of the house.

Far, far away from a place where the man she'd been kissing, only hours before, could rip his wrist open *with his fangs* and hold it out to a dying burn victim, so the man could clamp his jaws onto Bane's wrist and drink.

She felt herself being torn into two separate and opposing forces.

Ryan wanted very, very badly to run away from these people. These *vampires*.

But the part of her that was Dr. St. Cloud? *Dr. St. Cloud* wanted to stay.

Terror fought scientific curiosity.

Scientific curiosity won.

Dr. Ryan St. Cloud took a deep breath and crossed the room toward the three men.

The three *vampires*.

"I'm a doctor," she told Hunter Evans. "I'm here to help."

CHAPTER ELEVEN

Bane watched in mounting disbelief as the human pushed past her shock and fear, visibly schooling her expression into one of calm confidence, as she crossed the room toward him. Even in skimpy pajamas—even with wild hair and smudged makeup—she was every inch the professional.

Damn, but he had to admire that.

She knew what he was, and she was still walking toward him. Toward Hunter, who was clearly on the edge of a crazed, homicidal bloodlust that the Turn shouldn't be provoking in him this soon.

Hunter lunged in Ryan's direction, almost breaking free of Bane's hold.

"Oh, fuck no," Bane snarled. "Stay back," he roared at Ryan, hoping sheer volume would work where his attempts to enthrall her had not.

She kept coming, her only response a raised eyebrow. "This has a déjà vu feel to it, but I think you can't really expect *me* to listen to *you* when you ignored me so completely in the hospital. Also, you need to explain to me how you disappeared, but maybe later. Now." She took a deep breath and raised her chin. "Now, I want to examine my patient."

"Yesss," Hunter growled through a mouthful of blood, looking almost exactly like a hideous caricature of a monster in a bad vampire movie, which—for some strange reason—made Bane want to hide him from Ryan's view.

Why?

The answer, when it came, caught him completely off guard.

He didn't want her to see a monster and associate it with him.

The realization made his blood run cold—even colder than usual—and he filed it away, under *things to think about later or maybe never,* because the unbelievably fearless human was less than a foot away from him now, which meant that he could smell her and hear her heart beating far faster than her calm demeanor would have led him to expect.

And if *he* could smell her and hear her heartbeat... He tightened his grasp on Hunter a second before the man lunged at Ryan.

"Want!"

Bane caught his shoulders and pressed him down, and Luke, clearly suffering from blood-loss-induced exhaustion, based on the way his wrist was chewed up, got a firmer grip on Hunter's legs.

"This isn't good," Luke snapped, glaring at Ryan.

"Thank you, Captain Understatement," Ryan snapped right back at him. "Maybe you two can move out of my way so I can examine Mr. Evans and figure out what the hell you've done to him."

"Maybe you can move back across the room so I can get him under control," Bane gritted out from between teeth clenched so tightly he was surprised they didn't shatter. "He can smell you. Don't you get it? Your presence is aggravating his condition."

She looked uncertain for a split second, her gaze flashing to Hunter's face, but then Bane got fed up with the entire situation and made the decision for her, smashing his fist into the side of Hunter's head, knocking him out.

For how long, who the hell knew, but it solved the matter momentarily.

"Why did you do that?" Ryan demanded, outrage ringing in her voice. "You can't just—"

"I can, and I did. Now, maybe we can figure out why he keeps waking up when he should be out for three days. And we need some better restraints."

"No shit, Sherlock," Luke muttered. "And maybe you can explain why your human is here? I mean, play with them, fine, but keep them in your bedroom or at the club in the basement. We don't need her here."

Before Bane could answer him—or beat the shit out of him, which was his first inclination—Ryan pointed her finger at Luke's face.

"Hey. Asshole. Your bullshit lines didn't work on me at the hospital, and I'm sure as hell not going to listen to you now, when we're in a room filled with vampires. So, shut up, or I'll shut you up."

A peculiar feeling fizzled in Bane's chest at her words. Was it...laughter?

Pride?

What the fuck was happening to him?

Luke, inexplicably, grinned. "Hey, doll face. *We're* not in a room filled with vampires. *You* are. And my name's Luke, not Asshole." He flashed his fangs at her, still smiling, and Ryan took an almost-certainly involuntary step back, because then she immediately scowled.

His human was a fighter, then. The realization pleased him for the roughly two seconds it took for pleasure to turn to horror that he kept thinking of her as *his*.

"I can't...okay. I might need to sit down." Ryan made an abrupt right face, marched over to the far wall, and slid down to sit on the floor in a graceless heap, pulling her knees into her chest and wrapping her arms around them.

Everything about her body language suddenly screamed *defensive posture*, maybe an inch away from *helpless terror*.

The doctor had finally had enough.

Luke laughed. "Nice jammies, by the way, *human*."

Bane swung around, leading with his fist. He didn't aim for Luke's face but for a point about three inches inside his skull. When the blow landed, Luke's head rocked back, and his entire body lifted off the floor and flew a good six feet across the room before he hit the wall opposite the one where Ryan huddled.

"Keep your rude comments to yourself, or I'll be sure you're unable to speak at all," Bane snarled.

"You—" Luke gathered himself to leap off the floor, muscles bunching in readiness for attack, but then looked— really looked—at Bane and slowly dropped back down, wiping blood off his mouth with the back of one hand. "Fine. I have no idea what you're up to, but fine."

"My motivations are none of your fucking business, especially when you insult my...guest," Bane told him, substituting *guest* for *human* at the last second, cognizant of exactly what shit would hit the fan if the doctor heard him say that she was *his*—human or otherwise.

"I need to go home now," Ryan said quietly. Too quietly,

as if the fight and determination she'd shown had drained out of her like the blood Hunter had drained from Luke's wrist.

Bane blew out a sigh. He'd expected her to break. Had even wondered why it was taking so long.

The human brain had only a certain elasticity, in terms of being able to suspend disbelief.

Believe the unbelievable.

See the possibility in the impossible.

Hollywood, novels, and the internet had brought humans a long way toward what they'd accept as credible—on the page or on the screen.

Not so much in their reality.

If the monsters were real, then humans weren't the gods of their domains that they believed themselves to be. And human brains were absolutely not wired to go along with that.

So legitimate sightings of the supernatural were scoffed at as hoaxes. Mocked as the fakest of reality TV nonsense. Laughed at by skeptics, scorned by science.

But science, though hailed as the religion of the modern age, the true dogma in which to believe, with physics and chemistry the gospel of that contemporary church…

Science couldn't comprehend magic.

And monsters lived in the darkness of the interstitial spaces between science and magic—between logic and emotion.

Between life and death.

Twas brillig, indeed, but vampires, as well as the slithy toves, did gyre and gimble in the wabe. Lewis Carroll had gotten it partly right, but humans need beware of more than the Jabberwock.

Far worse creatures walked the night.

The problem was getting the humans to believe it.

Dr. Ryan St. Cloud was obviously crossing the threshold of scientific skepticism into belief, so the next question was plain:

Would her mind break under the strain?

Before he could come to a conclusion, Meara strode back into the room, her arms full of towels.

"All right, human. I've come to save you from the stink of stale wine and humiliation."

• • •

Ryan, still clutching her knees to her chest, opened her eyes at the female vampire's — Meara's — cheery announcement, when the words broke through the haze of hopelessness mixed with disbelief that had driven her to this position with her back literally against this wall.

"Quit calling me human. My name is Ryan. Or Dr. St. Cloud. Or even *you bitch.* Just not *human.* Got it, *vampire*?"

The vampire narrowed her gorgeous — and also glowing — eyes but then apparently decided to take Ryan's insult as a joke, because she threw back her head and laughed with what sounded like genuine amusement.

"She's got guts, Bane. I'll give her that. She smells like the place that a hangover goes to die, but she's got guts."

Ryan sighed and dropped her head back to her knees, her momentary spurt of rage-induced energy fizzling out. What was she thinking? Insulting vampires, even those who looked like Valkyries, was not a great way forward to a long and happy life.

"Cheer up, Doctor. Maybe we'll be great friends and watch movies and eat popcorn together," Meara said cheerfully.

Ryan tilted her head to stare up at the woman. "You like movies and popcorn?"

"And licorice. Not the black kind, though."

"Sure. I'll play along. You're a vampire who wants to have popcorn with me. What's your favorite movie?" Ryan gently thudded her head back against the wall, because it just seemed like the thing to do when one had conversations with *vampires* about *movies*.

"*Pride and Prejudice* with Colin Firth," Meara answered instantly. "I love the part where Elizabeth Bennet decides to fuck him after she sees the size of his house."

Ryan's mouth fell open. "What? You—that's not—that's not what happened. At all. She learned what a good guy he was, because of how he treated his servants—"

"He made them call him *The Master*. That's messed up," Meara said, striding over and tossing a pile of towels to the floor next to Ryan.

"And his sister—"

"He treated her like a helpless child. Plus he was too much of an asshole to stop Bingley's sisters from talking shit about Lizzie."

Ryan scowled at her. "You're so completely wrong about all of that, I can't believe it."

With the insightful, calculating part of her brain, Ryan was measuring distances to exits, wondering just how fast these creatures were, and wondering how fast she could get the hell out of this place.

The rest of her brain was blathering on about movies and trying not to freak completely out at the high probability of her imminent, horrible death.

"I can't believe we're talking about movies when Hunter might wake up any minute and go full bloodlust on us," the rude one Bane had knocked to the floor—Luke—snarled. He jumped up and made a point of straightening his clothes and then shoving his hair out of his face.

"Look. I'm sorry I insulted your human, Bane. My apologies, *Doctor*." This, with a flourish in her direction. "But we need to figure out what's wrong with Hunter and fix it, or do we even know if the Turn will take? If he goes through all this and dies anyway…"

He was right. She hated everything about him, but he was right. Plus, they clearly cared about the firefighter enough that she might use that for some kind of leverage.

She grabbed the towels and stood. "Good. Right. Show me to your bathroom, please, Meara? I'll get cleaned up and take a look at Hunter. Do you also have any clothes that might fit me? Um, sweatpants or something?"

Meara's perfect lips pulled back in a grimace. "As if I'd have *sweatpants*. And you're a good five inches shorter than me—"

"I'm five-six," Ryan told her, pointedly eyeing the woman's heeled boots. "And without those boots, I bet you're only five-eight. So…"

"Yes, but you're rounder than I am," Meara said, but not in a bitchy way, just matter-of-factly. "I'd kill for that cleavage, to be honest. Come on, we'll find you something."

She turned and strode out of the room, leaving Ryan rooted to the floor, heat flooding her body and undoubtedly turning her face hot pink, because she could already see the flush on her chest. But not so much with shame as with… pleasure? The most beautiful woman she'd ever seen envied mouse-like, boring Ryan for her cleavage?

Something that felt a bit like confidence tingled its way into her mind. She'd always been confident about her work, but her looks? Well, no. She was forgettable, and she knew it. Except for the wrong kind of attention, when she was a teenager growing into D cups before most of her friends even got training bras.

She'd never been the smartest, the fastest, the prettiest, the most charming.

She'd been *Boring Ryan.*

Ryan St. Grindstone.

She'd always been the person who could be completely and utterly counted on to work harder than anybody else. To be reliable and sensible and level-headed.

To definitely *not* be standing in a room filled with hot, supermodel-like vampires—*in her skimpy pajamas*—being complimented on her cleavage.

Although what the *hell* was she doing thinking about any of this under the current circumstances? She must still be drunk.

"Doctor? Are you coming or not?" Meara's impatient voice called out from down the hall, and Ryan suddenly realized that she was going on a mental flight of fancy in a room that was still *filled with vampires*.

She looked up and caught Bane's gaze and came to another realization: she wasn't the only one who'd been standing there thinking about her cleavage.

His eyes burned hot blue fire, and his body almost

imperceptibly strained toward her, even as he stood perfectly still, his hands clenched into fists at his sides.

"You should go," he growled, his gaze dropping to her breasts—tangible as a caress—and then back to her face. "You should go, *now*."

She clutched the towels to her chest and quickly walked out of the room, forcing herself not to run. When she took the left turn in the hallway to follow Meara, she heard the rude one's laugh again.

"From the look on your face, you're the one who's fucked, my friend."

Bane made a deep growling sound that made the tiny hairs on the back of Ryan's neck stand up. "Shut up, Luke, or I'll shut you up."

Luke's only response was more laughter.

Ryan paused, looking back toward the stairs behind her. She could escape down those stairs and out of the house and never, ever look back.

But Hunter Evans...she would not abandon him.

Meara leaned out of the last doorway on the right, at the end of the hall. "Are you coming, or is there something about looking and smelling like hell that's making you happy?"

Ryan sighed, took one long, last look at the stairs, and then headed toward Meara.

She'd get clean, she'd get a closer look at Hunter, and then she'd get out.

Call the police if she had to.

Protect her patient.

Never, ever see vampires again in her lifetime.

Except...why did she hate that idea so much?

CHAPTER TWELVE

Carter Reynolds, president of the Wolf Pack MC, stalked into the room, stared down at the battered and bound white-haired vampire lying in the middle of his clubhouse floor, and felt a killing rage rising inside him.

"Somebody better tell me, right now, who the *fuck* thought that breaking our treaty with the vampires was a good thing to do," he roared.

The twenty or so of his pack who'd followed him into the clubhouse dropped to their knees when his power washed over them, but nobody even tried to answer.

He'd known, when they rode up and discovered the sentries unconscious on the ground outside and the clubhouse door swinging open, that it would be bad. He'd expected *bad*.

He hadn't expected *now we're fucked all to hell*.

His head started throbbing in reaction to the fury pounding through his skull. There would be blood paid for this. "*Damn* it."

The vampire twitched, its face still hidden beneath a tangle of that pure white hair, causing the men nearest him to flinch and back away. The wolves all knew what vampires were capable of doing to anybody stupid enough to think a bloodsucker was down for the count.

They'd lost club members to just such stupid complacency in the past. But this—this wasn't on them.

And Carter didn't even know who this was.

"We didn't do this to you," he told the vampire. "If you'll hold still, we'll remove these chains, and—"

"I'd advise against it," said an icy female voice that sent revulsion skittering down his spine. "Consider him to be a gift."

The vampire's eyes, which had been fluttering open, closed again, and Carter turned to face the warlock striding toward him. She was definitely a warlock, although she'd been able to mask the stench of her magic until she was almost on them, and that was a new trick that signaled bad fucking times in the future.

"It's not my birthday," Carter said dryly.

His second, Max, started to rise, but he shook his head at her. Nobody needed to get in the scary warlock's path until he could figure out what the hell she wanted.

The warlock presented as young and beautiful like they almost all—male or female—did, whether they'd lived for decades or centuries, but Carter knew better than to trust appearances. His nose, even in human form, told a story of rot and death, not beauty.

"My name is Sylvie," the warlock proclaimed, in the tone of one giving him a great boon. She stared at him as if she expected him to bow or kiss her damn hand.

She was in the wrong place if she expected bowing and scraping. He'd been the alpha of this pack since he was nineteen years old, and he sure as hell hadn't gotten the job by backing down before predators.

He studied the face she wore. White skin, black hair. Black eyes, to match the blackened soul all warlocks carried, if they still had souls at all. Tall. Slender. Long legs. Just the kind of woman he'd give a second glance, except this wasn't a woman at all.

Warlocks were pure evil wrapped in a skin sack. And it was bad fucking news that this one had apparently decided to take an interest in his pack.

Or in him.

"We're taking over this territory," she said. "We could have use for you and your wolves, if you do what you're told."

Some of his pack began to growl, and she glanced dismissively at them and then laughed. "Oh! Please! *Please* challenge me. I love to play with puppies!"

With that, she flicked her fingers at Max, who fell over, her body contorting, her face grimacing horribly as a screeching howl burst out of her. Max smacked into the ground two seconds later and then—before Carter could even move—Max's wolf form burst free of her human body and crouched, shuddering in reaction, on the floor.

He could feel waves of shock equaling his own resonating from his pack. None of them, not even the strongest, could change that fast. The warlock had pulled Max's wolf out of her like she was selecting a chocolate from a box—casually and almost without thought.

Max shivered and turned dark eyes to him, and he could feel her pain radiating through his mind.

"We'll be in touch, Wolf," Sylvie said, turning those black eyes to him. "Discard the vampire however you want. He'll be in hell with the rest of his kind before very long, you can be sure of that. The Chamber is taking over this territory. And you'll either work for us or die."

With that, she strode back out of the room, pulling a veil of black smoke around her as she reached the door.

And then she was gone.

He pointed at two of his wolves, who both ran to follow her but returned almost immediately.

"She's gone. No car, no bike, no sign of her walking," Yerby said, shaking his head, shivers of reaction—or revulsion—wracking his muscled form. "The men who stayed outside to help the sentries are out cold, too. We need help to get them inside. Figure out if we need an ambulance."

Carter swore, fists clenching, but then nodded, and several of the pack ran to assist. He was grimly pleased to see no sign of reluctance from his people, in spite of the natural and pretty damn intelligent instinct to avoid anything to do with blood magic. When he looked down, the vampire was staring up at him with glowing silver eyes set in a surprisingly youthful face, considering the hair.

"I think we need to talk," the vampire said, snapping his bonds as if they were nothing and then leaping to his feet.

Carter held up a hand when he noticed some of his pack crouch into attack mode. The relationship between werewolf and vampire had never been an easy one, in spite of their current fragile truce, but the danger of warlocks blew through old rivalries like an icy breeze through a puff of smoke.

Then he nodded at the vampire. "I think you're right."

CHAPTER THIRTEEN

Bane waited until he heard Meara run downstairs before making his move, and every second lasted a hundred years.

He was surely losing his mind.

"Watch him," he ordered Luke. "Call Edge and get his ass back here to help. He can carry his weight in things that don't involve computers, too."

Luke's eyes gleamed with amusement and something that looked too damn much like pity. "Sure, boss. But if you go after her now, you may just be chasing after her for a long time to come. It's not very dignified of you."

"Fuck dignity," Bane snarled, and then he all but flew out of the room and down the hall, catching Ryan before she'd closed the door to Meara's bathroom behind her.

"No. Not here."

She jumped and then shot him a narrow-eyed glance over one bare shoulder, which naturally made him think hot, delicious thoughts of licking her creamy skin in that very place. Biting her...

No. Not biting.

"Not here, what? And will you please quit giving me orders, already? Your enthrally voice doesn't work on me, and overbearing men trying to tell me what to do is not a new tune in my particular symphony. I don't respond well to it. Not at work, and not in my personal life, and not... not in whatever this is."

"Your symphony?" She made his head hurt. She didn't

make sense, and yet the intelligence in her eyes was sharper than the silver blade in its sheath at his hip. She was afraid of him, and yet she was fearless.

She was plain, and yet she was the most beautiful woman he'd ever encountered.

As if drawn to the parallel, his own reaction to her was equally nonsensical. He wanted her to go away, before she pulled him further into her sensual, magnetic orbit.

He wanted her never, ever to leave him.

He wanted to fuck her while draining her dry.

"This must be what it feels like to go mad," he said, shaking his head once, hard, to dislodge any incipient insanity.

A flash of darkness slid behind her eyes, and her shoulders slumped just a fraction before she tightened her arms around the towels she held and turned to face him.

"You seem pretty sane to me." Her eyes darkened to a stormy blue, their intensity deepening. "No, Bane-who-is-not-a-hallucination-but-something-so-much-worse. I think you're not going mad. If anyone in this room is going mad, it is either me—for believing I'm in a house filled with vampires—or maybe Meara."

That caught him off guard. His sister was one of the sanest people he'd ever met. "Meara?"

Ryan waved her hand, the gesture encompassing the bathroom. "I have never seen anything messier in my life that wasn't the *before* on some TV show about hoarders."

He laughed and then froze in astonishment when he heard the rusty sound. He'd laughed more in the scant few hours since meeting this human than he had in years.

Maybe even decades.

Why?

And why did it matter? Why was he bothering to analyze a momentary pleasure?

Perhaps because he'd had so few of those in recent years.

Decades.

"Meara is rather careless of her things, but in her defense, she cleans her own rooms. She says she'd never inflict her messes on Mrs. Cassidy."

"Mrs. Cassidy?"

"Our housekeeper."

Ryan's lovely, full mouth fell open just a little. "You have a housekeeper? Is she a vampire, too?"

"No, she—"

"Does she know about you? Is she enthralled? Is she, like, your Renfield? Do you—"

"Enough," he protested, wanting very much to pound his head against the wall. "There are no Renfields. Bram Stoker has much to answer for, and I plan to tell him that the next time I see him," he said grimly.

"Well, I...*what?* The next time you see him? Bram Stoker is alive after all these... Oh. My. God. Bram Stoker is a vampire?" Her voice rose so high it was nearly squeaking by the end of her question.

"How do you think he got so much right?"

She rolled her eyes. "How would I know what he got right, since I thought *Dracula* was fiction until about an hour ago?"

Bane's breath caught in his throat. "You rolled your eyes at me."

"And I probably will again, when you say something

stupid." She blinked then and bit her lip. "Yeah, okay, probably not brilliant to call a vampire stupid. You're not going to kill me, are you?"

His gut tightened at the hard truth that he probably *would* have to kill her. She was immune to compulsion, and there was no other way to be sure she'd never give away their secrets. But...later.

He could always kill her later.

"We can discuss that at another time, Doctor," he muttered. "I'll answer all your questions. After you have a shower and dress. I believe you'd feel much more at ease if you were not so...lacking in clothing."

And why did he care if she felt at ease? His entire existence had been about making people feel uneasy. Also, he quite enjoyed her lack of clothing.

This woman was turning his life upside down, and he didn't like it.

Lie.

He liked it a lot.

She glanced down at herself and blushed, and then a little of her bravado seemed to drain out with the color ebbing from her cheeks. Bane suddenly, viciously, wanted to punch himself in the face for stealing her courage. He might have to kill her, but he didn't have to humiliate her.

"Just come have a shower, in my very clean and uncluttered bathroom, and then I'll answer any questions you have."

And then Bane, the most feared vampire on the entire East Coast, held his breath and found himself hoping, very hard, that the fascinating, infuriating human would follow him down the hall.

. . .

Ryan was a firm believer in *shoulds* and *should nots*, and so she quite definitely knew she *should not* be following a vampire down the hall to his bathroom. In fact, nothing about that sentence—or the actual doing of it—existed even in the same universe as Reliable Ryan, the woman who was never the brightest star in the room but could always be counted on to be perfectly dependable and dependably dull.

She'd never had an actual adventure in her life, although her job gave her moments of excitement and fierce satisfaction—saving a life never, ever got old. But a bona fide adventure? No, she'd always left that to other people.

Daring people.

The kind of people who'd be bold enough to, for example, *follow a vampire down the hall to his bathroom.*

"Is 'bathroom' code for 'the room where you drain the blood from your victims and then climb into your coffin to sleep'?"

He muttered something that sounded like "out of my mind" but kept walking. "No. Bathroom is code for 'the place where you can take a shower, so my sister quits giving me death glares for being rude to a guest.'"

"I'm a guest? Not an abductee?"

He actually growled in response but said nothing, so she decided to shut up, look around, and see what happened next in this part of the waking dream she seemed to be having. Now—with his back to her—would be a great time to start running.

To try to escape.

But he'd almost certainly catch her. She'd seen how fast he could move. And it would probably make him angry, and maybe vampires got vicious when they were angry.

He still hadn't promised not to kill her, she realized, and the thought sent a cold shiver snaking down her spine.

But, on the other hand, there was Hunter.

For now—and maybe they'd be her own version of famous last words—she'd see what she could see. She'd always have a chance to escape when daylight came and they all went off to sleep in their coffins.

If, in fact, any of that happened to be true in any way. Maybe they loved the sun and slept in beds with quilted bedspreads right in front of open windows.

Or, maybe, her hungover brain was starting to stutter into idiocy. She took a deep breath, tried to shake off panic and mental fuzziness, and looked around.

The hallway was as beautiful as the ballroom they'd come from. Rich, slightly faded Persian rugs that looked as authentic as the ones in her grandmother's—now Ryan's— home covered the lustrous hardwood floors all the way down the hall. Dark wooden panels covered the walls partway up, and then the most luscious wallpaper she'd ever seen, in a delicate pattern portraying a garden party in spring in perhaps the nineteenth century, continued to the high ceiling. A series of small tables, placed equidistant all down the hall, were resting places for large crystal vases filled with fresh flowers. Wall sconces held exquisite globes of what appeared to be hand-blown glass, lit from within with a warm golden glow. Considering her hosts were vampires, she was somewhat surprised not to see lanterns and candles instead of electric lights.

And I'm trying very, very hard to focus on the walls and light fixtures, so I can avoid thinking about the hot vampire leading me down the hallway (pick one: a. to my doom or b. to a bathroom), and especially so I can avoid staring at the amazing musculature of his incredibly fine ass.

Seriously, he could be a model for anatomical drawings, he's so perfect. How unfair is that?

"Very unfair," she said firmly, as if to convince herself. Sadly, she wasn't much of one to lie to herself, so she quit pretending she wasn't staring at his butt or at the muscles in his broad shoulders or the narrowness of the waist that led to his hips and...

...And there we are, back at his truly fine ass.

"Do vampires have to work out?"

This time, he stopped and turned to stare at her. "What?"

"It seems fairly impossible that you can have that unbelievably perfect of an ass...*anatomy*, unless you work out, or it's some vampire hocus pocus. I mean, your body is objectively perfect, isn't it? Is that some magical side effect? I'm asking for scientific and evidentiary purposes, you understand."

A slow smile of quite unfairly wicked sensuality spread across his quite unfairly beautiful face, and she wondered if it were possible for panties to self-destruct.

"Perfect? I like the sound of that, Doctor. Shall we discuss the perfection of your ass...*anatomy* while we're having this fascinating conversation?"

And just like that, ice water washed over the unbeliev-able recklessness that had been running through her hormonally overactive mind.

"Very funny. Nobody has ever called my overly round ass perfect, and I know it, so maybe we could quit with mocking the human who already has enough to deal with right now."

His eyes widened, and if he'd been human, she'd have said he was surprised. But he wasn't human, and she didn't know how to translate vampire facial expressions yet.

Maybe widened eyes meant "I'm going to suck your blood from your body until you're a dying, withered husk on the floor if you don't shut up."

She shivered and caught him noticing, so she raised her chin and stiffened her shoulders, refusing to show fear.

"I'm not mocking you, Ryan," he said quietly. "Shockingly enough, I find little about this conversation, or this situation, funny."

With that, he turned and opened a door, pushing it open and gesturing to her to precede him into it.

She leaned forward to try to peek around his very large body to see inside the room—hoping to see a bathroom, not a bare floor with chains on the walls, racks of torture instruments, and a drain—and was relieved to find instead a large, well-furnished room that looked more like a library than anything else.

"That's your bathroom?"

When she dared a look up at him, he was smiling. Just a slight quirk of the corners of his lips, but she knew the hint of a smile when she saw one.

"No, that's my study. My bedroom is behind it, and it has an attached bathroom."

She clutched the towels more tightly to her chest. "Your,

um, bedroom?"

He raised an eyebrow. "Yes. I promise not to ravish you on the way to the bathroom, however," he drawled, and she could feel the heat of embarrassment shoot through her veins and sparkle along her nerve endings.

Of course, he didn't want to ravish her. Men who looked like gods come to life didn't frolic about with women who looked like her. Also, since when had she even thought the word *frolic?*

He was throwing her completely off balance. *Ravish* her.
If only.
Damn.

"It never occurred to me that you would," she snapped.

"Liar. I can hear your heart beating. Don't you realize that? It speeds up and slows down depending on your emotional state, which isn't really necessary, since everything you feel shows on your face, little human."

"Now, you're just trying to insult me." She slipped past him and stepped into the room, which felt like one of the bravest things she'd ever done in her life.

Get clean, get a look at Mr. Evans, and get out.
Get clean, get a look at Mr. Evans, and get out.
Get clean, get a look at Mr. Evans…
Holy cow, this *is his* study*?*

It was enormous. Books on shelves lined every wall, and the ceilings had to be eighteen feet off the floor, just like in the ballroom. She gasped and turned in a complete circle. "This is the most beautiful room I've ever seen in my life. It's like Beast's library that he gifted to Belle. This is all yours?"

"If I say yes, does that make me the beast in your analogy?"

"More like the belle, O Gorgeous One," she muttered, but clearly he heard it, because that lazy, sexy, far-too-seductive smile widened. On the other hand, if she distracted him with flattery, maybe it would be easier to find a way out.

"So. You can leave now," she said, not having much hope.

Sure enough, he shut the door behind himself and leaned back against it, making her heart thud inside her chest.

She was trapped. In a room.

With a vampire.

And, even if he'd been only human, he was much bigger than her, which meant that she was unlikely to escape unless he allowed her to do so. The anger that rushed through her at the thought—the memory of hands on her ass in classrooms, of "accidental" brushes against her breasts by men "just reaching for the instruments," and the daily indignities and verbal assaults that came with simply being a woman in the world—that anger burned through the terror. She'd leave his room whenever she damned well felt like it, whether he *allowed* her to or not.

Ryan wasn't much for waiting for a man to allow her to do anything.

"You like it?" He watched her, waiting for her answer, but she'd gone so far past their actual conversation in her mind that she had to cast back in her memory before she could answer him.

"Oh. The room. Yes, it's…it's really lovely," she admitted.

And it was. The room had clearly been originally designed to be a library with a private study for the man of the house, and somehow, she knew it fit Bane to perfection.

It was all rich, mahogany shelves holding hundreds or even thousands of books, leather chairs, and a cherry-wood desk, not designed to be the centerpiece of the room but just a place to work, from what she could see. There were papers and files on it, and a sleek, silver computer, which made her laugh out loud.

"Something's funny?" His voice was low and husky and deep, and it curled around her senses like the soft brush of cashmere on bare skin.

"No, I just—it struck me as incongruous for a vampire to have a computer. It feels like you should have scrolls and a quill with an ink stand, you know?" She laughed at her own foolishness.

He studied her, the expression on his face as puzzled and yet rapt as if she were a particularly fascinating specimen of talking parrot or trained monkey. "Do you always say everything that comes into your mind?"

Irritation scratched at her. "No, I do not. I do not say, for example, *I'm sorry, Mr. Smith, but this cancer is inoperable, which makes us pretty damn worthless to you,* or *We really can't help you, Mrs. Jones, because your child is very ill, and we can't figure out why,* or even *I must be ridiculous to be alone in a room with a man who either believes he's a vampire, in which case* he's *crazy, or really is a vampire, in which case* I'm *crazy.* So no, Bane, which can't possibly be your real name, I *don't* blurt out everything that comes into my mind, and you really *can't* read every emotion on my face. Maybe now that we've gotten that out of the way, you can show me to your bathroom, which hopefully has a door that locks?"

He blinked, and then he started laughing.

Damn the man, even his laugh was beautiful.

"Do you really imagine that a lock would keep me out?" His voice was mild, but his eyes still sparkled with amusement.

"You don't actually think you're coming into the bathroom with me, I hope?"

"Hope. Ah. The last resort of disappointed humans." He stalked her across the room, a predator cornering his prey.

Too bad for him that she was definitely not prey.

"Then let me put it this way. You should stay out of the bathroom while I take a shower. If you can't promise that, then I'm out of here."

His eyes gleamed a hot blue that seared through her all the way to her toes.

"There is no *should* to a vampire, Dr. St. Cloud," he said, reaching out to touch her hair.

She yanked her head away. "Ask."

He froze, his silken brows drawing together. "Ask what?"

"If you want to touch my hair, ask me," she told him, hating that her voice sounded far more breathless than demanding, but still proud of herself for forcing out the words.

"Ah." He took a step back. "You demand consent?"

"Yes. I demand consent."

In a fraction of a second, he put his hands on her waist and lifted her into the air, pushing her back against the wall, until only Meara's towels and not even a breath of air was trapped between them.

"I am a vampire. I don't give a damn about your consent," he rasped.

Something heavy, with sharp, jagged edges, sank from her heart to her stomach, but she glared defiance at him.

"Then you will never, ever have it."

He tilted his head to one side. "Do you know that your skin glows when your emotions are heightened? I wonder why that is."

"I *what*?"

He leaned even closer and whispered into her ear. "I want you, little human, and I always, *always* get what I want. Do you think to tame me with your refusal? I am not human. The Turn stripped me of any gentle emotions that you might expect or prize. And you forget—I can hear your heartbeat. I can see your skin glow. I know that you want me, too."

"Put me down. Now," she gritted out. "Enough about this glowing skin lie. And you might want to remember that anger and fear make the heart beat faster, just as much as arousal, not to mention several varying degrees of cardiovascular disease. And yes, in case you're wondering, I just compared my feelings about you to my feelings about atherosclerosis."

Instead of putting her down, though, he threw her over his shoulder, opened another door, marched through an enormous bedroom that she was too furious and too upside-down to really see much of beyond deep, rich colors of midnight blue and burgundy. Then he shoved open the door to an equally large, though blindingly white, bathroom and, finally, put her on her feet.

"Here you are. You wanted to get clean. Strip. *Now*," he demanded, his voice hard and dark with anger or lust.

Or both.

Fine. Fury and a spectacularly misplaced wave of arousal were surging through her body, making her skin feel hot and tight. But *not* glowy. She glanced down at her arms, just in case.

No. Not glowing at all. Whatever the hell *that* was about. She bared her teeth at him. "Not this time, Vampire. Just go ahead and kill me. I'd rather die than get naked with you."

He took a step back, the fire in his eyes banking and then hardening to blue ice.

"Fine," he snarled. "Prepare to die."

CHAPTER FOURTEEN

Edge tilted his head and took a mental inventory: beat all to hell, but still alive.

Good enough, then.

The Were staring at him must be Carter Reynolds, president and alpha of the Wolf Pack MC. Luckily, the man was acting like he might be reasonable, although that wasn't what Edge expected from a werewolf.

He could feel his lips curling back from his teeth and forced his face into a neutral expression. Bane's reaction to the dying human, and then Evans attacking Meara…it was no wonder Edge had been blindly racing away from the mansion on his bike.

He should have flown, but flying was dangerous. Sometimes, after all, humans *did* look up.

The silver net that had flown across the highway and knocked him off his bike had been powered by the stinking fuel of blood magic, and the warlock had laughed in his face before her thugs had knocked him out and transported him here. If the crash hadn't beaten him up so badly, Edge could have easily overpowered or escaped the three men, but he hadn't fed in a while, and his recuperative powers were at a low point.

The warlock must have put him in a temporary magical stasis spell, too, once they'd carried him inside the building and dumped him on the floor. With a final whisper that if he moved, he died, and a searing pain from a burning blast of magic, she'd disappeared just before the wolves entered the room.

But he'd been awake for her conversation with Reynolds, pulling up the alpha's file in his eidetic memory.

Carter Reynolds: 32 years old, parents deceased, one sister living

Alpha, Savannah Wolf Pack MC, for 13 years

Reputation: Lethal

Second: Maxine Washington, goes by Max, female, 28 years old

Reputation: Also lethal

Pack status: 47 current members

Reynolds nodded at him again. "So, you said we need to talk. Talk."

Edge glanced around the room, and Reynolds took the not-very-subtle hint.

"My people can be trusted. If they couldn't, they wouldn't be here."

Edge shrugged, trying not to wince when one of his broken ribs protested the movement. "Fine. As you've seen, we've got warlocks. They want to kill us and take our territory."

Reynolds's eyes narrowed. He was a big man, thickly muscled and maybe six feet tall. He had very short hair, dark brown skin, and sharp brown eyes that missed nothing.

"I think you got that wrong, *vampire*. They want to kill *you* and take *your* territory, according to the lady. She gave you to us as a gift, in fact."

Edge laughed, but there was nothing happy about the sound that came out of his throat. "That would be the worst fucking present of your life, *wolf*. And I said *us*, because I've never met a werewolf who'd be willing to roll over and show his belly to a warlock. Or do I have that wrong?"

The second, Max, still in wolf form, crouched and snarled at him, but Reynolds held up a hand. "Easy, Max. He's an asshole, but he's not wrong. There's no way we're letting blood magic users encroach on our territory. From what little I've heard of this Chamber, they're seriously bad news."

Edge snorted. "Calling the Chamber bad news is like calling a tornado a little bit of wind. They're powerful practitioners with delusions of godhood, and they've sent at least one necromancer."

Reynolds swore and jerked his chin toward a door in the rear of the room. "A necromancer. Fuck *that*. Let's go into my office and chat. The rest of you, get busy. We need to find out more about these damn warlocks and what they want. Make sure all the families are protected. We may need to get them out of town. *Move.*"

They moved.

One thing you could say for a werewolf pack, after all: they followed chain of command.

At least until they didn't, and somebody ripped the alpha's throat out.

In the office, which was strictly utilitarian, with a couple of desks, each with its own computer, and a few filing cabinets, Reynolds pointed at a chair. "Sit. Want a beer?"

Before Edge could answer, Reynolds narrowed his eyes. "You'll get nothing else to drink here."

"I don't drink wolf. You all taste like wet dog."

Hot amber flared in the alpha's eyes, but he just waited.

"Yeah," Edge told him. "A beer would be fine."

The wolf got a couple of Savannah Brown Ales out of a small refrigerator, opened them, and handed one to Edge.

"Never thought I'd be drinking beer with a vampire."

Edge raised his bottle in a mock salute. "Believe me, it wasn't my plan for the day, either. Fucking warlocks."

They both drank, and then the wolf aimed a direct stare at Edge. "What do you know about them?"

"Unfortunately, not a hell of a lot. We wiped out a nest of them a few days back, north of here in the Savannah National Wildlife Refuge."

"We go up there and run sometimes," Reynolds said, his voice hard. "Fucking warlocks, indeed. They have time to kill off all the local wildlife?"

"It was definitely on the decline, but we think we got them before the situation was beyond repair. It was bad. Three warlocks are dead, but the worst of them — a necromancer — managed to escape. We're looking for him, but the Chamber is very good at covering its tracks."

Reynolds sat back in his chair, eyes narrowing. "That's bad."

"Bad. Yeah. If by *bad*, you mean apocalyptic. Listen, we should work together on this." Edge said this without consulting Bane first, because he knew that they'd be in perfect agreement on this one. They already had a truce with the wolves, and as much as he hated to admit it even to himself, even werewolves were better than warlocks.

Barely.

Reynolds thought about it for a minute, to his credit, and then he stood up and held out his hand. "Yeah. Even vampires are better than warlocks."

Edge almost grinned to hear his own thoughts paralleled so closely, but instead he stood and shook the wolf's hand. "We'll be in touch. We'll find out what we can during the night, and you take the daytime. We'll send these bastards back to the hell they worship."

Reynolds nodded. "This is our territory, and we're not going to let any fucking warlocks take it over. We're with you, man. Have Bane check in."

"Will do." Edge put the empty bottle down on the desk and turned to go, his mind running scenarios for possibly tracking the Chamber operatives through the dark web.

That's why he wasn't on guard against the wolf who attacked him when he opened the office door.

CHAPTER FIFTEEN

The doctor didn't run.

She didn't scream.

She didn't do anything that a thousand other humans had done when confronted with Bane in his most fearsome, almost-feral state.

Instead, she laughed in his face.

After the long, long moment it took for him to swallow his shock, he started laughing, too.

"Okay, that was a bit much," he admitted.

"*Prepare to die*?" She put one hand against the glass wall of the shower, as if she had to hold herself up because she was laughing too hard to stand upright.

"It wasn't *that* funny," he growled.

She wiped her eyes with the corner of one of the towels she still held. "Oh, no. It really, really was. I mean, kill me if you must, but spare me the melodramatic threats. You're no Inigo Montoya."

A dark spear of anger caught him by surprise. "Who the fuck is this Montoya? Is he your lover?"

Does he need to die?

Her eyes widened. "Is he my...are you kidding? Have you never seen *The Princess Bride*?"

The conversation was spiraling out of control, fast. On the other hand, the way she was laughing was doing extremely interesting things to her curves, and suddenly he forgot about everything but the way she looked and the way his cock was hardening nearly to the point of pain.

If she'd only quit laughing, maybe he could convince her to let him strip her clothes off her lush body and carry her into the shower, where he'd soap down every single inch of that pearly, nearly translucent skin until she begged him to put his mouth on her.

Interesting how the glow in her skin calmed down when she started to laugh. It was definitely a symptom of heightened emotion. He'd seen fear, anger, and—he hoped—arousal cause it.

He stood there, frozen, listening to her musical laugh, wishing she were laughing *with* him and not *at* him, and realized the truth: he'd started giving a damn about her consent exactly when she told him she'd never, ever give it to him.

He stilled. He'd never taken a woman's body without her agreement, but he'd taken blood from many people— both men and women—without their consent. Many, by force. He'd made them forget afterward, but that didn't mitigate his sins. He had done horrible things in his centuries in the dark, and he could never be redeemed for any of them.

Even to touch this brave human—this healer—would be a grotesque affront.

Darkness besmirching the sunlight.

She'd braved his wrath and even taken the knowledge of what he was—what all of them were—in stride, in her fervor to protect a man she knew only as a patient.

He should be on his knees to her for her courage, and instead he'd insulted and threatened her. He shook his head, trying to dislodge the copper taste of shame from his throat, but stopped when he realized how richly he deserved to feel it.

And then he backed up until he was just outside the room.

"I'm sorry," he managed to say, forcing the words past the boulder in his throat. "I was wrong."

And how long had it been since he'd uttered those words to anyone?

Her slightly hysterical laughter slowed and then stopped, and she drew in a huge, deep breath. "I—what?"

"I'm sorry. Please, lock the door. I'll stand guard, but out in my study. No one would dare to come into these rooms, in any case. You will be quite safe." He could barely manage to meet her gaze, so he didn't. He looked at the sinks—at the shower—at the towels she held.

"I'm...sorry," he repeated, almost strangling on the words.

And then he slammed the door between them, picked up his massive, carved, wooden bed and hurled it against the opposite wall, shattering the thick posts into kindling.

There was a long pause, and then her light footsteps came toward the door and stopped. For one wild moment, he thought she meant to come find him—to invite him into her shower. Into her arms. Into the sunlight that surrounded her.

But then the *snick* of the lock bit into him as if it had been the tip of a blade.

She didn't want him anywhere near her—and why would she? He'd broken into her home and abducted her. He'd mocked and threatened her. Even now, the sound of his temper smashing his enormous, two-hundred-year-old bed must have frightened her.

He wasn't just a monster—he was a child.

A fool.

"So be it, then," he told the empty room. "I'm a monster and a fool, and it's too far against my nature to try to be anything else, even for the delectable doctor."

He turned to face the bathroom door.

• • •

Ryan stared hard at the door she'd just locked, well aware of how flimsy a barrier it would be to the man who'd made the smashing noise she'd just heard. What had she gotten herself into?

Not that she'd exactly gone out looking for vampires to taunt about matters of consent, but she *had* followed him down that hallway. Maybe they could put that on her tombstone or on the outside of her cremation urn:

Here lies Ryan: If only she hadn't followed that vampire to the bathroom.

His voice, somehow sharp and raspy at the same time, interrupted her mental ramblings.

"I'll be in my study, if you need…if you need anything. There are clothes in the closet. Wear anything you want. You can roll up pants legs, or use a belt, or—"

When his voice trailed off, she heard a thud that sounded like he'd dropped his forehead against the door. She understood the inclination.

"Yes. Fine. Thank you," she called out, proud that her voice barely shook at all.

She'd argued *consent* with a *vampire*. He could have

killed her with one fang, probably, and she'd stood up to him.

Warmth spread through her. She had told him to stop—and he had. This man—this *monster*—who could take anything or anyone he wanted had stopped because she'd told him to stop.

She stood, wild-eyed and wild-haired, clad in nothing but her pride and skimpy PJs, and met her own gaze in the mirror as a smile started to spread across her face.

She'd never felt more powerful in her life.

CHAPTER SIXTEEN

Bane spent the longest twenty minutes of his life listening to the sound of the shower and then the small sounds of footsteps, drawers opening and closing, and the faint murmur of the doctor's voice when she talked to herself.

He couldn't make out the words, of course. Even his superior vampire hearing couldn't make out quietly spoken words from two rooms away, with two closed doors between them. But there was nothing wrong with his imagination, and the thought of Ryan St. Cloud in his bathroom—in his shower—using his soaps and shampoos on her deliciously wet skin and hair nearly had him crawling the ceiling in frustration.

He wanted to smash through the doors separating them and take the towels from her hands. Dry each inch of her body. Dry her hair and brush through the long waves. Find lotions and oils and whatever else women needed and tend to her. Pamper her.

Cherish her.

What the actual fuck was happening to him? *Cherish* her?

Ryan had been wrong. He really was running mad. If he started to see pigs fly or elephants dance, he'd skip whatever came next and just walk out into the dawn, saving hundreds if not thousands with his sacrifice. There could be nothing more deadly to walk the earth than an insane vampire as powerful as he.

And he was very much afraid that he'd go after the woman in his shower first, in a frenzy of territorial possession and lust, and fuck her until they were both dead of it.

She'd die so easily. Humans were far too fragile.

He'd kill himself from the guilt.

Yet more reasons why he should stay far, far away from her.

He was sunk so far in his black mood that he paid little attention to the sound of approaching feet, except to note that it was friend, not foe, until the tentative knock sounded at the door to the hallway.

He raised his head and tried to focus on anything but what was happening in that bathroom. "Come in, Mrs. Cassidy."

"Sorry to bother you, sir, but does the doctor wish to have breakfast? I've cooked up a fair feast, you know. It's still an hour till dawn, and I thought you'd all be hungry, after what you've had to do with Mr. Evans." She entered just far enough to be inside the room, but no farther. He'd made it clear that his rooms were his private sanctuary, although she'd gently bullied him into allowing her to come in and dust and clean every so often.

"I don't know—"

The other door, the one he'd been watching for nearly half an hour now, opened, and Bane shot up out of his chair.

"Breakfast, Miss? Doctor? The least we can do is feed you," Mrs. C said, smiling.

Ryan bit her lip. "I don't know—is it actual food?"

He took one look and wanted to bite that plump lip for

her. Wanted it more than he'd wanted anything else in his life. He forced himself to grab the edge of the desk with both hands to help keep him from moving toward her and then had to relax his fingers when he heard wood splintering from the pressure of his grip.

"It's actual food. We eat, Doctor," he said, drinking his fill of the sight of her.

She'd put on one of his plain, white shirts and a pair of his black trousers, and both were vastly too large for her. But she'd rolled up sleeves and pant legs and belted the waist with one of his ties, which should have looked ridiculous but instead fired his territorial instincts again at seeing her in his clothes.

Smelling her wearing the scent of his soap.

He wanted to toss her into his bed and spend hours touching every inch of that freshly washed, rosy skin. Use that tie and others to bind her to his bed and drive her to delirious pleasure with his hands.

His mouth.

His cock.

The bed that no longer existed except as a pile of scrap.

Damn.

She tried on a smile and crossed the room to Mrs. Cassidy, carefully walking a wide path to avoid coming too close to Bane. He deserved it, but it still pierced him in a way he didn't understand.

"I'm Ryan St. Cloud. I'm Hunter Evans' doctor. I don't really have time for breakfast, but thank you for offering. I need to see my patient and then go home. If you'll pardon me, I'll be on my way."

"I'm Mrs. Cassidy. Nice to meet you."

And then, before Bane even realized what was happening, Ryan slipped past Mrs. C and was gone.

"Damn that woman," he groaned, starting after her. "She never does what I expect."

Mrs. C moved aside to let him pass but didn't bother to hide her smile. "And how boring would that be if she did? I think it's about time you found a woman who challenges you."

"It's not—she's not— She's not a woman. She's a doctor." He didn't bother to argue any further, because nothing in his brain made sense, and he could already hear Mrs. C laughing behind him.

Apparently, it was the day for people to laugh at him. Usually, when that had happened in the past, there'd been a lot of the screaming and running Meara so liked.

Ahead of him, Ryan turned to enter the ballroom, and the next sound he heard was her shouting his name. He raced into the room and yanked her into his arms, fangs fully descended, muscles tense.

"What? What happened?"

Ryan, who'd started bullheadedly struggling to get away from him the moment he'd picked her up, pointed.

"Look!"

It was Hunter. Lying on the table. But not the Hunter they'd left in the care of Lucas such a little time before. Now, the former human, former firefighter looked like nothing more than a mummified skeleton, and an exhausted-looking Luke slept on the floor next to the table.

"What *happened* to him?"

Bane sighed with more than a little relief and released the doctor. "Finally. Now he can complete the Turn."

She whirled to face him. "What? This is *normal*? He looks like he died twenty years ago!"

"I know. The Turn devours the human blood of its host during the process, and then we will have to replenish his blood with ours. It's…tricky."

"Tricky? It's *tricky*?" Her beautiful blue eyes, so different in shade from his own, widened, and he lost the sense of her words when he fell into her gaze, drowning in the liquid dark—sinking into her intensity—into her passion.

How long had it been since he'd seen such passion?

How long since it had been directed at him?

"Can I examine him? Is there any point? Does he even have blood pressure like that?"

Why did she keep asking him questions, when all he wanted to do was watch the shapes her mouth made when she spoke?

She pounded a fist on his chest, snapping him out of his mental trance. "Hello? Are you even listening to me?"

"Not really," he admitted, reaching out to touch one long, damp strand of her hair and then pulling his hand back. He had not asked to touch it.

It occurred to him that this, at least, was one thing he could rectify.

"May I?"

"May you what? Bane, I have no idea what's going on here, but every medical instinct in my body, every ounce of education and training, is telling me that we have to get him to the emergency room. We need—"

"May I touch your hair?" The answer to his question was suddenly the most important answer in the world. "And believe me when I tell you that taking him to the hospital now would kill him. This is a vital part of the process and gives me reassurance that he will survive it."

Her enormous eyes were filled with doubt. "Are you sure?"

"Yes, I'm sure," he said, what little patience he had waning. "I've done this several times over the centuries, Doctor. Now. Your hair. May I?"

She blinked and then opened and shut her beautiful mouth a couple of times. "You want to touch my hair. Now."

"Yes. And I did ask," he pointed out, moving a step closer but careful not to crowd her.

"Is this really the time?" She put her hands on her hips and narrowed her eyes, but he could sense a thread of excitement and maybe even anticipation beneath her outward impatience. Not to mention the faint golden glow that began to shimmer faintly on—or maybe beneath—her skin. The doctor was no more immune to him than she was fully human, this much he knew.

And—in spite of himself—he treasured the knowledge. *Now*, he wanted to demand. Instead, he decided to coax.

Maybe even a monster was capable of learning?

"Please?"

She blew out a long breath, glanced back at Luke and Hunter again, and then squared her shoulders. "I think this is a bad idea, but because you said please. And because you stopped when I said no in that bathroom. And because of the shower and the clothes and… Okay. Just…okay," she finished, her voice all but inaudible.

He leaned in and inhaled her scent and completely forgot about manners and consent and coaxing.

"You will let me touch you whenever I please," he demanded instead, forcing every ounce of his power and compulsion into his voice.

She swayed a little but then quirked one corner of her mouth in a lopsided grin. "Keep trying. I'm sure somebody is going to listen to your enthralling voice sometime. And yes."

"And yes?"

She drew in another breath, this one shaky. "You can touch my hair."

He stilled to motionlessness and stood, drinking in the sight of her flushed cheeks. Her lush curves pushing at his shirt that she wore. Her bare feet and their silly purple toenails.

"Thank you," he whispered, and then he reached out a hand. Took one long, wavy strand and slid his fingers down damp silk. Released it and watched it spring back into its curl.

Immediately regretted the loss of its touch.

Her breath stuttered, and he could hear her heart speed up, could see the glow of her skin intensify, but she only nodded.

"And now, can we have breakfast?" Mrs. C's cheery voice rang out behind Bane, and he almost laughed at the thought that his housekeeper had been able to sneak up on him, unnoticed, when dangerous enemies had never accomplished the feat in all the centuries of his existence. He'd entirely forgotten she was in the hallway behind him.

Then again, he'd never faced such a distraction.

Ryan bit her lip again, and he had to fight not to touch her lips with his fingers or with his own mouth. He wanted to soothe the tiny bite with his tongue. With his kiss.

Instead, he smiled at her. "Breakfast? Please?"

Having once said the word, the second time was easier.

She offered a tentative smile of her own, and it was as if the sun itself had decided to shine through the roof of his home and down upon him. He wanted to curl up in the warmth of her smile and stay there for hours.

Days.

"Mrs. C," he said instead. "Do you see how the doctor's skin is glowing?"

"What?"

"Enough with the glowing," Ryan said, rolling her eyes.

"Bane, I think maybe you gave too much blood," his housekeeper said tentatively.

He blew out a sigh. Maybe he had. But...

"I made pancakes and bacon," Mrs. C coaxed, interrupting his train of thought.

"Well. I do love pancakes and bacon," Ryan said. "Is there coffee?"

"All the coffee you could ever want to drink," his housekeeper told his...*the*...doctor, who turned back to Bane.

"And Mr. Evans? He'll be all right? You're sure?"

"I'm very sure. This is not the first time I've done this," he repeated.

Her shoulders relaxed, just a fraction, but she finally nodded. "All right. I can't believe I'm saying this, but scientific curiosity is winning out over self-preservation." She shrugged, which did interesting things to her breasts.

Bane concentrated on trying very hard not to stare at them or—worse—take them in his hands. If she'd known how hard that internal battle was, she would have fled in terror. Luckily, she wasn't psychic, because she smiled at Mrs. Cassidy instead.

"Okay. In for a penny, as they say. Let's have breakfast, and you can tell me everything I need to know. Give me the *Vampires for Dummies* version, okay?"

With that, Ryan moved past him and toward Mrs. C.

"So, what kind of coffee? Do you have cream and sugar? Are there potatoes? Can you put garlic in the potatoes, or is that a no-no? And what can I do to help? I'm a pretty good touch with scrambled eggs and toast, and I can carve up a ham like nobody's business. Surgical skills translate into good kitchen knife skills, you know?"

Bane closed his eyes and drank in the sounds of their voices for a long moment as they headed down the stairs to the kitchen.

"This can't end well," Luke said quietly. Perhaps he'd been feigning sleep. "You know that, but I'm going to remind you, whether you kill me for it or not. You remember what happened to me."

"There will be no end, *well* or otherwise, because there's no beginning. She's just a diversion, and she may have some interesting medical information we can use. Don't you think it's about time we looked at our...*condition*... from a scientific perspective?"

Luke's laugh was filled with honest amusement. "Our *condition*? Do you really think we have a blood disease that causes what we are?"

Bane turned his gaze to the withered husk of the body on the table.

Another mistake?

Perhaps.

Probably.

Ryan, though...bringing her here was almost certainly a mistake, too. One that he admitted, if only to himself, that he was making with full knowledge of all the reasons why he should not.

But the touch of her hair...

"No," he finally said, offering up the only truth he could share. "There is magic in what we are. But perhaps there is science, as well. After three centuries, I'd like to know."

"And that's all?"

He wouldn't answer that question, though, not for Luke. Not even for himself. Instead, he nodded at Hunter. "Let's get him into the warded room, now. We can't watch him for every minute of three days, with everything else going on."

There was a club meeting coming up that night, and he was startled to realize he'd almost forgotten it until now. The club's mission was vital to who they were and what they did.

Luke, who was the vice president of the Vampire Motorcycle Club, nodded. "Yeah. We need to talk about the Chamber. Our people are wondering what the hell is going on, and the rumors are flying fast and furious."

Bane's vision skewed to a brilliant scarlet. "We need to find this Constantin. Fast. Any progress?"

"Not yet, but we will. Edge is on the job with the computers, and I've got word out to all the usual sources." Luke scowled. "This necromancer worries me, I have to admit. I wanted to talk about it when you came back, but you were busy with your human."

His human. He listened, focusing in on tracking the

sound of her voice, and was relieved to hear that she was in the kitchen with Mrs. C, undoubtedly still pelting the housekeeper with questions.

My *human. Luke said she was* my *human. Could it be possible?*

Even as his mind toyed with the idea, bleak pragmatism told him it was ridiculous. Ryan St. Cloud was a healer who lived her life in the bright light of day—he was a predator confined to the night.

She could never be *his* human.

His woman.

His *anything.*

"Let's move Hunter. And then I hear there are pancakes."

Luke grinned. "Who doesn't love pancakes?

They bent to lift Hunter together, although either of them could easily have carried the man to the reinforced room behind the tapestry on one wall of the ballroom's alcove. It was symbolic—they were a team. A family. And now, they were bringing another member into the fold, so they'd do it together.

As they crossed the floor, a random thought occurred.

"Luke."

"Yeah?"

"What's your favorite movie?"

Luke missed a step, almost dropping Hunter's legs. "What?"

Bane snorted out a laugh. "Never mind. Just something the doctor and Meara were talking about."

Luke nodded and thought about it for a minute, and then, after they carefully put the firefighter on a bed, closed and locked the door from the outside, and Bane re-activated the magical wards that would keep Hunter safely locked inside, he finally answered.

"*Cleopatra*. With Elizabeth Taylor."

Bane hadn't expected that. "Really?"

Luke grinned. "Yeah. Liz Taylor was hot."

"Can't argue with that."

"What about you?"

Bane shook his head. "I have no idea. Let's go have pancakes."

"You're not planning on having the delicious doctor for breakfast?" Luke dodged out of the way when Bane's fist shot out, and he held up his hands in laughing surrender. "Just kidding. I promise to behave."

With that, he headed toward the stairs. Bane followed more slowly behind him, his twisting emotions so tangled that he had no idea what he'd do if the primal side of his nature perceived any threat to Ryan.

Which was laughable, in any case, because the biggest threat to Ryan St. Cloud in this house — anywhere in Savannah — was absolutely clear. Not Luke, not Hunter.

The biggest threat to Ryan is me — and I still haven't decided if I can let her live.

CHAPTER SEVENTEEN

Ryan stared at everything. The enormous kitchen, built on the same scale as the rest of the mansion, wasn't the least bit historically accurate. Instead, everything in it was state-of-the-art, like Bane's bathroom. Where the bathroom had been marble and glass, this room was gleaming subway tile, shining quartz countertops, massive appliances, and a hanging rack of copper pots, with plenty of fresh herbs in pots lined up on the windowsills and potted plants of the decorative variety on other surfaces.

On the windowsills…

"How can you have windows? Do they, um, the vampires, not come in here?"

Mrs. Cassidy smiled. "It's a special glass Edge developed. It doesn't let in any of the harmful rays that might be a danger to them."

"Edge?"

The housekeeper's cheerful expression faltered. "He… you'll meet him later."

And then she turned quite deliberately to her pots and pans, signaling that she didn't want to discuss the missing Edge any longer, so Ryan continued her survey of her surroundings. In spite of being a showpiece of a kitchen, it was clearly well used, quite possibly the center of the house. A discarded copy of the *Savannah Morning News* lay folded on one end of a massive wooden table that bore the scars and scratches of decades of use. A pair of glasses exactly like the ones Mrs. Cassidy wore sat on an open cookbook on the counter. Heaps of pancakes, bacon, potatoes, and fluffy scrambled eggs already sat steaming on platters on the table, but no plates or silverware were out yet.

"Can I set the table?"

Mrs. Cassidy glanced at her, startled. "Oh. Well, that would be lovely, but you certainly don't need to do that. I mean, you're a *doctor*."

Ryan smiled. The elderly housekeeper, all white curls and comfortable roundness, had said *doctor* with tones of reverent awe that Ryan certainly didn't associate with herself or her job. But Mrs. Cassidy was from a different generation, and even Ryan's own grandmother had felt like that about her granddaughter's chosen profession.

She missed Gran so much. And somehow, she doubted her grandmother would be surprised by vampires. After all, she'd always believed in ghosts.

"I'm happy to do it. I feel very lucky to have someone else cook for me, to be honest. It's mostly protein shakes and cafeteria food in my normal life."

Mrs. Cassidy shuddered. "Those protein shakes should be outlawed. Nasty things."

"I have to agree with you there, but sometimes necessity wins out over luxury."

"It's a sad day when eating a real meal is a luxury, but you young people do things differently, I know that. The flatware's in the drawer in that sideboard."

Ryan turned around and caught her breath. The sideboard in question was rosewood, in an Art Deco style, almost certainly from the twenties or thirties, and definitely worth a fortune. She didn't know a lot about antiques in general, but she knew a bit about furniture from trips to estate sales with her grandmother.

"That's a stunning piece. Do you know who the designer is?"

The sound of heeled boots preceded Meara into the room. She grinned at Ryan, glancing up and down her cobbled-together outfit.

"Nice clothes. Maybe you could call it homeless-person chic? Here. I brought you a pair of sandals, since we seem to be about the same shoe size." She held out a pair of gold, strappy sandals that looked perfect for a night out on the town but not so much for breakfast with vampires.

Ryan refused to feel embarrassed about clothes at a time and place like this but appreciated the gesture of the shoes, which she immediately slipped on. "Thank you. And maybe. If homeless people wore Armani pants."

Meara laughed. "Point to you. And that sideboard is by Jules Leleu, from 1935 or thereabout. I always loved his style. I believe Bane won it at cards."

"He plays cards for antique furniture?"

Luke sauntered in. "He gambles on anything that happens to be handy. There was this one time in 1966 that—"

The man—vampire—himself strode into the kitchen, in all his casually arrogant, blond-god gorgeousness, and Ryan suddenly had to remember how to breathe.

"Shut it, Luke," Bane said, never taking that burning blue gaze off her face. "Ryan, are you all right? Can I get you anything?"

She shook her head, trying not to feel overwhelmed by

being surrounded by three vampires in a kitchen that sported an antique French sideboard that was probably worth as much as her entire townhouse. They were dangerous, and they were rich, and she was entirely vulnerable, and yet she was staying for breakfast?

Next she'd be having tea with werewolves.

Werewolves…

"Do werewolves exist?"

Nobody started laughing, like she'd expected. They traded glances that read a lot like, "How much can the human handle?" instead. She reached for a chair and fell into it, suddenly boneless. "Really? Werewolves? What else?"

"Many, many things, Doctor," Mrs. Cassidy said matter-of-factly. "Meara, dear, please get out the flatware. I think everyone needs a good meal inside them before we shock Dr. St. Cloud with any new revelations."

"Dr. St. Cloud agrees that might be a good idea," Ryan said slowly, her mind whirling. "Oh! And I'm sorry. I meant to set the table. I just got distracted by the…well. By the everything, I guess."

Many, many things?

What else had been hiding in the dark?

"Do you often speak of yourself in the third person?" Meara asked with interest, placing the silverware on the table. "Bit like the royal We, isn't it? 'Dr. St. Cloud would like her breakfast now.' 'Dr. St. Cloud thinks the patient in room 208 has a nice ass.'"

"Room 208 is in obstetrics, so definitely not that," Ryan said absently, her mind still on the fact that now not only vampires but other things actually existed. "What kinds of other things? Trolls? Leprechauns?"

Bane sat down next to Ryan and reached for her hand but then froze and rested it on the table instead.

When she realized what he'd been doing—preparing to comfort the human whose worldview had just exploded—a wave of welcome warmth spread through her. She dared to put her hand over his, where it rested on the table, and a spark of sensation raced from their joined hands all the way to her toes, causing her breath to stutter.

"Thank you," she murmured. "This is—this is a lot."

Those amazing glowing blue eyes—the color of the sky on a cloudless day—widened, and he turned his hand over and entwined his fingers with hers. "I'm not sure you should thank me, Doctor. I'm the villain in your story."

She gave him a long look. "You're taking too much credit. Maybe you can be part of a subplot?"

He pretended to glare at her, and she laughed.

"And now, I'm switching rapidly between wanting to laugh in wonder and wanting to scream in terror at this new world to which you've all opened my eyes."

When she looked around the table, she saw that they were staring at her hand and Bane's, clasped and resting on the table, with varying expressions of shock. Her face heated up, and she pulled her hand away.

"What—" she began, but Luke cut her off.

"We prefer the screaming," he said, heaping eggs on his plate.

"Screaming *and* running," Meara said, a sly smile on her face. "Can't forget the running. It's more fun when we get to chase them."

And, just like that, Ryan was back to *what the hell am I*

doing here mode.

"What—what happens to me now? Nobody knows about vampires and werewolves. Is this an 'I know too much, so now you have to kill me or lock me up forever in your lair' moment?" She swallowed, hard, against the boulder that suddenly seemed to be lodged in her throat. An icy tendril of fear whispered in her mind that she was damned right to be afraid, just like she'd been terrified the first time she'd placed a central line or performed a tracheotomy in the emergency room. Those had been firsts where she'd been in danger of killing a patient.

This time, the potentially imminent death was hers.

And he *still* wasn't denying it. In fact, the silence from everyone at the table was deafening.

Bane blinked, and then that unfairly sexy smile spread across his face. "My *lair*? I never quite thought of my rooms as my lair, but I guess I could try to set up a Bat Cave of sorts. There are a lot of secret underground spaces here in Savannah, many of which pirates used for smuggling."

Meara passed the platter of pancakes, and Ryan took two, even though she was sure she wouldn't be able to eat a bite, because she was suddenly starving in the "this may be my last meal" kind of way, she loved pancakes, and she wanted to keep up her strength, in case she was the next designee in the "running and screaming" agenda.

Plus, everything smelled delicious.

"So, how is it you eat food? It's almost dawn; will you fall into a deep sleep or...or die? When did you become vampires? Why? Are there lots of you? Bunny shifters?" That was the right tone. Flippant was good. It made her sound like a badass, right?

"We eat any food we want; I adore caviar. And chocolate, though not together," Meara said, taking a bite of eggs. "Bane and I have been vampires since the same night a little more than three hundred years ago. And no, usually only predators are shifters, like wolves. Lions, tigers, and bears."

"Oh, my," Ryan chimed in automatically, but her mind wasn't on movies.

Three hundred years?

"You look pretty good for being older than the entire country," she said, still stunned by the thought.

"Older than *this* country," Meara said.

Luke pointed his fork at Ryan. "How do you think Bane knows so much about those tunnels? He used them back when he was a smuggler."

"When he was a smuggler," Ryan said faintly. "Which was when, exactly?"

"Technically, he still is," Meara said. "Coffee?"

"Please. Or maybe something stronger? I feel like I need whiskey for this conversation." Ryan looked at Bane. "You're a smuggler? Today? And since when?"

He took a long sip of coffee and then looked at her. "You're asking a lot of questions about illegal activity for someone who's afraid to end up in my *lair.*"

Meara handed her a mug of coffee. "And no breakfast whiskey drinking. That would be a sign of a serious problem."

"Yes, nobody would want that," Ryan replied, only a hint of sarcasm in her tone.

"And, to answer your question, don't you think science

needs to know about you?"

A muscle clenched in Bane's jaw. "About my smuggling history?"

"No, of course not. I don't—I'm not the smuggling patrol. I would never tell anyone about that," she rushed to say. "About your...about what you are. You healed Hunter from burns that should have killed him. I mean, he might be dying now, but you healed his burns first, and..."

She finally shut up when she realized everyone was staring at her.

"It sounded better in my head," she offered, not knowing where to go from there. Why would they want to tell anybody about themselves, when they'd undoubtedly end up in cages and being dissected by government scientists?

"I might be inclined to let you study me," Bane said slowly. "Only you—nobody else could know—and only me. You stay away from the rest of my family. But it would be good to know the science, after all these long years."

Ryan caught her breath at the idea that he was even considering agreeing.

"It's not science. It's magic," Mrs. Cassidy said, speaking up from her post near the stove, where she was cooking something that smelled like fried grease and sugar—Ryan's favorite food groups.

"Well. Perhaps," Ryan conceded, because why wouldn't it be magic? There were werewolves, too, for Pete's sake. "But a lot of things that were thought to be magic in the past have been proven to be science. Maybe, if we studied exactly what happens to you—"

"*We*, Doctor?" Bane's voice suddenly had a dangerous edge. "Do you have any idea what would happen to our kind if multiple scientists find out about us? Would you like to know what has happened in the past, perhaps in vivid, brutal detail? Would you be so willing to see my family in cages, being tortured and experimented upon? When I said just you, I meant it."

"No, of course, I don't want to see any of that. But—" She glanced around and then swallowed whatever she'd been about to say.

Read the room, Ryan. Keep this up, and you might be in serious trouble.

"I...I'm sorry. Yes, just me," she muttered, taking a bite of pancake that still looked and smelled amazing but now tasted like sawdust in her mouth.

Bane put his fork down, turned in his chair until he faced her completely, and pinned her with a searing gaze. "We won't be analyzed, dissected, or tortured in the name of science or progress, Dr. St. Cloud. Don't doubt the lengths to which I'll go to ensure that this never, ever happens. If you enjoy Savannah when it's not a miles-long patch of scorched ground, you'll never bring up the idea of other scientists being involved again."

Ryan turned away from him, unable to bear the contempt on his face.

Meara's expression was kinder but wary. "This is too much, I know. It's why we never tell humans anything about us. Ryan, don't worry. Of course, we'll compel you to forget, right after breakfast, and take you home. We wouldn't have told you otherwise."

Bane shook his head. "Compulsion doesn't work. Luke and I both tried. It brushes off her like water off a duck. Even when I reinforced the push with touch, she broke through it in minutes. We'll have to think of another way."

"You'll not kill a doctor," Mrs. Cassidy blurted out, waving a spatula at them. "I won't have it."

Ryan's neck tightened at the baldly stated assumption that killing her was an option. Somehow, coming from the sweet, kind housekeeper made it frighteningly more real.

Of course, it's real. Because: vampires.

Bane smiled at his housekeeper with apparent fondness. "No, of course, we won't. We just need to think about—"

But Ryan didn't get to hear what they needed to think about, because that's when the kitchen erupted into chaos. An elderly man and an enormous dog that looked like a cross between a wolf and a Sasquatch burst in from the door on one end of the kitchen, and a white-haired man who appeared to have been beaten nearly to death burst in from the door on the other end.

The dog immediately started to bark and advanced on her, ears back, teeth bared, and a growl like thunder issuing from its throat. It—he—hurled his enormous, furry body between Ryan and the stranger, as if protecting her.

The injured man fell to the floor before anyone at the table could get to him.

"Tommy. Get Bram Stoker out of the kitchen if he can't behave," Bane ordered. "Edge. What happened to you?"

"Your dog's name is *Bram Stoker*?" Ryan didn't wait for an answer; the question was irrelevant. The second the man pulled the leashed dog back, Ryan was out of her chair and across the room to the injured man.

"Hot water and clean cloths," she snapped. "And call 911—no, scratch that, I guess that's not an option. Sir? Edge? I'm a doctor. Can you tell me what happened to you?

Were you beaten? Shot? Do you feel any broken bones?"

The man, whose face was far too young for the fall of white hair that framed it, turned startlingly silver eyes up to her and scowled. "Get the hell away from me, human."

Bane crouched down next to them and grabbed the man's jaw. "Shut up and let her help you. What happened?"

"Little problem with a wolf who'd been forced to shift by a warlock. Oh, and the warlock crashed my bike first. Not a big deal." Edge flinched when Ryan started to unbutton his shredded shirt to see his torso, and his hand shot out to grab her wrist. "I don't need your help, I said."

"Too bad. You're going to get it anyway. Now take your hand off my wrist, or I'll punch you right in this puncture wound," she threatened, feeling something fiercer than her normal bedside manner was called for.

A hint of amusement gleamed in his silver gaze, but then he sighed and shook his head, turning his attention to Bane. "It doesn't matter. I'll heal. But Bane—you need to know. The necromancers are still here, or at least one of them. She walked right into Wolf Pack MC and dumped me there and told Carter Reynolds that I was a gift."

Bane scowled at him. "Did Reynolds take her up on it?"

"Nope. We had a talk. The truce holds. The wolves want nothing to do with the Chamber, either, and Reynolds had the same reaction to a necromancer that we did. Since we were on the same page about all that, I almost asked him about joining up on the drug runs but figured that could wait for another day."

"Are you sure you're okay?" Meara knelt down on the other side of the injured vampire and put a hand on his shoulder, but he jerked away from her touch and would not look at her.

"I'm fine."

"*Warlocks*? And *drugs*?" Ryan rocked back on her heels, shock and revulsion almost choking her. "You—you're not just vampires, but you're drug dealers?"

She glared at Bane, thoughts of the addicts she'd treated burning in her mind. "Tell me the truth."

He said nothing, just stared at her, his face set in an expressionless mask.

"Tell me, damn you. Are you a drug dealer?"

His eyes flared red, and she flinched.

"Yes, Dr. St. Cloud," he said, biting off each word. "We use the Vampire Motorcycle Club as a front to run drugs."

Meara started to say something, but Bane sliced a hand through the air, cutting her off, still staring at Ryan. "Vampires and drug dealers. Fine crowd you've found yourself in, isn't it?"

"Better vampire than drug dealer, any day of the week," she said, ice freezing her veins. "If you're sure he'll heal on his own, then I'm out of here."

She jumped to her feet and turned to go but found the dog blocking her way.

"Bite me or get out of my way, but I'm leaving. Now," she told him, only belatedly realizing that the vampires in the room could take that as directed at them, too.

The dog fell to his side and rolled over, legs up in the air, tongue lolling out of one side of his mouth, and gave a gentle *woof*.

"He wants a belly rub," Mrs. Cassidy ventured. "He likes you."

"I like him, too, but I also want to wake up in my own

bed and find that all of this was just a very bad dream," Ryan said. "We can't always get what we want, though, can we?"

She leapt over the dog and started running for the door. Movement blurred past her peripheral vision, and then Bane was in front of her, blocking her way.

"I'm sorry, Doctor, but I won't let you leave me. Not like this." His eyes blazed red, terrifying her, and then he leaned down until his face was inches from hers. In a lightning-quick move, his hand shot out and took hers. "Sleep now."

As Ryan's knees gave out, and she felt herself falling into the dark, she faintly heard first Meara's voice and then the rumble of Bane's response.

"She won't forgive you for that, Brother."

"I could never deserve her forgiveness. I may as well earn her hatred."

CHAPTER EIGHTEEN

Ryan woke up in a place that was decidedly not the kitchen she'd just run from. It looked, instead, like the armory of the militia in a scary movie.

The walls were bare brick, lined with shelves and racks, all of which held a dizzying array of weapons. There were guns, but not as many as she would have expected, given the feel of the room. Mostly, there were swords.

And knives.

And…would those be called daggers?

All of this she took in at a glance, while scanning her surroundings from the bench she lay on, to figure out where the hell she was this time. At first, she thought she was alone in the room, but by the time she shoved herself up and off the bench, she caught sight of Bane in a corner, seated on a stool, holding a long-bladed knife in one hand and a rectangular sharpening stone in the other.

He stood, too, putting the knife and stone down on a low table, and then waited for her to speak.

"If you ever put me to sleep again like that, I'll find a way to hurt you," she said, rage pulsing beneath each word. "You asked me for permission to *touch my hair*, and then you do this? Again?"

His eyes, glowing brightly in the dimly lit room, turned to blue ice. "Do not push me too far," he said quietly. "I am not human—do not forget it."

Every word was a threat. Even his *existence* was a threat.

But somehow, for some reason, she was not afraid. Stupidity? Perhaps. Or maybe familiarity did indeed breed, if not contempt, a certain lack of giving a crap.

But then again, the drugs. The thought infuriated her all over again.

"No, you're not human. You're a bloodsucking drug dealer," she spat out, looking for the exit. "Where are we? I need to get out of here, now. Or are you going to kill me, now that I know about your criminal enterprise?"

"Bloodsucking is a little unfair. I didn't call you a coffee-sucking human. Why do you keep asking me if I'm going to kill you? You must know on some level that you will not like the answer."

"I'm not afraid of you," she shot back, lying through her teeth.

"That would make you brainless, and I know that's not true. Perhaps we can leave it as I will not kill you *yet*."

She drew in a sharp breath. "Yet. Oh, that's great. And better brainless than a drug dealer. If you'd seen what I see at the hospital, from drug use…"

"If you'd seen what I've seen, from the *lack* of drugs," he countered. He looked at her for a long moment and then took a step toward her, and she took a step toward the door, keeping the same amount of space between them. He immediately stopped moving but still said nothing.

"I want to leave, Bane. If you're not going to kill me, you have to let me go." She took another tentative step toward the door, waiting for him to attack her, put her to sleep again, or decapitate her with one of the many blades that could so easily slice through skin and muscle, tendon and bone.

"I'm not a drug dealer. Not in the way you're thinking," he finally said.

She took another step, but her stupid curiosity won out, again, and she stopped before reaching for the door handle and turned to face him. "How can you be a drug dealer but not a drug dealer?"

"I—we—life is a long wasteland of dull nights, when you live for centuries," he said, shoving a hand through his hair.

"You turned to a life of crime because you were *bored*?"

"No! Well, yes, but there was more to it than that." He started pacing, careful not to walk any closer to her.

"Do tell," she drawled, leaning back against the door and folding her arms. "This should be good."

He shot her a look. "Sarcasm. Yes. Thank you."

She waved one hand in a "go ahead" motion.

"There was a child. She was ill."

She waited. And waited. "Look. If you want to tell me—"

"She was my sister," he said, rushing through the words now. "Jane. She was very, very ill. A form of childhood cancer, I think it must have been, although we did not know that then. There was no treatment that would help."

A stab of pain pierced her stomach, as it always did when a child was involved. Doctors weren't gods. They couldn't save everyone. Ryan knew she was supposed to be calm and objective when she lost a patient, even a child, but she'd never learned how to do that.

"And what happened?" she asked, her voice gentle. She could tell by the look in his eyes that he, too, had felt real pain for the child.

"She died," he growled. "What else? She died, as so

many children died then and so many still die today."

He bent his head, averting his face from her gaze, and his shoulders bowed.

She wanted to go to him, for some insane reason. Comfort him. She knew this feeling of loss and pain. But there were no words that could form the shapes of healing. Only time could do that. And if he still hurt from her death after three centuries...

"If it had only happened today." He clenched his fists and pounded them down on a table. "I have more money than I could ever need in a thousand years. If my human family had lived in this time, I'd have found some way to help. You have medicines and treatments today... All cancer does not have to be fatal."

"That's true, but even today, so many die from cancer. Too many," she said, finally reaching out to touch his arm. "I'm so sorry, Bane."

"All these centuries, it has haunted me, somewhere in the back of my mind," he admitted, his face drawn into harsh lines. "But several years back, when I looked up from my own narrow view of the world, I learned that so many can't afford the medicines they need. In this century, with its wealth of science and medicine that earlier centuries would have seen as miracles or magic—in this century, *children still die from not having money for medicine*. It's obscene."

She agreed with every word out of his mouth. It was why she dedicated two days of every week to working in the free clinic. But still...

"I agree with you. I'm sorry, though, but I still don't see what that has to do with you becoming a drug smuggler."

He shrugged. "I fund purchases of mass quantities of medicines. And then we—Meara, Luke, Edge, and I, together with some of the members of the Vampire Motorcycle Club—smuggle the prescription drugs down the eastern seaboard from Canada, and we provide them to a select group of free clinics that we have connections with, like the—"

"The Delacourt Free Clinic downtown," Ryan gasped, making the connection. "Meara Delacourt—you—she's *that* Delacourt?"

His smile faded. "And now, yet again, I've provided you with a secret that I can't wipe from your memory, which endangers both my people and your life. What am I going to do with you, Ryan St. Cloud?"

"Trust me," she whispered, her framework for understanding him having just been shattered and rebuilt to separate dimensions in her mind. "Trust me and let me help you—help Hunter Evans. Let me try to understand, try to study—"

His eyes shuttered. "Study *us*?"

She shook her head, frustrated. "No. Well, just me. And only you. Like you suggested. But not to report to some governmental agency or shadowy cabal—"

"*Cabal*?" His eyes sparkled. "Would they meet in a *lair*?"

"Okay, I watch too many movies," she admitted, her words tumbling over each other as her mind caught fire. "But yes, maybe if I can study you, I can help you understand how the Turn works. Maybe we can figure out how to use this gift you have of healing in a way that could benefit even more people—"

"I don't give a damn about benefiting people," he

growled. "I'm so far from caring what happens to anybody but those who are mine—"

"To benefit *children*, then," she said, without missing a beat. "Without disclosing your secrets."

A muscle in his jaw clenched, and he looked away. "Fine. For the children, then," he muttered.

He glanced down, and she realized that somehow, without even noticing it, she'd taken his hands in hers. She forcibly stopped herself from backing away from him. If she showed him fear, he'd never believe her. Never trust her.

Never let her help.

And, she suddenly realized, she'd never wanted anything more in her life than she wanted him to let her inside his world.

Reliable Ryan wanted an adventure.

And this man used his immortal life to help children get the medicines they needed.

"Please?"

His eyes widened, and then he glanced down at his hands in hers and then back up at her face. "It has real power, doesn't it? That word. *Please.*"

"I hope so. Let me in, Bane. Let me look at your blood under my microscope. Let me help you understand what you are."

"It's dangerous to be part of my world," he murmured, leaning down until his forehead touched hers and closing his eyes. "What kind of monster am I that I'm even considering it?"

She closed her eyes, too, and breathed in his enticing scent. Pine trees, perhaps? And sandalwood?

He sighed and squeezed her hands so tightly that it almost hurt and then released them.

Her eyes flew open, and she caught her breath at the intensity of his gaze.

"If I say yes, you have to promise to keep what we are a secret," he said, his voice quiet and somber. "I can't—I won't stand by and watch you put my family in danger."

She didn't even need to think twice. "I promise. You're trusting me. You deserve my promise and my secrecy."

Before she could take even a single step back toward the bench, he put his hands on her waist and effortlessly lifted her to sit on the table behind her. A purely primal, feminine satisfaction that she'd never experienced before spread warmth through her chest, and she smiled at him. "Super vampire strength, huh?"

Those golden eyebrows drew together. "What?"

"You know," she muttered, already regretting the conversation. "Lifting me so easily. I'm a lot, I know."

The memory of her last boyfriend, nearly two years ago now, making a loud "oof!" sound when she sat on his lap at a party burned through her, and she could feel her face turn hot.

Bane, unexpectedly, laughed. When her gaze flew up to meet his, she could almost touch the desire flaring in his glowing blue eyes and slightly bared teeth.

"Oh, beautiful one. Men of this age are fucking weaklings. In my day, you'd have been pursued for your gorgeous hair, your blue eyes, and even your brilliance, but—most of all—for that lovely round ass that I constantly have to fight to keep from grabbing."

Heat of an entirely different sort than embarrassment

seared through her, and she had to bite her lip to keep it
from trembling. He was so close to her, standing practically
between her legs, and he looked like *that*, and he'd just said
that he wanted to grab her, and suddenly that delicious
heat raced through her, straight to her core, and she could
feel tingling all the way from her breasts to her…to her…

"I want to kiss you again, Doctor." His voice was smoke
and velvet, and it wrapped around her in a sensual caress,
until she caught herself leaning into him, turning her face
up to his like a flower turning to the sun, and then the
irony of comparing him to the sun—a being so completely
of the night—snapped her out of her trance, and she jerked
back.

"I have to call the hospital," she blurted out.

A muscle clenched in Bane's jaw, but he moved back a
half-step, and the dangerous electricity between them
subsided enough for her to think clearly again.

Thinking is overrated.

"The hospital?"

"I'm due to work today and have coffee with my friend
Annie before my shift, and I can't just not show up because
I disappeared into thin air with a strange man."

He nodded, his expression solemn. "I *am* a very strange
man."

She smiled just a little, in spite of herself. "Bane. I'm
already on thin ice at work after I spent last night inter-
rogating everybody about Mr. Evans. They all think I
need a serious vacation. How did you do that?"

"Luke used compulsion. Edge used computers. Between
the two of them, there's no record of Hunter being there."

Her head started to hurt again. All those hours, thinking

she was going crazy. "Anyway, why did you save Mr. Evans? You're all big on 'we only like humans for the running and the screaming,' but he's definitely human, or at least he was, and—"

"It's a long story."

"I have time." She folded her arms across her chest. "Unless you need to get to your coffin or something."

He slanted an amused look at her. "I don't have a coffin. But I'm starting to think you have some kind of coffin fetish, the way you keep bringing it up."

She shrugged. "I like horror movies."

"This explains a lot about you. You're not afraid of us, because you're attracted to the dark. Horror movies, night shifts at the hospital. You're practically one of us already."

She watched the shape of his lips as he spoke. The curve of his shoulders where they met the muscle of his arms. The movement of his throat.

Attracted to the dark.

Maybe.

And he was the dark come to life.

"I'm attracted to *you*," she blurted out, feeling almost as if she were caught in the enthrallment he'd tried and failed to use on her before.

He put a finger under her chin and lifted her face until he could stare into her eyes. "You don't want anything to do with me, Ryan. I'm dangerous."

"I'm sitting here surrounded by blades of every shape and size, and yet I've probably sliced into more human bodies than you have," she told him, reaching up to put her hands on his shoulders, suddenly needing help to balance herself where she sat. "Maybe *I'm* the one who is dangerous."

"Certainly to my peace of mind," he growled. "Ryan, I want to kiss you again."

Suddenly unsure, she turned her head away from the longing stamped plain on his beautiful face.

"Tell me about that," she said breathlessly, pointing at a random knife on a rack nearby.

"I—what?" he said, rasping out the words. "You want to know about daggers?"

"I want to know about your world, which seems to contain more knives than a chef's kitchen." And she needed to catch her breath, but she didn't tell him that. "So, tell me."

He said nothing for a moment or two, breathing hard, and then he held out his hand, and the knife soared through the air and the hilt smacked into his palm.

"Fine. Ask me. I'll trade each answer for a kiss."

Her hand flew to her mouth. "I'm—I'm not sure I'm ready for that."

He smiled, his eyes glowing blue fire. "I didn't say the kisses would all be on your mouth."

CHAPTER NINETEEN

Bane heard Ryan's heart speed up and tried not to let his triumph show on his face. He wanted her. Quite possibly more than he'd ever desired anything or anyone before.

But he needed her to accept him. To welcome him.

To *invite* him into her world.

Into her life.

Into her *body*.

He had to fight to keep his fangs from descending, just thinking of how it would be to ease her down beneath him, naked and willing and oh, so wet for him.

"I'm not sure that's fair," she said, swallowing hard. "I don't, ah, have that many questions."

"Well, then you'll be safe, won't you?" He leaned closer and inhaled her scent, which was a mistake. She smelled like summer and sunshine. She smelled like she belonged to him—like she was already his.

Persuasion, after all, was nine-tenths of seduction.

Her breath stuttered, and she turned her face to the side, leaving him to contemplate taking her earlobe between his teeth and nibbling on it, just until…

"Okay. Tell me about that one. What is it?"

Words, again, damn it. Too many words.

"Bane?" She pointed at the knife in his hand. "That one?"

He ground his teeth but then remembered the bargain. A question for a kiss.

"Should I answer you first or claim a kiss and then answer?"

She blushed, a fascinating dusky pink dusting her cheeks. "Answer first, I think."

Answers, not kisses. He took a step back, away from her heat and light and warmth. A step back toward the cold darkness of his life.

"Ask me anything."

He wanted her to ask him to rip her clothes off, so they could discover what passion between them could be. But he wanted her to feel safe with him even more than he wanted to satisfy his own desires.

Before he could take another step—either forward or back—she reached out and grabbed his shirt, and he froze.

"No," she whispered. "I want—I wish—answer me first, and then you can kiss me."

His gaze slowly, oh so slowly, traveled down to where she had a grip on his shirt, and it felt as though her fingers branded him through the fabric.

"Question," he growled, his mind empty. His body on fire from her touch.

What would it be if she were ever to touch his naked skin?

He might spontaneously burst into flame.

"The—the dagger," she said, more confidently now. "Tell me about that dagger, and then…then you can kiss me."

"The dagger." He cleared his throat and tried to focus on the knife instead of on the pulse in her throat. "Yes. That's a Bowie knife, actually, not a dagger. Jim Bowie invented it. It has a particularly long and powerful blade with this reverse-edge curve." He offered it to her. "Would you like to hold it?"

She shook her head. "Not particularly. It looks very sharp."

"It is. Sharp," he repeated, too entranced by the curve of her cheek to make any sense at all. By all the curves of her lovely body. The curve of her breasts beneath his shirt. The curve of her hips in his trousers.

His necktie was the only thing holding those trousers up—the only thing hiding her creamy skin from him...

He raised the knife slowly toward her chest, and she gasped.

"Bane?"

"One kiss for one question," he told her, carefully touching the tip of the blade to the placket of the shirt. "I didn't say where."

A twist of his wrist and the button popped off the shirt and fell to the floor, and the gentle pressure of her breasts strained against the opening. He gazed down at the hollow between the curves and forgot how to breathe.

"I—I did agree," she whispered, and when he looked into her eyes, they were fever-bright.

"So you did," he said, dropping the knife to the floor, and then he said nothing else, because his mouth was busy.

He pressed his lips to the swell of one breast and was rewarded by the way her body trembled beneath him. When she tightened the hand holding his shirt and then clutched his shoulder with her other hand, he gathered her into his arms.

"I don't understand this," she murmured when he finally, regretfully, raised his head, since he'd only bargained for one kiss per question. "How is my entire body on fire like this, just from a kiss? I don't even particularly *like* sex."

Bane smiled. "You don't like sex? Your body is so responsive that you were clearly *made* for sex."

She blushed again but then frowned. "Don't...you don't have to do that. The false flattery thing. I know it's what men do when they want sex—"

"I give a compliment when it's true and only then, believe me." He traced the curve of her shoulder with one finger, delighting in her shiver. "Ask me another."

"What?"

"Another question. Ask me another, so I can kiss you again."

"Tell me about being a vampire. How does it work? Are you all magic? And you can disappear, like you did in the hospital. How did you do that? Did you wake up with magic powers? Will Hunter Evans be able to do all those things?" She paused to draw breath, and he held up a hand.

"I think that was more like five or six questions." He pushed a strand of hair behind her ear and leaned forward to whisper into it. "So I'll answer them one at a time."

He ran his hands down her arms, watching her reaction. Barely suppressing a shout of triumph when her eyelids fluttered shut at his touch. "Yes, all vampires have magic, as far as I know. Or we *are* magic. Either way, the vampires that I know all gained certain powers when we Turned. None of them are exactly the same, either, and I don't know how or why that is the case."

He leaned forward again, closed his eyes, and inhaled. Reveled in her scent. Her warmth.

"But I—"

"No. My turn." He put his mouth on the curve of her neck, just over her pulse, and touched his tongue to her skin. When her heart rate sped up, he found himself fighting to keep from plunging his teeth into her vein.

He yanked his head away from her neck, panting. Shocked at his loss of the control it had taken him three centuries to develop.

Then taken her three minutes to demolish.

He put his hands on the table on either side of her hips and touched his forehead to hers. "I don't know what Hunter will be able to do. As you've seen, his Turn isn't progressing in the same way that I've seen before. I don't know why, before you ask."

"What about the others? What can they do?"

Her cheeks were flushed, her eyes bright, and her hair mussed. She looked like she'd just been thoroughly bedded, and he wanted nothing more than to make perception into reality.

But not here.

Not on an old wooden table in a room designed for weapons of war. It would not be war they waged between them, when he took this woman into his bed.

No, it would be something far older and more passionate than mere war.

"Bane?"

"No," he said abruptly. "I won't tell you secrets that aren't mine to tell. But now you answer me: in your home, you told me to take off my clothes. Is that offer still open?"

She blinked and glanced around. "I—here? I mean—"

"No. Not here. It would be the matter of a minute to take you back to my bed," he rasped out, skin and flesh and nerve endings all aching at the idea that she might say yes.

Unexpectedly—although what about this woman was ever expected?—she laughed. "I'm not the kind of person that this happens to. I'm old Reliable Ryan. Men as beautiful as you are never take notice of someone like me."

"You find me beautiful." He wondered if a face could crack from smiling so hard. "Clearly, you're a very perceptive and intelligent human."

She actually growled with frustration, and he wanted to roll around in the sound.

"Bane! You know you're beautiful. I've never seen anyone more beautiful in my life. It's ridiculously unfair, and either you're a genetic miracle or it's something about being a vampire."

His smile faded. "So, I'm only beautiful to you because I'm not human?"

"You're more human than any man I've ever known," she said softly. "You protect your family. You help sick children. You save the life of a man who was burned nearly to death. Don't hide behind this pretense of being a monster."

The words cut into him like a double-edged blade. Was her good opinion won so easily? Was she a fool that she couldn't see who he really was?

Worse, was the addition of touch and sensuality actually accomplishing the compulsion she'd resisted before? Maybe he should test that.

"Put your hands on your head," he commanded her, putting a strong push behind the words.

"Put your hands on your own head," she said, rolling her

eyes. "I thought we were past this."

Not compulsion, then. She actually found him to be human-like. Human enough to allow him to touch her.

To kiss her.

"Stay." He stepped back a pace and took a deep breath, needing a clear head. "Stay and study me. Tell me what you discover. Let's discover if science can analyze magic, if maybe my blood can help you learn how to cure disease."

"You'd trust me? With your secrets?"

"You could never share what you learn. Never tell the scientific community or anyone else. Could you be content with that?"

"Keep your secrets, or you'd have to kill me?" The light in her eyes dimmed. "We're back to that?"

"If I can't trust you, I'd have to do worse than kill you," he told her, forcing the words from his throat.

"Worse?" She paled, and her hand crept to her throat. "What's worse?"

"I'd Turn you. If you were one of us, you'd never tell our secrets."

"No! I can't... No. Promise me that you won't do that." She shook with tension or fear at the mere idea, making him realize that she must believe him a monster, to be so afraid to become what he was.

Which, of course, he should have expected, so he had no idea why his stomach suddenly felt hollow. But she deserved an answer, so he considered the question and then gave her the truth, when he so easily could have lied. "Yes. I promise you that I won't Turn you, so long as you don't disclose our secrets. Will you agree to work with me, and me alone, on those terms?"

She stared into his eyes for so long he was sure the answer would be no, but then she nodded. "Yes. I'll work with you, and I promise never to tell anyone about vampires."

She held out her hand, and bemused, he shook it.

"So professional, Doctor."

"Yes. So. I think we should get back." She bit her lip. "I need to go get some things from my place—some clothes—and some things from the hospital, so I can get started. I want to analyze your blood, first, and—"

"Would you like to see my club?"

"I—what?"

He could tell by the faraway expression in her eyes that she'd been miles away, making lists in her fascinating, scientific mind.

"My club? We're downstairs from it now. I can show you around, if you like."

"Sure. But, isn't it daylight now?" She bit her lip again, and a swelling of warmth spread through his chest when he realized why she'd asked.

She was worried.

For *him*.

"Yes. Dawn broke twenty minutes ago. We—vampires—can always feel when the sun rises and sets. But there are no windows in the club, and the door opens into an entry with another door. It's quite safe, but thank you." He smiled at her. "It has been a long damn time since anyone other than my family has worried about me."

"Maybe it's time that changed," she said softly, returning his smile, and he could have sworn he heard the sound of the concrete blocks he'd built into a wall around his heart start to crack.

"Maybe it is," he murmured. "Shall we go up?"

"After you," she said brightly.

He pretended not to notice when she slipped the Bowie knife into her pants pocket. If a blade helped her feel safer in the midst of monsters…

The most human man she'd ever met.

He could work with that.

CHAPTER TWENTY

Ryan waited until Bane's back was turned before sneaking the knife into her pocket. She had to stab hard to make a hole in the bottom of the pocket, so the full length of the blade would fit in, and then walk very carefully so she didn't slice her leg open. The only kind of blades she was used to were scalpels, and she didn't carry those around in her pocket.

He'd agreed. Only for the children, but still, he'd said yes to letting her study his blood, and she wanted so very badly to do it. To study him. To see how the secrets of his blood might be able to help cure incurable diseases. To learn about *magic,* after a life spent with no magic at all.

It was as if all her secret dreams of adventure were coming true—dreams of meeting a man who could fulfill the darkest fantasies she held deep in a hidden corner of her heart.

Of her soul.

And now here he was. In the flesh, so to speak. Magical and miraculous. So beautiful that, scientifically, he almost couldn't be real. And yet, somehow, he *was*. He not only existed, but he wanted *her*. She'd felt the evidence of it pressing up against her core when he stood between her legs. He'd kissed her like a man who truly wanted her—touched her with reverence and longing.

She knew this was true, because she'd had experience with the opposite. With perfunctory kisses. With touch fueled more by alcohol than desire.

No, Bane wanted Ryan for herself—not just because she happened to be available, like a few of the less-than-memorable experiences she'd had after nights out. And—even more miraculously—he made her want him as well.

The entire situation was impossible, and yet she was damn well going to talk herself into trying to believe it. At least for a little while, she could be the type of woman who went on wild adventures. Who rescued the prince from his tower. Who made friends with the dragon and rode off into the sunset. Maybe not to live happily ever after—but to live happily and magically for just a little while?

What *wouldn't* she give for that?

She would leave Reliable Ryan behind and become wildly, fearlessly *unreliable* in all the best ways.

By the time she came to this terrifying and tantalizing conclusion, Bane had led her up to the top of the staircase and into a freezing-cold space that looked like the NASA control room.

She'd never seen so many computers in one place in her life. "What could you possibly need all this for?"

"More questions?" Bane's smile was downright wicked.

She blushed, in spite of herself, because she knew exactly what he was thinking. More questions meant more kisses, and not necessarily on her mouth. That led her to thinking about some places that she'd very much like to feel his kisses, and then she had to clench her thighs together against the answering heat.

"Coming?" Bane stood at the door waiting for her. She almost could've sworn his gaze flickered to the pocket where she carried the knife, but that must just have been her nerves. After all, he didn't have eyes in the back of his head, so how could he know?

Unless x-ray vision was another power?

All of a sudden, she felt the headache rushing back. She'd barely touched her food before Edge had come crashing in, she hadn't slept, and all that wine was still working its way through her body. Not to mention the adrenaline that had been coursing through her at each new revelation. What she needed was oxygen, headache medicine, and about a gallon of water. Plus more coffee.

Lots more coffee.

Stat.

But Bane was still waiting, now with a hand held out to her, so she took a deep breath and smiled.

At the door, he suddenly paused. "I forgot to grab a carving knife I was sharpening for Mrs. C. Wait here."

Ryan sighed, watching him go.

Wait. Sit. Stay.

Roll over, human.

The man needed to learn a few things about this particular human, and she needed to stand up for herself before she actually rolled over for every barked order he issued.

She pushed open the door and walked into the room beyond.

As if on cue, most of the people in the room, which consisted of two kinds: 1) scary men wearing Vampire Motorcycle Club vests and 2) scary women wearing Vampire Motorcycle Club vests, turned to look at her with varying degrees of surprise. Most of them looked like people she wouldn't want to meet in a dark alley.

As opposed to the vampire *you're hanging out with now.*

One of the biggest guys, who had a full beard, long hair in braids, and a scar bisecting the dark skin of his right cheek, swaggered up to her and looked her up and down.

"Who the fuck are you?"

Behind him, she could see people grinning. Okay. Intimidate the outsider. Well, that was fine. She'd been the outsider a lot in her life. Never mind that this behemoth had a good foot of height and at least a hundred pounds of weight over her.

She smiled up at Bigfoot. "I'm Dr. Ryan St. Cloud. Who the fuck are you?"

He scowled down at her for a long moment, and then he threw his head back and laughed. "Good one, Doc. I'm Jenks. Welcome to the VMC. Beer?"

She glanced over at the clock on the wall, surprised. "It's seven-thirty in the morning!"

"Right. Whiskey?"

A tall woman with short brown hair, golden-brown skin, and the muscular physique of an athlete elbowed Jenks out of the way. "She doesn't want whiskey for breakfast, you dunderhead. Don't give our guest the wrong impression of us."

The Amazon held out her hand. "I'm Marisela Torres. Welcome. Coffee?"

Ryan shook her hand and smiled. "I'd love a cup of coffee. Hold the whiskey. And it's nice to meet you both."

Marisela flashed a gorgeous smile. "Same. The dunderhead is my husband. And you're here with?"

A rush of wind and a chill in the air warned Ryan that Bane had arrived, so she wasn't surprised when he put an arm around her shoulder. "*She's here with me.*"

She knew that voice—or was it *Voice?* He was project-ing his compulsion out to the entire room.

And it pissed her off.

"Maybe you could just pee on my shoe next time," she said sweetly, moving out from beneath his arm. "I'm sure *that* would mark your territory."

Bane slowly turned his head and pinned her with a slightly wide-eyed gaze, which, coming from Mr. Stone Face, must signify total shock.

Marisela burst out laughing. "Guess she told you, Boss. Now stand aside while I get the doc some coffee."

When the woman strode off toward the bar, Ryan leaned closer to Bane to whisper in his ear. "Are they human or vampires? And you named your club the *Vampire Motorcycle Club* but you'll kill me if I give away your secret?"

He casually dropped a kiss on the top of her head. "These are all humans, because having human members is a good front if anyone ever starts to get suspicious," he murmured, his breath in her ear causing shock waves of pure lust to sizzle down her nerve endings. "And the name? The best place to hide anything is in plain sight."

Ryan blinked. "Your brain works in fascinating and mysterious ways, doesn't it?"

Bane didn't respond but simply stared at her as if she were an especially intriguing puzzle he needed to work out. She shook her head and walked off to join Marisela, who reached over the polished wood and plucked a coffee pot off a warmer, pulled two mugs down from an overhead rack, and poured coffee for them both.

While Marisela did that, Ryan studied the place. It was a large, high-ceilinged room decorated in what she thought of as Ye Old English Pub. Tables with chairs were scattered about, there was a huge stone fireplace, a couple of pool tables, and two dart boards. The twenty or so people in the room were drinking coffee and sitting around in small groups, chatting. Two of the men were playing pool, and two women and a man were shooting darts.

It was the least motorcycle clubby scene she could ever have imagined.

"Not really *Sons of Anarchy*, is it?" Marisela said, smiling and holding a mug of coffee out to Ryan. "There's cream and sugar there."

"Thanks." Ryan added both sugar and cream and then took a long sip before responding. "I guess so. I don't know anything about motorcycle gangs—"

"Clubs."

"I—what?"

Marisela put her mug down on a coaster on the gleaming wood surface of the bar. "Club. We're a motorcycle club, not a gang. You're thinking of Hell's Angels and the scary criminals in movies, right?"

Ryan slowly nodded. "Yeah. I guess I was. But—"

"But?" Marisela's deep brown eyes studied her.

Ryan leaned closer and spoke very quietly. "I know about the drugs. That's actually illegal, right?"

"No. It's heroic," Marisela said, her smile fading. "Which you'd realize, if you weren't a rich doctor."

"Rich?" Ryan's first impulse was to laugh, thinking of her massive student loan debt, but then she thought about it. It was true, she'd never had to worry about money, or food, or health care.

Her gaze involuntarily went to Bane, who was deep in discussion with Jenks and a few other club members. He glanced up at her and smiled, and the men around him fell silent with varying looks of shock on their faces.

Guess he wasn't the type to smile much.

Or ever.

She didn't know how to feel about that. About any of it. So she decided to ignore it.

"Maybe you're right," she finally said, turning back to Marisela. "What do you do when you're not here?"

"I'm a professor at SCAD. Painting and portraits."

"That's wonderful! Maybe I've seen some of your work at one of the shows?" The Savannah College of Art and Design was an integral part of the city, and Ryan had always loved the annual film festival and attended as many of the art shows as she could.

"I had a self-portrait in the Perspectives show a couple of weeks ago," Marisela said, suddenly looking a little shy. "I'm sure you didn't—"

"Oh my God! That was you!" Ryan put her mug down, studying the other woman's features. "The six-foot-long nude of you reading in the window seat? I *loved* that painting. You're so talented."

Marisela's smile was blinding. "Thanks. I appreciate it."

"Not me," Jenks called across the room, but he was grinning. "I don't love other men looking at my beautiful naked wife."

Bane met Ryan's gaze and started prowling toward her, dangerously graceful. She suddenly realized that his eyes, although still beautiful, weren't glowing anymore. He must be able to control that, to hide it from the humans?

"You love it, you Neanderthal," Marisela told Jenks, laughing. "He kept saying, 'That's my wife,' until I made him leave," she confided to Ryan.

"He *should* be proud. It's amazing, and you're so beautiful in it. I could almost feel the sadness—"

Marisela's eyes clouded.

"Oh, I'm so sorry," Ryan stammered. "I didn't mean to bring up—"

"No. You pour your soul into your art, and if you're brave enough to put it out into the world, your truest wish is to make people *feel* when they encounter it. Thank you for telling me." Marisela lightly touched her arm.

Bane didn't stop his approach until he was standing only inches from Ryan. "I would *not* be happy if other men saw *your* nude body," he growled.

Ryan blinked, speechless. This was not the kind of conversation she'd ever had in her life.

Marisela shook her head. "Peeing on shoes again, Boss?"

That snapped her out of it. "You—" She elbowed Bane in the side. Hard. "You don't get a say in anything I do with my body, nude or otherwise."

He leaned closer and put his cheek on the top of her head, inhaling deeply. "You smell like sunlight," he murmured. "It makes me want to do many things with your body, naked *and* otherwise."

Jenks, who'd walked over to join them, grinned at Bane. "So, you're letting us meet your old lady?"

"Hey!" Ryan narrowed her eyes. "I'm not old!"

Most of the people in the room, many who'd been

watching Ryan surreptitiously or openly, started laughing, and she was caught off guard for a second, but then she started to laugh, too.

Bane, however, didn't. His hand shot out, and he grabbed Jenks by the shirtfront and lifted him so high into the air that the man's shoes barely touched the floor, as casually as if he were picking up a napkin. Then he locked his gaze on Ryan.

"He insulted you. Do you want me to kill him?"

CHAPTER TWENTY-ONE

A red sheen washed over Bane's vision, and he had to turn his head so the humans wouldn't see it. The humans other than Ryan, who was looking at him with some concern, her lovely eyes gone dark and questioning.

She put a hand on his arm—*the arm that wasn't lifting one of his trusted club members into the air; what the fuck was happening to him?*—and shook her head.

"Seems a little extreme," she said dryly. "Maybe you could just arm wrestle."

He released Jenks, who, luckily, took it as a great joke and started laughing. "I always knew that when you finally fell, you'd fall hard. No insult to your lady, my friend." He clapped Bane so hard on the back with one giant hand that the blow would have knocked a human a few feet across the floor. "Been working out, huh?"

"Men. Am I right?" Marisela's expression was wary as she flicked her gaze between Bane and Ryan. "Can't live with them, can't take them out back and beat some sense into them. Wait! Maybe we could…"

Ryan smiled and moved subtly to position herself between Bane and the other two. "Maybe. But other things are much more fun. Bane, are you ready to go?"

Shock froze him in place for a moment. The doctor had just placed herself between him and perceived danger—he'd been a warrior long enough to recognize the move.

She was trying to protect *him*.

Her instinct was to protect him from *other humans*, even though she knew he was a vampire.

Heat smashed through him at the realization that this small human was *trying to fucking protect him*. Beauty trying to protect the beast.

She was a goddess. A warrior goddess.

"Yes," he managed to rasp out. "Yes, let's go now. I called Mr. C from the office. He should be here now."

Marisela tilted her head. "When did you get here? I didn't see your car or any of your bikes when we arrived."

"Tommy dropped us off around six," he said, figuring none of them would have been here that early.

Marisela nodded, but her eyes had a speculative look in them that he didn't like. She was very smart—maybe too smart. If she discovered too much about him, he'd have to compel her to forget.

Luckily, Ryan was the only human he'd ever met with total resistance to compulsion, although it did wear off after long periods of time on some people. Those were the ones he'd had to kill. He didn't want to have to kill Marisela.

Or Jenks.

"You should bring her on one of our rides," Jenks offered, rocking back on the heels of his boots and grinning like a fool. As usual, the big man was completely oblivious to any undercurrents in the conversation. Subtlety was not his forte. "Has he shown you, Doc? The prez has a sweet collection of rides."

Marisela smacked her husband lightly on the side of his head. "You know Bane doesn't ride during the day with his eyesight."

"Oh, yeah. Hey, Doc! You can fix his eyes, right?"

"I'm not an ophthalmologist," Ryan said, smoothly covering up the fact that she'd had no idea he'd told them his eyes were too light-sensitive for daylight. "But I can certainly see what we can figure out."

"We should go now," Bane said, taking her hand in his and managing not to reveal how the electricity in that simple touch flared throughout his body.

"You come back anytime, Doc," Marisela said. "I'll buy you a drink, and we'll make fun of the men in our lives."

Ryan's smile transformed her face—what he'd stupidly thought of as her rather ordinary, everyday human face—into a picture of such beauty that Bane had no idea how every man she'd ever met wasn't following her around, begging for her attention.

And then, just like that, the idea of such a trail of men flashed a searing arrow of rage through him.

Wrong.

He wasn't angry. He was jealous.

Jealous?

In a daze, he nodded to the club members as he led Ryan through the room to the doorway, still holding her hand as if he had any right to do so.

Right to do so? He'd be damned *if anybody could stop him from holding her hand, or holding any other part of her luscious body, and oh, sweet fuck, he was actually jealous.*

Still in shock over the fierce and conflicting emotions he was feeling—about a human he'd *just met*—he sent his senses out ahead of them and was relieved to feel Mr. C's solid presence and hear the purr of the limo. He led Ryan through the inner door and then, just as he put a hand on the door to the parking lot, she stopped walking. "Wait! It's past dawn! We can't—won't you burn up?"

"And *again* you try to protect me." He swung around and pulled her into his arms, surprising a delightful squeaking noise from her. "Who sent you to be my temptation, Dr. Ryan St. Cloud?"

Her gaze dropped to his mouth, and she licked her lips, which made his cock instantly harden. "I don't—I don't know what that means."

"It means you're my miracle, and I don't know what I'm going to do with that," he muttered, releasing her and taking a deep breath. "We should go before Jenks follows us out into the parking lot. He likes you."

"I like him, too." She caught her breath when the door opened, allowing the dawn sun to wash into the dark space, but when he didn't immediately explode into flames, she relaxed her tight grip on his hand and followed him out of the club.

Wasting no time, Bane strode the three paces to the limo, which was waiting between neatly parked rows of Harleys, and yanked the back door open for her. Ryan, true to her stubborn nature, stopped short and shoved his shoulder. "You first, please."

He ignored his first instinct, which was to pick her up and toss her in the damn car, and gave in. As soon as he folded his frame into the backseat, she climbed in next to him.

"Home, sir?" Mr. C said, smiling at him in the rearview mirror. "You must be getting tired."

"Yes, thanks."

"Hello, Mr. Cassidy," Ryan said.

"Hello, Dr. St. Cloud. Lovely day, isn't it?" With that, Mr. C started to whistle and then pushed the button that raised the darkened glass—sun-proofed like the windows—between the seats, something he'd never done before in the decades that he'd been driving for Bane. "Just for a bit of privacy, sir."

"Whatever you're doing to me, you're clearly doing to my staff, too," he told Ryan, shaking his head. Bit of privacy? Did the man think Bane was going to jump her in the backseat in the fifteen-minute drive to the mansion?

Actually, the jumping was a good idea, but the fifteen minutes part was just insulting.

"I was worried about you catching on fire," Ryan said. "You need to tell me more about what being a vampire actually means. I saw that you can eat food and drink coffee. Now you can go out in the daylight. I'm guessing you don't sparkle?"

Her lips quirked, as if she fought against smiling, so he pretended to glare at her. "Meara told us about that craze. Trust me, I'm not Edgar Cullen."

"Edward."

"What?" The glimmer of amusement in her eyes had distracted him into losing track of the conversation.

"It's *Edward* Cullen, not Edgar. Edgar was the poet with the decidedly dark imagination."

He watched her lips move as carefully as he'd once watched the coast from his ship for signs of English soldiers. So lush, those lips. If she'd only wrap them around his cock...

He groaned. Loudly.

"What? Did the sun hurt you after all?"

When she leaned forward in alarm, he shifted in his seat to relieve the pressure from his pants.

"No. I just—never mind. I met Poe once. Odd guy."

"You met *Edgar Allan Poe?*"

"In a bar. He was babbling on about some raven, so drunk he couldn't stand upright. Good poet, though."

"Creepy guy. Didn't he marry his cousin when she was just a child?" She wrinkled her nose in a grimace.

He shrugged. "In those days—"

"No. Don't 'in those days' me. Marrying a girl that young was *never* right." She pointed at him, her eyes narrowed. "Don't even try to argue this one."

He grabbed her hand and kissed it, loving the way her eyelids fluttered at his touch. "I was going to say that in those days, people married their cousins. It was legal. I don't think anyone knew enough about genetics to be concerned. The pharaohs used to marry their siblings, after all."

She sat back and folded her arms. "Right. So now you're telling me that you were around for the early days of ancient Egypt."

"I do read books, Doctor," he said, amused. "You're not the only educated one in this car. Mr. C has a degree in botany, for example."

"And you? Did you go to school?"

His amusement faded. "No. No, I was more of a school of hard knocks graduate, as you—"

"Don't say humans!"

"As you *Americans* would say."

"But—you're not American? Your accent is, well, not Southern so much as vaguely New England boarding school, but not British." She tilted her head and stared at him, as if a closer perusal would prove the truth of his origins.

"I was born in the British countryside, and you've already heard about Jane. My childhood is an ugly story I don't care to share any more of," he said abruptly, looking away from the trace of hurt that briefly shadowed her face. "About vampires. Some basics. We can't bear the sun at all for the first hundred years or so. The older we get, the more...not immunity, but defense, perhaps, we have. Meara is more able to stand exposure than I am, but only for a few minutes at a time, in the early morning or late afternoon. Direct exposure to the noon sun for longer than maybe ten minutes would kill us. And, most of the time, we must sleep during the daylight hours. Just after Turning, we can't be awake at all when the sun is up. Now, I can stay awake, but it's really tough and it makes me weak."

She listened so intensely he could almost see her desire for a pen and paper to take notes.

"What about blood? Do you need it? And do you—" She glanced at the dividing glass. "Do you eat your help?"

Just the sound of the word *blood* coming from her lips made his thirst start a lazy swirl inside him that he had to shove away to focus on her question. "Yes, we need blood. Not that often the older we are. And no, I never have and never will take blood from anyone who works for me, although they've offered before when things got rough."

"Rough? Rough in what way?"

He shrugged. "We've come home at dawn a time or two in bad shape."

She studied him, her gaze meeting his, as if trying to

peer into his brain and learn his secrets. "Are they all like you? The people in the club. Even Jenks and Marisela?"

He laughed at the idea of beach-loving Jenks being a vampire. "No. Lots of them are human. The humans ride in the daylight. The vampires at night. Some in both crews help with the drug runs, depending on circumstances."

"Do they know about you? The humans? About what you are?"

"No."

She nodded. "Ah. The eyesight problem. That's how you cover up not going on daytime rides with them? How do the others—do you all pretend to have eye problems?"

He laughed. "No, of course not. We maintain that the 'mystique' of the VMC lies in the pretense that we're really vampires, so we can only ride at night. We're successful enough that they are happy to go along with it."

"Successful?" This time, it was she who turned away for a moment, no longer meeting his gaze. "The drugs, you mean? You make profits from that?"

"Ryan." He waited for her to look at him, suddenly, urgently needing her to hear what he had to say. "There is no profit in what we do. I fund the rides, and the drugs, and the payments to the club members out of my personal accounts. If you believe anything I tell you, please believe that."

She sighed, and her shoulders slowly relaxed. "Thank you. I—I know it might not be important to you, but it is to me."

He understood. She was a healer. She was goodness, and light, and kindness.

He was a killer disguised as a man.

But for the children…for them, he could still find some small remnant of his lost humanity. For Jane.

"They don't know you're a vampire, but they respect you. They listen to you," Ryan said, changing the subject.

"Yes. I couldn't be the club president if they didn't. Some of them, like Jenks and Marisela, came to the club because the name amused them, and then they stayed because they liked the people and the mission. Others came from other MCs, the criminal gangs that you no doubt imagined, where the rules are harsh, and the punishment for breaking them is vicious. They help us out with other jobs, sometimes," he said, not about to tell her more about the damn warlocks.

"But the people in your club. None of them—"

"None of the dangerous ones ever come to the club this early in the morning," he said, knowing what she was wondering. "For all of them, if they can't listen to me, they're out. The financial benefits from being in the VMC are enough to make most of them fall in line, and the ones who succeed are the best of them. Jenks and Marisela are trying to have a baby, and it's not working. Her insurance doesn't cover the things they need. Their VMC payments do."

She put a hand on her chest and blinked rapidly. "Please, sir! No more of your fancy talk of charity and helping people, I do declare," she said in a comically broad Southern accent, pretending to fan herself. "A girl can't hardly *breathe* around all your awesomeness!"

Bane found himself laughing. Again.

Not understanding what was happening to him—what this woman was doing to him—but more than willing to go along for the ride.

He gave her his best lustful villain smile. "Well, fair maiden. You're asking a lot of questions. You know what the cost is for each one."

Ryan tilted her head and gave him a flirty little smile. "Maybe it's your turn to pay the price. You've asked me a few questions, too."

Bane suddenly found it hard to swallow. "The price?"

"And kisses aren't necessarily all on your mouth," she reminded him saucily, stealing his breath and his ability to think straight. "How far is it to your house?"

Before he could think, or talk, or do anything rational at all, the fierce, brilliant, and oh-so-delectable Dr. Ryan St. Cloud looked him in the eye. "I'd like to touch you now."

He smiled. "I thought you'd never ask."

And then he took her hand and put it on his cock.

CHAPTER TWENTY-TWO

Old Reliable Ryan would never do this!

Ryan froze, shocked at her own audacity, and felt her cheeks go up in flames. She'd always been easily embarrassed and quick to blush, but putting her hand on the...*enormous, very hard, really huge, oh my goodness*... um, package, of a man she'd only met the night before was so shockingly out of character for her that it was a wonder she didn't spontaneously burst into fire right there in the limousine.

Bane's eyes flared such a hot blue, she almost expected to feel his gaze searing her skin.

"Oh, Doctor. You're in so very much trouble now," he growled, and surprise mixed with terrified anticipation caused her fingers to convulsively tighten around him.

Throwing gasoline on a fire would have had less of a reaction.

Faster than humanly possible—faster than thought itself—Bane lunged at her. He pulled her into his arms and onto his lap, and then he slanted his mouth over hers and took her captive with a blazingly hot kiss that shattered her defenses and blew up any idea she'd ever had that she didn't really like sex.

This kiss was better than sex—at least, better than any sex *she'd* ever had. His mouth laid claim to her—burning. Almost feral.

He kissed her like she belonged to him.

Like he'd never let her go.

She dug her fingers into his hair and pulled him even tighter, wanting to climb inside him—inside the passion and wonder and pure hunger he ignited in her. She moaned, or he did, and the sound was swallowed up in the kiss, where air and sound and feeling and *wanting* danced and sang in the space between them.

And then the car door opened.

"Oh! I, ah, I didn't know—um. I'll just close this back up, shall I?" Mr. Cassidy slammed the door shut, but not before Ryan wrenched her head away from Bane, gasping for breath.

"I—You—"

"He's fired," Bane growled, pulling her back to him, back into the kiss, back into pure, sensual pleasure.

He kissed her until she forgot why she shouldn't be sitting in the backseat of a limo kissing a man—a vampire— she'd just met.

He kissed her until she forgot her own name.

When they finally, reluctantly, paused to gulp in long, deep breaths, she was more aroused than she had ever been in her entire life. Her nipples were hard points scraping at the fabric of her shirt, and she had to clench her thighs together against the throbbing that all but demanded she rip Bane's pants off—the ones he wore *and* the ones she wore—and beg him to fuck her.

"Bane," she said, his name a talisman or a revelation on her lips. "I *need* you."

"I need you, too." He kissed her again, a gentle, cherishing kiss, and then pulled back and rested his forehead against hers, breathing hard. "But not here. I can't—you're too important for me to take in a car."

He'd spoken as if the words were being wrenched out of him, and she responded with a gasp of laughter. "I don't know about important, but I can tell you I've never before in my life wanted sex as badly as I do right this very second. Wanted anyone as much as I want you. Right now, right here, hell, in the middle of the parking lot, I don't care, but oh, please, please, don't stop now!"

Before he could refuse, she shifted a leg and straddled him, and *finally*, all that lovely huge hardness was centered right where she wanted it.

Where she *needed* it.

And then, completely involuntarily, her body jerked in reaction to every single nerve ending being massively over-sensitized, bucking against him. She gasped and tightened her arms around his neck, clinging to him, helpless to do anything else but ride the wave of need. Oh, dear lord, she was on the verge of an orgasm, and she hadn't even touched his bare skin yet.

"You're going to kill me," he rasped, grabbing her butt and squeezing, pulling her even closer, moving her up and down against his hardness.

She could feel her body going up in flames, her mind melting into a puddle of lust and need and sheer carnal desire. "Need you," she moaned, shocked by the dark, husky sound of her own voice. "Need you so much."

Suddenly, as if her words had broken something in him, Bane flipped her over and onto her back on the long, leather seat.

"Yes. Now." His eyes were glowing blue flames, and when his lips parted, she could see the tips of his fangs, which should have terrified her, but instead the sight pushed her completely over the edge of reason into insanity.

"Now," she demanded. "Take me, do me, fuck me, now, now, now, please, oh my God, please, now."

His smile was so brilliant—so wicked—that she wondered it didn't light up the world.

"You said *please*," he growled.

And then he took hold of her shirt—his shirt that she wore—with both hands and ripped it apart. Buttons flew everywhere, but he paid them no attention, because he was staring at her breasts the way a man dying of thirst in the desert might stare at water.

"You're a goddess," he breathed, and he captured the tip of one breast in his mouth and licked it and sucked it and blew air on her nipple until she wanted to scream or beg, until she was twisting and squirming in the seat.

And then he did the same to the other breast, using his clever fingers on the one no longer getting attention from his mouth, pinching and teasing and stroking her nipple until she thought she might orgasm on the spot.

"Bane, Bane, Bane," she panted, helplessly aroused, helplessly jerking her body against his, where he held her firmly down. She couldn't move, couldn't reach his cock, which she was desperate to get her hands on, couldn't think, couldn't breathe. She could only feel, and feel, and *feel*, until she thought she might die from the pleasure of it.

When he lifted his head, an expression of such sheer male triumph was stamped on his face that she almost laughed, but then he reached into her pocket and snatched out the knife she'd forgotten she'd stolen—*borrowed*—and held it up between them.

"I never liked that tie, anyway," he growled, and then he sliced through his tie that she'd been using as a belt, tossed the knife on the floor, and yanked the pants off her body so fast she almost didn't know what was happening.

"Are you wet for me, Dr. St. Cloud?" His voice was dark seduction itself, and she found herself caught almost hypnotically in a haze of desire that was far more potent than any compulsion he'd tried to use on her.

"Yes," she whispered. "So wet. Please...*please*." She didn't even know how to ask for what she wanted, only that she wanted it so very badly. "*Please*."

But when she tried to reach for his belt, he stopped her, and now she heard the rasp of an almost-feral desire in his voice. "No. Right now, I'm going to put my mouth on you and lick the honey from your body. I'm going to tease you and taste you and suck on your plump little clit until you scream my name, and then I'm going to make you come again and again and again."

She almost came just listening to him talk about what he was going to do to her. "I—oh—"

He smiled so wickedly that she knew she'd somehow fallen into a trap. "But it's like your hair, Ryan."

"My—my hair?"

"I need your consent. Tell me yes. *Ask* me to do it. Ask me to taste you. Ask me to suck on you until you come in my mouth."

"I—I—I can't...I've never—" She almost cried with frustration. She needed him now, but could she make herself say such things? She'd never...

He reached down between their bodies and slid one

finger into the wet heat of her body, and she arched up off the seat in reaction, crying out.

"Well? Tell me, Ryan. What do you want?" He moved his finger, sliding up, spreading her wetness on her clit, but pulling his hand away when she cried out again.

"Tell me," he demanded. "What do you want?"

"I—I want you," she moaned. "Yes, all of that. Taste me. Suck me. Make me come. Make me scream. Please, please, *please*."

But, by the third "please," he'd put his mouth on her, and coherent thought fragmented into shards of such exquisite pleasure she thought she might die from it. His tongue was a revelation, and his fingers delved inside her, stroking reaction after reaction from her, until she was shivering and moaning, mindlessly whipping her head back and forth on the seat.

In the car—we're still in the car, some remnant of sanity tried to shout at her, but she told sanity to go to hell, and instead she clenched her hands in his hair and pulled his head closer to her.

He was taking her—claiming, in the most primal way possible, the very core of her body, and all she wanted was more and more and more, and then he licked a swirling motion around her clit, just before he closed his lips on it and sucked, hard, and she shattered beneath him, riding a crest of such powerful pleasure that it was almost pain, and she did, she did, she *did* scream his name, over and over, coming and coming and coming until she thought she might die from the sheer ecstasy of it.

And when her body finally began, just the tiniest bit, to calm down from the tidal waves of earthshaking orgasm pounding through it, Bane lifted his head and stared into her eyes.

"Tell me to bite you, Ryan. *Please*," he demanded, his voice stark, his expression gone feral.

She didn't hesitate for a single second. "Bite me, Bane. Now," she ordered him, feeling more powerful than she ever had in her life. Claiming what she wanted from him yet again.

She turned her head and pushed her hair away from her neck with a hand that was still trembling with aftershocks, but he bared his teeth, fangs now fully descended, and shook his head.

"Not your neck."

Then he bent his head back down and sucked her clitoris back into his mouth, one more time.

And then he bit her.

Ecstasy poured through her like molten gold, spreading from the most sensitive part of her body, and Ryan disintegrated from a being of conscious thought into a tornado of blazing sensation.

He sucked, hard, and she could feel the pull of his mouth drawing blood from her body, and a screaming orgasm smashed into her with the force of a tsunami, hammering a frenzy of pleasure into her and through her until she was afraid she couldn't survive it.

She screamed as the orgasm peaked, a sound beyond his name, beyond words, her entire body arching up off the seat, and Bane finally stopped biting her, stopped sucking on her, stopped destroying her, and sat up, pulling her into his arms as she shuddered through the aftershocks.

She clutched at his shirt, only then realizing that she

was nude and he was still fully dressed, which might have made her feel embarrassed if she hadn't just experienced the most mind-bending orgasm—*orgasms*—of her life.

When she looked up at him, dazed, he was studying her with a look of wide-eyed wonder on his face. "Your blood," he whispered, so quietly that she almost didn't hear him. "Your skin…what *are* you?"

It took a long time for her breathing to calm down enough for her to speak, and then she found that she felt suddenly, ridiculously shy and couldn't bring herself to look at him. "I don't—what?"

He paused and then shook his head, his laughter a warm rumble beneath her cheek. "I think you just discovered that you really do like sex after all."

She couldn't help it. Her innate sense of humor broke through, and she started to laugh, too. "I'd find that hard to deny right now. But I—we're still in the car."

Oh my God.

"We're still in the car! Are we parked on the street? Oh no, what will Mr. Cassidy think?" She was too limp with pleasure to be nearly as mortified as she ought to be, considering what had just happened and how everyone in the house would almost certainly know what they'd been doing.

"Oh, this is insane. I have to get dressed right now!" She grabbed at what was left of Bane's shirt and pants that she'd been wearing and dressed as best as she could, tying the shirt together since the buttons were gone. "How are we going to explain this? I mean—"

He snorted.

No, wait.

That wasn't a snort.

She whipped her head around to stare at him, and he was...sound asleep.

He was *asleep?* After *that?* He hadn't even—they hadn't—it had been all about her, and he must have...

Daylight. Vampire.

Right. He was a vampire, it was now mid-morning, and so it was probably perfectly natural that, after giving her the most mind-bending orgasm of her life, he'd fallen asleep.

She started to laugh.

This was definitely down the rabbit hole territory. Old Reliable Ryan would have fallen over dead at the shock of it all.

The new Ryan felt like the queen of the world.

She leaned over and gently kissed his beautiful mouth. "All right, Sleeping Beauty. Let's figure out how to get you inside. I'll just rest my eyes for a moment, until the world stops spinning, and then we'll definitely do...something."

She curled up against him, her body still pulsing with aftershock, and closed her eyes. Just for a moment.

She was so tired...

When she woke up two hours later, Bane was still sleeping. She watched him for a while, unable to understand how her life had gone from dull to dangerous in the space of so short a time. How a man—a vampire— had blown through her safe, ordered world like a gale- force wind.

She wanted to touch him. To kiss him. To hold him.

Instead, suddenly shy, she very quietly and carefully opened the car door to discover to her great relief that they were in a dimly lit garage, not in a parking lot in broad daylight. She'd find help getting Bane out of the car or find out if she should leave him here, and then she'd go to her place and the hospital for clothes and supplies.

She nodded to herself, decisive, ignoring the bizarre reluctance she felt at the thought.

I don't want to leave him, even for a little while.

She was in serious trouble.

CHAPTER TWENTY-THREE

The second Ryan started to leave the car, Bane's eyes snapped open.

"Usually guys only fall asleep after sex that they, ah, participated in," she said, feeling her face heat up.

He breathed deeply, inhaling the scent of her arousal— her pleasure. His cock, which hadn't fully subsided during his brief slide toward unconsciousness, stood at attention again, ready and willing to take what it had been so cruelly deprived of.

He wanted her again. Wanted to make her silky skin glow again. To drink the champagne of her blood. In all his centuries, he'd never tasted anything like her blood.

Or were his feelings for her making him hallucinate? Were *taste* hallucinations even possible?

He discovered that he didn't care, not even a little

Leaning forward, he slid his hand around the nape of her neck, drawing her to him. "If you think I didn't *participate* in that, you're really, really wrong. I may need to give you a refresher on your anatomy classes. That was me between your legs, with my mouth on your—"

"I know!" She smiled so brilliantly it lit up the darkest part of his heart. "I was there, too. I mean, I was sort of there. Mostly, I was floating somewhere in space, out beyond Saturn, watching supernovas cartwheel through the sky, while my brain exploded. Not that you need more fuel for your arrogance, but...*wow*."

Damn, but she was beautiful when she blushed. Her cheeks and chest turned the exact color of an English rose in the springtime sun, a sight he hadn't seen in far too long. He *had* to kiss her. He had no choice.

And so he did, bending his face to hers and gently taking her mouth. Where before it had been all passion and heat, this kiss was softer. Gentler. A simple reminder that such goodness existed in the world—in his *life*—and he could reach out and touch her in such a way.

She can never leave me.

The thought shocked him, as much for its intensity as its meaning. He'd only just met this woman, and now he wanted to keep her forever? He had no more right to possess this woman than he did to possess the sun itself.

And yet, to bask in her warmth...forever...what wouldn't he sacrifice for that?

"Bane?" From her tone, it wasn't the first time she'd spoken his name. "Are you okay? We should get you to your, ah, coffin?"

Her nose wrinkled, in spite of her obvious attempt to keep her expression neutral, and he started laughing.

"No. No coffin, no grave dirt, no turning into a bat. I can fly, but never in the shape of a rodent, or any other shape, for that matter. What you see is what you get."

Her mouth fell open before he finished speaking, and her eyes lit up with pure glee. "You can *fly?* Not just, you know, hover?"

"Yes—"

"Do you grow wings?"

He blinked. "No, I'm not an *angel.* I—"

She clutched the front of his shirt and shook him.

Actually shook him. "There are *angels*? Oh. My. God. Annie is going to die! Can you fly with somebody? Like Superman and Lois Lane? Can you take me, I can't believe I'm going to say this, rational thought insists that there is no possible way you can do this, but can you take me flying? With you?" She paused to gulp in a breath. "*In the air*?"

He stared at her for what felt like a long time. "You're not at all what I expected," he finally said.

Right there, right before his eyes, her excitement started to fade. She released his shirt and moved back then turned to leave the car. "Yeah," she said sadly. "I get that a lot."

He grabbed her shoulders and pulled her back against him. "You're far, far more wonderful than I could ever imagine a human to be," he breathed into her ear, not resisting the opportunity to kiss her neck.

The scent of her skin and the pulse of the blood racing through her veins combined into a powerful aphrodisiac, driving him to take. To possess. He clenched his jaw against the urge and forced himself to relax his grip.

He realized he cared about not frightening her, when he'd cared about so little for so long; the epiphany shone like a jewel in his mind.

In his *heart*? Surely not.

She turned to look at him, her beautiful ocean-blue eyes sparkling again. "Really?"

"Really."

"So, about falling asleep earlier…"

He motioned to her to precede him out of the car. "Giving enough blood to effect the Turn in someone is very draining."

She snorted out a laugh. "I see what you did there. *Draining.* Vampire puns, for the win."

"I didn't actually intend that," he said, chuckling. "You must be good for me."

"Well. I know how you can thank me," she said, flashing a saucy grin. "You can take me flying."

"Maybe not right now."

"Fair enough. I need to stop by the hospital, go home, and get some food and sleep, and then get my medical bag and come back to see if I can do anything for Mr. Evans. If you—"

Bane slammed the car door behind him, his vision starting to haze into a red sheen. She could not leave him.

She *must not leave him.*

"No."

Her brows drew together. "What do you mean, no? No to which part. No to flying? That's okay, but—"

"*No to all of it,*" he commanded, putting his hands on her arms and using his most powerful mental push.

She stared at him for several seconds and then backed away. Then she put her arms straight out in front of her body and started walking jerkily toward the door to the house, her eyes wide, her mouth hanging open.

"Yesss, Master," she droned, jerking her head back and forth.

He froze. He'd never encountered such a reaction. What had he done? Had his push been too hard? Had he permanently damaged something in her mind?

She made a sound, and he realized she was choking. He'd *broken* her. He'd broken this human—this woman— who'd come to mean so much to him in such a short time.

He raced over to take her into his arms but stopped short when he realized that she wasn't choking at all.

She was laughing.

At him.

Doubled over laughing, in fact.

"Oh, oh. Oh, Bane," she gasped, still laughing. "What, did you think that you'd zombiefied me?"

Before Ryan, nobody but Meara had dared to laugh at him for three hundred years, and this woman did so—openly—again and again.

And he *liked* it.

Warmth swept through him, threatening to dissolve the block of ice he called a soul. Threatening to offer him a chance at the most terrifying thing in the world.

Hope.

He suppressed the smile trying to break free and instead, pretending that she'd injured his dignity, he brushed past her to open the door.

"Zombies don't exist," he informed her, using his haughtiest voice.

In response, she stood up on her tiptoes and kissed him right on the mouth. "Oh, honey. You're priceless. If you could have seen your face."

Still laughing, she entered the house, calling out a hello to Mrs. C, who was walking up the stairs with a load of laundry. Bane's housekeeper stopped and handed Ryan a bundle of clothing, shooting Bane a scandalized look, probably due to the buttonless, beltless way he'd brought Ryan back.

Bane just stood and watched them, and then he slowly brought his hand to his mouth to touch his lips. She'd laughed at him.

She'd kissed him.

She'd called him *honey*.

He realized, standing stock still in the doorway from his garage, of all places, that he would kill for this woman. He'd kill to protect her. He'd kill to *keep* her. His vision flared red again—just for a moment—and then subsided.

He knew what he wanted. What he must have.

Now, it was all about strategy.

• • •

Hunter was worse.

Not only was he not in the trance-like state he should have been in, he seemed to be growing more and more feral. Bane could hear him crashing against the walls and door in the safe room from all the way downstairs, where he was waiting for Ryan to come out of the bathroom in whatever clothes Mrs. C had given her.

"Ryan. I have to check on Hunter. Stay here." He sped up the stairs, entirely unsurprised to hear her open the door and follow him. Did the woman ever listen to anybody?

Edge sat slumped in a chair outside the safe room, head in hands, eyes closed. He looked up blearily when he heard Bane arrive.

"He won't stay down. I've given him blood three different times, and each time he sleeps for less time between feedings. It's full-on day now; he should be out." Edge shook his head. "Hell, I should be out. But he keeps... Well. You can hear him."

Everybody could hear him. Hunter was shouting for Bane each time he hurled his body at the wall.

"I should check his vitals, at least," Ryan said, walking up to join them. She wore a pair of soft black pants that Meara liked to wear for exercising and a loose, bright purple T-shirt that said *Savannah Pirate House* on the front.

He considered himself a big damn hero for not staring at her lush, braless breasts, barely contained by that soft fabric.

"His *vitals*?" Edge sneered at her. "He's a vampire. What comparative data do you have to judge his vitals?"

Ryan bit her lip but stood her ground. "Nevertheless. Maybe I can find some way to help him. It's agreed that I can study Bane, and only Bane, but maybe there's something I can do for Mr. Evans. It can't hurt to at least try."

Edge suddenly raised his head, sniffing the air, and then his gaze arrowed in on Bane. "You fucked her? First, you tell her our secrets, knowing she can't be made to forget them, and then you fuck her?"

Ryan flushed a hot red. She wouldn't have known how keen vampire senses were.

Edge *definitely* didn't realize the fine line he was treading.

Bane needed to teach him a lesson. So he slammed his fist through the wall, right next to Edge's head.

"You will apologize to the doctor," he said, very quietly— so quietly that Edge's silver gaze widened.

They all knew what happened when Bane's fury grew so powerful that his voice turned quiet and deadly.

People died. Vampires died.

Everybody died.

Edge inclined his head. "Yes. I was out of line. Chalk it up to exhaustion and blood loss." He stood and held a hand out to Ryan. "I'm sorry, Doctor. That was rude, and, worse, you didn't deserve it."

Ryan nodded and shook his hand, and Bane had to fight himself to keep from yanking her away from the other vampire.

"I totally understand. Not at my best here, either," she said, head held high. "I'd still like to check on Mr. Evans, if you don't mind."

"Whatever. It's up to Bane. I need to get some sleep." Edge shoved a hand through his hair and then headed toward the hall. When he reached the doorway, he paused and shot a narrow-eyed glance back at Bane. "I'm not wrong, though. And you know it."

And then he was gone.

Ryan touched his arm, and Bane glanced down to see her glaring at him, her cheeks still flushed.

"You could have mentioned that vampires have heightened senses of smell."

He couldn't help himself. He leaned over and kissed her. "You need to stay well back when I open the door." But then, considering her usual response to being ordered about, he continued. "*Please*. He'll be able to smell your blood—the bloodlust is extremely heightened during and just after the Turn—and it will make things more difficult."

She studied his face and then nodded. "Of course."

"It's important. He—" Bane's mind, already prepping his argument, caught up with what she'd said. "You will?"

A thud and a shout from the warded room made her flinch, but then she shrugged. "I'm not unreasonable. If me being nearby will make things worse, I'll go stand over there. It's going to make it hard for me to examine him, though."

"Once he's asleep again, we'll see if we can make that happen."

She walked over to the far wall and turned and leaned against it.

He took a deep breath and opened the door, braced for Hunter to charge him in an escape attempt.

Nothing happened.

He took a cautious step into the room, which had been entirely trashed, from the chair to the bed to the walls themselves, and caught sight of Hunter, huddled in a far corner.

"It hurts so much, Bane." The man raised his head, which Bane was shocked to see looked like a skull barely covered with skin. Hunter's eyes glowed a dark red, and his nails had grown out, which made sense, given the deep, scoring claw marks on the walls and, in one corner, on the ceiling.

The ceiling that was twelve feet off the floor.

"Maybe basketball will be your superpower," Bane said, attempting a feeble joke, but any humor faded as he looked at what was left of his friend.

"Hurts. You didn't tell me it would hurt so much," Hunter growled, and Bane felt every single word as a black mark on his soul.

He'd done this.

And now it was up to him to fix it, when he had no idea what was wrong.

"I'm sorry. This isn't how the Turn should be happening. I know that is no comfort to you, but—"

Hunter lurched up to stand, staring past Bane. "Blood. I smell—it's so good. Want. Need. *Need! Now!*"

Hunter shot across the destroyed room, and Bane braced for impact.

"Need!"

"No," Bane commanded. "*No, you will not go near her. Take my blood. You only want my blood now.*"

"Want your blood now," Hunter said, so brokenly that a spear of self-loathing sliced through Bane. If he'd left his friend to die, as humans did, the firefighter would be at peace now.

But he'd be dead.

No.

Bane's fangs descended, and he bit into his own wrist before Hunter could savage it. "Here. Take what you need."

Hunter lunged, grabbing Bane's arm with newly enhanced strength. He drank and drank, gulping in the blood that he shouldn't have even been awake to need for another two days. And then, mid-gulp, he glanced up at Bane, eyes widening, and then slowly toppled to the floor, dislodging his new fangs from Bane's wrist as he fell.

Just like that, he was asleep again.

Bane bent to feel for his pulse and was relieved to find it steady. Inhumanly slow, which meant the Turn was in fact taking effect, but still steady. He bent and lifted Hunter into his arms and put him down on what was left of the slightly shredded mattress lying up against one wall.

When he looked up, Ryan was in the doorway, horror stamped on her expression. "What have you done to him? He was better off in the hospital than like…like *that.*"

She didn't add "you monster," but the words hung,

unspoken, in the air between them.

He'd known she'd one day look at him with horror and disgust. He'd just hoped it would be some day far, far into the future.

Not today.

Not now.

"I wanted him to live," he began, but she cut him off.

"No. Not now." She rolled up her sleeves and walked into the room.

Shock froze him in place. After seeing that—seeing what Hunter had become—she *walked into the room* instead of running away.

She was a warrior, and he wanted to worship at her feet.

Instead, he rose and silently watched her approach.

"Now," she said. "We figure out what's wrong and how we can fix it."

CHAPTER TWENTY-FOUR

Mr. Evans—Hunter—had destroyed the room. It looked like a tiger had been let loose in it. She glanced at Bane's wrist. No, not a tiger. A feral vampire. But she'd think about distractions like that later, when she wasn't in the room with him.

When the scent of freshly spilled blood wasn't thick in the air, carrying with it such a heavy weight of ancient superstition and very modern fear.

"I need my kit," she mused, crouching down to examine him.

Bane blocked her from touching Hunter by the simple expedient of lifting her bodily and flashing across the room and out the door.

"Not now," he growled, his eyes twin blue flames. "I don't know if he's truly asleep again or just taking a brief respite before he continues to dismantle the room and anyone who enters it."

She made a growling sound of frustration right back at him. "I need to examine him, Bane. And at least let me bandage your wrist."

But when she looked again, she saw the wounds fade to fine, white lines on his skin.

"We heal pretty quickly. Even those marks will be gone tomorrow."

She inhaled a deep, shaky breath. "Okay. Okay. Well, if we can discover what property in your blood drives your metabolism—your healing—imagine the implications for the rest of the world."

He held up a hand before she could get any more carried away. "Maybe, and I still agree to let you try—only on me—but I seriously doubt it. I think magic explains more about our status than science, Doctor."

Ryan, who'd started pacing back and forth, turned to stare at him. "You don't know that! We don't know anything until we analyze anything and everything we can learn about what makes you—" She waved her hand, apparently to encompass both him and the state of being a vampire, all at once. "What makes you, *you*. Certainly, a blood sample isn't going to tell me why you can *fly*, but it might tell me about your sensitivity to the sun." She pointed at the open door. "It might tell me if sedatives will work on him, to help get him through this Turn that you don't know why he's not doing properly. Or, at least, maybe it could help when you want to…if you want to do this again in the future to someone else."

She swallowed, hard, and an expression of barely concealed panic crossed her face. She must have been remembering what they'd talked about before. Her visceral reaction to even the thought of becoming a vampire told him more than her words had done.

To so powerfully reject the idea of becoming like him told him a lot.

None of it good.

He dismissed the thought and closed and locked the door before Hunter could wake up again. "I don't know about sedatives. He's in a kind of magical stasis during the Turn—or, at least, he's supposed to be. Right now, he's caught between human and vampire, and I don't know what might work on him. It's not like I've ever had medical assistance during the process before."

"I need to get to the hospital and get my bag. Get some supplies." She paused and leaned against the wall, shoulders slumping. "Clothes. And I need to do it soon, before I keel over. That nap was fine, but not enough."

"You can sleep in my room," he decreed, which had the expected effect of her complete disregard.

"Maybe, but you destroyed your bed. Nice job, by the way." She shook her head. "Temper, much? Second, I need clothes and my things. Finally, I need to get some supplies and equipment, if I'm going to do any kind of effective job at studying you—"

"But—"

"Which you *said* I could do," she continued, steamrolling right over his attempt to interrupt the flow of words. "So, there you have it. Shall I call a car, or can Mr. Cassidy drive me? And do you have anything less conspicuous than a limo?"

He pressed his fingers to his temples and closed his eyes, just for a second or two, but when he opened them, she was still standing there.

Still waiting.

Still *real*, even though he didn't deserve such a gift.

"I can't let you go," he said, stalling while he tried to come up with a reason that she'd accept. "I—my family! You know too much about my family. Secrets that aren't only mine. I can't just let you walk out of here, knowing that you might change your mind and tell someone about us."

Her beautiful smile slowly faded. "I thought we were

past this. I thought we had a certain measure of trust between us after, you know, I let you put your *teeth* on my…private parts."

She blushed again, to his amusement, but then memories of her *private parts* seared a flash of heat through him. "I'd like very much to do that again. Let's go to my room, for now, and then later—"

"No." She shook her head. "There is no later if you can't trust me."

And there it was. The gauntlet, thrown down by a woman who hadn't even lived in the days of duels over breaches of honor. She'd called him out, and he had no choice but to respond, with his trust, though, instead of swords at dawn.

"I—yes," he rasped out. "Yes, I trust you. Do you—do you swear to return?" Each word was ground glass shredding his throat. "I can't go with you, in case Hunter gets worse."

Her eyes widened, and she slowly crossed the few paces separating them. Then she reached up and touched his face. "I've seen you angry, and arrogant, and aroused. But I think this is the first time I've ever seen you vulnerable."

A chasm opened up in his gut. "Monsters are never vulnerable."

"You're not a monster, and yes, I swear I'll come back," she whispered, and then she kissed the corner of his mouth.

From the doorway to the hall, the sound of slow clapping interrupted whatever he'd been about to do to her.

"Am I the only one getting a *La Belle et La Bête* vibe here?" Meara leaned against the doorway, studying her fingernails.

"Quit calling me a beast," Ryan said, grinning at his sister. "Hey, you want to ride to my place and the hospital with me, to make Bane feel better? You can sleep in the car."

Bane stood, stunned, as Ryan started toward Meara. She would do that? Invite his sister along, just to *make him feel better?*

He could never deserve this woman.

Fuck that.

He flashed forward and pulled her into his arms. "If you're the beast, what does that make me, Doctor?"

"It's Ryan, okay? You don't have to keep calling me 'Doctor' after you, after we, well. You know." She grinned, blushing. "And, duh. Obviously, you're Beauty. It's totally unfair, and quit making me admit it."

"I'll go with you. Meara can stay here."

"You will not. You need to take care of Hunter. I'll be perfectly fine," she told him, eyes snapping with the beginning of temper.

He bent his head to hers and took her mouth in a searing kiss, not stopping until she was trembling in his arms, and then finally raised his head, his own temper flaring. "If you're lying to me about returning, Heaven itself will not keep you safe."

Her eyes narrowed dangerously. "If I punch you in the head for these melodramatic comments, you won't feel all that safe, either. I took boxing lessons once, you know."

Before he could think of a single response to that, she kissed his cheek, twisted out of his arms, and ran down the stairs with Meara.

Luke followed Bane to the landing, and they watched

Ryan and Meara chat with Mr. C and then head into the garage. Just before she left, Ryan smiled up at them and waved, and then she was gone.

"You know better," Luke finally said.

"Don't."

"Claiming her? What were you thinking? What *are* you thinking? She's human. She'll grow *old* and hate you when you don't. Or, worse, she'll beg you to Turn her and…"

Bane waited for the rest of the sentence. Was unsurprised when it never came. "And she'll die. Like your lady did, Luke. It's been fifty years. Don't you think you could take a chance again?"

Luke's laughter singed the air with its bitterness. "Like you did? What happened the last time *you* fell in love?"

The last time Bane had *thought* he was in love. With a woman who'd had all of Ryan's fire but none of her goodness. She'd betrayed him. Tried to kill him, so she and her lover could rob him of all he had.

He'd killed the lover but left her alive to suffer for it.

And then she'd died in a fire. In *the* fire.

And he'd never trusted a woman with his heart since.

"Meara told me. Seventeen ninety-six. The fire that destroyed all of Savannah. Almost nothing was left, and certainly nothing was left of you," Luke said, speaking aloud the ugliness that had iced over Bane's soul more than two centuries before. "So, why her? Why now?"

It was a good question. Unfortunately, he had no answers, so he shrugged. "The heart wants what the heart wants? Get some rest. We need to find that necromancer. Tonight."

The expression on Luke's face was priceless.

When Bane reached his room, though, the smile faded, and he looked at his hands, which had started to shake. He was dangerously long past feeding, and he'd given too much to Hunter. Plus, he hadn't gotten nearly enough sleep lately.

Let's quit lying to ourselves, shall we? You're shaking like a junkie who can't get his fix—except your fix isn't drugs, but Dr. Ryan St. Cloud.

It was true. He'd had to fight his own instincts with everything he had to keep from stopping her. To keep from imprisoning her in his rooms, tying her up, tying her down, never, ever letting her go.

He crossed to a mini-refrigerator and took out two bags of blood, heated them with a swift pulse of magic, and then downed both, one after the other. There was one problem solved. Now, to sleep.

It wasn't until he'd shoved open the door to his bedroom that he remembered his bed. "Temper, much?" she'd said. He smiled at the memory.

He yanked the mattress and some blankets into a pile, walked into the bathroom to wash his hands, and stumbled to a stop at the sight of her clothes, forgotten on his floor. Almost in a trance, he bent to pick them up, his hands clenching convulsively on the scraps of silk. Silk like her skin. Like the warm, wet honey that he'd tasted while he pleasured her.

Forget sleep. He needed her. Again.

And again and again.

He might not survive this separation.

MEARA! KEEP HER SAFE FOR ME!

A moment or two passed, and then he could hear his

sister's laughter in his mind.

ALREADY? YOU'VE GOT IT BAD, BROTHER.

She wasn't wrong.

I'LL KEEP YOUR HUMAN SAFE FOR YOU. YOU CAN RELAX NOW. WE'RE ALMOST AT THE HOSPITAL. WE'LL BE BACK SOON, BANE. HAVE A CARE: IF YOU HOLD ONTO HER TOO TIGHTLY, YOU'LL EITHER LOSE HER OR DESTROY HER.

He knew that. It was part of what terrified him.

Meara was the strongest fighter he knew. He could trust her to keep Ryan safe—at night. But even Meara was severely weakened during the daytime.

He gently placed Ryan's discarded clothing on the counter next to the sink and forced himself to crawl into the bed and close his eyes. He needed to recharge before they went after the necromancer tonight; the warlock was too dangerous to face in a weakened state.

When his head touched the pillow, he fell almost instantly into a deep sleep, where he dreamed of Ryan, lying broken and bloody on the ballroom floor, dying in his arms.

"If you want to protect her, you have to let her go," Meara told him.

"I'll never let her go!" he roared. *"She is mine. Nothing is more important than what I want!"*

"Yes. You keep saying that, and you keep killing her. Over and over and over."

Bane moaned in anguish, tightened his arms on his cherished, dying love, and looked down at her precious face.

Ryan's eyes snapped open. "Why do you keep killing me?"

And then she died.

When he woke up, his face was wet and his throat ached, but he shook his head hard to dislodge the remnants of the nightmare. "No. It was just a dream. None of it was real. She's mine."

Her beautiful, dying face flashed into his mind from his nightmare, and he roared out his denial.

"*No*! It will never happen. She's *mine*."

When his heart quit racing, the inexorable pull of sleep pulled him back under, and yet again, he dreamed of Ryan, dying in his arms.

And then he dreamed it again.

Again and again and again.

CHAPTER TWENTY-FIVE

Constantin put himself into a state of deep meditation in order to commune with his god, reach his true center, and focus his consciousness until he was as one with the universe.

Also, he wanted to fuck with the vampire.

He sent yet another blast of insidiously hypnotic magic through the conduit he'd prepared, into the heart of the vampire's home—into his mind. Into his dreams.

Then he opened his eyes and started laughing.

"What is it?" Sylvie, lounging on a blue velvet couch and licking blood off the face of the human who owned the house they'd taken over, shot him a lazy glance. "Doing foul deeds for fun time again?"

"I don't know exactly what Bane is dreaming about, but it's sure as hell not good," he told her, reaching for his glass of champagne. The human's wine collection was truly fantastic.

She laughed. "Bad dreams can drive even vampires insane. I once caused an entire village of them to set themselves on fire, back in Italy in the late 1700s. I can tell you—"

"You already have," he interrupted, sick to death of her stories. "Big fire, started in the church, blah blah blah."

Sylvie narrowed her eyes but didn't dare talk back to him. The power structure was clear between them and in the Chamber as a whole: Constantin was the master—the one who made the plans and carried out strategy. He wore twelve-thousand-dollar bespoke suits and handmade shoes of English leather.

She wore slut-black leather pants and high heels from Hookers R Us.

But damn, she was vicious. And in their job, vicious was good.

Vicious was *excellent*.

He was distracted, though, by what he'd seen in the servant's brain. "There's a human."

Sylvie shoved the homeowner off the couch and used his back for a foot stool. "What human?"

"A woman. A…doctor. Bane's attached to her somehow. It's not clear. The old man is fighting the spell." He stood and started pacing the enormous room, curling his lip at the chrome and glass decor. Apparently, the interior designer had died sometime in the 1990s and the place had never been updated.

Constantin was a man who liked his simple pleasures: fine wine, elegant and expensive homes, and the sheer joy of raising a corpse and commanding it to do his bidding.

"She can't be important to him," Sylvie scoffed, stretching like a cat. "They only use humans for food, except for their servants. He's probably just fucking her before he kills her. We can't use a human as leverage over a vampire, Constantin. It would be like trying to use a pork chop as leverage over a hungry lion. It might annoy him for a minute or two, but then he'd turn around and rip your throat out and to hell with the pork chop."

He sneered at her. Her metaphors were as tiresome as the stupid Goth clothes she'd been wearing for the past forty or so years.

"Well, this *pork chop* is a doctor, and the Minor demon followed Bane to a hospital, didn't he? So maybe the pork chop is more important than we know. Put somebody on her."

"But—"

"*Now.*"

She stalked out of the room, careful to swear at him beneath her breath so he couldn't quite call her out on it. Or so she thought. One of these days, he'd decide he was tired of her insubordination, tired of her mouth, and tired of her stupid clothing choices.

And then *she'd* be the pork chop.

He started laughing, and the human cringing on the floor started to weep.

Constantin smiled. He loved it when he made the pork chops cry.

CHAPTER TWENTY-SIX

"Why don't you ride up here with me so Meara can sleep in the back and you can look out at the scenery?" Mr. C opened the door to the front passenger seat and smiled at Ryan.

She glanced at Meara, who waved her in and then yawned before climbing into the back and pulling the door closed. Before they even pulled out of the garage, though, Meara rolled down the privacy glass and tapped Ryan on the shoulder.

"Really? In the *car*?"

Before Ryan could answer or even have time to wish a hole would open up in the floorboard and swallow her up, Meara pealed out a laugh, leaned back, and powered the window back up. Face burning, Ryan resolutely stared out the side window so she didn't have to see Mr. C's expression.

"Don't mind them, Doc," he said cheerfully. "They just don't understand human embarrassment after all these years. When they found out Mrs. Cassidy and I were out skinny dipping in the pool, we didn't hear the end of it for weeks."

Ryan thought about how long ago that must have been, given the Cassidys' ages.

"And that was just last month." He shook his head. "Why have a pool if you don't sneak in a midnight swim once in a while, I say."

"Last month," she said faintly.

Wow. Even septuagenarians had more exciting love lives than she did.

Not anymore.

Her thighs clenched as she remembered exactly what they'd been doing in that backseat, and she realized she'd put up with any amount of embarrassment for another round of *that.*

Mr. Cassidy pushed a button, and both of their windows rolled down, letting in the steamy fall air. "Too beautiful to always be cooped up in the dark when you don't have to, am I right? Especially in these parts."

In the light of the morning sun coming through the window, though, he looked tired.

"Is it a lot, trying to keep vampire hours?"

He glanced over at her, his smile fading. "No, not usually. We get plenty of sleep. I've just been fighting a bug, I think. Pretty tired."

"Do you want me to take a look?" She didn't want to be pushy, but maybe he was hinting, and she'd be glad to check him out.

"Oh, no, no. I'll have a nap later, and I'll be fine. See what's over there?"

Ryan decided to keep an eye on him and take his temperature later, when she had her bag. She looked out the window, realizing that she really had no idea where they were, and then sat up straight in her seat. "Hey! That's Bonaventure Cemetery! I didn't realize we were all the way out here. It's so beautiful."

"Yep. The house is right on the Wilmington River, too, just down a ways from Bonaventure." He glanced over at her. "The cemetery doesn't frighten you, does it?"

"No. I think it's one of the most beautiful places I've ever seen," she admitted. "My gran took me there a lot when I was a little girl, to pay our respects to the dead, as she used to say. She claimed she saw ghosts there all the time, but I've always been a scientist. I've never believed…" Her voice trailed off when she realized what she'd been about to say, and Mr. C laughed.

"Never believed in ghosties or haunts or things that go bump in the night? Betcha feel a little bit different now."

She returned his grin. "I kind of do, Mr. Cassidy, I have to admit."

"Go on and call me Tommy, then. Meara does. We're not much for formality, Doc."

"And please call me Ryan."

"Sure thing, Doc." He chuckled and then pointed. "And that's the clubhouse, just there, of course. Bane has hinted a time or two that there's an underground tunnel that used to go from the mansion to the area just beyond the clubhouse, but I think he's pulling my leg."

"Where do the other vampires live?" She glanced hastily at Mr. C. "I mean, if that's okay to ask. I don't want you to give away any secret vampire resting places."

When he started laughing, she groaned, realizing that most of what she thought she knew about vampires came from *Buffy*.

"They live all about, in regular places like everybody else, so long as they have safe rooms. Only Bane, Meara, Edge, and Luke live at the house with us."

A tasteful sign sported the outline of a motorcycle, drawn in gold. It read VMC and nothing else. The clubhouse was long and low and looked a little bit like a fancy version of a country store. There was a front porch with rocking chairs and benches all down its length that she hadn't seen before, which meant that she and Bane must have come out a side or back door earlier. The parking lot started in front and wrapped around to the side, and it was dotted with maybe a dozen bikes.

She thought about Marisela and smiled. Maybe she'd found a potential new friend there.

"To the hospital? Savannah General?"

"Yes, please. I need to pick up some things and then go home. Or you can take me to my place for my car, first, if you have things you need to do."

He shook his head. "Nope. I'm at your disposal. If I left you alone, Bane would have my head. He's a bit protective of you, in case you hadn't noticed."

"I feel that way about *him*, too," she murmured, wondering when exactly that had happened. Sometime between hearing about the free clinics and having her mind blown in the backseat of this very limo, she suspected.

Before long, they were pulling into the visitors' parking garage at the hospital. Mr. Cassidy found a spot in a dark corner that was the farthest from the elevators and stairs and parked the car lengthwise across two spaces.

"Here you go, Doc. I'll stay in the car with Meara. Text me when you're on your way out? I'll give you my number."

She blinked, suddenly realizing she didn't have her phone. Hadn't had her phone in almost twenty-four hours... and hadn't missed it at all.

Technology: 0, Vampires: 1

The window between the seats suddenly rolled down,

and Meara popped her head up. "I'm not going in with you. Too many windows, and hospitals and doctors' offices smell like death. No offense."

"Why would I be offended? I actually wasn't going to ask you to come in. Much quicker if I just run in alone. But if you dislike doctors' offices so much, why did you build the free clinics? Why not fund art galleries or something like that?"

Meara gazed at her through sleepy eyes for a moment and then shrugged. "I give money to the arts, too. But as far as the clinics, it was those or donut shops. Clinics don't make my ass wide."

Ryan, whose ass was at least a little bit wider than it might have been, thanks to her fondness for donuts, had to laugh. "That's a lie. You're as much of a do-gooder as Bane is."

"Bane? A do-gooder?" Meara stared at her in patent disbelief. "Are we talking about my brother? Tall, blond, rips the arms and heads off warlocks for fun?"

"*What*?" Again with the warlocks. She needed to find out what the hell that was about. But not now. She blew out a sigh. "Look. I want to hear more about this. Later. But now I need to go inside, get a few things, and then we can go to my place. My spare bag with keys to my house is in my locker, since I didn't exactly bring my purse with me when your brother *abducted* me."

Meara rolled her eyes and rubbed her index finger and thumb together. "*Whatever*. Tiny, tiny violins playing sad songs for you."

"I'll be back soon," Ryan promised, rolling her own eyes. "But I can't text. I left my phone at home when Bane kidnapped, ah, whisked me away."

Meara turned serious. "If you don't come back, I don't know what Bane will do. I've never seen him like this before."

Ryan doubted that. He'd lived a very long life. "Over a human, you mean?"

"Over anyone. Ever," Meara said, and the bleak expression on her face told Ryan that she didn't think it was all that great that it was happening now.

"I'll be back," she repeated. "I promise."

Meara nodded. Then she curled up on the seat, her eyes closed before her head touched the leather.

• • •

The hospital, oddly enough, looked exactly the same as it had every other time Ryan had been inside it, which seemed impossible, given how her world had shattered and reformed into an entirely different version of reality.

She wondered how many of life's greatest epiphanies came with this sense of disjointedness—this feeling that the world was slightly off-kilter from the way she'd left it. And the hospital didn't smell like death, *thank you, Meara,* but like antiseptic and healing.

Like home.

Perhaps it was a matter of perspective. The patients, some in pain and filled with despair, might see it differently. She just knew that she and her colleagues did their very best to help and to heal. To offer hope to those who had little.

Sometimes, discovering an accurate diagnosis was the

beginning of finally being able to conquer an illness. But sometimes—often—her surgical skills were required. She cut into live bodies, like a psychopath or a serial killer, which was hard for some people to understand. Certainly, some of the guys she'd met through friends or dating apps had a very hard time with it.

Bane, though, hadn't seemed to be deterred one bit by her chosen profession.

Of course, he also had no problem with cutting—biting—into live bodies. She didn't know how to feel about that, either, so maybe those men she'd dated hadn't been so wimpy, after all.

She kept walking, waved at people, and said quick hellos, but didn't stop to talk, intent on getting to the residents' lounge before she had to field too many questions about her unusual attire. She grabbed a lab coat off the first laundry cart she saw and pulled it on, relieved to have her unrestrained breasts covered up. She hadn't been able to get away without wearing a bra since she was about thirteen years old.

Like not wearing a bra *is what's unusual about today.*

She snorted a laugh and quickly turned it into a fake cough when she saw a couple of med students giving her odd looks. Probably wondering why Old Reliable Ryan was wandering around in fancy sandals, laughing to herself.

Rounding the final corner, she ducked into the residents' lounge, delighted to see that it was empty except for her very best friend in Savannah, Dr. Annie Coates, the finest pediatrician Ryan had ever met.

"Where have you been, girl?" Annie put her hands on her hips. "I texted you a dozen times. I covered for you, but

I was starting to worry!"

"Let me run and change, and we'll talk." Ryan hurried to her locker, before anybody else came in, and grabbed her backpack that contained her spare keys, and the extra sets of scrubs, sneakers, and socks she kept at the hospital. She also had a bra in there, thank goodness. She was tired of bouncing with every step she took.

After she changed into clothes that made her feel like herself again, she walked back out to chat with her friend. Annie was five feet, four inches of trouble packed into a slender, graceful body with an angelically innocent face that belied her great talent for mischief. She'd been a ballet dancer, professionally, until she'd turned twenty-five and realized that her shelf life in dance would probably be over soon, thanks to frequent injuries. Then she'd whizzed through college and medical school, done her residency here in Savannah, and stayed to build a practice, even though her family called Atlanta home.

"Thanks! I was—" Ryan broke off, staring at her friend. "The braids! Those are new. I love them!"

Annie did a twirl. "I'm going with box braids for a few months, trying it out. I'm looking forward to going back to natural, but this transition stage is a pain."

"Well, they look amazing with your killer cheekbones." And, of course, they did, just like everything Annie wore or did with her hair, because she looked exactly like the ballerina princess she'd been before. Ryan loved to hear stories of all the little girls who had been so excited to meet a ballerina who looked like them, instead of always seeing only white dancers.

"Misty Copeland is doing God's work," Annie liked to

say. They'd made a deal to go see Misty dance in New York one day soon.

Ryan wondered what Annie would say if she found out about vampires.

Probably nothing good, and she sure as hell wouldn't want Ryan to have anything to do with them. She might like Meara, though. Annie was joyfully bisexual and had a special thing for tall blonds of every gender and skin tone.

Ryan was discovering that she had a thing for tall blonds, too. Or at least one of them.

"What is that smile on your face? Oh my God, you got some. Finally! Praise the lord and pass the lubricant. Who is it?" Annie ran over and threw her arms around Ryan in a quick hug. "Tell me right now. Is it that new resident in the ER?"

"No! Doctor Douchehead? Euwww!" Ryan shuddered. "Why would you think I'd be attracted to an arrogant asshole like that? He mansplained a simple surgical procedure to me last week, and I finally had to tell him that after he'd finished his residency, we could talk. Jerk."

Annie tapped her foot. "Then who? And don't tell me nobody, because I recognize that glow, my friend."

"I—it's so new, I don't want to talk about it yet, okay?" Ryan knew she sounded honest, because it was the truth, as far as it went. She certainly didn't want to talk about Bane. She couldn't share the truth, for one thing. For another, she found that she wanted to hold the secret of him to herself for a while longer.

"Well." Annie grinned at her. "Fair enough. Gotta run, break over, those kids need their ballerina doctor. But my birthday is this weekend, remember? So when we go out for drinks, you have to spill all."

"I will," Ryan lied.

She would spill nothing.

Instead, she would, to quote Elizabeth, after Darcy proposed and she turned him down, have *so much to conceal.*

CHAPTER TWENTY-SEVEN

Ryan popped into HR and told them she had to take emergency leave for a week, due to a family emergency—it was no problem, she was assured, since she had several weeks of leave built up. Old Reliable Ryan worked all the holidays, after all, so the doctors with families could be home. Then she made another, more surreptitious, stop to get a few of the supplies and some equipment that wouldn't be missed here but would be very helpful at Bane's place.

After that, she found herself rushing out to the parking garage, almost afraid that the car—and Meara and Mr. C, her links to Bane—would have disappeared into the dark abyss of her imagination, where she'd dreamed them up in the first place.

She ran up the three flights of stairs, raced across the aisles, and then stopped, a sound almost like a sob escaping her throat.

It's still there. I didn't dream him.

This is all real.

When she got closer, Mr. C popped out of the car and made as if to walk around and get the door for her, but she waved him off.

"I'm good. Sorry if I took too long."

"No worries. Meara slept the entire time, and I've been caught up in a killer game of Scrabble."

She gave him directions to her house, and they chatted a bit about her job at the hospital, Meara still asleep in the back. She told him she worked at the clinic two days a week, usually.

"I can't believe I've worked there for more than a year and finally meet the woman who founded it...and she's a vampire."

"They're good people," he said, taking a turn quickly before a carload of drunk tourists from Michigan could sideswipe the limo.

Savannah was a hot tourist destination. Ryan usually avoided them, but it was always fun to catch a ghost tour once in a while or buy a round of drinks for a bachelorette party in town for a destination wedding.

"Have you known Bane and Meara for a long time?"

"Luke, too. We've been with them for more than sixty years, now, I guess. Well, I have. Mary Jo has been with them all her life. Her parents and grandparents ran the house before her. I married up, you might say." He grinned at her, eyes twinkling.

"Married up?"

"I was fresh out of the Army and couldn't find a job other than working at the filling station. What you call the gas station these days. When she drove in with an almost-flat tire, I took one look at her and fell so hard I never came back up for air to this very day."

"That's all it took?"

"That's all it took. I believe in love at first sight, you can be sure of that." He threw a sly glance her way. "I bet Bane does, too, now."

She couldn't bring herself to smile. "I'm sorry to say it, and no disrespect to you and Mrs. C, but I don't believe in love. My parents...my father pretended to love my mother but treated her so badly that she... Well. It didn't end well. I find it's safer not to venture anywhere near anything that looks like romantic love."

Ryan had learned a valuable lesson in all those years of pain, though: it was better to protect your heart than risk it being shattered on the rocks of someone else's contempt.

Meara sleepily chimed in from the backseat. "That's a lonely way to live your life, Ryan."

Ryan stiffened but glanced back at her. She didn't need pity from anyone, especially not a vampire who'd apparently spent hundreds of years alone. "I don't see you doing any better."

"I'm only alone now because I chose to be," Meara said, her eyes darkening.

"What does that mean?"

The vampire shook her head and sank back against the seat. "A story for another time, Doctor."

They drove the rest of the way to Ryan's in silence.

• • •

It took her almost five full minutes to convince Mr. C and Meara to return to the mansion without her. She was perfectly able to drive her own car back there and intended to do so. She finally asked them if they planned to drag her into the car, and Meara rolled her eyes.

"So dramatic, human." She waved a hand at Mr. C, who looked concerned but ultimately acquiesced, and then turned a serious gaze on Ryan. "See you later. But remember what I said. If you betray my brother, I don't know what will happen to him...or to you. I like you, but I love my brother. I won't take well to anyone hurting him."

"I'll be there in a few hours," Ryan said, exasperated, and then she slipped out the door before she had to sign a blood oath or promise her firstborn child.

Vampires.

She ran up the stairs, unlocked her door, and all but collapsed into the familiarity of home. It should have been so welcoming. So reassuring. And yet...

It was not.

Her townhouse smelled abandoned, like stale wine and mustiness, as if she'd been gone for a month instead of not even a full twenty-four hours.

There, her phone lay discarded on the coffee table, probably flashing with texts and notifications and all the things she wondered if she'd ever care about again.

All those years of plodding along. Of sporadic bouts of bleak depression and loneliness. Relationships that never got off the ground. And now—now, she was on the wildest ride of her life.

And suddenly, out of nowhere, life had handed her a gift. The promise—the reality—of what shining adventure— what *gift*—her life might bring, if she could survive just one more hurdle.

And if her shining gift just happened to be a deliciously hot vampire with glowing blue eyes?

"More power to me!" She laughed a little, in spite of the tears she almost hadn't realized were running down her face. If she ever decided to quit practicing medicine, she could have a career writing greeting cards.

Suddenly, she didn't want to spend one minute more than necessary in this lonely place. She changed into her favorite red sun dress and rushed through her bathroom and bedroom, stuffing clothes and toiletries in a bag, grabbing the cherished medical bag that Gran had given her, and—at the last minute—taking the four unopened bottles of wine she still had and putting them carefully in a tote.

Vampires might not drink wine, as far as she knew, but she had a feeling she was going to need quite a lot of it in the coming days. Suspension of disbelief came so much easier with wine, and she and Meara had a date for movie watching, after all.

Maybe *Interview with the Vampire*.

She snorted out a laugh at the thought of Bane's opinion of Tom Cruise as Lestat, and then she locked up, packed everything in her ten-year-old Prius, and headed out for her date with a vampire.

There's the title of my memoir:

Date with a Vampire: Dr. Ryan St. Cloud's Introduction to a Strange New World (before she died a bloody and horrifying death).

She laughed out loud, with only a touch of trepidation beneath her amusement, and switched on the radio so she could sing along. Another thing she hadn't done in…years? The first song that came up on the Oldies channel was "Walking on Sunshine."

Because, of course, it was.

She smiled and sang all the way to Bane's house.

CHAPTER TWENTY-EIGHT

Bane had been up and pacing his study floor for an hour, pushing away the memory of the nightmares and making calls. To contacts of his in the city, who all claimed to know nothing. To Edge, who never slept much during the day, anyway. Edge had been surly and barely verbal on the phone, responding only in the negative.

No, he hadn't been able to find anything out about the Chamber's presence in Savannah.

No, he hadn't discovered where the necromancer had gone to ground.

No, and no, and no. No useful information of any kind.

When Bane had asked him what the hell computers were good for, anyway, if they couldn't find out this basic information, Edge had graphically informed him exactly what Bane could do with his laptop.

That had pretty much ended the conversation.

Luke was asleep. Meara was asleep. Almost none of Bane's connections were answering their phones, and those who were had nothing to say.

And — worst of all — necromancers had no problem walking around in the daytime. Their powers were weaker than at night, but there were a hell of a lot of very bad things that Constantin could be up to while Bane was trapped in his house.

He hurled his phone to the floor and left his rooms, fleeing both his feeling of utter uselessness and his recurring nightmares of murdering Dr. St. Cloud.

Ryan.

Dying in his arms. Again and again.

He knew they were only nightmares and yet—and yet. He never dreamed. Almost never. Meara had told him his daytime sleep was more akin to a coma than true sleep, and he was "bloody well hard to wake up out of it."

Why now?

He'd had premonition dreams before, it was true, but he refused to believe this was one of them. He didn't want to kill her—would do anything and everything in his power to avoid it.

Unless she betrayed you.

And then he'd have no choice.

Denial rose in his throat, burning like bile. *No.* He'd never harm her. He'd pack up and take his family far away from Savannah, if it came to that. Edge could be sure that nobody would ever find them again. The doctor would be mocked, and nobody would believe her if she tried to tell her story to a world that didn't believe in vampires.

That won't work. If she betrays me, I'll have to kill her. There's no other choice.

He stumbled to a stop, disgust and self-loathing rising like bile in his throat. *Perfect.* All she'd asked for was his trust, and here he was already plotting how to destroy her when she inevitably betrayed him.

Proving, yet again, that he was a monster—even when it had nothing to do with fangs or magic.

She deserved so much better than him, a small, seldom-heard voice in the back of his mind tried to insist. The resurrection of his long-dead conscience?

"Never," he snarled, as if responding *out loud* to the voice in his head were in any way normal.

When he heard the garage door open, he flew down the stairs, his feet never touching the ground, and yanked open the door. Mr. C was climbing out of the car. Meara, too.

And no one else.

"Where is she?" He barely restrained himself from grabbing the man by the throat. "*Where is she?*"

Before Mr. C could answer, Meara smacked Bane in the shoulder. "Hey, dumbass. Fighting below your weight class there. If you want to bully someone, try it with me."

He whirled and got right up in his sister's face. "Where. Is. She?"

Meara, proving yet again that she had no sense of self-preservation, yawned and rolled her eyes. "She's at her place, getting some of her things. She promised to follow in her car as soon as she could."

Bane barely managed to keep from putting his fist through the concrete wall of the garage. "And you *let her*?" he roared.

She shoved him, knocking him back and away, and he realized that she'd lost her temper, too. "I must be to put up with you for all these years. Look, Bane. Your human is smart and honest, so far as I can tell. Better than *you* deserve, to be sure. She promised she's coming back. You need to trust her or you'll lose her. And you know you can't travel through Shadow during the day, so don't even try it."

With that, she pushed past him and left the garage. "I'm going to bed. Call me if you need—no, you know what? Just don't call me. I don't need this *merde*." She stalked off, calling him creative names in the French slang of three centuries before.

Bane watched her go, all but vibrating with rage and terror. A hand clasped his shoulder from behind.

"Now, there, son, your sister's right. You just have to trust the Doc. She's a woman of her word, I can tell, if a bit sad. You going off half-cocked and acting like a raging bull isn't going to help her trust you any, right?"

Bane briefly closed his eyes while Mr. C walked around to face him, trying to let himself believe. Trying to understand why it felt like his world was ending.

"Thank you," he finally said, and then he felt worse when the man's shoulders almost imperceptibly relaxed, as if he'd been afraid Bane would hurt him.

Tommy smiled, but his face was still pale. Maybe Bane really had frightened him. A wave of shame washed over him. "I'm sorry. My…emotions are in a roil from this woman, and I don't understand why, but I'd never harm you. I'd never survive Mary Jo's wrath if I did."

"That's the truth. More scary a woman you'll never meet—human, vampire, or werewolf." He patted Bane's arm. "I told the doctor our story, and she said the saddest thing. She said her life has been such that she doesn't believe in love at all."

Bane stared at him, unable to speak a single word.

"Terrible thing, that. Maybe you can help change her mind." With that, he winked and trudged off, undoubtedly to join his wife and plan more skinny-dipping adventures or something equally likely to make Luke's head explode.

Bane's lips twitched. That had been quite the night. Maybe if—

The doorbell rang, and Bane flashed through the house faster than thought. If some unlucky salesman stood at the door, he might not live to see another day.

He put a hand on the doorknob, and Mrs. C came rushing down the hall.

"Don't you do that! It's three o'clock in the afternoon. You'll get far worse than a sunburn, for sure."

But it might be Ryan.

He growled at his housekeeper, who flapped a dishtowel at him.

"Oh, hush." She moved in front of him and opened the door, but he didn't wait to see, because he already knew. He could *feel her heartbeat.* It was Ryan.

Ryan.

Ryan had come back to him. She stood, silhouetted by the sun, as if an angel had come to visit. An angel with long, dark waves of hair, wearing a simple red dress.

His angel.

He reached out and yanked her into his arms, barely noticing the sun burning his exposed hands. Her bags and boxes went flying, except for one she clutched tightly that made clinking noises. He buried his face in her hair and tightened his arms around her until she made a protesting noise.

"I'm glad to see you, too, but you're cracking my ribs, Bane."

He breathed her in—her scent first calming him and then wrapping itself around his nerve endings and seducing him into fantasies of silken skin and passion—and then finally opened his eyes to see that the front door was closed and Mrs. C was nowhere to be seen.

"I can't breathe, either," he confessed, staring into the blue eyes that seemed to see directly into his soul. Touching the lips that he dreamed of touching his body in so many ways. "You came back to me."

She smiled "I told you I would. I said you could trust me."

But he *couldn't*. Couldn't trust that she'd come back to him again. Couldn't trust that he'd survive it if she betrayed him.

Didn't know how to control the waves of relief and gratitude and terror for what might have been—she could have been harmed, she could have run away, she could have been in a car accident. Humans were so fragile.

"*Please don't leave me again*," he commanded, using his *Voice,* even though he knew it didn't work with her. Tightening his arms around her again. "*I can't bear it.*"

She sighed. "And here we are back at this, again. You can't keep me prisoner, Bane. We can't be…friends, if you treat me this way."

"Of course, I can keep you prisoner. And I want to be very much more than your friend."

Her lips flattened. "Remember trust?"

"I don't know how to trust." His body was shaking—actually shaking—as if he were caught in a tempest.

What the fuck is happening to me?

He couldn't do this. Couldn't be this person with zero control.

Couldn't let her see the power she had over him.

He forced himself to release the grip he had on her arms and stepped back. "So. You brought wine? You think you'll need to drink to put up with us?" His voice was a hoarse rasp, but Ryan gracefully pretended not to notice.

Her smile was shaky, but she gamely held up the tote. "Yes. Well, I didn't know if you'd have wine around, and it might be helpful. I brought some sedatives, too, and some gear to draw blood, so we can start investigating and see what we can find out. Also, how does Meara feel about *An American Werewolf in London?*"

He laughed in spite of the turmoil in his mind, collected the bags she'd dropped, and started up the stairs to where Hunter hopefully still slept but stopped when he realized she wasn't following him. He glanced back and saw her watching him with an expression of almost unbearable sadness on her face.

"Bane. I promise you can trust my word. Please believe that."

A lump the size of a boulder was somehow in his throat. "I'll try, Ryan. I'll try."

And he would. If he could just figure out how.

• • •

Luke was stretched out on a couch he'd dragged across the room, reading one of his beloved thrillers.

"What's *A Girl* doing this time?" Bane asked him. "Riding on a train, looking out a window, being dead, being frozen, or being gone?"

Luke closed the book and yawned, stretching. "Solving her own murder, I think. Not very far into it yet."

Ryan entered the room and nodded to Luke. "Hello again. How's Hunter?"

"Entirely quiet for the past hour. Are you going to check

in on him?"

"I'd like to, if that's okay."

Luke rolled off the couch and shrugged. "Not my call. You can hang out here with me while Bane checks on him, if you want, though."

Bane glared at him. "Find your own woman. This one is mine."

Ryan sighed. "And now we're back to the shoe peeing."

Luke glanced between the two of them, puzzled, but Bane started laughing. He couldn't help it. His emotions— the same emotions he'd thought had died long ago, rusted by their complete lack of use, or perhaps even incinerated by the knowledge of terrible deeds—raced up and down between delight and despair like a child trapped on a roller coaster…in *Hell*.

He might not survive knowing Dr. Ryan St. Cloud, but it was certainly going to be fascinating to try.

He walked past Luke, who was staring at him, open-mouthed, and listened at the door before opening it.

Silence.

Hunter was either asleep or preparing an ambush. Vampires were especially cunning just after the Turn. Bane cautiously opened the door, first making sure Ryan was still behind it, and looked in, to find Hunter, lying still as stone, on the mattress where Bane had left him earlier.

He *listened* for a moment, in case a speeding heartbeat disguised ill intent, but the man's heart beat exactly as slowly as it should for one in the midst of the Turn. Was it possible the process was finally proceeding as it should?

"He looks a little better."

He shot a hand out to block Ryan from walking into the

room. "Let me check on him first."

Every fiber of his being told him to keep her away, but he had agreed, as she was sure to remind him, and he was afraid that she'd take refusal now as another sign of his lack of trust.

Hunter was completely out cold, though. Literally cold—his body temperature had dropped considerably. Once the Turn was over, he'd warm up to a not-quite-human temperature, but for now his body was conserving energy for the process of becoming vampire.

"Is this what it's supposed to be? This comatose state?"

"Yes. Maybe now he'll finally progress as he should," Bane said, but his unease was growing. Nothing about this Turn was going according to plan. Had it been the burns? Edge had been tortured nearly to death, but with blood and skin loss, not burns. Did it make a difference?

How could he ever know?

"Can I draw your blood now? There's no point to try a sedative on Mr. Evans, it looks like, but I could experiment with their effects on you, if you'd be willing to take a bit of a nap."

No.

Not if it means seeing you die again.

He schooled his features to impassivity before he turned to face her. "Yes, I'd be willing to try, given certain conditions, just not now. Today is—will be—extremely busy. And yes, you can take my blood. Let's get out of here, first."

"Sounds good," she said, and he waited until she left the room to move away from Hunter, just in case. That's when he saw the basket on the floor behind the door, filled with bags of blood.

Meara, probably. It was the kind of thing she'd think of. He should have thought of it, though. He was slipping. Missing details.

Yet another example of how this human woman is taking up far too much space in my mind.

And yet that was exactly where he wanted her to stay. In his mind—and in his bed.

He closed and locked the door and leaned against it, a wave of weariness sweeping through him. He hadn't slept much, except in fits and starts, since the battle with the warlocks.

"You look like shit, man," Luke said. "You'd better get some sleep before the big meeting tonight, especially if we can find Constantin and get to kick some warlock ass."

"What," Ryan said, in a dangerously quiet voice, "exactly, does that mean?"

When Bane shot him a dirty look, Luke put his hands up in surrender. "Sorry, man. Hard to know which secrets you've told the human and which you haven't." With that, he strode out of the room, whistling.

I need to remember to kick his *ass the next time we spar.*

Ryan carefully transferred the bags containing her equipment to one hand and pointed at him with the other. "Okay, let's have it. Which secrets are you keeping from *the human* this time? I know there must be hundreds, given what you are and how long we've known each other, but maybe we can start with the *kicking some warlock ass.*"

The frantic sound of toenails scrabbling up the steps interrupted whatever he'd been about to say, and Bram Stoker came joyously bounding into the room and hunched his body in the telltale sign of a dog who was getting ready to leap. And he was aimed at Ryan, who wasn't much taller than the dog.

"*STOP!*" Bane commanded, and the Irish Wolfhound slid to a stop, all but falling over his own oversize feet. Then he sat there, his tongue hanging out of his mouth in a goofy smile, waiting for someone to tell him what a good boy he was or rub his belly, staring up at Ryan with a look of utter devotion.

Not a bad life, really.

"Saved by the dog?" Ryan shook her head at Bane. "Not for long. Shall I set up in your study? Come on, Bram Stoker. I have some ear scratches with your name on them."

And then, not waiting for Bane to answer, she marched out of the room, head held high, the dog devotedly trailing after her, and Bane caught himself smiling.

Again.

"Right there with you, buddy," he told the dog and followed the parade down the hall to his rooms.

CHAPTER TWENTY-NINE

Ryan set up her equipment, including the astonishingly expensive portable spectrophotometer she'd borrowed, on the long reading table in Bane's library. She talked to the enormous dog as she worked, explaining the principles of what she planned to do, knowing that Bane was listening, but not ready to speak directly to him until he told her about this dangerous meeting he was apparently planning.

She wanted to know about the warlocks, too.

"I suspect that there is some form of iron-deficiency anemia at work here, Bram Stoker. Yes, you're a good boy." She petted his head, which came up almost to her shoulder. "What are you? A wolfhound crossed with a wooly mammoth?"

Bane threw himself down on the enormous leather couch and watched them, still saying nothing.

"So, I'll do a CBC—that's complete blood count test—to see if you have lower than normal red blood cell counts, hemoglobin or hematocrit levels, or mean corpuscular volume. If that's the case, then I might be on track." She glanced over at Bane, who looked far too sexy for her peace of mind, sprawled out on that couch, all long, lean muscles and gorgeousness. "Ready for me to draw your blood?"

He tilted his head and crooked his finger at her. "I'm ready to kiss you again, so I can discover if it's really possible that the taste of your lips can set my entire body on fire, like I seem to remember happening in the car."

She felt her face get hot and her nipples tighten but shook her head, swallowing hard. "In a minute. I want to test a sample of your blood and do some research, so I can see if I can figure out exactly what is happening with you. The magic versus science conundrum is fascinating."

"Fine," he drawled, rolling up a sleeve.

She took a quick blood sample, careful not to look into his eyes when she did it, in case he magically made her clothes disappear just from the heat of his gaze. Not that she didn't want that to happen, exactly, but right now she wanted to take refuge in science while she figured out exactly what was happening to her.

She reached for a bandage, but he stopped her with an amused glance.

"Oh. I forgot," she murmured as she watched the tiny puncture mark on his arm vanish. "How wonderful that must be."

"Wonderful," he repeated, and when she glanced up at him, he was staring at her breasts. Her breath stuttered, and she quickly backed away and retreated to her equipment.

"If I find that your red blood cells are a different size, shape, or color from those of normal human red blood cells, that gives us a place to start. Of course, I'm limited by what I can do here, since we can't exactly go to the hospital and run tests."

She tapped her finger against her chin, thinking. "Too bad, really, because a sample of your bone marrow would tell me so much. But I don't see how we can do that, just yet, and anyway, if we start here, we can determine what we might want to do next. Does that make sense?"

He said nothing.

"Bane! You have to at least answer me—" She turned to face him and saw immediately why he hadn't replied. He was sound asleep, and Bram Stoker, who'd apparently abandoned her mid-blood-test speech, was sprawled out on the rug next to the couch, out cold with all four legs in the air.

"And, yet again, I have bored you to sleep. This is not the best basis on which to build a relationship," she murmured, and then she froze, blood vial still in her hand.

Relationship?

With a vampire she just met, she was thinking the R word?

"Okay, that's it. I need food. I'm delirious."

She carefully put everything on the table and quietly, so as not to disturb them, walked to the door, and slipped out, carefully closing it behind herself. If Mrs. C didn't have any food handy, she'd order something delivered, but she needed to eat something now and then maybe catch a nap before her brain got any fuzzier.

There was plenty of time for everything else later.

The hallway was deserted, but then again, it was mid-afternoon, so probably everybody not human in the house was sleeping. She resisted the urge to go check on Hunter and wandered downstairs toward the kitchen, where she found Mrs. C presiding over a pot of soup and pulling fresh loaves of bread out of the oven.

"Oh, wow, I might actually faint dead on the spot from how good that smells," she moaned, leaning against the doorway. "Can I help with anything? And maybe get something to eat? I'm starving."

The housekeeper/cook/all-around everything, from what Ryan could tell, was pink-cheeked from the oven's heat. She smiled at Ryan and waved her to a chair.

"Have a seat, Doctor. I'll dish you up a bowl."

"Oh, no, please don't wait on me. I can—"

"You can sit yourself down and let me enjoy the pleasure of serving food to a lovely guest is what you can do," the woman said firmly, so Ryan hastily sat herself down and watched as Mrs. C carved a big hunk of steaming hot bread that smelled deliciously of rosemary and put it on a plate.

Then she handed the plate to Ryan and pushed a ceramic crock and a butter knife across the table. "Get started on that, and I'll dish you up some soup. Do you like potato leek?"

"I love potato leek," Ryan said, and then she was too busy moaning with pleasure as she bit into the bread to talk.

Mrs. C put a large bowl of creamy soup, chock full of potatoes, leeks, and plenty of herbs, down in front of Ryan with a soup spoon.

"There you are. Eat up. Would you like some sweet tea?"

Sweet tea was the Southern drink of choice, but Ryan had never quite gotten the taste for it. It was like drinking liquid sugar with a bit of lemon to her, but she almost felt guilty declining. "Just a glass of water, please?"

"Certainly."

For several minutes, Ryan ate one of the most delicious meals she'd ever had, while the housekeeper bustled around the room, periodically patting Ryan's shoulder, humming, and placing little plates of fruit, cookies, and a slice of pecan pie on the table.

"Ahhhh," Ryan said, contemplating the pie. "This is my favorite Southern food in the world. I could eat pecan pie every single day and be happy."

"That's my grandma's recipe," Mrs. C said, finally taking a seat with a mug of tea and her own slice of pie. "Bane always loved it when she made it, so Mama and I made sure to keep up the tradition."

Ryan slowly put her fork down on the side of her plate. "Hearing you so casually say something like that reminds me how absolutely surreal this situation is. Your *grandmother* baked this pie for Bane, who looks young enough to be your son."

The other woman laughed. "That's kind of you, but he looks more like my grandson these days. And maybe I shouldn't tell you this, but my great-grandmama cooked for Bane and Meara, too."

"And Luke?"

"No. Luke never came around until the sixties. He was a refugee from somewhere else, from someone very bad, I think, but he never talks about it, and I respect his privacy." She sipped her tea. "Ah. As cold as we keep the house, I do enjoy a hot cup of tea."

The house was quite chilly, but Ryan kept her place cool and hospital temperatures were always low, so she hadn't particularly noticed it.

She took a bite of pie and briefly closed her eyes in total bliss. "This is the best pecan pie I've ever tasted. You're amazing."

"Thank you," Mrs. C said, dimpling. "I do love baking.

I'm not nearly as excited about cooking, but I love making bread, too."

"I'd weigh a thousand pounds if I ate here very often," Ryan said glumly. She ate another bite of pie to cheer herself up, though, so it was fine.

"You don't have to worry about your weight, young lady. You have those lovely curves that men love, like I did."

"Like you still do, from what I hear about you and Mr. C skinny dipping." Ryan grinned.

"Well, that's as may be. The secret to a man's heart isn't only through his stomach, after all. Other organs give you a more direct line, as you'd know, being a doctor and all. Tommy's not feeling so well today, though."

Ryan could feel herself blushing. "I only hope I can be as wonderful as you some day," she said fervently. "You're my hero. And if you'd like me to look at Tommy, check his vitals, and look at his throat, I'd be glad to do it."

This time, it was Mrs. C's cheeks that turned pink. "Oh, get on with you. And thanks, but I'm sure Tommy's fine. He just needed a nap. Lots of excitement around here lately. And I'll give you pie every day of the week, if you help my family."

"Your family?"

"I've known Bane and Meara since I was a little girl, you know. Uncle Bane and Auntie Meara, then. Now, they feel as much like my kids as my daughter does."

Ryan took another bite of pie. "Where is your daughter? Does she live here, too?"

Mrs. C responded with a peal of laughter. "Oh, goodness, no. She'd never be content to keep house for someone. My Molly is studying art restoration in France.

On a full-ride scholarship that Bane provided for both her and two of her art student friends, mind you. They live together in an apartment he and Meara bought them in Paris."

"That's amazing," Ryan said, meaning it. A full scholarship would have made a huge difference to her bottom line. As things stood, she was going to have to sell her grandmother's townhome and move into a tiny apartment just to pay off her student loans.

"It certainly is. And the fact that Molly learned French from a native speaker didn't hurt any when it came time for the interview with that French museum director, let me tell you. She said *s'il vous plait* and *merci beaucoup* and there she was, in for the degree and the internship, both."

"That's really terrific. Have you been over to visit?"

Mrs. C sighed happily. "Not yet, but we're going over in December for Christmas, and Bane is paying for that. He actually growled at us when we said we could buy our own plane tickets. He's an amazing man, Doctor."

Ryan added this story to the cache of information she was gathering on the man who'd invaded her home—*and her heart?*—so easily. "He certainly is," she agreed after she swallowed the final bite of pie and stood to carry her plate to the sink.

"*Ryan*." Startled at the intensity with which the housekeeper had called her name, Ryan turned to see that the woman was twisting her hands and frowning.

"Please don't hurt him. He…he means so much to us, you see. I don't…please don't hurt him."

Ryan wanted to promise, but she didn't know how. What would—or even *could*—hurt such a man? So she simply smiled, nodded, and patted Mrs. C on the shoulder.

"I'd better get back up there. Thank you for the meal."

When she glanced back, the housekeeper sat, shoulders slumped, staring down at her hands, and Ryan had the distinct impression that her answer, or lack of one, had been enormously disappointing. She blinked back the tears that suddenly threatened but didn't go back to try to offer comfort. She was terrible at that.

No, being a disappointment was very much more in her wheelhouse.

She stopped and looked at the front door for a long time, thinking of her Prius and escape sitting right outside. Trying to make the decision.

Stay? Or go, before she lost her heart—and maybe her life—to a vampire?

CHAPTER THIRTY

Bane woke up in a cold sweat for the first time in three hundred years.

And vampires don't sweat.

"Ryan!" He bolted up off the couch and called out for her before he was even fully awake, only to trip over the dog, who'd woken, too, and was looking frantically around for whatever the threat might be.

Bane somersaulted in midair, landed on his feet, and finally noticed Ryan on the other end of the long couch, curled up beneath a blanket, sound asleep. His heart rate and breathing slowed down instantly; seeing her alive and well helped dissipate the terrible memory of yet another dream of her dying.

His first instinct was to sweep her up into his arms, but the bluish, almost bruised hollows beneath her eyes told him how much she needed to sleep. For her, even more so than for him, the past two days had been exhausting.

The memory of his dream sent shudders of dread down his spine. Bram Stoker, catching his mood, sat down and started to howl.

"Stop!" He snapped his fingers at the dog and pointed to the door. The dog, fairly well trained for a not-quite-year-old pup, instantly stopped making that hideous noise and trotted over to wait by the door, panting softly.

Ryan had never even twitched. She truly must be completely worn out. He'd leave her to sleep while he and

Luke went to the club for the meeting. If they teamed up with the Wolf Pack MC, as Reynolds had agreed, they'd have a better chance of finding the warlocks.

He bent down and kissed her, so gently she wouldn't even feel it, more for his reassurance than hers. And then he adjusted the blanket around her shoulders.

"I'll be back soon, Dr. St. Cloud, and then we'll explore whatever this is between us," he murmured.

She snuggled deeper into the blanket and made a little humming sound that went straight to his cock. What kind of noises would she make when he was finally inside her? Maybe he should stay here and wait for her to wake up, so he could find out.

Bram Stoker let out a soft woof from the door, which probably meant he needed to go out and water the lawn, and Bane took it as a sign. He opened the door and followed the dog out of the room and then, only hesitating for a moment, turned and locked the door.

Locked her in.

If she woke before he got back, he'd catch hell for it, he knew. Dr. St. Cloud was not the type to stand for what she'd surely consider to be imprisonment. For his own peace of mind, though, he had no choice. If she decided to go check on Hunter by herself, and he woke up in full bloodlust mode...

No. She'd sleep, and she'd be safe, and he'd cope with any consequence when he returned.

He found Meara downstairs in the parlor, picking out a tune on the baby grand piano. The Steinway had cost him half a million dollars twenty years before, but it made his sister happy, so he considered it well worth the price. She could have afforded a dozen Steinways, but it had pleased him to give it to her.

When one's sister was immortal—and a millionaire many times over—finding Christmas gifts became problematic.

"'As Time Goes By?' Feeling sentimental, Meara?"

"A kiss is never just a kiss, is it, Bane?" She sang along with her playing for several lines and then trailed off. "I don't know. Seeing you with the doctor has made me feel lonely, I guess."

"Jean-Claude was a very long time ago," he said, wondering why he was suddenly having conversations about *feelings* with everyone in the house, when his own had only just barely returned from the ashes.

Meara restlessly shoved back the lace sleeves on her plum-colored silk shirt, and he inhaled sharply and then walked over to take her wrist in his hand. The veins were stark black against her pale skin.

"You need to feed. Or there must be blood in the house—"

She pulled her hand away and shook her head, her hair flying with the vehemence of her denial. "You know I don't drink blood out of *bags*, Bane. It tastes like plastic, and it makes me sick."

"Then take from me." He held out his wrist, but she shoved it away and leapt straight up into the air, landing lightly on top of the piano in her bare feet.

"No! I told you five years ago I'd never take blood from family again. Why don't you listen to me?" Her fangs descended, making her look both feral and hauntingly beautiful. "I'm tired of all of this. The club, the people around all the time. The *boredom*. I need to have some fun. I'll go out and find someone to eat later and try not to leave any bodies in my wake."

He knew she was baiting him. Knew she'd only take a little from any one human, and that she'd compel them to forget. But, for some reason, she wanted to fight, and the only thing different in their lives was Ryan.

"Do you hate her?" The words felt like he was ripping them straight from the center of his chest, but he forced them out. Meara was his *family*. "I can give her up, if you—"

"No, you can't." Her fangs retracted, and she laughed. A real laugh. "You can no more give her up than you can give up drinking blood. You forget, brother, I've known you for more than three hundred years. You worked for my father while we were still human. And never once, in all that time, have I seen you act the way you do with the lovely doctor."

He said nothing.

Because she was right.

Dr. Ryan St. Cloud had stolen her way inside his defenses. Not only did he not know *how* to push her away, his entire being rebelled at the idea of even trying.

"Right." She smiled at him, but with far too much sadness in her eyes, and then she jumped down from the piano and kissed him on the cheek. "*Ne t'inquiète pas, mon frère*. I'll get someone to eat. But I'll wait for you to get back from your meeting, so I can keep an eye on the lovely doctor for you."

"Don't tell me not to worry. Worrying about you is part of the deal. And don't wait too long. Ryan's asleep, safely in my rooms, and she's not going anywhere. Go feed before you spend time with her."

"Afraid I'll snack on your girlfriend?"

"Of course not."

Probably not. It *had* happened before, though...

Meara's eyes suddenly widened. "She's *not going anywhere*? You didn't lock her in, did you?"

He averted his gaze, suddenly interested in polishing a speck off the piano keyboard.

Her peal of laughter startled him into looking at her.

"Oh, you truly are in trouble. She won't easily forgive you for that, you know."

"I don't give a damn," he snarled, suddenly tired of the entire conversation. "Better that she's angry with me rather than be too *dead* to be angry."

Meara backed away from him a step. "You've *never* been like this before."

He blew out a sigh. "I know. I think I'm going insane. I don't understand what it is about this human."

"This *woman*," Meara corrected him.

"Yes." He thought about it. "I think...I think she's the bravest woman I've ever met. She accepted what we are and marched right in to save the man she thought of as her patient. She *came back* when she could have been free of us, forever."

Meara sent him a sly smile. "Maybe not forever. I was already planning to abduct her for you if she didn't return. But yes, she has a lot of courage. Maybe too much."

"Almost as much as you." He leaned forward and kissed her forehead.

"I rather like her, your human." She sighed. "All right. I'll feed, and I'll look in on her, and I'll even try not to let her know that my pigheadedly stupid brother locked her in his room like a child. How's that?"

"I know she's not a child," he muttered, and she laughed again.

"No, brother. *You're* the one acting like a child here, jealously guarding a favorite toy. Be careful, Bane."

"Always looking after me." He grinned at her and flicked a strand of her hair, like he'd done when they were children.

She threw her hands in the air. "*Somebody* has to do it."

He watched her start up the stairs, and then he called for Luke.

ARE YOU READY?

Luke's response came immediately.

ALREADY OUTSIDE ON MY BIKE. LET'S GO.

After one long last look at the stairs, Bane headed out the door. They needed to figure out the necromancers' plan and destroy it. Destroy *them*. He wasn't about to let them get a foothold in Savannah or anywhere near his territory. They could stay in the Old World and keep their problems, politics, and death magic on the other side of the ocean.

Even after he climbed on his Harley, his eyes strayed to the upstairs window behind which he knew she slept. *His* human. Maybe he should check in on her once more...

But Luke revved his bike and took off, and Bane couldn't let him stand alone at this meeting. Meara would protect Ryan.

He took one long, last look at the dark window, and then he roared off into the night, the closest he could ever come to flying while still on the ground. First warlocks, and now necromancers. They needed to find Constantin and the woman who'd attacked Edge, and then they needed to destroy them.

And after that, he might need to find a way to take a trip to Europe and *personally* deliver a message to the Chamber.

. . .

Meara decided to check on Hunter before she released poor Ryan from Bane's insane imprisonment scheme. To her surprise, Edge was there, slouched in a chair outside the safe room instead of locked up with his precious computers as he usually was.

"Well. If you're here, I'll be going," she said, turning to leave the room.

"That *is* what you're good at," he called after her, with so much bitterness in his voice that she stopped and turned to face him.

"What?"

"Running away from me. It's your special talent." His face was all bleak lines and harsh angles in the dim light, but his silver eyes shone as if reflecting the entirety of the moon. "Will you ever forgive me for what happened when Bane Turned me? If I'd known he might *die*, I'd never have let him try, Meara."

Suddenly her hunger and exhaustion caught up with her, and she sighed, resisting the urge to move closer to him so she could reach out and touch a strand of his long, white hair. The hair that had gone from black to white overnight after what had been done to him. "I've already forgiven you, Edge. I just want you to stay out of my way."

"*Why?*"

If she didn't know better—didn't know him to be an emotionless bastard with ice—or nanotechnology—running through his veins—she might have thought she heard anguish in his voice.

More than likely, it was just contempt.

"Why?" he repeated, moving closer, all shining beauty and heated demand. "Because I used to work for the government? Because I'm a scientist?"

She laughed in his face. "I like scientists. They're crunchy and taste good with ketchup."

He didn't even crack a smile. "If you hate having me here so much, I'll leave. I won't inflict myself on you any longer."

She closed her eyes against the weakness threatening to make her stumble forward and collapse into his arms. His strong, muscular arms.

That she definitely was not noticing.

"Don't be dramatic," she finally told him, leaning back against the wall. "I don't hate having you here. I don't even notice you most of the time." With that, she gathered up her last reserves of energy so she could go. Maybe she'd even drink some of Bane's plastic blood.

Desperate times…

"Really?" Edge leapt across the room and slammed his hands to the wall on either side of her head. Caging her in. "You don't even notice me?"

Staring at her with eyes turned to silver fire.

"Notice *this*," he snarled, and then he captured her mouth with his own and *took*.

Plundered.

Savored.

He kissed her as though he were conquering her, and God help her, she loved it.

Reveled in it.

She plundered his mouth right back. Took his head in her hands and pulled him deeper into the kiss. Wrapped a leg around his thighs and yanked his body to her, so that there was no space between them, no air, no room for thought or regret or razor-sharp memories of past pain to intrude.

There was only Edge and Meara and this kiss—this passion—that was blazing like wildfire between them. Why hadn't she known, why hadn't she—

"Meara?"

The sound of Ryan's voice snapped Meara out of the sensual haze into which she'd willingly plunged, and she pulled away from Edge and his deep, drugging kisses.

"What?" His gaze was unfocused, and he stared into her eyes and then down at her mouth. "More."

She put a hand on his chest. "No."

He ignored her and bent his head to her again. "But—"

"I said *no,*" she shouted, and she threw her hands into the air—hurled her power at him—and levitated him a good six feet off the ground, where she pinned him to the wall with the sheer force of her rage-fueled magic.

"Did you think my only power was to become invisible? To live my life unseen, like so many other nameless, faceless women who have to skulk in the shadows to avoid the attentions of men like you?"

"Men like me? Meara," he said, his voice a husky croak.

"I'm sorry. No, I never thought anything of the sort. I've wanted you for so long, and I—but you kissed me back, and I thought—"

"Yes. I did. But then I said no."

Ryan entered the room then, or maybe she'd already been there, witness to Meara's extraordinary lapse of judgment. She looked at Meara and then up at Edge, still hanging against the wall, and then she nodded, as if she saw this sort of thing every day.

"No means no, dude," she told Edge. Then she shifted her attention to Meara. "Also, where's Bane? He and I need to have a little chat about locking me in *for my own good.*"

From the look in the human's eyes, Meara had an idea it wouldn't be a comfortable chat for her brother. But then again, she'd warned him.

"Maybe let the nice computer guy down now," Ryan ventured. "We could have pie and talk about how men are pigs."

Abruptly, Meara started laughing. She'd always been able to see the ridiculousness in a situation, even when the joke was on her. She released her power, and Edge gracefully dropped to the ground and landed lightly on his feet, which was annoying.

She'd much rather he'd fallen on his ass.

"If you'd just bend your knees, touch one hand to the ground, and stick the other one straight out in the air behind you, you'd have a great superhero pose," Ryan told Edge, who stared at her as if she were an alien species from another planet.

Meara shook her head. "There are no heroes here. So.

You said something about pie?"

When they left the room, she could still feel Edge's gaze burning into the back of her neck.

"I wish you could teach me that trick," Ryan said, starting down the stairs. "There's this new guy at work, Doctor Douchehead, who could really use a lesson just like that."

Meara shook her head. "That's a very unfortunate name. Perhaps he's suffered enough."

Ryan started laughing and explained about the name, but Meara tuned her out. Her lips still throbbed with Edge's kiss, and she had to fight herself to keep from going back and finishing what they'd started.

If he'll ever kiss you again, after what you did to him.

That was the trick, though, wasn't it? Finding a man who could celebrate you for your strength instead of rejoicing in your weakness. She didn't want a man who was strong enough to protect her—she wanted one who was strong enough to stand with her while she protected herself.

While they protected each other.

But if she hadn't found that in three centuries, what made her think she might now?

CHAPTER THIRTY-ONE

"You don't have a brother, do you?"

Ryan blinked. "No. Only child. Why?"

Meara sighed. "No reason. Okay. Enough of this. We're going out."

"We are? I don't have anything to wear," Ryan said, scrambling for a reason why she didn't want to go out on the town with the supermodel vampire standing next to her. She was used to being ignored in bars, standing next to Annie in all her dancer's body splendor, but she had a feeling she'd wind up with actual boot prints on her scalp from all the men trying to climb over her to get to Meara.

She was already having self-esteem issue about her ordinary looks compared to the supermodel's brother.

Who had locked her in his room. Get back to the point here.

"Bane locked me in his room," she said. Again. "My father used to do that to my mom and me 'for our own good.' Not only am I claustrophobic, in a big way, but I am furious that your brother did that to me when I'm a grown-ass woman, and if he thinks—"

"He's gone," Meara said, looking bored by the conversation. "You look fine. The red dress looks good with your hair. But we're not going out clubbing. We're going shopping. I have a ball to go to tomorrow night, and I need a gown."

"You have a ball to go to," Ryan said slowly, wondering

when she'd gone from *Alice in Wonderland* to *Cinderella* and whether it would be a good choice for vampire movie night. Since she was going to *kill* Bane for locking her in, maybe he'd like a chance to watch Prince Charming chase all over the country for a foot that fit a glass slipper first.

"Yes. It's a charity thing for the clinics. And since we've discovered that you work for me, you have to do what I say, because I'm your boss," Meara concluded, her eyes sparkling and her lips still swollen from whatever had been going on with the silver-eyed hunk of broodiness in the ballroom.

Oh, for Pete's sake. Now *she* was doing it. Hanging out in *ballrooms*.

Still… "I don't think that's how that works," she told Meara. "I actually volunteer my time. You—the clinic— don't pay me, so I don't work for you, so I don't have to do what you say."

Meara whirled around, in one of the spooky vampire superfast moves Ryan supposed she'd now have to get used to, and bared her…fangs. "Then do what I say because I'm a *vampire,* and I'm *hungry*, and you're starting to look like dessert."

She did look hungry. Ryan swallowed whatever she'd been about to say and changed tactics. "Did I mention how much I'd love to go shopping for your ball gown with you?"

Meara smiled, her fangs retracted now. "Perfect. We'll get you one, too, and you can be my plus-one."

"I can't go to a ball. I'm supposed to be off work for a family emergency. Plus, I'm not really the ball type. Don't you want to take, ah…" *The guy whose tongue was down your throat* didn't seem polite. "Edge. The sexy guy with the white hair?"

"No. That was a momentary lapse of judgment. Come on. We'll take my car."

Meara's car turned out to be a sleek BMW convertible that she immediately jacked up to maybe a hundred miles per hour past Ryan's comfort level.

"You know, I don't heal like you, so when we crash and burn, please tell Bane that my last words were *you shouldn't have locked me in your room*," she shouted over the wind rushing past.

Meara rolled her eyes, which seemed to be her signature move, and took a turn on two wheels. Or maybe only one.

Ryan wondered what horrible way she'd be murdered if she threw up in a vampire's luxury car. Then she figured maybe she'd just close her eyes until they arrived at whatever store in Savannah sold ball gowns at nearly midnight.

When the car squealed to a stop, she cautiously opened one eye.

"We're here. Hop out." Meara leapt out, and Ryan unclenched her death grip on her seat belt and followed her onto the sidewalk.

"Whitaker Street? What will be open here this time of night?"

"Nothing is open to the *public*," Meara said, saying *public* in the tone of voice that Ryan used when saying *infectious diseases*. "But she'll open for me, and she'll even give me a little snack."

Ryan perked up. "Pecan pie?"

"Not exactly."

By the time Ryan followed Meara into the unmarked

door at the top of the short flight of steps, the vampire was already fangs deep in her snack—who turned out to be the owner of the boutique.

Ryan wandered around the small shop, not wanting to stand there and stare like a voyeur, but not knowing what else she should do, either. From the sounds the woman at the door was making, she was *very* happy to let Meara "snack" on her, so Ryan didn't feel like she should interrupt.

On the other hand, did "first, do no harm" include allowing a fellow human to be used as food?

Her mind flashed back to when Bane had bit *her*, in a far more sensitive location than her neck, and how it had felt, and she shivered.

Yeah.

Neither Meara nor the human woman would appreciate being interrupted right now, for sure.

A few minutes later, they were done. Meara murmured something to the woman, who shook out her cloud of red curls and walked over to Ryan.

"Hello! Welcome to Katrina's. I'm Katrina, as you probably guessed. What lovely breasts you have! I think Christian Siriano or Zac Posen for her, don't you, Meara?"

Ryan's face instantly flamed with heat. "Um, thanks?"

Meara looked at Ryan with interest. "Ooh. Yes. In red. It has to be red, don't you think? With that hair and skin, I think red."

Ryan cleared her throat. "So, I can't afford a designer gown. To be honest, I can't afford a designer handbag. Or even a wallet. So, let's just focus on your dress, Meara."

The vampire picked up a slim, long, emerald-green sheath dress and held it up against her slim, long, Valkyrie-like body. "I think I need this, Kat. And yes, show her whatever you have in red. Add it to my bill, please."

"Of course," Kat cooed, just as Ryan said, "Oh, no, definitely not."

Meara pointed at Kat. "Or maybe a sapphire silk? With her eyes? Low-cut bodice, for sure," she said, ignoring Ryan completely.

Ryan took a deep breath and tried again. "Meara. I appreciate your generous offer, but—"

"No, you don't."

"I—what?" Nonplussed, she stared at the vampire. "What do you mean?"

Meara shrugged and handed a tiny beaded handbag to Kat. "This, too. And those emerald teardrop earrings."

"Meara," Ryan tried again.

"No. You don't appreciate the offer, because you're too damn proud. And you have some silly human idea of what's yours is yours and what's mine is mine, and whatever. I have enough money to buy Louisiana. I'm buying you this dress."

Ryan blinked, feeling distinctly bulldozed. "Why would you want to buy Louisiana?"

"Have you ever eaten gumbo in New Orleans? That's reason enough."

Ryan shook her head and bowed to the will of Hurricane Meara. She could always return the dress later. She sank into a chair, accepted the glass of champagne Katrina handed her, and let the conversation flow over and around her.

Nothing about this adventure was anything that Reliable Ryan would ever do, in a million years, so she suddenly wanted to experience all of it.

"Bring it on," she told the two women airily. "Cinderella had nothing on me."

Meara grinned at her. "I've always wanted to be a fairy godmother, but my brother is definitely no Prince Charming."

Ryan took a long sip of champagne. "More like Prince Arrogance, really. But damn, he'd look hot in a tux."

"What a great idea!" Meara pulled her phone out of her pocket—the first time Ryan had seen any of the vampires use phones—and tapped out a text. "There! I told him he's going with us tomorrow."

Ryan, starting on her second glass of champagne, smiled. "Sounds great to me. Can he dance? He was secretly a European prince back in the day, right?"

Meara's expression was priceless. "Prince? Prince of the stables, maybe. He worked for my father, with the horses."

"So, no dancing," Ryan mused, trying to fit this information into her mental file labeled *Bane*.

"Oh, he can dance. My father was a *conte*. I taught him to dance after we Turned."

"You taught your father to dance?" Ryan picked out a pastry from a china tray Katrina offered her.

"No! Pay attention! I taught *Bane* to dance. He hates getting dressed up, but he will for you. And you'll want to look beautiful for him."

Ryan found she liked the idea of that. *Very* much. She smiled and drank champagne and tasted pastries, and then she tried on gowns that almost certainly cost as much as she made in a year.

Because why not? She was *Unreliable* Ryan these days

and loving every minute of it, and she would very much love for Bane to see her as beautiful, too, even if only once.

An hour later, slightly drunk and entirely shocked at how many packages Katrina would be messengering over to them the next day, Ryan followed Meara back out the door and down to the street.

That's when the shifters attacked.

CHAPTER THIRTY-TWO

Bane leaned against the bar, and Luke and Edge took positions on either side of him. Nine of their best fighters—all vampires—sat at tables, drinking beer, talking quietly, and watching the door for the unprecedented sight of a pack of werewolves walking into the Vampire Motorcycle Club headquarters.

"It's going to be bad if the warlocks have already taken any of the wolves," Luke muttered.

Edge nodded. "Carter Reynolds is a major strength, but his people don't have any natural immunity to blood magic, like we do."

"None of us but Bane have much, either, as we just discovered," Luke growled.

"I guess we're about to find out," Bane said, hearing the bikes roar into the parking lot.

A few minutes later, Reynolds sauntered in, with a casual expression on his face like he walked into the middle of a dozen vampires every day and twice on Fridays. Behind him, several of his pack members, including his second, Max, followed him, belligerence and defiance an almost-tangible wave around them.

"We're here. The party can get started," Max called out, her cheerful expression and freckled nose belying what he knew about her deadly skill as a fighter.

Most of the wolves and a few of the vampires laughed.

"It was her role to break the ice," Bane said quietly.

"Now, we'll see the show of power."

Sure enough, a big guy who was built like a bulldozer crossed with a bear started snarling the minute he reached the center of the room.

"You don't look so tough to me. Look like a bunch of wimps," he growled, staring at Luke and then Edge, but careful not to meet Bane's gaze.

Bane nodded to Reynolds. "Okay. We've gotten the preliminaries out of the way. Can we talk now or do you need to pee in the corner first?"

A shadow of a grin crossed the alpha's face, and then he returned Bane's nod and motioned to his man to stand down. "Let's do it. I'm a busy man. Things to do, people to intimidate."

"I know I'm intimidated," Bane said in his driest voice, and the werewolf laughed.

"I can see that. All right. What do you know?"

Bane nodded, and one of his club members walked behind the bar and started handing out bottles of beer to the wolves. He and Reynolds took seats at a table in the middle of the room.

"The warlock named Sylvie appeared in the middle of your clubhouse without anybody scenting her?"

The alpha's eyes flared hot. "She knocked your vampire off his bike and dragged him to our place, and he couldn't fight back?"

Bane shook his head. "I'm not trying to start a pissing contest, and I'm not casting blame on you or your wolves. This is a special fucking party trick from a necromancer. Ordinary warlocks can't pull it off easily, if at all. Vampires can't detect necros, either, when they don't want to be seen or smelled."

The alpha accepted a beer from one of his men. "Yeah. That was exactly it. Dropped your guy off and called him a gift. Then she left. I've been waiting ever since for the other shoe—or, in her case, spike-heeled boot—to drop."

"No word?"

Reynolds took a long draw on his beer. "None. You?"

Bane filled him in on their encounter at the wildlife preserve. "Nothing since then, which doesn't make sense. Usually, when they come in force, they want you to know. Warlocks are more like hurricanes than spring showers. There's no way this Constantin and Sylvie came on their own, unless they were just scouting, but taking such aggressive action either means they have an army to back them up or—worse—they're so powerful they believe they're a fucking army all by their own damn selves. Have you dealt with necromancers before?"

"Never. My dad had, though, he said. When he lived in Louisiana. Baton Rouge. Took the entire combined force of all the supernaturals in the city to get rid of them—and that was for only two of them."

"We have at least two here, and the master, Constantin, is extremely powerful. We took care of three ordinary warlocks, but Constantin and this Sylvie are clearly necromancers, which is a big fucking problem."

"Zombie magic? Pulling up the graveyards?" Reynolds's eyes narrowed. "That is some unpleasant shit, especially in an area filled with cemeteries like Savannah."

Bane drained his beer. "Yeah. Zombie shit. This is going to get really bad before it gets better. We need to coordinate or she might take over some of your wolves."

Reynolds leaned forward, his face hardening to stone. "My wolves are not—"

"Your wolves are incredibly tough, but even two of my vampires, who have at least a small amount of natural immunity to blood magic, fell hard and fast to Constantin. Do you or your wolves have that?"

The alpha reluctantly shook his head, a muscle in his jaw jumping.

Bane leaned forward. "In Europe, the worst of the warlocks sometimes had entire packs of werewolves under their control. Alive or dead, didn't matter to them. Is that what you want, just so you can prove you're tough? To watch Max's corpse be operated like a puppet by one of these bastards?"

The wolf's eyes flared a hot amber, and Bane thought he'd gone too far, but as he watched, Reynolds visibly gained control over his anger.

"No. Never. So, let's figure out a plan. First, we'll—"

But Bane didn't get to hear Reynolds's plan for what they'd do first, because that's when the howling started.

• • •

The parking lot looked like a scene from a gangster movie. At least ten werewolves, in various stages of turning to wolf, were attacking the VMC sentries who stood guard outside the clubhouse. Reynolds bellowed orders at his people, but they acted like they didn't hear him, even when he forced a wave of pack magic through the area that was so powerful even the vampires felt it.

Bane grabbed the alpha's arm and shouted at him, to be

heard over the howls and screams. "They can't hear you. They're enthralled. Bound to the warlock."

"How do we break the spell?"

"We kill the warlock. Until then, you can only restrain them—or kill them."

Just then, a huge gray wolf raced toward them and leapt through the air, aiming what must be a couple hundred pounds of snarling bulk directly at Bane. Reynolds shoved him out of the way and threw himself into the path of the werewolf, shifting as he moved, and both wolves crashed into each other with a fury of claws and teeth.

Bane had never in his long life seen a werewolf who could shift that fast, but he didn't have time to think about it, because more were coming at him.

"Don't kill them, if you can help it," he shouted at his vampires. "This isn't their fault."

"Sure. That's going to be a fucking walk in the park," Edge snarled, just before he whirled around and punched a wolf in the head so hard it flew back five feet and crashed to the ground.

Bane crouched, waiting for the three werewolves in wolf form racing toward him from three different directions to get within leaping range. The minute their paws left the ground, he flew up into the air, just out of reach, and shouted out a wordless cry of triumph when the three of them smashed into each other and knocked themselves out for the count.

But then he sped into the clubhouse and yanked a bag of restraints out of a locker. Before the fighting even died down, Bane had restrained seven of the werewolves so fast they almost didn't even know what was happening.

He tossed the bag to Luke and walked over to Reynolds, who stood over two of the fallen wolves, growling at them when they tried to move.

"Only two of yours are dead," Bane told the alpha. "One of mine, I see. Those warlocks have a lot to pay for."

Reynolds, still an enormous black wolf, threw back his head and howled for his fallen.

"I'm with him," Edge snarled. "We need to take these bastards *down.*"

Bane nodded grimly. "Yeah. We do. But first we need to find them. Where the *fuck* could they be? Go!"

Edge raced off to try to find the warlock or necro who'd cast the spells. Luke walked up to Reynolds, offering the restraints in his hand to the alpha.

Reynolds shifted back to human with what looked like only a minimum amount of effort and shook his head at the chains. "No. I'll handle this without that."

"I've never seen anything like the power of your shift," Bane told him. "Maybe you'll be able to break the magic binding with your alpha call, given enough time. It's worth a try, at least. I've heard of it being done by the most powerful pack leaders."

The werewolf caught a pair of sweatpants somebody threw at him and pulled them on. "It is worth a try. Thanks to you and your people for not killing them outright."

"We try not to kill our allies," Bane drawled. "We're going out hunting. You do what you need to do with your people and then give me a call so we can coordinate efforts. I'm guessing you have more than these who might still be in danger?"

Reynolds swore. "Yeah, we have four who didn't show

up, but I don't know why."

Bane's phone buzzed in his pocket. He started to ignore it but then thought, *Ryan.* But when he pulled it out to look at it, it was Meara, and it was a pin with her location.

Wolves. Hurry. Ryan's here.

"I may have found your wolves," he snarled and then shot up into the sky, headed for Whitaker Street.

CHAPTER THIRTY-THREE

At first, Ryan had no idea who or what they were, the four men who detached themselves from the shadows edging the street and coalesced into a choreographed quartet of menace around them. But in the light from the streetlamps, the *Wolf Pack MC* on the patches embroidered on their vests gave her the *who* of it.

The *why* was less clear.

"What is happening?" She looked to Meara, who was—shockingly—smiling, her fangs glinting in the golden light.

"Oh, boys," Meara purred, moving to stand between Ryan and danger. "Did you ever pick the wrong women to try this on. If you wanted to mug somebody, you should have stuck to Broughton Street."

"Shut up, bitch," the tallest one snarled, and Ryan instinctively edged closer to Meara, who sighed.

"Okay, as much as I'd love to kill you all, I don't want my human to get hurt. So how about this?" Her brilliantly golden eyes gleamed with inner fire. "*Go home to your mommies.*"

Compulsion didn't work on Ryan, but she knew it would on others, so she watched eagerly as...nobody moved an inch.

"Yeah, my mother is dead, bloodsucker," one of them growled.

"Then you can go to the cemetery and spend the night apologizing to her that you grew up to be such an asshole,"

Meara said sweetly.

He growled, low and feral, but one of his friends put a restraining hand on his arm.

A different one stepped up. "And we're warded against your magic, so you can give up on compulsion now."

"Warded?" Meara scanned the group. "Since when do shifters use magic for warding? And don't we have a treaty with your MC? What is this? Have you gone rogue?"

"Enough questions. Our new mistress told us we need to make a *point* with Bane."

"New mistress? She doesn't stink of rot, does she?" Meara said, taunting them.

"The mouthy one is his sister," the ugly one—*ugliest* one—said. "The other one doesn't smell like vamp. She must be food."

"Do we kill them both here?"

The big one grinned with a mouthful of broken teeth. "They're going to die, sure. But nothing says we can't play with them first."

"Incorrect," Meara purred. "*I* say you can't."

Ryan, who'd been frozen for a few minutes while this all happened, reached into her purse, but not for her phone. This didn't seem like the kind of situation that 911 would help.

"I also say you can't," she said. "And I'm sure as hell not food."

The four thugs cracked up. Apparently, they weren't used to the *food* talking back. Ryan realized she had never been so afraid in her entire life.

Which might be over soon, actually.

"Here we go," Meara sang out, and three of the men—

shifters?—headed for her, claws starting to extend, so yeah, shifters.

There are freaking werewolves in Savannah, Ryan's amped-up brain shouted at her, but she had to focus, because *yes*, there were *freaking* werewolves in *freaking* Savannah, and one of them was coming *straight for her.*

Meara sprang into action, and it was like a martial arts movie on steroids. If Wonder Woman and Bruce Lee had a baby, it would be Meara. She kicked and punched and twirled, and two of the attackers were down on the ground, groaning, before their friend even reached Ryan.

Right.

Time to focus.

She burst into tears. "Oh, please don't hurt me, sir, please. I'm a doctor, I can't be part of this, please, if you'll just let me give you my money, let me get my wallet…" She dug in her purse, shaking violently and cringing away from the oncoming shifter.

He let loose with a truly nasty laugh. "Pathetic. I can't believe Bane's sister would put up with even food who was so cowardly. Maybe I'll break your neck now and do the world a favor."

He reached out, almost casually, with one huge, meaty hand, and the tips of his claws scratched her face. Ryan ducked beneath his arm, cold and steady, all pretense over, and brought up the scalpel she'd hidden in her purse earlier, back at her place, back when she thought that *vampires* were the scariest things around.

And she sliced it across his carotid artery with every ounce of strength she had.

When he hit his knees, arterial spray splashing

everywhere, she blinked, and a kind of false calm came over her, which meant she was probably going into shock.

Which I deserve, because now I'm a murderer.

Before she could process that thought, the shifter made a horrible groaning noise, and then *he stood back up.*

He *stood up*, after she'd just sliced open his carotid. He had to be dead—she'd killed him.

Somehow, though, he was *still moving.*

Yeah. *Now* she was going to die.

He took a staggering step toward her, but she was frozen in place, unable to move. Facing her own death without the ability to run, hide, scream, or fight back, because this was impossible, this could not be happening, this was *insane*.

A horrible roaring noise filled her ears or maybe her mind, like the death train at the end of the world was bearing down on her. She had about two seconds to think *so this is how the world ends*, and then the shifter looming in front of her suddenly flew up about twenty feet into the air and then hurtled back down to the middle of the road.

And landed on his skull.

Even Ryan, who'd seen horrible, horrible things while working in a hospital, had to look away from that, and when she turned her head, all she could see was Bane. He yanked her into his arms and flew with her about twenty feet away, kissing the breath out of her, and then he set her down on her feet next to a tree and raced off to help Meara.

"Stay there," he shouted back at Ryan and, for once, she had no desire to do anything else.

"I don't need your help," Meara yelled at Bane, but then

she screamed, and Ryan automatically started toward them, still clutching her scalpel, with some idea of helping.

Ryan St. Cloud, superhero, who thought she could help the *vampires* defeat the *werewolves*.

She shouted out an almost-hysterical laugh and started to run, but by the time she got back to where the shifters had attacked them, the three Meara had been fighting were all dead, and Meara was lying on the sidewalk, the side of her throat ripped open.

"Meara!" Ryan raced over to her. "I—damn. I don't have my bag or any supplies. We need to call an ambulance—"

Bane put a hand on her shoulder. "Watch."

"What?" But she looked at the ugly gash on Meara's neck just in time to see it seal itself into a jagged red line and then fade even more, as far as she could tell in the dim light and with all the blood splashed on Meara's skin.

Bane crouched down next to his sister. "You must take my blood. You're in desperate need."

Something was certainly wrong. Meara's veins were snaking dark lines beneath her skin, and she looked like she'd lost twenty pounds in the last ten minutes.

"No," Meara croaked. "No blood from family."

"Damn it, Meara," Bane snapped. "This is an emergency situation."

Ryan swallowed, hard. This sounded like an old argument, but Meara might not have time to stand on this principle. There was, however, another option.

"Take mine," she whispered, and both of them whipped their heads around to stare at her, in inhumanly fast movements.

"What. Did. You. Say?" Bane's eyes shone bright, ruby

red instead of his usual blue, and Ryan suddenly wondered if she should be afraid of this man who'd just saved her life.

The man who murdered someone right in front of my eyes.

She blew out a shaky breath and gathered her courage. "I said take mine. So long as it's not, you know, all of it, you can take my blood to help you heal."

Meara reached up and touched Ryan's face. "So easily you offer what no one has freely given in more decades than I can count. You truly are a gift, Doctor."

Ryan tried to smile. "Oh, I think we should be on a first-name basis, if you're going to have your fangs in my throat. Or, um, could it be my wrist, instead? I just don't want to look like I have a giant hickey, and—"

The sound of a motorcycle roaring up interrupted her inane babbling, thank goodness. Bane and Meara must have expected the arrival, because they didn't look concerned.

It was Edge. He dismounted the bike and raced over to them then fell to his knees and scooped Meara into his lap, swearing the entire time.

"If you won't take Bane's blood, take mine," he told Meara, savagely biting at his own wrist.

"No," she protested, but Ryan could see how her gaze fixated on the blood now dripping from Edge's arm.

"*Yes.*" He put one hand behind the nape of her neck and held her in place while he sealed his wrist to her mouth, almost forcing her to drink. After a moment, she did.

Ryan sank back on her heels, blowing out a huge sigh of relief. Admittedly, part of her relief was at not getting bitten, but—somehow, in such a short time—Meara had become almost as important to her as Bane.

Bane.

Where had he gone? She looked around to find him standing over her, staring down at her with those terrifying, glowing, scarlet eyes.

"You're bleeding," he growled.

"What? No, it's his blood, the...oh." She reached up and touched her cheek, which she only then realized was stinging. "Yes, I guess I am, but just a little. He scratched me before I...before I—" Her teeth started chattering; she was definitely going into shock.

"Your *blood*," he said, his voice a dark roll of thunder and need. "Want it. *Want it now*."

Meara shoved Edge's wrist away from her mouth and tried to stand, but she was still shaky and fell back against him.

"Brother," Meara said, cajoling. "No. Not her."

"*Need*," he growled, and now Ryan was starting to feel the fear even through the shock.

Edge put a hand out. "Bane. Stop. You've been around human blood before. You can control this. You need to stop. You're scaring her."

Bane ignored him completely and crouched down and scooped her up in his arms, staring down at her with an expression gone entirely feral. "Not like this. Not like *her*. Tastes like sunshine and champagne and happiness." He closed his eyes and drew in a huge breath. "Tastes like *everything*."

Edge and Meara lunged forward, probably to help her, or maybe to stop Bane, but he sliced his hand through the air in an imperious gesture, and both of them flew back through the air and bounced off the car behind them. Then he made another gesture when they sprang to their feet, and they froze, unable to move.

Bane's fangs snapped down. "I take what I want," he snarled, grabbing a handful of her hair and pulling her head back to bare her throat to him.

"No!" She reached up to touch his face, in spite of her shock—in spite of her fear. "No, Bane. I don't think you would ever forgive yourself, so let me tell you this," she told him. "It's not taking if I freely give. Take what you need."

He smiled, his red eyes flaring even hotter, and then he drove his fangs into her neck.

CHAPTER THIRTY-FOUR

Bane's brain exploded at the first taste of her blood. So sweet, so full of life and light and everything he'd ever wanted. He wanted *more and more and more.*

He *needed* her blood. Needed her.

It's not taking if I freely give.

She freely gave her blood to him. She'd even offered her blood to save his sister.

And he was killing her.

He froze, forcing his fangs to retract, and swept his tongue across the puncture marks to help them heal. Ryan's eyes fluttered open, but she looked so, so weak.

How much had he taken?

"How can you trust me when you see what a monster I am?" The anguish in his voice cut through the night.

"Because I see beneath the monster to the man," she whispered, almost boneless and weak as a kitten in his arms.

He wanted to kiss her, but not with her blood staining his lips like the evil of his past stained his soul. He could never deserve this woman. He should tell her that, as much as the monster inside him howled denial.

"Ryan—"

She offered him a shaky smile. "Maybe let Meara and Edge go before I have to kick your ass."

He could never deserve her, but he was damn well going to try.

He released Meara, who was spitting mad, and Edge, who glared at him and then silently strode to his bike and stood waiting, gaze fixed on Meara as if she were his north star.

Bane's attention returned to Ryan, all but asleep in his arms. Ryan, who had trusted him. Trusted him *not to kill her*, after she'd watched him kill those shifters. Not just trusted him, but freely gave her blood.

She was a fool to give anything to a monster—even if she claimed to see the man.

"I'm going home," Meara said, ice dripping from every word. "I'm getting in my car and driving it at a ridiculously fast speed and going home to shower the stink of shifter off me. Bane, you and I are going to have a long, *long* talk, my brother."

He nodded, barely looking up. "I'm…sorry."

"And you—*what*?" Silence followed, as if he'd shocked her to speechlessness. Maybe he had. Apologies were not exactly his fucking specialty.

"I'm *sorry*. I really am, Meara, and I'll make it up to you, but right now I'm taking Ryan home, and then I'm going to find these necromancers, rip their heads off, and shove them up their asses," he snarled.

"I'll go with you," Edge said, his voice pure ice. "They dared to touch Meara. All of them are going to die tonight."

Meara sighed. "Let's regroup at the house. These said they have a new alpha, so clearly something is going on that we need to find out about. Let's not go off half-cocked just yet."

"It would be better to find out the facts first. And, Meara, they said new *mistress*, not new alpha. Is that the same?"

Ryan murmured, awake again.

"No, it's not," Edge said. "They must have been talking about Sylvie, the warlock who attacked me, unless there are even more of them around."

"She must be a necromancer, too," Meara said grimly.

Ryan pushed against Bane's chest. "Put me down, please."

"Never," he swore, tightening his arms. "I leave you alone for a few hours, and you start a fight with a shifter pack."

She sighed. "Yes. That's exactly how it happened. And we still need to talk about how you locked me in that room."

"Oh, *mon Dieu*. Not this again." Meara threw her hands into the air. "I'm out of here."

"I'm with her," Edge said, firing up his bike.

"They touched you," Bane told Ryan, his brain locked onto that fact. "They have to die."

"Let me down now, please. I am perfectly capable of standing on my own two feet."

Instead, he called to the Shadows and stepped into the Between, still carrying the woman he'd just proven he'd kill for. Knew he would die for.

When the vortex closed around them, Ryan screamed, startling him so much that he lost his focus, and they tumbled out of the Between before reaching their destination.

Into a cemetery.

The cemetery, to be precise.

"Are we in Bonaventure?" Ryan was trembling in his arms, now clutching his shirt. "And what the *hell* just happened? Was that some freaky kind of vampire transporter? Did you just beam us up? Is that how you disappeared with Hunter Evans? And maybe give a person a warning before you pull shit like that?"

She paused for long enough to suck in a huge breath. "And you'd better put me down. I feel like I'm going to throw up."

• • •

Ryan bent over and put her hands on her thighs, taking in deep, calming breaths, for three or four minutes. Whatever Bane had just done to them had felt like being swept into the middle of a tornado. It was even worse than Meara's driving. And that was on top of the shock of blood loss to her body…she really needed to be resting and drinking orange juice, not standing in a cemetery with a vampire.

A burble of a laugh escaped her lips. *Standing in a cemetery with a vampire* was another good title for her memoir. That, or a good name for a rock band.

And yeah, wow, the blood loss had fuzzed her brain.

"They touched you. They all have to die," Bane repeated, stalking back and forth, looking like nothing so much as an avenging angel, especially here, surrounded by monuments to death.

Given the fact that he was a vampire, his eyes were still glowing that bright scarlet, and they were standing in the middle of the freaking cemetery, the impression might not be that far off.

"I killed one," she blurted out. "Or, at least, I thought I killed him. If he'd been human instead of a shifter, I'd be a murderer."

The shaking threatened to take over again, and she could feel the hyperventilating coming on. She hadn't had a full-blown panic attack since the time she'd been trapped in a dark elevator for three hours during a power outage in New York, but this was shaping up to be a whiz banger of one.

"One," she counted, closing her eyes, and then she took a slow, steady breath. "Two."

Exhale. "Three."

Breathe in. "Four."

And so on, until she got to fifteen and felt the edges of the panic attack subside. When she opened her eyes, Bane stood inches away from her, staring at her with eyes that had changed from red to blue. Maybe her relaxation technique worked on vampires, too.

The thought forced a slightly hysterical laugh out of her. "I defended myself from a *werewolf.* With a *scalpel.* I was awesome!" She punched a fist in the air. "I pretended to be terrified—well, that wasn't so much pretense, I really was terrified—but I pretended to be helpless, and then I ducked under his arm and stabbed him. I was *attacked*, and I *defended myself*. I *am* a superhero!"

The fury stamped on the hardened planes and angles of Bane's face told her more plainly than words that he definitely didn't agree.

Screw him. She was freaking Super Ryan, who could battle werewolves with a spare scalpel she just happened to be carrying in her purse. Well, okay, she'd put it carefully into the inside pocket of her purse when she'd stopped at her place, because she was brave but not naïve, and she'd been willingly going back to a house where vampires lived, but still.

"Super Ryan," she repeated, and—much to her shock—
he started laughing.

A real, actual laugh, filled with amusement, not mockery.
He threw back his head and laughed, and she watched him
in wonder, touching her neck where he'd bitten her. How
did she reconcile the two sides of this man?

This self-proclaimed monster and the man who'd so
passionately made love to her?

How can I be falling in love with him?

She must have made a sound when the epiphany
smacked her in the face, because Bane stopped laughing
and looked at her, still smiling.

"Super Ryan. Yes, you definitely are. To think I asked
Meara to protect *you*. You're a one-woman fighting machine."

Warmth from his praise spread through her, which was
terrifying, considering what she'd just realized about her
feelings for him. Instead of responding, she deflected. She
was very good at that.

"It's nice to hear you laugh. You don't do that often
enough."

He raised an eyebrow. "I laugh."

"Yeah, but more in a *bwah ha ha* kind of way, not real
laughter." She shrugged. "Not a big deal. Just nice to hear
it."

But, as she spoke, his smile faded. "What do I have to
laugh about tonight? You and Meara could have been
killed by those shifters." He reached out and gently took
her shoulders in his hands. "Worse—far, far worse—I could
have killed you."

A hint of red flared in the centers of his pupils. "I am so sorry, Ryan. I have no excuse for what I did. For what I almost did. I don't understand why the scent of your blood calls to me so strongly. Maybe—"

"Oh, I get it," she interrupted. "Tons of vampire novels and movies all combine to tell me that I'm your *fated mate.*" She put on a movie-trailer announcer voice. "*In a world where vampires are real, one brave doctor proves to be the undoing of a gorgeous denizen of the night.*"

Then she bowed with a flourish, grinning at Bane when his mouth fell open. Mr. Stone Face didn't get her humor, evidently.

"Maybe you are my fated mate. You think I'm gorgeous," he said smugly.

"Duh." She rolled her eyes. "Me and everybody else on the planet, probably."

"Also, denizen of the night? You're a very strange—"

"If you say *human*, I'm going to punch you," she warned him, narrowing her eyes.

"Woman."

"I get that a lot," she admitted. "Hey. Since we're here, let's stroll around. I love this place. It reminds me of my gran, before…before she died."

"Is she here?"

"You mean is she buried here? No. She wanted to be cremated." She blinked back tears.

"I'm sorry." He held out his hand, and she took it, wondering at the comfort she drew from such a simple touch. "But I meant, is *she* here? Does her spirit still walk here, to be close to you?"

She gave him a sideways glance and started walking.

"Of course, not. I don't believe in ghosts," she said automatically, the same denial she'd made so many times since moving to Savannah, where every other person claimed to be a psychic or medium.

But—this time—she froze, realizing that she was denying the existence of *ghosts* to a *vampire*. The vampire who was holding her hand.

"I guess I need to rethink that."

They strolled along in silence for a few minutes, and Ryan found herself calming down, the adrenaline of not one, but two near-death experiences slowly working its way out of her body. She'd experienced the fight-or-flight reaction first-hand tonight and learned which way she'd go when worst came to worst.

In spite of the horror she still felt over actually trying to kill that man—even though he'd tried to kill her first—she also felt the faintest tinge of…pride.

She'd protected herself.

Sure, Bane had come in and finished the werewolf off after he'd pulled a "bad guy in the horror movie who won't die" routine, but she—Dr. Ryan St. Cloud, ordinary, unimportant, Reliable Ryan—had stood up to a monster and come out alive and on top, at least for those few, precious minutes.

She stopped and turned to face Bane. "You were right."

"Always." He reached out and pushed a strand of hair back behind her ear. "About what this time? And we need to get you home and cleaned up. You still have blood on your face," he said, his voice darkening.

She shook her head, impatient. "It will keep. Listen. You were right. I *am* a goddess. I stood up for myself tonight, in a way I never have in my life. Not just—not just the violence. But my sheer refusal to back down. I realize I give in and give up far too often in my life. In my job. Always expecting to get the worst end of the stick. Always willing to accept less, because I feel like I *am* less."

"You're definitely not less," he said. "You're absolutely amazing."

"Thank you. But that's something I needed to see for myself, you know? And now I do. Not that I'm amazing, exactly, or maybe that I am because *everyone* is amazing. Nobody, ever, should be willing to accept *less*. Even though it took something so terrible happening for me to learn this lesson, now that I have, I'll never back down or give up on myself again."

"You deserve everything, my warrior goddess," he murmured, and then he pulled her into his arms and captured her mouth in a kiss.

This time, though, *she* claimed *him*.

She kissed him like the warrior goddess he'd named her, proud and strong and wanting to share her strength with this man—this monster.

Her monster.

When they finally broke apart to breathe, both of them were breathing hard.

"If you don't want me to strip you bare, right here in the middle of the cemetery, we need to leave right now, or else you have to stop kissing me like that," he growled, and she loved the rasp of hunger in his voice.

"Anticipation adds spice to everything," she countered. "Let's walk some more. I need air, and I love the smell of the flowers and the river. The sound of the insects and the owls. Bonaventure at night is like a secret world where you might turn a corner and see fairies at any minute."

He pulled their joined hands to his mouth and kissed her fingers. "They prefer to be called Fae."

Ryan's world turned upside down, for the third or fourth time since she'd first found a vampire in her patient's hospital room.

"They *what*?"

CHAPTER THIRTY-FIVE

Ryan stared at the vampire who had just so casually dropped the existence of *fairies* into the conversation.

"They prefer to be called Fae. And are you sure you don't want to get naked right now? We could walk down by the river and find a secluded spot and—"

"Bug bites. On my ass. Just no. And did you really say *they prefer to be called Fae*? What kind of world do I actually live in?"

"That, my beautiful one, is a conversation for another night."

They wandered around, up and down the paths, until they came to the tomb of Little Gracie Watson, and Ryan pulled Bane to a stop.

"She was only six when she died," she said, staring at the beautiful monument, said to be an exact likeness of the child. "My gran told me the story of the famous little girl, so beloved by so many, who was left here all alone, because her parents went back to New England after she died. When I was six, I begged to be allowed to leave my doll here, so Gracie wouldn't be so lonely."

Bane's hand tightened on hers. "You had a kind heart even then. Did you leave it for her?"

Ryan nodded. "I did. It made me feel somehow comforted, and I remembered her in my bedtime prayers for a long time. God Bless Mama, and Grandma, and Little Gracie, and Fred."

"Fred?"

"My neighbor's dog. I was never allowed to have a pet; my father forbade it."

"Ah." He smiled, but only a little. "Gracie would have liked little Ryan very much, I think. She was a lovely, cheerful child."

Ryan dropped his hand. "You *knew* her?"

She didn't know why she was shocked. Of course, he could have known her. Gracie had lived in the 1880s.

"Not knew, no. I only met her once, when I had a business meeting one evening in the hotel her father managed. She was dancing in the lobby and singing a little tune." He smiled at the memory, gazing at her sculpture. "I remember thinking that I'd never seen a child so filled with light and joy, since I'd first met Meara."

Ryan leaned her head against his shoulder.

"Good night, little one," he murmured as they turned to go, and Ryan's throat tightened with tears she was determined not to shed.

No monster would be so gentle when bidding farewell to a child he'd met once, more than a hundred years before.

"Tell me about her," she urged. "Meara, as a child. She must have been the most ridiculously beautiful child who ever lived."

Bane chuckled. "She was very beautiful and very wild. Her mama died when Meara was very young, and her papa spoiled his only child's every whim. Almost any other child would have become hateful and arrogant, but Meara merely saw it as her due and continued to treat everyone with the same level of kindness and interest."

"And you worked for her father?"

He shrugged. "Not as official as that. My family died of

the plague when I was eight—my parents and my older brother. My sister had been gone for a while by then, as I told you. I spent the next couple of years scrapping and stealing on the streets of London, trying to stay alive. Sleeping on rooftops, near chimneys when I could get a place, because they stayed warm even on cold nights."

She wanted to cry, thinking of an eight-year-old boy, homeless and starving, trying to stay alive in eighteenth-century London, but he was telling the story in such a matter-of-fact, calm way that she didn't want to derail the conversation. She was so hungry, though, to learn more about this man who'd become the center of her world in such an impossibly brief span of time.

"When the count traveled to London on business, he brought Meara with her. I first saw her when she was riding in a carriage, throwing pennies out the window to the little ones who scrabbled in the street. I'd never seen any girl so clean and beautiful." He laughed. "I thought she must be an angel. That was before the first time she gave me the rough side of her tongue, believe me. Meara in a temper can strip a man's hide from his body with a few well-chosen words. Or an entire stream of them."

"She is forceful, I'll give you that," Ryan said, remembering that a ball gown in her size would be delivered to the mansion by noon, in spite of her protests.

"Anyway, one of his stable lads fell sick and died, and I managed to be in the right place at the right time. They took me with them when they continued their travels, and—for the first time in years—I had a warm place to sleep that I didn't have to fight for, in the stables, and more than enough food to eat every single day."

"Is that why family meals at your house are such a feast?" Ryan thought back to how she'd splurged on groceries when she finally escaped her father's house and could eat whatever she wanted without having to listen to his blistering diatribes on her weight. She also knew that children who grew up in food-insecure households often developed eating disorders when they could afford to buy and binge on all the food they wanted.

Bane's grip on her hand tightened and then relaxed. "Perhaps. Oddly enough, I've never thought of it in those terms, but it is true that having a fully stocked larder has always been a requirement in my homes. You never forget the feeling of a belly so empty that it burns or the ache of the constant fear that you won't survive another night."

"What…what was your name? The name your family gave you?"

He stilled. "You know, I'm not sure I even remember it."

Ryan stopped and put her arms around him and just stood there, holding him, for a very long time. When she stepped back, she tried not to let him see that her cheeks were wet, but he touched her face with one finger, his face softer than she'd ever seen it.

"You honor me with your tears, Ryan, but that was a very long time ago."

She nodded and managed to swallow the lump in her throat, and they walked on, in companionable silence, toward the entrance. Several minutes later, as they approached the main gate, Ryan looked up at him, struck by a thought. "When did you come to Savannah?"

"In the early 1700s. And how we came to travel here— that's a long story, and one I'll share with you another time."

"Have you ever been back?"

"No. I can never see England in the sunlight again, so it seems not worth the bother of trying to travel there."

"You have money. You could charter a plane."

"Yes, but it's probably better to stay on this side of the ocean and defend what's mine. Also, there are...other reasons why vampires can't easily travel to other geographic locations, but that's also—"

"A story for another time. Okay, I get it." She yawned unexpectedly, her face all but cracking with the force of it. "I think I'm ready to go back to your house or my house, somewhere I can get a shower and some sleep. Is it— should we walk?"

He shook his head. "I asked Luke to send Mr. C. He should be pulling up outside the gate by now."

"How...when did you do that? Do you even have a phone?" She hadn't seen him make a call.

He bent his head to hers and pressed a brief, gentle kiss to her lips. "It's more super-secret vampire stuff, as you like to call it. I reached out, mind to mind."

She blinked. "Well. That's just creepy."

From behind her, a woman started laughing. "Oh, honey. You have no idea."

Bane spun around and thrust Ryan behind him. "You must be Sylvie. You stink of grave rot. I'll give you one warning. Get the fuck out of Savannah. This is *my* territory."

The necromancer—because who else could it be?— smiled. "Yes, I *must* be Sylvie. And here, vampire, you are in *my* territory."

With that, she slowly raised her arms and started to chant.

And the dead of Bonaventure Cemetery started to rise.

CHAPTER THIRTY-SIX

"This is not good," Bane said calmly while considering his options.

"You think?" There was an edge of wild hilarity in Ryan's voice, understandable under the circumstances. She'd just survived one attack, only to be faced with another.

After just learning that vampires existed.

And werewolves.

And warlocks.

And the Fae.

She was doing pretty damn well not to be curled up in a corner sucking her thumb, which was what most humans would do when confronted with necromancy on top of everything else he'd thrown at her.

All around them, the dead were rising. At least a dozen of them, he noticed with the corner of his mind not preoccupied with watching Sylvie. So, this necromancer's reach wasn't all that powerful.

Or else she thought it would only take twelve of them. If so, she was vastly underestimating him. Or would be, if he'd been alone. Now, his only priority was removing Ryan from danger.

"Time to get you the hell out of here," he told her, grabbing her hand and calling to the Shadows...which failed to respond.

Sylvie laughed. "I can feel you trying to call to your dark

powers, Nightwalker. But my magic reigns here."

"So that makes you the queen of dead things, Necro-mancer? Your mother must be so proud."

Ryan's hand tightened on his. "Maybe don't taunt the scary, evil witch until *after* we find a way out of this?"

Sylvie stopped chanting and snarled. "How dare you call me a witch, human? A demon bred with my human ancestors to create my line. I'm no pathetic, nature-magic-wielding human *witch*."

"Sorry," Ryan shot back. "My magical references come from *Harry Potter*. Now, why don't you put the nice dead people back so we can talk this out?"

The necromancer aimed a wide-eyed look at Bane. "She's very annoying. Why haven't you killed her already?"

"Why don't I kill *you* already?" He yanked Ryan close to him and shot up into the air. He'd fly her to safety and come back to deal with this trash.

"I don't think so," Sylvie said, and a bolt of foul magic slammed into him, knocking him out of the air and back to the ground. He turned over in midair, so his body struck the ground first, cushioning Ryan, but it was a jolt.

"Are you okay?" He jumped up, not willing to be caught on the ground when a necromancer and her new army were on the march, pulling Ryan with him.

"I'm fine," she gasped. "Behind you!"

Bane spun around to find that three more reanimated corpses, two of them not much more than skeletons, were shambling up on them from behind. He grabbed a skull in each hand and crushed them together, pulverizing the bone.

"Two down," he called out, and then he ripped the head

off the final body and hurled it into the air with so much force it went sailing over the nearby trees.

"Bane, three. Zombies, zero," Ryan said, crouched in a defensive posture and whipping her head from side to side to scan for more attackers.

"You can give up now," the necromancer sang out gleefully. "I'll send these after you, and then more, and more, and more. We have all night, after all. And if I keep you here until after sunrise…well. Then I'll get to play with your human."

"The human is not down with that plan," Ryan said, defiance in every line of her body. "Why don't you go back to the hole you crawled out of?"

Sylvie turned her attention to Ryan, just as six more corpses surrounded Bane to attack. "*What* did you say to me, blood bag?"

"You heard me. Also, where do you buy your clothes? At the Halloween rejects store?"

"I thought we weren't taunting the necromancer," Bane said, lashing out to pummel the nearest corpse, which collapsed onto the ground, its spine still in Bane's hand.

"Reanimate *that,* bitch," Ryan shouted, pointing at the fallen, spineless, body. Then she whirled to face Bane, her back to the necromancer. "I'll distract her. You take care of the zombies."

"That's an *awful* plan." He launched a spinning kick into the air and smashed a zombie into the one behind it, taking them both down.

"It's a *great* plan. Trust me, I'm a doctor," she said, making no sense at all, but—with five more newly animated bodies heading for him, he didn't have time to talk about it anymore.

Sylvie, he noticed, kept a careful distance away from him, which meant, luckily, that Ryan was also a careful distance from Sylvie. Until Ryan decided to pick that moment to step closer to the necromancer.

"Stay away from her," he shouted, just before three corpses rushed him, and he found himself covered with dead bodies that were pummeling him all at once, with inhuman strength.

"Oh, no, *please*, little human," Sylvie purred. "Come to me, and let's play."

"Play with this, bitch," Ryan shouted, and then she *ran straight at the necromancer,* holding that useless scalpel in her hand.

"No!" He desperately fought his way free, gathering up his magic to strike out—if he could at least knock Sylvie out, if not kill her, her power over the dead would be interrupted.

But he was too late.

The warlock sliced the air with one hand, and a burst of powerful magic sizzled through the air, aimed directly at Ryan.

And, helpless to get there in time, Bane had to watch as every ounce of that foul power smashed into the woman he'd just now realized he loved.

"No," he howled, destroying the final corpse that lurched in front of him, blocking his view.

But then a fountain of silvery white light cascaded up from the area where Ryan had just been struck down, and Bane had to shield his eyes against it, even as he raced toward her. The light shimmered and then coalesced around Ryan, who wasn't dead.

She wasn't even down.

She was standing in the middle of a swirling tube of pure light, holding her arms out, a look of total astonishment on her face.

Behind her, Sylvie was on the ground, cringing away from the light.

Bane recovered from his shock for long enough to check behind himself for more zombies, but they were all down. The foul power that had reanimated them had disappeared, and—right in front of his eyes—they sank back down into the ground beneath where they lay.

"Bane?" Ryan's voice was shaky but clear. "Would you like to explain exactly what is happening to me?"

"I'd like to know that, too," Sylvie said, so quietly that Bane could barely hear her. And then she made a circling motion with one hand and disappeared.

Bane slowly approached Ryan, who was still glowing, but the fountain of light had diminished until it wasn't much more than a glimmering outline of light surrounding her.

"Are you harmed?" He reached out to touch her, but the light jolted him with a severe electrical shock and knocked him back a step.

Ryan gasped and turned her hands over and back, staring at them in wide-eyed wonder. "This…this isn't some residual side effect of hot vampire sex, is it?"

He barked out a laugh. Of all the reactions he could have expected her to have, that wasn't even in the top hundred.

"Definitely not." Then he turned, sensing a familiar

presence, as Luke raced over to them and skidded to a stop a good ten feet away from the still-glowing doctor.

"What the hell is going on now?"

The epiphany slammed into Bane with the force of a speeding truck. "Oh no."

Ryan pointed at him with one glimmering finger. "Don't you 'oh no' me. The last thing I need to hear right now is 'oh no.'"

"I'm sorry, but this isn't…this is…Oh, hell." He shoved a hand through his hair. "Or, should I say, the *opposite* of Hell."

Luke and Ryan both stared at him.

"What?" she shouted.

"When every other solution is impossible, what remains is… Oh, fuck it. You're Nephilim."

Luke started swearing and backed another two steps away from Ryan.

"I'm *what*?"

"Your daddy was an angel," Luke told her. "A freaking angel. We're fucked."

Ryan, the glow finally beginning to fade, wrapped her arms around herself and bit her lip. "I don't… No. You're wrong. My father was a financial consultant."

Bane shook his head. "I'm sorry, but no," he said gently. "The light, your ability to deflect blood magic, the glowing skin, even the taste of your blood…you're Nephilim. Which means your father—your biological father—was an angel."

Ryan blinked but said nothing. Then she blinked again and swayed where she stood. Bane tried to get to her, but the light smashed him back again.

Luke just stood and stared at her for a long minute and then started laughing. "You know, I can't imagine Daddy is going to be happy about his little girl hooking up with a vampire."

Ryan took a stumbling step toward Bane, the glow finally diminishing. "An angel?"

He clasped her hand with only a minor electric charge this time and then pulled her into his arms. "We'll figure this out, I promise. We'll— "

But she was suddenly boneless in his arms. She'd fainted. Or maybe the Nephilim power appearing had drained her. He wasn't sure.

The only things he was sure of were that she was Nephilim, the necromancer would probably figure that out any minute, and a pissed-off papa angel might be on his way to tear Bane into multiple tiny pieces.

The world was suddenly a more complicated place.

"Fuck *that*. I'll never let you go," he whispered into her hair. And then he stepped into the Between and took her home.

CHAPTER THIRTY-SEVEN

Meara and Edge crowded into Bane's room, barraging him with questions.

"Quiet," he growled, carefully putting Ryan down on the new bed that had magically appeared in his room while he was out. He made a mental note to give Tommy a raise for installing a new bed and removing the remnants of the old one so quickly.

"Do you think we should take her to her hospital?" He pulled a blanket up over her still form but couldn't force himself to move away from her.

"What would we tell them? 'Hey, doctors, our human actually turned out to be Nephilim, and she burned out using her magic angel powers, please fix her?'"

Meara's sarcasm made Bane want to punch something, but she was right.

Human medicine had no solution to this.

"I won't give her up." He turned to glare defiance at his sister and Edge. "I don't care who her father is. She's mine."

"*She* might have something to say about that now that she knows what she is," Edge pointed out before backing away, hands held up placatingly, when he saw the expression on Bane's face.

Meara gave one of her elegant, very French, shrugs. "We shall see. You know the history, right?"

Bane shook his head. "No, I never paid attention when you were telling me about the conversations you had with those monks in France. What history?"

She sighed. "I knew it. Anyway, you know, of course, that the original vampires were the progeny of demons mating with humans, right?"

"Of course," Bane said.

"What the fuck?" Edge's silver eyes widened. "Nobody thought to tell me they were Turning me into a demon?"

"Don't be ridiculous," Meara said impatiently. "We're a separate race now."

"Oh, fine. I just have a demon great-great-grandmother."

Bane slanted a look at Edge, who sighed but shut up and made a go-ahead motion with one hand.

"So, as you also know, Nephilim are the progeny of angels mating with humans. But it doesn't descend in genetics. The only Nephilim are those with an angel father. That's why we thought there weren't any being, ah, *made* anymore."

"Apparently Ryan's father was a naughty angel," Bane said. "But how could she never know until now? Wouldn't her powers have manifested before?"

"She probably didn't have to battle a lot of necromancers or zombies in her medical training," Meara drawled.

"The things she's mentioned about her father…I wonder if he knew she wasn't his child. It would explain why he treated Ryan and her mother so badly," Bane said slowly, staring down at Ryan's pale face for a long moment before turning to his sister.

"And what about us? I mean, the pairing of vampire and Nephilim?"

She laughed. "Oh, that's easy. Never. *No way, no how, forbidden, taboo.* Almost as bad as the inconceivable idea of demons mating with angels to the scholars who supposedly wrote down the rules. There was some kind of treaty between angels and demons."

"There are rules?" Edge closed his eyes and groaned. "Why didn't anybody tell me about the rules?"

"Because they're archaic," Meara snapped. "Have you ever run into any angels or demons? Even two hundred years ago, the monks believed the Nephilim were no more, and nobody has seen one since, as far as I know."

Bane raised an eyebrow. "You keep up with the monks?"

"They're scholars, and yes. They have a website, and we email periodically." Meara shrugged again. "What can I say? I've always found the history—our history—fascinating."

Bane reached down and smoothed a strand of hair off Ryan's cheek. "Are we in trouble?"

Meara nodded. "Partly, it depends on who her father is. There's a slim chance he won't smite you on sight. But yeah. We're pretty much fucked. An angel will definitely know the rules."

"Fuck him," Bane growled. "He broke some rules himself. And he abandoned his daughter. Let him try to come for me."

After that, they left him alone to watch over Ryan, probably going off to research on their computers how to fend off a smite attack. Bram Stoker came galloping down the hall and shot across the study to the bedroom, where he jumped up on the bed next to Ryan.

"Should have made a no-dogs-on-the-bed rule," Bane told the hound, who grinned a doggy grin, tongue lolling out, and ignored him totally. Then Bram Stoker turned

around three times, curled up on the end of the bed next to
Ryan's feet, and fell asleep.

Bane, on the other hand, was all but flying from the
effects of the night's battles and—even more so—from the
blood he'd drunk from her veins. The richly delicious,
almost unbearably sweet taste of it still lingered, phantom-
like, in his mouth, and now it made sense. The tiny taste
he'd had before, when he'd made love to her, hadn't been
enough to let him know exactly how special it was. How
special *she* was.

The more he fixated on Ryan—and her blood—her
Nephilim blood—the more he worried that he wouldn't be
able to resist jumping on her.

Putting his mouth on her.

His teeth in her.

His *cock* in her.

All of it—forbidden. The treaty Meara had mentioned,
so ancient he doubted anyone even remembered what the
penalties were. Because nobody today thought they'd need
to know. Of course, it was probably bloody death. Everything dealing with angels and demons involved bloody
death.

Vampires—created originally by the breeding of
demons and humans. How the hell had he never known
this?

Nephilim—the children of angels and humans. That,
he'd known, but in the same way he'd known ancient
Rome once existed. Not as a fact that would show up in his
life.

In his bed.

The pairing of vampires and Nephilim? Never. *No way,*

no how, forbidden, taboo. Almost as bad as the inconceiv-able idea of demons mating with angels.

And yet, here they were.

I need to get the fuck out of here.

This time, he very deliberately did *not* lock the door behind himself.

In the hallway, he found Luke talking quietly to Edge, who had stationed himself in front of Meara's door.

"Standing guard over my sister?" He thought he was speaking in a calm, mild voice, but Edge's narrow-eyed reaction clued him in that maybe he hadn't been.

"Your sister doesn't need me to guard her. I just—I don't want to leave her alone yet. Especially since we're all going to die any minute now, since you're fucking a Nephilim."

Bane snarled at him, and Edge shook his head. "Later. We're going hunting."

Luke's eyes lit up. "Necromancers?"

"You bet your ass."

Meara wrenched her door open and stared out at them. "Go. And call me when you find them. I want to be in on this kill." She glanced at Edge and then quickly away, but it was enough for Bane to see that something had happened between the two of them—something more than the blood sharing after the attack. "Bane, I'll go to your room and watch over your angel girl."

He could feel two warring urges inside himself. Should he go wipe these necromancers off the face of the planet or stay and be sure Ryan was safe?

She could only be safe if the necros were gone. He'd deal with the imminent daddy issues later.

"We'll take the bikes," Bane said. The other two couldn't

fly, at least not far, and he wanted them to stay together, in case of ambush.

"Should we call any of our vampire club members? Some of them are scary motherfuckers," Luke said.

"Not for this. None of them are scary enough to face necros. Warlocks, maybe, but not this. And if the Chamber sent many more than these two we know about, we're all fucked," Bane said grimly, voicing the threat he hadn't wanted to acknowledge.

If the Chamber came in real force, they might all be dead in a matter of days. But he'd sure as hell take as many of them as he could with him. Luke and Edge said nothing, no doubt silenced by the specter of an army of warlocks.

"I'd hoped those unholy bastards had decided to stay in Europe after the last time we stopped them from invading," he admitted as they headed down the stairs.

Luke snorted. "Fucking Brexit."

Bane grinned. Sometimes black humor was the only kind that would do.

"Speaking of *unholy*." Edge aimed a narrow look at him. "What the hell are you going to do about Ryan? If the warlocks figure out what she is, they'll never stop coming after her. Nephilim blood would fuel their rituals for years."

"*If* they kept her alive," Luke growled. "Imagine what power killing a Nephilim would give them."

"They'll never get their hands on her," Bane told them, his voice ice. "We're going to kill them. Tonight."

They headed out to the bikes, and then three of the deadliest predators to ever set foot in Savannah went hunting.

. . .

Six hours later, though, they had to admit defeat.

The warlocks, wherever they were holed up, had covered their tracks very well. Everyone they asked claimed to know nothing and then, when compelled to answer, gave the same response.

Nothing, nothing, nothing.

The Wolf Pack alpha called and reported the same. "Not a clue. Nobody knows. And my wolves that they infected are trying to kill us, each other, and themselves, in spite of the restraints. I'm still trying to break the binding myself, but it doesn't look promising. We need to kill Sylvie, or Constantin, or both of them, and we need to do it now."

"My thoughts exactly." Bane hung up and shook his head. "Nothing."

"I need to get to my computers," Edge told them.

They stood in the ruins of the Noble Jones house on the Isle of Hope, eight miles south of Savannah. It had been a last-ditch effort, since they knew the wolves liked to run the marshes of Jones Narrows at night during the full moon, so they'd thought maybe the necros had found it.

No luck.

Again.

"How will computers help?" Luke asked Edge, who just grunted.

Bane knew better than to even ask. The former government scientist was a wizard with those things, working his own kind of magic on the internet's darkest corners. If there was intel to be found, he'd find it.

"Nice place, this," Bane said, inhaling the fresh night air.

"Maybe you can bring your lovely doctor to a twilight picnic here sometime," Luke said, sarcasm dripping from every word. "You know, right before her daddy shows up and smites us?"

"Shut the fuck up about smiting," Bane said. "You should have seen her tonight. She went after one of those shifters with a tiny little scalpel."

Luke shook his head in disbelief. "What? A cut from a blade that small would heal on a werewolf in a minute or two."

"She didn't know that. And she got his carotid on the first try. All she knew was that they were trying to kill her and Meara, and she was determined not to let that happen. She's incredible. She tried to pull the same trick on the necromancer. That's when the woman blasted her with blood magic. Defending herself from that is what seems to have unlocked Ryan's power."

Edge brushed his hands off on his pants and then headed back to the bikes. "Yeah. She's brave, I'll give you that. But she's also Nephilim. So, on one hand, she's incredible, but then on the other hand, there's the smiting. You need to clear the fuck away from Dr. Ryan Angel-Baby St. Cloud."

But Bane had the crystal-clear feeling that it was far too late for that. And now that it was almost dawn, the overwhelming need to get back to her pushed him out of his reverie and back on his bike.

He needed to see his...angel.

CHAPTER THIRTY-EIGHT

Jasmine, aged three, was a tear-streaked bundle of unhappiness whose mother had brought her into the clinic for a possible ear infection. Ryan tried to cover her wince when the teenaged mom carried her child, screaming and kicking, into the exam room.

Maybe coming to work after only a few hours of sleep—not to mention the werewolf attack—hadn't been the best idea.

Especially adding in the necromancer attack—with zombies.

Or finding out that she, herself, might be *part angel*... Yeah. It would have been understandable if Ryan had said no when the clinic admin, not knowing anything about Ryan's fake family emergency, had begged her to come in, since two other doctors were out with the flu.

And now here was Jasmine, clearly in pain, who needed her doctor to pay attention to *her*, rather than to Ryan's own increasingly bizarre *Grimms' Fairy Tale* of a life.

"Hey, sweet pea. Let's see if we can help you feel better, okay?" She automatically dropped into her soothing doctor voice. "Can you sit up on the table for me, like a big girl?"

Big girl or no, Jasmine was having none of it. She shook her head, which made her wince and cry even harder.

"That's okay. You sit here with Mommy while Dr. Ryan has a quick look into your ears."

Sure enough, it was a raging ear infection. A Mom Diagnosis was rarely wrong in cases like this.

"We're going to have to put her on the pink stuff," she told Mom, who was nodding.

"She's had that before, about six months back. I wish she'd stop getting these awful ear infections. This is the fourth one she's had!" Mom—Tyra—blew out a sigh and snuggled her little girl. Ryan glanced at the chart again. Though only seventeen herself, Tyra had been diligent about vaccinations, well-child checks, and bringing Jasmine in when she was ill. Ryan had met a lot of adult parents who weren't as careful.

"She'll be fine," she told Tyra. "Her fever's a little high, though. We don't like to see 101.5 last very long. Alternate the acetaminophen and the ibuprofen—baby Tylenol and the baby Motrin—like it says on this sheet, and Jasmine should be feeling better very soon."

Suddenly, the child sat up straight, stopped crying, and stared up at Ryan, the tears glimmering in her lashes. She held out her hand and pointed one chubby little finger. "Shiny!"

Tyra laughed. "That's her new favorite word. Everything is shiny. Tin foil, the car window in the sunlight, whatever. It's all shiny."

Ryan smiled at Jasmine. "That's a great word!"

But before Ryan could move on to her next patient, the child lunged at her, pushing free of her mom's grip. Ryan dropped the chart on the floor and caught the girl before she took a header.

"Wow. Okay. You have to be careful, sweetheart."

"Jasmine!" Tyra patted her chest over her heart. "I swear

she's going to give me a heart attack one of these days."

But Jasmine wasn't paying attention to her mother or to what Ryan was saying. The child put her hands on Ryan's cheeks and stared into her eyes.

"Shiny," she whispered. "Shiny lady."

Ryan smiled, but suddenly she felt a powerful sensation of warmth, and it felt as if something inside her was reaching out to the little girl. Something warm and comforting.

Something...*magic*?

Whatever it was, it surged between them, carried from Ryan's face to Jasmine's hands, and the little girl's sturdy little body, which had been tense with pain, relaxed completely.

Jasmine's eyes opened wide. "Oh, that feels me better, shiny lady."

"It's Doctor Ryan, Jazz, and you need to come to Mommy now," Tyra interrupted, giving Ryan an apologetic smile and taking her child.

"Doctow Wyan feeled me better, Mommy," Jasmine babbled, and Tyra gave her a distracted pat.

"Yes, I know. Let's go get your medicine now, okay? And then you can have some ice cream."

Ryan suddenly jumped into action on a hunch. "Tyra, just a moment. I want to check her temp again."

The mom looked confused, but she nodded. Ryan whipped out the thermometer and placed it to Jasmine's forehead and then smiled up at Tyra, dropping the thermometer in her pocket. "Okay. Just double checking. You're good to go. They'll fill these prescriptions up in front at our pharmacy desk."

Tyra bit her lip. "Are they very expensive? It's just, I don't get paid till next week, and—"

"No charge."

Ryan smiled and waved bye-bye to Jasmine, who continued to peer at her over her mother's shoulder, mouthing the word "shiny."

When they'd walked out of sight, Ryan pulled her hand out of her pocket, clutching the thermometer she'd used to take the girl's temperature.

The thermometer that had read 101.5 on Jasmine only minutes earlier but had read 98.6 after the *shiny lady* touched her.

• • •

The rest of the day went by in a whirlwind, and she was far too busy to think about magic or supernatural creatures or special healing powers. Normal cases came in and got normal treatment.

Normal, normal, normal—everything her life suddenly wasn't anymore.

After her last patient walked out of the exam room, Ryan stretched, her back sore from a very full day. The clinic staff was bare bones even when nobody was out sick, so today had been a whirlwind. It was sometimes hard to find people with the time and inclination to donate that time to indigent patients.

Although, now that she had an idea of how much money Meara and Bane must have, she might put in a word that they hire more full-time staff doctors instead of depending on volunteers for so much.

Suddenly, to her surprise, she realized that she actually wouldn't mind being one of them. Her mind started to race with plans for what she might do if she had the chance to work here full-time. There were better policies and procedures that could be put in place and implemented. Higher standards of care. Better patient follow-up.

She shook her head. Always trying to think ten steps ahead, and now she only had to convince her new vampire friends to more fully fund their free clinics, instead of spending so much money on convertibles and mansions and ball gowns.

She glanced at her watch and grimaced. It was already seven, and she'd promised to be back by six p.m. when she ran into Mr. C in the kitchen at five in the morning. Bane hadn't returned yet, but Mr. C had convinced her that Bane, Luke, and Edge were fine, just "doing a sweep," whatever that meant.

The vampires would want to talk to her about the attacks and about Ryan's new Nephilim status, but Ryan wasn't ready for that conversation, and she didn't know when she would be. Still, time to woman up. She grabbed her bag, said good-bye, and rushed out to her car. When she pulled out her phone, she had eighteen missed messages, all from VMC ENTERPRISES.

Ouch.

She sighed, ignored the messages, and drove back to the mansion, preparing to face the music, hoping that the sight of her in the red ball gown made Bane forget that she'd been out of touch all day.

Except, *necromancers.*

She was probably out of luck.

She pushed the speaker button and called Bane, who answered almost before it rang.

"Where the *fuck* are you?"

She looked at her phone in disbelief and contemplated stopping for a cheeseburger and fries. Lots of fries.

And a beer or three.

"Nope," she finally said.

"What?"

"I said, nope. You do not get to tell me I'm a warrior goddess one day and then try to control my life the next. Or speak to me like that. And may I remind you, you never checked in with me when you were gone all night."

"But—"

"*And*," she continued, speaking right over him, "we still have to talk about that time you locked me in your room."

Silence.

"Bane?"

"Did Meara let you out?"

She pulled out onto Route 80. "No, I let myself out. My father used to pull that nasty little trick, so I learned to be fairly competent at picking locks. But if you think it's in any way a good thing to do something that makes me compare you to my asshole father, you're sadly mistaken."

"He's not your father."

"That actually makes me feel better," she snapped, making the turn at the light.

Another, longer, silence.

"I'm sorry," he finally said, just when she was about to hang up.

She sighed. "I forgive you, so long as you never do it again. There. Was that so hard?"

"You have no idea," he said fervently, and she burst out laughing.

"Are we going to talk about what we discovered about you last night?"

"No," she said firmly. "My capacity for new revelations ran out somewhere around the zombies. We're going to go to this party with Meara, and maybe even dance, and then we'll talk."

"Okay. Come back to me now."

"And there you go, ordering me around again." She sighed again, loudly this time, to be sure he heard it, and he laughed.

"Teaching a three-hundred-year-old vampire manners and consideration is going to be a full-time job, Dr. St. Cloud. I hope you feel you're up to it." His voice suddenly dropped low, all silken sin and seduction, and Ryan pressed down a little harder on the gas.

"I'll give it my best shot," she promised. "Maybe we can start tonight?"

"Perhaps. But first, we have a ball to attend. I hear you were questioning my ability to dance."

"I didn't —"

"Even stable boys can learn to waltz, Ryan. I look forward to showing you my…techniques."

And with that double-entendre hanging in her ears, he clicked the phone off.

Ryan blew through the speed limit all the way back to the house.

CHAPTER THIRTY-NINE

Bane forced himself to take a cold shower, for the third time that day, after talking to Ryan on the phone, just so he'd have some chance of not leaping on her and tearing her clothes off the second he saw her. But, then again, no.

Could a vampire have sex with a Nephilim? She hadn't electrocuted him yet, but that was before her powers were unlocked. Maybe a simple touch would kill him.

Maybe it would be worth it.

He was so finely attuned to her presence now that his skin tingled with electric sparks when he felt her drive up, but he stayed in the shower, face turned up to the cold spray. He would not humiliate himself over this woman.

He would *not*.

Each step she took—each word she exchanged with someone else in the house, before running to him—was torment. Each moment she spent *not* coming to him—torture.

He turned the temperature of the water to icy.

And then—finally—she was there.

Framed in the doorway to the bathroom, wearing blue scrubs with pictures of tiny animals on them, looking tired, and beautiful, and hesitant, and beautiful, and shy, and oh so incredibly, fuckably beautiful.

She bit her lip, and his cock came to fully rigid attention. "Hello. I'm back. Is Hunter doing okay?"

"He's still sleeping normally. Not that I'm particularly

pleased that you're looking at me, naked, and thinking of another man."

She smiled, her eyes flickering as her gaze skimmed his body. "Trust me, I'm not thinking about anybody but you. Um, do you want company?"

He changed the water temperature to one that would be comfortable for her creamy, delicious, glowy—*glowy? Oh, shit*—skin.

"You have no idea," he said, repeating his comment from earlier, and it made her laugh.

He reached out and barely touched her cheek with the tip of one finger, ready for the tiny bite of electricity that snapped at his skin. "You're starting to glow again."

Her breath caught in her throat. "Oh! I don't—will it be safe? For me to touch you?"

"*Please*, please try," he said, and he could hear her heartbeat speed up.

She stared at him, and he could hear her breath hitch when her gaze reached his cock. "Oh! Is that…are you…"

He wrapped his hand around its thickness and stroked once, hard. "You do this to me, Ryan. Please come join me. Let me touch you and taste you and fuck you. Let me do everything to you."

She blinked several times, and then her hands went to the waistband of her pants, and she slowly slid them off her hips and down her legs. Then she stood and pulled her shirt over her head and stood, shy but undaunted, in nothing but tiny blue scraps of silk.

He thought that waiting patiently for her to come to him might kill him, but he was afraid to go to her. Afraid he'd frighten her or drive her away. Instead, he held out his hand, in one of the most heroically restrained actions of his entire life. "Please."

She stared at him, poised for flight, but then she finally, *finally* nodded. "Yes."

And, wonder of wonders, miracle of miracles, she walked over to him and took his hand. She still wore her underclothes, which might have felt to her like protective armor against his ravenous gaze, but he could work with that. The glow was still barely there—just a hint of incandescence—but it was growing brighter by the moment.

He framed her face with his hands, catching his breath at the pinch of her power, already growing sharper. "I'll try not to overwhelm you. I don't know how to do this—I don't know how to feel so much. It has been a very long time since I let anyone close to my heart. But this...Ryan, what I feel for you compared to what I felt before is like comparing a tsunami to a dripping faucet. I am buffeted by what I feel for you. By my hunger for you, whether you're human or Nephilim or whatever else. *Please*. Please help me."

She trembled in his arms, the electric feel of her power sparkling against the drops of water on his skin, but she didn't look away. "It's so much, isn't it? Maybe too much. I feel so many things for you, too. Things I never expected to feel for anyone, ever. Just touching you is like grabbing hold of a hurricane with both hands and trying to find a way to hang on."

He grinned. "Well. If you really need something to hang on to, I have some ideas."

He moved his hands, caressing her shoulders, and her arms, and then sliding his hands around her waist and settling them on her lace-covered ass and pulling her body against the unmistakable evidence of his hunger for her, holding his breath in hope that her power would not rebuff him.

That she would not deny his claim on her body.

His claim on her heart.

Ryan gasped. "Wow. I mean, *wow*. But physiologically, I'm not sure that something that big is going to fit inside my—"

Before she could start listing the scientific names for genitalia, Bane gave in to the urge he'd been fighting since he heard her car in the driveway.

He kissed her, and his heart soared in his chest.

He kissed her and pulled her more fully into the shower. His mouth still covering hers, he moved so that she stood beneath the hot shower spray, which beat on her back and shoulders while she stood with his body wrapped around hers, ignoring the pain of her magic biting at his skin.

She shivered and clutched his shoulders, her Nephilim power slowly gentling from electric shock to a soft, buzzing sensation, and he stopped kissing her—just for a moment.

Just for long enough to say the words he seemed to be forgetting, since his mind was doing cartwheels in sheer ecstasy.

"Ryan. I want you. Please tell me you want me, too."

She shivered violently and stared up at him in silence, her gaze filled with an emotion he wished he could name. She shivered again, and he flicked the faucet to a warmer temperature.

"Are you cold?" He wondered if the glow flickering along her skin warmed her.

Wondered if it might consume him.

Wondered if he cared.

She looked up at him with those enormous blue eyes that he thought he might drown in. "I feel like I'll never be cold again."

"Ryan—"

"Yes. I want you, too."

Triumph swept through him, but kissing wasn't enough. "I need to touch all of you. Please. Tell me I can."

She bit her lip, and he immediately had to kiss her again, so it was several long moments before she could give him an answer. When he let her breathe again, she smiled brilliantly.

"Yes. Yes, Bane. Yes to touching me, yes to everything. Please. I want it *all*."

He whooped out a sound of pure joy and then snapped his fangs down and bit through the front of the fabric keeping him from putting his tongue on her nipples. When the shredded fabric fluttered to the ground, he took her breasts in his mouth, first one and then the other, and sucked on them until she shivered like she was about to come right there and then.

"More," she moaned, and he was happy to comply. He bent down and bit through the lace side of her underwear and pushed it down her legs and then looked his fill of her wet, naked body.

She opened her eyes and caught him staring, saw the primal possession that must be stamped on his face, and she blushed. "Bane. I want—"

"And I want to give it to you," he said, sliding one hand between her legs.

She moaned again but then put a hand on his to stop him. "No. I want—I want to pleasure *you* now."

Disbelief rocketed through him. "You think it's not pure pleasure, touching you?"

"I want to do more." She smiled at him and slid one still-glowing hand down his chest. "I want to do everything. Bane—I'm safe. Do we have a condom?"

He blinked, trying to focus. "Condoms. No, I don't—we can't catch any human illness or father children, so we don't need them."

She paused and then took a shaky breath. "Okay. That's a lot to think about. Later. For now..."

He watched her hand, completely hypnotized, as it continued down his body. As it wrapped around his cock. He jerked, his head falling back from the electric rush of the contact. Her touch branded him with pleasure. Her laughter brought him back to life.

Her kisses filled him with more warmth than he'd ever known in the bleak emptiness of his entire existence.

A nasty voice in the back of his mind asked him what he'd do when she finally realized what a monster he was and left him. Or when her angelic father showed up and tore her from him.

No.

He grasped her shoulders and pulled her up on her toes until they were face to face. "Don't leave me, Ryan."

"I'm not going anywhere," she said, but it wasn't enough, not nearly enough to counteract the sudden terror that enveloped him.

"Promise me," he demanded. "Swear it."

She stared into his eyes for what seemed like an eternity, and then she nodded. "I promise."

He wrapped his arms around her and held her tightly for a long, long while, until he could force his traitorous body to stop shuddering. And then, when he finally relaxed his grip, she flashed him a very naughty smile, bent down, and took his cock in her mouth.

He groaned, long and harsh, and his hands tangled in her hair, holding her in a gentle grip that she could escape at any time—desperate to feel all of it. Everything. Her lips and tongue tasted him, and then she gave a tentative suck, and a stronger one, and a sound he'd never made before wrenched its way out of his throat.

He was drowning in sensation—sure he might die from it—and then she wrapped one hand around the base of his cock and took his balls in her other hand, stroking and stroking, and licking and sucking, applying pressure and movement and friction, and he was almost certainly going to climb out of his skin, she was *driving him mad*.

He bucked against her, helpless to stop himself, sure she'd stop what she was doing since he was basically fucking her mouth, but instead she tightened her grip on his cock and moved her hand up and down in short, strong strokes, sucking his cock, licking the head, still stroking his balls, until he had no idea how he was still standing, and the stars themselves pinwheeled behind his closed eyelids and he shouted, he was coming, he was coming so damn hard his brain would surely burst, and she sucked on him and licked him and sucked it all down, and he convulsively jerked, again and again, beneath her hands and mouth, until finally, he was drained of both seed and strength.

This time, it had been he who shouted *her* name.

He stood there, leaning back against the tile wall, touching her hair and her face, gasping in air, unable to think or breathe or speak, and she stood and put her arms around his neck.

"Bane," she said proudly, her beautiful face alight with a smile. "I *am* a goddess."

Before she could say another word, he was fucking her.

• • •

Ryan gasped when Bane yanked her up off her feet, put her legs around his waist, and drove his cock inside her. First, she lost her breath.

Then she lost her mind.

And her body—all of it—lit up from within with sensation.

Lit up with actual, honest-to-angel, light.

"You—*ohhhhh,*" she said, her eyes rolling back in her head. "Am I hurting you? The electric shock, I, you, *ohhhhhhh.*"

"Definitely not hurting me," he growled, thrusting into her body again and again. Kissing her face, her neck, her lips.

"You certainly recover quickly. I didn't think—oh, *yes*— that the blood supply to the corpora cavernosa could—"

"Ryan," he growled.

"Yes?"

"Shut up."

"Okay."

Normally, she would have protested, but her body had different ideas and kept arching up to meet his deep, deep thrusts, and he was holding her and driving his body inside her, over and over, in a timeless rhythm that had little to do with skill or finesse and everything to do with *want* and *need* and *now*.

She felt her inner muscles accommodate him, pulsing around him, welcoming his invasion into her most private place, and she leaned her head back and moaned, closing her eyes, becoming a creature of pure sensation—pure pleasure—pure desire.

Slowly, and then with an almost-impossibly rising heat and frenzy, her passion rose to meet his, and they came together in a symphony of magical sensation.

"More," he growled. "Take more of me. Take *all* of me."

And she nodded, widening her legs even further, adjusting the angle of her hips to accommodate his size. When he took immediate advantage, thrusting deeper and harder than ever before, she cried out and dug her nails into his back, urging him on. Urging him to take her with him to the next crest, to the next orgasm, to the next adventure.

This was the most wildly *unreliable* she'd ever been, and she reveled in it, she wanted it, she *demanded* it. His body was all long, lean muscle and beauty—so much beauty—and he was hers, blood and bone, heart and soul, in this minute, in the foreseeable future, in her dreams, in her reality. She kissed him, or he kissed her, again and again, drinking in his mouth and his heat and his need and making it her own, until she couldn't breathe, couldn't think—until she turned into a being made up of pure, incandescent desire.

"Now," he demanded, gasping for breath. "Come for me,

Ryan. I want to feel your hot, wet body squeeze my cock. Come for me *now.*"

And she did, she came *screaming*, and everything that she was and ever had been shattered into a prism of brilliant light that lit the room like the brightest day.

Almost immediately, he shouted out his own triumph, pounding into her and convulsing, bucking his hips against her, coming and coming, until both of them, shuddering and panting for their next breaths, floated slowly back to earth together.

When the corona of light surrounding them finally dimmed, she melted against him, and her legs, feeling boneless, slid down from around his waist. He leaned his head back in the miraculously still-hot running water and let it run down his face. Then he pulled her into his arms again and kissed her, long and slow and gentle.

"Maybe sex is just better with Nephilim," she mused, barely able to think.

"Ryan."

She kissed him again, leisurely and oh so satiated. "Yes, Bane?"

The expression on his face was the epitome of smug male satisfaction, but she had a feeling her face carried the female version of that exact same look, so she let it slide.

He flashed a wicked grin. "How's *that* for a corpora cavernosa?"

CHAPTER FORTY

Ryan draped her boneless body over Bane's in his new bed and snuggled up against him and into the multitude of pillows that Mrs. C must have arranged—men never thought of pillows—and sighed in sheer, blissful contentment.

"I can tell you quite honestly that I have never, ever had sex like that," she said, her mind still completely blown.

He grinned. "Just call me Captain Orgasm."

"I'll never call you Captain Orgasm."

"Your Highness, the king of Orgasmia?" He put one arm behind his head and stretched, still with that ridiculously smug grin plastered all over his face.

She lifted her head and stared at him in disbelief. "You do realize that I have access to scalpels? And sedatives that can quite literally stop your heart, right?"

In a vampire-quick movement, he flipped her over and pinned her to the bed and then started kissing her neck. "Violent little thing for a baby angel, aren't you?"

"Hey!" She poked him in the chest. "*I'm* not the one who bit *your* neck."

His smile faded. "Ryan. I'm so sorry for that. I promise to never—"

"No." She put her fingers on his lips. "Don't make any promises that might be hard to keep. Let's play this by ear, okay?"

Bane dropped his head to her shoulder and groaned.

"It's not that I don't forgive you," she rushed to tell him.

"It's just—"

"Not that. It's Meara," he said, yanking the sheet up to cover them both.

"What?"

The door banged open, and Meara came striding into the room. "I wondered what was taking you so long," she said, glaring at them. "Bane, get your naked self off my plus-one. We have a ball to get ready for."

Ryan giggled like a fool. "We already had our own ball."

"I can see that," Meara snapped, but a smile played at the edges of her lips. "Get up. We need to get dressed."

"First, we *need* to talk about the fact that Ryan is a Nephilim," Bane growled. "That's more important than some stupid dance."

Ryan, who'd been hiding under the covers, closed her eyes. "I'm not going to the ball, Meara. I'm exhausted, and I'm really not the ball kind of person. Why don't you take Edge?"

Meara leapt onto the bed and stood staring down at them. "We're *all* going to the ball. Do you want to know why?"

Bane narrowed his eyes. "Get off my bed, Meara. And why don't you leave my bedroom while you're at it?"

Meara lightly jumped back down to the floor but showed no signs of leaving. "We're all going to the ball because the necromancer is the *host*."

Bane sat up. "What did you say?"

"You heard me. I just happened to dig out the invitation today. *Sylvie Chambers* requests our presence, blah, blah, blah. *Sylvie Chambers,* Bane."

Ryan gathered the covers against her chest and sat up,

too, and asked the obvious question, even though she was sure she wouldn't like the answer. "Why is that important?"

"*Chambers.*"

"Oh. On the nose, much?" Ryan's wonderful mood slowly drained away. "Is she taunting us? Or pulling a *Gatsby* to get us to attend her party?"

Bane's entire body went rigid. "Damn them. Fine. Now get out so we can get dressed. But Ryan is not going anywhere near the place."

Ryan sighed. "Not again. Look—"

"They've probably figured it out by now, Meara. And you know what necromancers would love to have? The blood of a Nephilim. She's staying here."

"My blood?" Ryan narrowed her eyes. "You need to explain—"

Meara spoke over her. As usual. "You'd leave her alone, at a time like this?"

"I am *right here*," Ryan shouted.

The two of them glanced at her and then exchanged a glare that seemed to carry an entire conversation within it, and then Bane nodded. "Right. So. Ryan. How would you like to attend a ball with me?"

"Why not? I already have a dress."

• • •

As it turned out, she also had a makeup artist, a hair stylist, and the shoes, jewels, and even underwear that went with the dress. Meara had insisted on a blood-red silk gown with a fitted, plunging bodice—to "show off the girls!"—and Ryan had to admit it was the most beautiful, flattering garment she'd ever worn in her life. There was a discreet slit in the front of the voluminous skirt, and the delicate shoes had three-inch heels that Ryan hoped she'd be able to walk in, let alone dance.

Unfortunately, her mind spent more time churning over the revelation that Sylvie and God only knew how many other warlocks and necromancers would be at the party than it did on appreciating her party dress.

By the time the various professionals were done with her, though, she was awestruck and even secretly thought that she might look almost as good as Meara, and though half her brain was consumed over worry about Sylvie and her necromancer pals, the rest of her brain was distracted by the most movie-perfect makeover of all time. When they steered her over to the full-length mirror in Meara's salon-sized dressing room, she took one look and almost fell out of her fashionable new shoes.

"That's...that's *me*?" It *couldn't* be her. Not Reliable Ryan, who lived in scrubs at work and yoga pants at home. Who rarely wore makeup, except on the occasional evening out with Annie. Who had never, not once, been the belle of any ball—or even the center of attention in a campus pub.

And who now, evidently, was half angel and sleeping with a vampire.

She pushed away thoughts of how a life could change in less than a week and focused on her reflection. Her hair was pulled back and partially up, leaving long curls to frame her face, and she had smoky eyes and shiny lips. Her skin glowed like it never had before...actually, on second thought, she'd had that glow before they applied any makeup at all.

She had Bane to thank for that. Bane and her long-lost, apparently heavenly, father.

Tears started to burn at the back of her eyes, but she forced them away, because she didn't want to ruin her makeup. She whirled to face the team of helpers who'd arrived to prepare her and Meara for the ball.

"Thank you! Thank you so much. I can't—you're both amazing. I've never looked so good in my entire life. You're both wizards!"

"They're not wizards," Meara called out from the other room. "No beards, no familiars."

The makeup artist, Candice, looked puzzled. "What?"

"Oh, she likes her little jokes," Ryan said hastily.

"Anyway, we're not wizards," Jane said, putting her hair tools back in her rolling case. "You have great hair and good bone structure. You just need to play it up a bit. And, of course, Meara is so gorgeous she's practically not human, you know what I mean?"

"I know exactly what you mean," Ryan said, wondering what the women would think if they ever found out just how *not human* their client actually was.

Probably some of the running and screaming Meara had mentioned when Ryan first met her.

"How much do we owe you? I'll go get my purse."

Jane waved her away. "Meara keeps us on retainer. And she includes tips, too, so you're good. Just put in a good word for us to your fancy friends tonight, if anybody asks, okay? We working girls need all the help we can get these days."

"I hear you," Ryan said, but she could tell from their discreet glances at each other that they thought she was a rich socialite or something.

"Well, thank you again. I can't tell you how much I appreciate it."

They showed themselves out, and Ryan went back to admiring herself in the mirror because, damn, she was worth admiring.

"Warrior goddess, indeed," she murmured. "This is almost a *Pretty Woman* moment, except without the prostitution."

Meara came out of her bedroom then. "What *are* you talking about? You do realize you're a very odd human, right? Or—I guess I can't say that anymore, little Nephilim."

"You could lose the 'little,' too." She turned around and actually gasped out loud. "Meara! You're too beautiful to even be real!"

The vampire wore a coppery-colored sheath that hugged her slim form and perfectly complemented her amazing golden eyes. Her hair was twisted up in a knot, she wore ridiculously high heels and simple jewelry, and the entire effect was stunning.

"I know," Meara said, preening, but then she whistled. "Why, Dr. St. Cloud. You're an absolute beauty. My brother is not going to know what hit him."

"Neither will Computer Guy," Ryan said, grinning.

Meara looked away, a faint blush staining her perfect cheekbones. "Not that I care."

"Of course not," Ryan agreed, tongue firmly in cheek.

Meara narrowed her eyes but didn't rise to the bait. "Shall we go, then?"

"We shall. But the hardest part of tonight might be

negotiating the stairs in these heels." Ryan laughed. "I'm not exactly good at this. I wear sensible shoes at work."

"Sensible shoes." Meara shuddered. "We need to get you a new job."

"Speaking of that," Ryan began, thinking of the clinic and her new abilities. Her new plans.

"Later. Now, we go dance."

. . .

Bane paced back and forth at the bottom of the stairs, from the kitchen to the salon, changing his mind at least a hundred times about allowing Ryan to attend this damn ball with him.

Not that she'd let him get away with the idea of "allowing" her to do anything.

But if Constantin and Sylvie had an army backing them up, he didn't want Ryan anywhere near the place.

And yet, he didn't want her to be alone, where he couldn't protect her, if the necromancers were coordinating an attack on him.

"Damn them," he snarled.

Edge shot him an impatient look from his perch on a chair in the parlor. "Damn who, exactly? The Chamber? The warlocks? The shifters? Meara and Ryan, who have been making us wait here, dressed up like penguins, for more than an hour?"

Bane stopped pacing and grinned at the scientist. "Hey. You may be a penguin, but I make this tuxedo look *good*."

Edge rolled his eyes. He'd definitely been hanging out with Meara too much.

A slight noise alerted him to Ryan finally arriving at the top of the stairs, and he walked out to the hallway to wait for her.

And then, for the second time that day, the bottom fell out of his world.

It wasn't the clothes.

It wasn't the paint on her face.

Or the way her hair was done, or the fancy shoes.

It was the sheer joy—the confidence and delight—in her expression when she looked down at him that punched him right in the gut. She was *his*, this woman, this fascinating, infuriating, warrior goddess; he knew it utterly and completely in that moment, and his heart expanded in his chest until he thought it must burst free of skin and bone and fill the room.

Mine.

"What do you think?" She held her skirt up and showed him her shoes. "Pretty much a Cinderella moment, right?"

"You're the most beautiful woman I've ever known, but that has nothing to do with the dress," he told her, his sincerity ringing in his voice.

Her answering smile lit up the world.

CHAPTER FORTY-ONE

Bane stared up at the front of the historic mansion and remembered when the home had been built, back in the early 1900s, along with so many of the homes that were now registered in Savannah's National Historic Landmark District.

Maybe that made *him* a national historic landmark, too.

Ryan took a tighter hold on his arm and sighed after Tommy, departing in the limo. "I vote we go watch movies and order pizza. This is not my kind of place. Too fancy."

Meara, standing very carefully not too close to Edge, snorted. "Our house is both bigger and fancier than this one, and you're very comfortable there, considering what you were doing just before I came to get you."

"Enough, already," Edge growled. "Can we just go in and get this over with?" The scientist had been unable to take his eyes off Meara ever since she'd appeared at the top of the stairs in that dress, and he'd strongly and repeatedly made his objections to the plan known on the drive over. "And we took the damn limo, like a bunch of fools," he continued. "How exactly do we make a fast getaway in a limo?"

"Luke is bringing your car now. It will be parked just across from Forsyth Park, there," Bane said, pointing. "Surely the Ferrari is fast enough to qualify as a getaway car?"

They believed that Bane could carry Ryan off through

the Between, if need be, because he hadn't wanted to burden them with the knowledge that Sylvie had been able to block his access to the Shadows.

This might not even be anything to do with Constantin and Sylvie, though. As Edge had pointed out more than once, there were roughly thirty-two people named Chambers for every hundred thousand Americans, according to the census data.

When he'd said *census data*, Meara had started swearing in French. From the way Ryan had flinched, she had a fairly good grasp on the language, too, at least when it came to *pig-brained ass of a diseased rodent* and other colorful expressions. Edge, however, had just looked baffled, as he so often did around Meara.

"Now, we join them and go inside," Meara said, nodding at the stream of Savannah's elite who were streaming into the mansion. "And we see what's what, because this is clearly no *census data* Chambers."

Bane nodded. "I smell it."

Ryan glanced up at him, puzzled. "Smell what?"

"Rot," Edge snapped, and then he offered Meara his arm. "Shall we?"

Now absolutely convinced that this was a terrible idea, but having none better come to mind, Bane led them into what was almost certainly a trap.

"We should at least dance before the shouting and the killing starts. After all, when am I going to look this good again?"

He glanced down in disbelief, only to realize that Ryan was attempting a joke, a fake smile pasted on her gorgeous face. Damn, but she was brave. He impulsively bent to kiss her cheek and lingered to whisper in her ear.

"Maybe later, we can dance naked, and you'll look even better."

She blushed, and her smile deepened and turned into something real, just in time for them to walk past the first of what was sure to be several levels of security: two large men dressed in dark, police-like uniforms.

SHIFTER, Meara sent telepathically, and he nodded.

But the shifters, who should have known what they were, said nothing and barely even looked at them as they walked past.

BLOOD-THRALLED, he sent to Edge and Meara, who nodded.

Ryan elbowed him in the side.

"What was that for?"

She smiled brightly, as if she were telling him something delightful. "Stop doing that. The secret vampire telepathy. I want to know what's going on, too," she said very quietly.

Fair enough. If he'd been a human walking into this, he'd also have wanted all the information he could get. Hell, he was a powerful vampire with magic in his own right, and he wanted all the information. Or, at least, more than he had now.

He put an arm around her waist and pulled her closer then bent to kiss the top of her head. "The security guards are shifters, but they seem to be thralled. No sign of any warlocks yet, in spite of the smell of necromancer."

She laughed, as if he'd told her something funny, and he realized she was good at this—at *going undercover*, as she'd called it in the car. In fact, she fit into his world far better than any human ever had before.

He wasn't sure what to do with that, but now certainly wasn't the time to analyze it.

Now was the time to beware.

• • •

The inside of the mansion was far more showplace than home, and Ryan gasped when she saw it. Decorated for the party with flowers and tiny, twinkling lights wherever she looked, the house was like a dowager lady displaying her wealth to her best advantage, and the rich, glittering people mingling inside were the jewels in the old girl's tiara.

She wondered how many parties this house had seen. How many love affairs had begun or ended right here in this ballroom or out on the terrace, beneath the bright, indifferent gaze of the stars. Probably more than she could count.

"It would be interesting to read about the history of this house," she told Bane, who shrugged. He was so extraordinarily beautiful in his tuxedo that she could barely tear her gaze from him. She wanted to stare at him and touch him and shout at anybody else who even looked at him.

And there were a *lot* of people looking at him, damn them. But…there were a lot of people looking at her, too.

"Why read about it?" Bane asked, and she had to think back to what they were talking about. "Humans built it, lived in it, and died in it, much like any other house. They just spent more money while doing so."

She sighed. "I can tell you're going to be too much of a sappy romantic for me, Bane. It's all hearts and flowers, all the time."

He tightened his grip on her waist. "If you want romance, I can throw that man who keeps staring at your breasts out the window," he said darkly.

She followed his gaze. "Bane, violence is not romance. Anyway, that window is closed."

"*I know.*"

She grinned. "Come on, let's look around. It's the normal, human thing to do when you get invited to a place like this, so it won't even look suspicious that we're wandering about, unlike Meara, who is stalking around the place like she's a general on patrol."

Edge was doing his best to keep up with her, but Meara was moving at a pace that was too fast and too graceful to be fully human. Ryan just hoped nobody noticed until they found what—or who—they were searching for.

"I have a better idea." He pulled her along with him to another enormous room, maybe another ballroom or grand salon. A string quartet was playing, and some people were dancing.

"May I have this dance?" He bowed, just as if he truly had been the European prince she'd first imagined him to be, and she put her hand in his and followed him onto the dance floor.

When he put his other hand on her waist and began to move, she snapped out of the romantic haze that the entire situation had put her in and admitted the horrible truth. "I don't really know how to dance like this, Bane," she whispered urgently, sure she'd trip and make a fool of herself at any second, since not only was she now dancing—was it a waltz?—but she was *dancing backward and in high heels.* "Or, you know, at all."

"Trust me," he murmured, and she did; somehow, she did, and somehow, she was dancing, following his lead. And so the stable boy who grew up to become a vampire led the lonely little girl who grew up to be a doctor in a dance, in one of the most opulent homes in all of Savannah.

And—for several precious minutes—it was magical.

She stared into Bane's eyes and imagined she could see forever. She'd promised never to leave him. That didn't sound like *temporary*. Didn't feel like *disposable*.

Forever, or at least as long as she wanted, until she grew old and faded away, as humans did, and Bane lived on without her. She flinched from the thought of that, tried to push it out of her mind, but then wondered, for the very first time: how long did Nephilim live?

No. Too much to think about now, when danger might be all around them.

Later. Later, she'd look for answers to all of this. For now, she'd enjoy this dance.

"I love this," she told him. "Dancing. I wish I could give you a gift as wonderful as the gift of this dance."

He pulled her into a twirl, and her incredible dress swirled around her, and then he bent his head and kissed her, right there on the dance floor, never missing a step, making sure that she never missed one, either. "The only gift I need, Ryan, is you."

When the music ended, at least the music in the room— the music in her heart still sang its wordless melody of hope and light *and…love?* —Bane nodded toward the stairs.

"If there are warlocks here, they'll be up there somewhere, keeping an eye on everything. We should go look around. Remember, at the slightest sign of trouble, you run. Got it?"

She nodded, slightly off-balance from his abrupt switch from sweet words to steely warrior, but she knew how important this was—they'd finally explained fully about the warlocks on the way over—so she turned her mind to cataloging everything and everyone she saw, so she could hopefully be of some help.

But in the end, the necromancer, or at least the necromancer's flunky, came to them.

The man was rather short, with ordinary brown hair and an ordinary face. He looked like an accountant or a middle manager for an insurance company. He wore a plain suit, not a tuxedo, and he stood, unsmiling, waiting for them to notice that he'd followed them into a relatively small, second-floor library.

When Bane whirled to face him, the man said nothing, just pulled back his sleeve to show the triangle tattoo on his left wrist. Bane immediately put himself between Ryan and the stranger.

"You know who we are," the little man said in a calm, pleasant voice. "I've been sent to tell you that we are claiming this territory. Leave or die."

Bane's eyes flashed red, and he bared his fully descended fangs. "And if I kill you and toss your body into the Savannah River?"

The man shrugged. "It would make no difference to anyone but myself, as you probably know."

"Take this message back to your masters. This is my territory, and I'll defend it to the death. If they know anything about me at all, they know what that means."

The man inclined his head and turned to leave the room, but when he reached the doorway, he glanced back and fixed his mild gaze on Ryan. "Remember, perhaps, that those you care for are not as invulnerable as you might wish. And now, Sylvie and Constantin know it."

And then he was gone.

Bane raced after him but stopped when he reached the door, scanned the hallway beyond in both directions, and then shook his head.

"He vanished. Warlock games," he said grimly, striding back across the room to Ryan. "We're leaving. Now."

Then he gazed into the distance with the expression that Ryan had learned meant he was communicating telepathically with the others. After a moment, his attention returned to her.

"Right. We're traveling through the Between. This time, no screaming or fighting me, please. Is that enough notice?"

"Wait—does it—"

But he didn't wait. Shadows came from nowhere to coalesce around them, and Bane swept her up into his arms and stepped forward into a hurricane. All Ryan could do was hold on.

CHAPTER FORTY-TWO

When they arrived back at the house, stepping out of the Between and into the ballroom, Bane's first inclination was to carry Ryan off to his rooms, strip off every inch of her finery, and console himself with the pleasure of her body.

Ryan, however, had other plans.

"Have I mentioned how much I hate traveling like that?" Ryan sat down on a bench and pulled off her shoes with an expression of blissful relief and then glared at him. "How can you stand it? I feel like my molecules are being scrambled."

He shrugged. "It doesn't affect me that way. Perhaps because you're human? Meara has had no problem traveling with me, either."

She sighed and then glanced at the door to the safe room. "Bane, we should check on Hunter."

He felt a nasty tug of guilt. With everything happening, he'd almost forgotten about his friend and the Turn. And tonight should be the night Hunter came out of it. When he opened the door to the safe room, however, the firefighter still slept in the deep coma of the Turn.

"Maybe since he only truly entered this state later, he'll be in it longer?" He looked at Ryan, as if being a human doctor meant she'd have any idea about this.

"I do have some thoughts about the anemia that his blood test showed me, but I need to compare his sample with yours to draw any valid conclusions," she told him, putting on what he thought of as her doctor face. She'd start talking about carotid arteries or corpora cavernosa any minute.

Ridiculously, he found that he liked serious Dr. St. Cloud very much. And that made him want to take her to bed.

Everything made him want to take her to bed. Maybe it was the angel blood? But no—he'd felt like this when her magic had been bound.

"Why don't we go to my rooms and try that naked dancing we talked about earlier?" he murmured after safely sealing the door to the safe room again. But when he tried to kiss her, she slipped away, shaking her head.

"Keep the tux on for a little while longer. I like you in it," she whispered. "And stay right here. I have a surprise for you."

With that, she ran lightly down the stairs, barefoot this time, and he heard her calling out a greeting to Tommy and Mary Jo. Maybe she wanted some food?

But in only a few minutes, she raced back up the stairs, followed by the Cassidys. Mary Jo was grinning like a delighted child, but Tommy looked exhausted or ill. He was walking behind Ryan, so she didn't see it, because Bane had no doubt that when she did, she'd slip into doctor mode and take care of Mr. C.

Like she kept taking care of *him*.

"I have a gift for you, Bane," Ryan said, clasping her hands and all but dancing with glee. "But you have to close your eyes for a minute."

"Nothing good ever started like that," he muttered.

Bram Stoker picked that moment to gallop into the

room, barking, so it took a minute to get him to calm down. Ryan leaned over and kissed the top of the dog's silky head, and Bane realized he was feeling envious of a dog.

Mrs. C started laughing. "Oh, I can think of a few things that got started with closed eyes. When you gave us those cruise tickets, we found ourselves alone on the deck one night, and—"

"Okay, okay," he said hastily. "I'm closing my eyes. What now?"

"Hold still," Ryan said, brushing against him and then startling him by putting some form of hat—no, helmet, definitely helmet—on his head.

"Hold out your hand," she demanded, and then she put a cylindrical object on his palm.

Then Bane heard whispering, giggling, and rustling noises, before Ryan finally spoke again.

"Okay. Open your eyes."

When Bane, feeling unsure and vulnerable, opened his eyes, he took one look and shouted an unintelligible sound, and then he looked around again. "What the *hell*?"

Somehow, through some magic he already knew must be science, he stood, in bright noon sunlight, directly in front of Buckingham Palace.

He was back in London.

He was *back in London*.

He whirled around, and the images stayed with him. He was *inside a movie, in the daylight, in London*.

And he had Ryan to thank.

He held out the hand not holding the remote, because, of course, that's what he held. This must be a virtual reality device; he kept up with technology, so he'd known about them.

But he hadn't *known* about them.

She took his hand, and he held on as if to a lifeline while he stared in wonder at the milling crowds of tourists and the guards, standing impassively, and the cars going by, while he listened to the sound of Big Ben in the distance.

"You can go almost anywhere in London, well, anywhere that they've mapped," she told him, and he could hear Mary Jo chuckling.

"Were you all in on this?"

"The doc went out on her lunch break and bought the system, and I set it up for her while you were at the party," Tommy said quietly. "Got a chance to see where Molly lives, too. Thanks for thinking of that, Doc. Awful nice of you."

It was beyond *nice*. It was the kindest thing anyone had ever done for him. That she would think of Tommy and Mary Jo, too, was astonishing. No, not astonishing or even unexpected.

It was pure Ryan: pure grace, and joy, and kindness.

"Try the Tower of London," she urged him. "It's exactly right! I even followed the path through the place where they keep the crown jewels!"

Bane discovered how to work the control, still holding tightly to her hand, and he spent the next half hour exploring London...both the London of his childhood, which was still there, albeit superimposed by a veneer of modernity, and the London of today, built on the sturdy bones of buildings created by architects long dead.

"There! There's the church where the priest would give us food if we could perfectly recite the Lord's Prayer." He grimaced, remembering how many times he'd gone hungry at first, too damn stubborn to offer up his prayers for the pompous ass's satisfaction.

"And if you didn't?" Ryan's voice was filled with outrage on his behalf, and yet another cracked, barren inch of his long-dead heart split open and came back to life.

"No food. Sometimes they'd beat us out in the court-yard."

"Those bastards!" This was Mrs. C's voice speaking. Anything to do with harming children would stir her mama wolf instincts.

"Agree," Ryan growled. And then, softer, "Bane. If this is bringing back bad memories—"

"No!" He laughed and pulled her close for a hug, careful not to smack her in the face with his bulky helmet. "No, a thousand times no. This is the most amazing gift anyone has ever given me."

He heard the click of high heels over the rushing sounds of London traffic in his headset, and his sister spoke up.

"Well, that's saying a lot, considering I bought you that Lamborghini last year," Meara said. "What the hell are you wearing?"

Reluctantly, he pulled the headset off, feeling like his face might split in two from the enormous smile he couldn't seem to shake. "I was in London, Meara. In the *daylight*!"

Ryan smiled shyly. "You gave me this amazing dress, Meara. And the hair and the styling…I wanted to give you Paris."

His sister stared blankly at first Ryan and then at Bane. She wasn't much for technology, so she might not even know such a thing as VR existed. Behind her, Edge scowled, no doubt kicking himself for not thinking of doing this for her.

Ryan took the equipment from Bane's hands and made a few adjustments, and then she asked Meara to close her eyes.

When Meara opened her eyes to find herself in Paris, in the daylight, she gasped. "Oh! Oh, *mon Dieu!* Oh! *Notre-Dame de Paris!*"

"It's Notre Dame before the fire," Ryan said. "So probably just as you knew it."

Bane then was treated to the fascinating experience of watching Meara rediscover the city of her childhood, in the full light of day. When Ryan walked back over to stand next to him, he realized her face was wet, and he hugged her to him.

"I'm sorry," she said, her voice muffled by his jacket. "I'm an easy crier these days."

"Never apologize to me. Your tears are merely your heart's goodness overflowing."

She sniffled, and then she looked up at him, her eyes shining. "Did you really like it?"

"I *love*…it," he said, catching himself from making the declaration right there in the ballroom in front of everyone. Knowing he'd tell her the truth, soon.

He loved her. He'd fallen in love with her. He wasn't sure when, exactly, it had happened, but he'd fully realized it upon seeing London. Feeling the full impact of the wondrous and incredibly thoughtful gift Ryan had given him. And again, while watching his sister, hearing her cries of joy at seeing her beloved Paris again. He'd never forget this moment, if he lived to be a thousand years old.

And if the Chamber kills me? Then what do I have to give Ryan?

He tightened his arms around her. Tomorrow. He'd think about that tomorrow and plot and plan his attack and counterstrike. It would take time for his message to get back to the higher-ups in Europe and for them to decide on a measure and implement it. He'd also need to protect them all from Constantin and Sylvie.

Tonight, though, he just wanted to enjoy being here, with his family. With Ryan.

"This is amazing!" Meara shrieked, spinning around in a circle. "Where can I go next?"

"The software has settings for most major cities in the world and all the major historical sites," Ryan offered. "Maybe—"

"The Taj Mahal!" A few seconds later, Meara's peals of laughter rang through the room. "An elephant just walked right by me!"

"Ooh! I'd like to see that," Mrs. C said. "And what about the Blarney Stone? The west coast of Ireland, where our people come from?"

"And what would *you* like to do now, Doctor? Anything you want is yours." Bane spoke quietly, since everyone else was chattering excitedly about the VR. Everyone but Edge, who continued to brood in a corner, scowling. Bane felt a moment of sympathy for the poor man. Meara would lead him on a merry chase.

Ryan put her hands on his face and looked into his eyes

and said, "Anything?"

"Anything," he said, fantasizing about what *anything* might encompass.

"I'd like to go to my apartment so I can check my mail and water my plants."

He blinked and then started to laugh. "Well, I did say anything. Shall we get changed and go?"

She stopped him with a hand on his chest. "This time, let's take the car."

Before they could sneak out of the room, though, Tommy collapsed, moaning, to the floor.

Bram Stoker rushed over to him and started sniffing him, barking like a fool, and Mrs. C tried to pull the dog away.

Bane went to help her, but then he paused. "Wait. Look!"

The dog was nosing Tommy's front pocket and whining.

"I don't want to go all *Timmy's down the well* here, but is it possible that there's something in his pocket that is causing this?" Luke grimaced. "I mean, it's just a thought, with warlocks around. I know they use charms and stuff sometimes."

"No, it's a good idea," Bane said. He knelt and reached into the old man's pocket, and something in there burned his hand.

He swore viciously but managed to hang onto the metal object for long enough to get it out of the pocket and toss it across the room.

Meara stalked over to it. "A gold coin. Looks extremely old. It stinks like magic, too."

But Tommy was still moaning, and he'd started jerking

and twitching with what looked like the beginning of convulsions.

"Out of my way, please," Ryan said briskly. She knelt down next to Tommy and put a hand on his forehead, and the man's eyes flew open. He stared at her with wild eyes, and then he started screaming.

"None of that," she told him, and then, with a quick glance up at Bane, she put both hands on Mr. C's cheeks and leaned closer to him.

And then she—both of them—started to glow.

Within seconds, it was over. The glow vanished, and Tommy, looking tired but less gray and drained than he had before, sat up and hugged his wife.

"You're a miracle," Mrs. C said to Ryan, utterly awed.

"I'm a doctor," Ryan said, smiling. "With maybe a little extra juice."

"I don't know what happened to me or where I got that coin, but I could feel it was wrong," Mr. C muttered brokenly. "I tried to take it out of my pocket, but I couldn't, and I tried to ask for help, and I couldn't do that, either. I'm so sorry, Boss. It was—somehow, I could *feel* him, inside my brain. He was trying to send you nightmares."

Bane felt like he'd been punched in the gut. He'd definitely had the nightmares. And now, here was the proof that he'd failed to protect his own people.

"I'm so sorry, Tommy. I should have warded you, as well as the house. Both of you. We'll do that before you leave the house again, okay? For now, you should get some sleep."

Luke helped the Cassidys down to their quarters, and Meara, who'd left the room, came back with a bandanna in one hand and a small wooden box in the other. She carefully wrapped up the coin and dropped it into the box.

"I'll go online right now and ask the monks for the proper way to destroy that," she told them.

Edge touched her arm. "I'm coming with you, if that's okay."

She nodded, and they headed down the hall toward Meara's room and the waiting computer.

"This is bad," Ryan said. "I guess this means we're not going out?"

Bane pulled Ryan into his arms. "They know this place, not yours. I think it's safe enough. And thank you for giving me London. You *are* a miracle."

She sighed. "The miracle needs a cheeseburger. You up for a drive-thru?"

CHAPTER FORTY-THREE

After devouring a fast-food meal, Ryan surprised herself by dozing off in the car on the way to her place, worn out from a long day and the healing—healings?—she'd done. Staying up all night might be fun when she could sleep all day, but she'd worked a full shift at the clinic, and her life had been more than a little draining this week, too.

Heh. *Draining.* Now she was doing it.

"Was that your Nephilim power? Did you—have you learned how to channel it?"

She yawned. "I don't know. Maybe? Something happened at the clinic with a sick little girl, and I just thought—maybe it was instinct—that I could help Mr. C. I'm glad it worked."

"It's definitely something for you to explore," he said lightly, but his grim expression didn't match his tone.

When Bane pulled the sleek car—his; he'd refused to ride in the Prius—to a stop outside her townhouse, she stretched. "Maybe we can get a nap, too."

His quick grin was almost predatory. "Is *nap* code for *get naked and see what happens*?"

She laughed, but it turned into another yawn. "No, it was pretty much just nap. It has been a very long day. But maybe I could be convinced."

"I've scanned the area but feel nothing out of the ordinary. Still, we know necromancers can mask their presence, so let's move quickly."

They quickly exited the car and raced up the stairs, and when she unlocked her door, she was relieved to see that her housekeeper—her one monthly splurge, since she worked such long hours—had been there. The place smelled like lemons instead of stale wine.

She reached over to flip on the light switch and tossed her keys in the bowl on the table by the door.

And then the world exploded.

• • •

Lights, flashing.

Darkness.

Pain.

Bane's face, a cruel slash with red, red eyes.

Darkness.

Pain.

Annie, bending over her, tears welling in her beautiful eyes.

Darkness.

Pain.

The O.R.—except the perspective was all wrong. She was on the table, instead of standing over it, and Meara's piano was crushing her chest. She couldn't breathe, and they wouldn't listen to her. Nobody wanted to dance; the music was dying.

Darkness.

Pain.

Annie, again, this time in a brightly lit room filled with flowers.

Trying to speak. Her voice broken and rusty. "Bane?"

Tears on Annie's face. "Oh, honey, I know there's pain. But you're alive, and you're going to stay that way. It was touch and go there for a while, but we got you back."

"Bane," she tried again but then slipped back into the darkness and the pain. So much pain.

A nurse, one of her favorites. Henry.

The pain, again—and then the coolness of relief.

She let the ocean of waiting dark pull her back down. Bane would come. He'd said *forever*.

He would come.

• • •

He didn't come.

But, at dawn, her father did, and he took the darkness and the pain away.

CHAPTER FORTY-FOUR

Bane lost his mind to berserker rage when the explosion harmed Ryan, and he never found his way back to reason.

When the bomb came through the window, he'd thrown himself between it and Ryan, but he'd been too late, too slow, too useless, too fucking *arrogant* in his belief that he could protect her. He'd expected magic, not technology. The walking dead, not human-made explosives.

By the time his body had healed itself enough that he could open his eyes, the humans with their fire trucks and ambulances had arrived, and he'd had barely enough strength to conceal his presence from them. He'd watched them take her, hooking her up to needles and tubes, knowing that he was too broken and weak right then to try to heal her himself.

Knowing that she'd never once even evinced interest in the Turn, as applied to herself, so he had no right to force it on her, even to save her life. And she was Nephilim, which meant the Turn wasn't even an option.

That was the realization that had sent him into the darkest reaches of hell.

She could have *died*, and it would all have been his fault.

Entirely his fucking fault.

After the ambulance had screamed away with its precious cargo, he'd managed to call the Shadows and crawl into the Between. Managed to make it to his house, where the byways dumped him out in the middle of the ballroom, where everyone still gathered.

Bram Stoker let out a mighty *woof* when the blackened, smoke-smothered *thing* that was Bane's broken body fell into the room. After that, Bane switched into and out of moments of lucidity while Meara and Edge and Luke all gave him blood, since theirs was so much more powerful than bagged blood.

While they talked over him about retaliation and revenge and plots.

When he finally looked up at them, finally had enough strength back to stand, he only said three words:

"They all die."

That night, Death rode the highways of Savannah, borne on currents of air and on steel horses. Bane, Meara, Edge, and Luke tracked them all down—every single one of the blood-thralled humans and any of the werewolves still at large—any and all who were bound to the necromancers.

They killed them all.

They found the man who'd made the bomb and killed him, too.

The Chamber's messenger, they found in a hotel on the river, cringing in a corner when they smashed through the door to get to him.

"I'm sorry! I'm sorry. It wasn't supposed to happen," he babbled. "They called it off, once they learned what she was, but it was too late. The bomber was already on the job. But Constantin would never, they know what she is. Please. Please! They don't want her harmed, they just…"

His frantic begging faded off when he realized that what he'd been about to say—that they only wanted to abduct her for her blood—was no better.

"Where are they?"

The man cringed, and hopeless tears started to roll down his face. "I don't know. They don't trust anybody with that kind of information."

Bane left the messenger alive so he could deliver a *new* message.

"You tell Constantin, Sylvie, and the Chamber this," he told the terrified messenger, whose mask of calm had vanished at the sight of Bane's blood-covered face. "I will salt the entire eastern seaboard of this country with their ashes if they *ever* set foot here again." He picked the man up by the throat. "*Do. You. Understand?*"

The coward cringed and babbled and huddled on the floor after Bane dropped him, and Meara looked down at his cowering and crying with utter contempt.

"I think he understands," she told Bane.

"Not enough. Not yet," he roared.

Meara stopped him before he could do more than break one of the man's arms.

"He needs to *die.*"

"I know, but not yet. Not until after he delivers that message. He's nothing, Bane. Let's go."

And then, having found and destroyed some of his prey, but with no way to track the necromancers, Bane returned to the roof of the building opposite the hospital and planned to stand guard over Ryan until dawn forced him into the dark.

• • •

Meara joined him later that night, climbing up to where he sat in his lonely vigil.

Locked out of Ryan's life. Her heart.

Her sunlight and goodness.

By his own choice.

He'd watch over her every single second of every single night, and he'd hire professionals to watch over her all day. Mercenaries. Hardened men who would throw themselves in front of a bullet, for what Bane would pay them.

He'd already reached out to the local witches' coven to ask that they ward her in every way they could possibly imagine. Her home. Her car. Her friend, Annie. Hell, he'd pay them enough to ward the entire fucking hospital.

"You can't do this," Meara said gently. "Torture yourself. Why don't you just go to her?"

"Because I can't keep her safe if she's anywhere near me," he managed to say, with a voice gone rusty with disuse. "I've known all along that I might have to kill her. Now I know that being with me might do the job for me. I can't do that. Not to her."

"Doesn't she deserve to make that choice herself?"

"No."

"They know what she is. They'll come for her, whether she's with you or not."

"That's why I'll make sure none of them can ever get anywhere near her. If they step foot in Savannah again, they die."

"Bane—"

"*No.*"

He closed his eyes against the concern on her face. When he opened them again, Meara was gone. He waited until the dawn began to strengthen, almost past the edge of when he could safely travel through the Between, and then he went home with plans to pace the floors, reading hourly check-ins from the security team, until dusk.

When he walked into the house, Hunter, pale but strong, stood staring at him with glowing red eyes. He shouldn't have been able to be awake past dawn, but nothing else about Hunter's Turn had gone according to tradition, either, so Bane wasn't surprised.

"You survived the Turn." Bane wanted to feel glad, but only a dim sense of relief made it through his grief.

"Yeah. Harder than I imagined, though." Hunter's lips pulled back in a grimace, and his new fangs extended.

"I'm sorry for that. I had no idea it would be such an ordeal, or I wouldn't have—"

"Don't say that. I'm glad not to be dead."

"Not dead is good," Bane agreed grimly.

"They told me. About what's happening. The doctor and the Chamber. Everything we have to face." Hunter stumbled a step and put a hand out to steady himself.

"*We* don't have to face anything. You should leave. Get far away from Savannah and everyone who knew you here. Running into people from your life before can be difficult. And you don't need to be any part of this coming war, either."

Hunter's eyes flared an even hotter red. "You don't know me at all if that's what you believe."

Bane whirled and smashed his fist through the wall. "I don't know *anything*. Don't you understand? I love her. I love her, and I put her in danger."

"Seems like her own Nephilim nature is putting her in

danger now," Hunter said, folding his arms over his chest. "You're just going to leave her out there on her own?"

"Not on her own. I have people protecting her night and day," he snarled. "She's better off away from me, though."

"Is she?" Hunter shook his head. "You're a damn fool to let her go."

"You don't understand," Bane snarled. "She's in danger just from being near me. The Chamber will never stop coming after my territory."

"And what does that matter? You think your pride or your damn *territory* matter one fucking bit compared to losing someone you love? Ask me about Hope someday, and I'll tell you what pride is worth." Hunter's face was stark with remembered pain. "It's worth exactly nothing, my friend. Exactly nothing."

Before Bane could respond, the hours-old vampire turned his back and walked away.

CHAPTER FORTY-FIVE

Two days later…

When Meara finally answered her phone—and Ryan had only gotten the number by sending Annie to threaten Katrina the shop owner with a lawsuit—she didn't open with hello or how are you. Instead, she only spoke six devastating words.

"He doesn't want to see you."

"Meara! Just tell me. Is he okay?"

"He's…he's alive."

And then she hung up.

Ryan finished dressing, having finally talked the doctors into releasing her, although they couldn't understand how she could have healed so quickly. It's not like she could tell them that she'd been *literally* touched by an angel.

Her father. *Ramiel.*

One of the Fallen.

He'd only stayed for less than a minute, healed her, and said he'd be back. And every minute of every hour since then, she'd tried—and failed—to remember exactly what he looked like. There had been light.

Lots of glowing, golden light.

Warmth.

An overwhelming sense of tremendous power and tremendous peace.

And then she'd woken up the next morning, completely healed. It had taken some fast talking to keep anyone from checking her bandages or repeating any x-rays. In the end, only the fact that she was a doctor on staff and was threatening to check herself out AMA—Against Medical Advice—convinced them to let her go. Annie had gone home, finally, to get some sleep, so now was the time to escape.

She was going straight to Bane's house, and he'd damn well see her and talk to her, whether he *wanted* to or not. She was furious.

Livid.

Who the hell did he think he was to make her decisions for her?

Because that's exactly what this was. He was afraid, because she'd been hurt. He didn't want her to get hurt again.

She got it. She felt the same way about him.

But Bane had said *forever.* And *promise you won't leave me.*

And, unless she was totally crazy, he'd been about to tell her he loved her. Now, though, he thought he could get rid of her so easily, for her *own good*, no doubt.

"Oh no, you won't, you arrogant ass," she told her empty room.

She was *Nephilim*, not some ordinary human he could brush off. She'd kick his *ass* if he even thought about trying. Moving slowly, in case anybody saw her and wondered why she'd healed so *miraculously*—talk about your puns—she picked up her backpack and headed out.

She had a few stops to make on her way to convince a vampire that he needed her in his life.

CHAPTER FORTY-SIX

The doorbell rang at five minutes past sunset, and Mrs. C called out that she'd get it.

Bane, pacing the floor from kitchen to parlor and back, over and over, with brief breaks to check his phone for status reports, barely registered his housekeeper answering the door until she called his name.

"What do you mean, she left the hospital? Where the fuck is she? What am I paying you a damn fortune for if you can't keep track of one wounded woman?" he shouted into the phone.

Mrs. C leaned around the open door and stared at him, wide-eyed. "Bane? I—it's for you."

"Send them away," he snarled and kept pacing.

"*Nooo*, I think you need to see this."

He started to snap at her, but Mary Jo didn't deserve to bear the brunt of his rage, so he walked over and yanked the door open.

A young man holding the strings to what looked like dozens of balloons stood on his porch.

"Are you Mr. Bane?"

Bane just looked at him, and the boy's face paled.

"He is," Mrs. C said, smiling broadly.

Traitor.

"I have to sing, dude," the boy said, shrugging. Then, much to Bane's horror and Mrs. C's amusement, he burst into song.

Happy birthday to you
Happy birthday to you
You're wrong, wrong, wrong, but I'm coming for you
Happy birthday to you

Bane stared at him, willing him to stop. Wondering why his own skin was trying to leap off his body. When the kid finally quit making that hideous noise, Bane glared at him and said the first thing that came to mind.

"It's not my birthday."

And then the reason electric sparks were jumping off Bane's nerve endings stepped out from the side of the porch, where she'd been hidden.

"Don't scare my balloon guy," she said, a little smile playing on her luscious lips.

Ryan.

He automatically started to reach for her but then came to his senses. First, because he needed to stay away from her. Second, because he didn't want to burst into flames right there in front of the singing messenger.

Ryan smiled at him, her entire heart in her eyes, and then she handed the boy a fistful of cash. "Thanks."

"Sure. Good luck." The kid glanced at Bane and then leaned over to whisper to Ryan, handing her the balloons. "He's *hot*."

"I know," she said, smiling.

"It's not my birthday," Bane repeated, like a fool, after the kid left.

She ducked under his arm when he belatedly tried to block her from coming inside. "But you *are* wrong, and I *did* come for you, so the song was mostly right."

Mrs. C hugged Ryan, glanced at Bane, and then took

the balloons. "I'll just go…bake a pie or something. Make some soup."

"I don't want to see you, Doctor," he said, his voice harsh, hating himself for the necessary falsehood. His mind shouted out a plea that was entirely the opposite:

Please come back to me, before I die of loneliness.

Ryan poked him in the chest. "Liar. You love me. You said *forever*."

"I was just trying to get in your pants, *Nephilim*," he lied, his heart shattering. Vicious and cruel, both, should be enough to drive her away. It was for her own good. For her safety.

For her *life*. "Worked, didn't it?"

She blushed but stood her ground. "I got in your pants, too, *vampire*. No. *No*. You don't get to choose my life for me."

She took a deep breath, and he had to physically step away to keep from touching her. To keep from falling to his knees and begging her to stay.

Instead, he said nothing at all.

"I don't know how it happened so fast, but I'm in love with you, Bane," she said, each word a knife in his heart. "But I want to be your equal, not the poor woman you have to protect. I'm not going anywhere until you admit you love me, too. And we already know you can't use compulsion on me. You'll have to bodily throw me out of the house to get rid of me, and even then, I'll keep coming back and coming back and coming back. You *love* me. You all but admitted it. What are you going to do about it?"

He slowly blew out the breath he'd been holding during the speech that had shredded his soul. He knew her tenacity, knew she meant what she said. So he changed his tactics and went for honesty.

"Yes. I love you. But how I feel doesn't matter. These are *warlocks*. Worse—necromancers. And they don't hesitate to hire humans with guns and bombs. The Chamber wants my territory, and now that they know about you, they want you. They want your blood. You need to move. I've just been waiting for you to heal, so I could send people to help you pack up and leave town. Far away from me and far away from Savannah. *Do you hear me*?" He was shouting by the end of his damn speech, shaking her by the shoulders, but he didn't see an ounce of fear on her beautiful face.

No, what he saw was defiance.

"I'm not going anywhere without you," she shouted right back. "And I don't care about the damn warlocks."

CHAPTER FORTY-SEVEN

Before Bane could even think up a response, the door blew off its hinges so hard it smashed against the wall.

"That's all right, Doctor," drawled the necromancer standing on Bane's porch. "We care about you."

Bane yanked Ryan out of the way and slammed every bit of magic he could channel at Constantin in a punishing torrent—and every bit of magic he could channel was a *lot* of fucking magic.

The warlock flew backward, but he regained his equilibrium in mid-air and hurled a spell at Bane, who easily dodged it, just before he saw what was coming up from the river toward the house.

"Oh, *fuck*."

It was an army of the dead. Walking up out of the river and trudging toward them, no doubt intent on killing every single one of them—except for Ryan. The necromancers would do far worse to her.

"Over my dead body," he growled, realizing it was all too likely. There must be more than a hundred of them, trudging inexorably closer and closer, step by shambling step.

Ryan ducked beneath his arm to see, and then she started shouting. "Meara! Edge! Luke! *Everybody!* We need all hands on deck!"

"Not you," he snarled at her. "You go upstairs and hide. Now!"

"Fuck *that*! I'm Nephilim. We fight!" She pointed. "And there's Sylvie. I owe that bitch."

A deep, roaring bark sounded from the kitchen, and Bram Stoker flew out of the doorway and started toward them, his fur standing straight up and his lips curled back from his teeth. The Cassidys were right behind him, and they both carried shotguns.

"If it's a battle they're looking for, we're going to give them the fight of their lives!" Mrs. C shouted. Her cheeks were flushed, and she had boxes of ammo sticking up out of her apron pockets.

Her husband nodded, face grim. "We've defended this house before, and we'll do it again. No way do those bastards hurt any of our family."

Bane had no words, so he just shook his head and stepped out onto the porch. "Constantin, is this all you've got? I thought you'd bring some of your warlock friends. Instead, you're hanging around with a bunch of dead bodies because nobody alive wants anything to do with you, right? The Chamber must be scraping the bottom of the barrel to send the likes of you."

"I don't need help, Nightwalker." The necromancer turned and flung his arms out in a ridiculously melodramatic gesture that encompassed the oncoming dead. "Take the vampires, my people. Take them all, but keep the woman alive."

Meara's voice rang out from the roof. "I'm your Huckleberry."

A shadow of confusion crossed Constantin's face. "What?"

Beside him, Ryan laughed. "Good one, Meara! We'll

watch that one later tonight, after we kill these assholes!"

Just then, Sylvie jumped down from where she'd been hiding in the branches of one of the Southern Live Oaks and stalked toward them, the dead parting in a wave before her. "You didn't forget me, did you, you stupid Nephilim whore? I'm going to drain you dry, over and over, and make such delicious magic from your blood. Maybe even from your bones. You don't need all of those arms and legs, after all."

Ryan shuddered but then rolled up her sleeves. "If you want me, come and get me, Necro-Bitch." She started forward, shoving balloons out of her way, but Bane caught her by the back of her shirt.

"*No.*"

She laughed and then grabbed his face and kissed him, hard. "Nice try. But you don't get to tell me no about this, either." And then she twisted out of his grasp, jumped off the porch, and raced toward Sylvie.

Bane roared with frustration, but before he could go after her, the fight was on. The first swarm of the undead had reached the lawn, and he waded in, blasting them with magic and also using his hands, feet, and the long knife that had been sheathed at his side to stop them any way he could while he fought his way toward Constantin.

Edge and Luke descended on the horde of zombies like twin waves of destruction, swinging swords that they'd started carrying after the attack in the cemetery. And Meara—watching Meara was like taking a master class in graceful killing. She flew, danced, kicked, and twirled in an arabesque of destruction, and wherever she moved, the undead went down and stayed down.

But it wasn't enough. The more corpses that they stopped, the more that kept coming up out of the river. Constantin—far more powerful than Sylvie—must be calling bodies from every cemetery for miles around.

He was still doing it, too. Protected by a group of his undead, he stood with his eyes closed, still chanting. Waves of foul blood magic flowed out from where he stood.

Bane needed to get to him. *Now*.

But he also needed to protect Ryan. *Now*.

And he was suddenly, desperately afraid that there might not be time to do both.

• • •

Ryan's Nephilim magic—for that's what it surely was— came easily to her call now. Whether something about the explosion had finished clearing whatever block or binding had kept her from her power before, or whether meeting her father in person had done it, she was ready and willing to use the magic of life and light against the forces of death and darkness.

"Apparently, Nephilim are *freaking poets, too*," she shouted at Sylvie, who was stalking toward her, the zombies falling away from the path between them.

"Bring it, little angel spawn," the warlock spat. "I'm going to enjoy torturing you for what you did to my face."

She tilted her head toward the light, and Ryan saw for the first time that the entire right side of the warlock's face had been horribly burned.

The healer in her felt bad about it, for a second or two.

The warrior in her wanted to shout out her triumph.

"Nobody could have deserved it more," she called out, taunting the evil bitch.

"I'll show you what *you* deserve!" Sylvie shrieked, throwing her hands into the air and then *shoving* them toward Ryan, who could feel the wave of magic even before she saw and smelled the stench of the dark shadows arrowing toward her.

"Nice try!" Ryan raised her own hands and built a wall of light with her mind a mere second or two before she built it in reality. The cloud of blood magic broke harmlessly against it like an ocean wave against a stone seawall. Even the rank stench dissipated.

"Good beats evil every time," she shouted, laughing. "Now, let's try this!"

With that, Ryan imagined a battering ram made of pure light and hurled it at the warlock, who watched, seemingly frozen with shock, only dodging at the last possible moment.

"Not so fast, Nephilim. I've been doing this far longer than you," Sylvie purred, and then she started throwing spear after spear of magic, each more powerful than the last, at Ryan, who was using every ounce of her brand-new power to block them.

When Sylvie jerked her chin to the side, Ryan was too exhausted to even wonder why, until the zombies crashed into her from behind, taking her down to the ground, face first.

Suddenly, Sylvie was standing above her, and the last thing Ryan saw was the warlock's boot coming for her face.

Behind her, Bram Stoker howled.

CHAPTER FORTY-EIGHT

Bane saw Ryan go down, heard the dog howl when several of the undead started hitting him, and, still covered in the animated corpses attacking him, roared his fury out to the skies. Meara screamed and shot over to Bram Stoker, dealing destruction to the undead in her path, but more of them kept rising up out of the river, coming and coming and coming.

Bane spun in a 360-degree turn, slicing a pointed wave of magic around him as he went, decapitating and cutting any undead near him in half. Then he shot up into the air to go to Ryan, but another wave of necromancy smashed into him and knocked him back down.

"I expected more from a vampire who's rumored to have defeated the Chamber before," Constantin shouted, sneering.

A wave of black despair threatened to swamp Bane. Ryan was down. If she died…

If she died, the world could *burn*. A berserker rage rose in him and the tips of his fingers began to glow as red as he knew his eyes must be. The necromancers would die, now.

Everyone would die.

Before he could hurl the blast of power gathering inside him at the necromancer, Bane heard Ryan's voice rise above the cacophony of the battle. "I'm fine, Bane. Kick his ass while I take care of this one."

Relief and a fierce burst of pride swept through him

and gave his magic far more power than he'd ever had before. He levitated up and up, until he was floating nearly six feet over the heads of the incoming dead.

"Oh, look, the vampire can fly," Constantin sneered. "I don't know why I was afraid of you. You're nothing. You're *nobody.*"

"Who I am is the vampire who's going to kill you," Bane told him, the fire of his rage amplifying his voice, until it boomed across the field of battle, making everyone freeze and look up at him. Then he smashed his magic out over the field in a bone-shattering wave that destroyed all the corpses between himself and Constantin.

Still more kept dragging themselves out of the river and onto the bank, though. More and more and more.

"You're not powerful enough to defeat me," the necromancer shrieked, forcing his magic into the dead, compelling them to do his bidding.

"You picked the wrong battle, necromancer." Bane hurled a bolt of magic at Constantin and then shielded himself from the return shot. He leapt up into the air again, deflecting Constantin's attacks, and sent another bone-crushing wave of power at the oncoming dead.

"There are more coming!" Luke shouted. "Look over there, behind the trees, in the direction of Bonaventure!"

Before Bane could locate the new threat, a roar like thunder preceded thirty or more motorcycles that poured into the driveway and yard. The Vampire Motorcycle Club had arrived—and they'd brought some of the werewolves with them. The vampires and wolves jumped off their bikes and started laying waste to the hordes of undead, smashing through them like the Georgia Bulldog offense on a really great fucking day.

Bane looked across the field and smiled. "Now it's just you and me, necromancer."

Constantin, starting to look a hell of a lot less certain than he had before, took a step back. "I'll live to fight another day, vampire. And we *will* have your territory. The Chamber is moving into North America, and we're starting *here*, just like we did hundreds of years ago." He raised his arms again, but this time, Bane could feel the necromancer call to his dark magic.

And he was ready for it.

Instead of trying to block or defend, he stepped sideways into the Between and—half a second later—stepped out directly in front of Constantin's ugly, sneering face.

"Not this time, asshole."

And then he ripped the necromancer's head off and, using an extra *push* of magic, set it on fire and hurled it all the way down the hill into the river.

• • •

Ryan caught the warlock's boot in both hands and twisted, hard, because she'd learned self-defense a long time before she'd ever been involved with magic, warlocks, or vampires. Then she punched her in the side of the knee, dislocating her patella and knocking her to the ground, where Sylvie lay clutching her leg and shrieking.

Ryan jumped up off the ground. "That's *anatomy class*, you witch!"

Sylvie, her shrieks turning into whimpers, started to

chant, and Ryan crouched down and punched her in the face. "I don't think so. You're done here. Give up, or I'll really hurt you."

"I will. I surrender! Please don't hurt me anymore," the warlock begged, tears starting to run down her face.

"That's what I thought." Ryan stood again and turned to find Bane—to see what was happening—and suddenly, Meara raced past her, carrying a freaking *sword*.

Before Ryan could utter a word, Meara swung the sword with one powerful motion, and Sylvie's head rolled off her shoulders and down the hill.

Ryan stared, speechless, and then slowly turned to face Meara. "What? But…but I defeated her. She was—"

"She was getting ready to stab you in the back," Meara said, pointing to a slim dagger still clutched in the headless body's hands. "And the blade is undoubtedly poisoned, because that's what they do. *Putains de démonistes.*"

Ryan started shaking with the aftershock of adrenaline and a healthy dose of belated fear, but then she whirled around to find Bane, only then noticing that every single zombie—and there must have been hundreds of them— was down. The magic that had animated them was gone.

"Bane!" She grabbed Meara. "Where is he? Did he—is he?"

A rush of wind from directly above her alerted Ryan to his presence before she saw him. Before his feet even touched the ground, he was pulling her into his arms.

"You're unharmed?" She frantically searched him for evidence of any injury. "I was so afraid for you!"

He closed his eyes, clutched her to him, and started swearing in something that sounded like Old English. "*You* were afraid for *me*? I'm an extremely powerful, three-hundred-year-old vampire! I was terrified for *you*. Never do that to me again!"

She started to kiss him but then stopped, frantic again. "Bram Stoker! Is he okay? The zombies—"

Rowf!

The dog, limping only a little, came galloping over to them, leaping over the piles of bones and bodies on his way. She knelt and hugged his giant, furry neck and cried a little, but then she checked him for injuries.

Bane, his hand on her shoulder, as if he couldn't bear to stop touching her, blew out a deep breath. Meara walked up and stood on Ryan's other side, facing the carnage on the grounds.

"Brave boy. He'll need a few sutures. I'll take care of it inside," she told Meara and Bane.

When she stood, giving Bram Stoker one final hug first, she finally got a real look at the extent of the destruction.

"Oh my God," she whispered. The remains of hundreds of corpses, two warlocks, and three men wearing MC vests covered the grass.

A tall, dark man who carried himself like a leader—like a warrior—walked over to them.

"Reynolds," Bane said, holding out his hand. "Thanks for the backup."

They shook hands, and Reynolds nodded to Meara and Ryan. "We lost one of ours and two of yours, I'm sorry to say. But better this than the thousands of people Savannah would have lost to these monsters."

"I'm sorry for your loss," Bane said. "And thanks again. Do you want to borrow a truck to transport your man?"

The alpha nodded, and Luke, bloody but alive, walked over to them. "I'll take care of it. What are we going to do with all these bodies and skeletons, though?"

Bane started to shake his head, but then a beam of brilliant light pierced through the night sky, spearing to the ground directly in front of them, and a voice like thunder shattered the night sky, causing everybody still on the field to flinch.

I MAY HAVE AN IDEA ABOUT THAT.

Ryan, her heart rate still not quite back to normal, smiled.

"Hello, Dad."

CHAPTER FORTY-NINE

Three hours later, Ryan stepped out of the shower and smiled at Bane. "Am I a badass or what?"

He held out a towel, grinning, loving everything about having her here, with him, safe.

And *naked*. Especially naked.

"Oh, you're definitely a badass."

"I'm hoping my father will show up periodically to actually teach me how to be what I am instead of just popping by in times of crisis," she said, toweling off her hair and then wrapping a dry towel around her luscious body.

"I hope we don't have any more times of crisis," he said fervently, pulling her into his arms and holding her so tightly she could never, ever escape. "I saw you go down when Sylvie attacked you. I love you, Dr. St. Cloud, and don't you ever frighten me like that again, or I'll have to take desperate measures."

"Such as?"

"They're so desperate, I haven't even dreamed them up yet."

She laughed, and he kissed her, because he couldn't help it.

He kissed her, because she'd brought life, and love, and hope into his heart.

He kissed her, because he intended to spend eternity kissing her.

And then pulled off the towel she wore, wrapped a blanket around her, lifted her into his arms, and flew out the open window. Holding her tightly in his embrace, exactly where he planned to keep her, forever.

She clung to him, but there wasn't a trace of fear on her beautiful face. Instead, she let out a joyful whoop.

"We're flying! Bane, we're flying!"

He laughed and flew up and out over the river to show her the beauty of the moon on the water. To give her the sky.

To give her the world.

"I love you, my warrior goddess. And I choose you, now and forever, to be part of my life. We'll fight our battles together."

"I love you, too. And you promise to let me stand by your side, till death do us not part, and never lock me in a room again?" She kissed him and then started laughing. "And take me flying whenever I ask? Wait! Do you think angels—Nephilim—can fly, too? I need to ask my father, if he ever shows up again. Or maybe just try it!"

He groaned, getting the sudden visual of his fearless doctor jumping off the roof of the house to experiment with flying.

"Maybe only try it when I'm with you, okay?" He kissed her again. "And anyway, why would I bother trying to lock you in? I hear you're great at picking locks."

"I'm great at a lot of things," she told him in a very sultry voice. "Maybe when we're done flying, I can show you a few of them."

He shouted out a laugh, tightened his embrace, and flew higher and faster, showing her Savannah—their territory, their *home*.

Their future. Together, forever, for the rest of their lives.

"I am *very* unreliable," she suddenly said, biting a very sensitive spot on his neck and then throwing her head back, laughing. "Savannah is beautiful from up here, too. Almost as beautiful as you."

"Almost as beautiful as *you*," he growled, his body hardening, his mind hazing over with need. "Also, exactly how unreliable are you?"

"I don't—*oh*!" Her eyes widened when his fingers stroked over the center of her heat and then slipped inside. "You can't—oh, *yes. Yes*, you can. Please."

He slowed the speed of their flight, pulled her leg higher on his waist, adjusted his pants and the edge of her blanket, and then thrust inside her all the way to the hilt, growling with the sheer pleasure of claiming this woman. His woman.

Now, here, and always.

"Oh, my, oh, *oh*!" She shuddered, digging her fingers into his shoulders and tightening her body around his cock. Then she started moving her hips, at first in a slow swirl and then bucking against him, harder and harder, her eyelids fluttering with the sensation.

He drove into her, joy and triumph and possession and, far more important, *love* in every movement. In every touch and murmur.

She clung to him and conquered him, returning every bit of his passion. Returning every ounce of his love. Together, at last—as they meant to go on always—they claimed each other, there in the night sky.

He laughed when her skin began to glow.

"If there are reports of UFOs in the news, that will be my fault," she said, gasping, but then she had no more words, and neither did he, except *yes* and *more* and *now* and then the syllables of each other's name were jewels on their tongues, and the night sky lit up around them and inside them with the power of their completion.

When they could finally breathe again, she pulled his face to hers and kissed him, long and sweet. "This is going to be the best year, ever," she said, stretching. "I think I want to kiss you again."

His cock sprang back to instant attention. "I think I want to let you. Any time and any place you want."

She gave him the most wicked smile he'd ever seen and then deliberately looked down at his erection.

"And not necessarily on your mouth."

He groaned, turning them midair to return home, as his warrior trailed a hand down his chest. And lower. "Not to change the subject, but what did your father say to you about me? I'm suddenly expecting him to show up any minute and smite me for this. Although, for some reason, I can't actually remember what he looked like."

"Yeah, he has that effect. He seemed to be okay with you, but there were generalized threats of bloody death if you ever hurt me. Now shut up about my father."

He started to answer, something about the *bloody death*, maybe, but then she wrapped her hand around him, and his body turned to liquid fire. Again.

"You're going to have to marry me, you know," he told her.

"Oh! Really?" Her eyes lit up. "Are you asking? I'm getting a flying proposal?"

"Do you want me to get down on one knee?" He pulled her to him and kissed her again—long and deep—and she moaned.

"Maybe later," she said. "For now, yes. A thousand times yes. Yes and yes. You said you'd give me forever, and I plan to hold you to it."

"Forever and ever and ever," he said, pulling her closer and staring down into her beautiful eyes. "I love you, Dr. St. Cloud."

"I love you, too," she said, joy in every syllable. "Forever."

For the first time in centuries, Bane was glad to be immortal, now that he'd found the woman he planned to spend eternity loving.

Forever was going to be *wonderful*.

"Wait? Does your father have to give you away at the wedding? That may be a problem."

"Shut up and kiss me now," she demanded, pulling his head down to hers, as they flew back through the window into his—their—home.

And so he did.

Forever was his new favorite word.

EPILOGUE

A phone rang in a brightly lit conference room in London, and the man who answered would have appeared to the casual visitor to be in his early seventies.

This was irrelevant, since Lord Alastair Neville was not, strictly speaking, a man, and he never, ever had casual visitors.

He neither offered a greeting nor waited to hear one. "Is he dead?"

After listening to the response, the man gently placed his phone on the table, exactly parallel to the pen that lay next to it, and then he turned to look at the twelve other people in the room, all of whom, like himself, wore the triangle on their left wrists.

"We have a problem."

ACKNOWLEDGMENTS

Thank you to my amazing team at Entangled: Liz Pelletier, Stacy Abrams, Jessica Turner, Bree Archer (oh, that cover art!), Meredith Johnson, Lydia Sharp, Curtis Svehlak, and Jessica Meigs (sorry about my comma abuse problem!). We had to rethink publishing to cope with the pandemic, and you are all rock stars!

To my agent, Kevan Lyon: Thanks for your patience and sense of humor.

To my readers: Thank you for being part of my worlds for so many years. I appreciate you more than I can ever say.

To Navy Guy, College Princess, and Law School Ninja: I love you more than the universe.

Author's Note: I thought long and hard about incorporating the pandemic in this book but ultimately decided against it. So many readers write to thank me for the small oasis of respite and pleasure that my books provide in challenging times, so I honored that by keeping the world of the Vampire Motorcycle Club coronavirus-free. I offer my best wishes and hopes that you and your loved ones are safe and well.

FURY
UNLEASHED

Maccus Fury, a fallen angel, is trying hard to keep his sanity. Seems being an assassin might be catching up with him. Now, Heaven, or Hell, has sent a beautiful assassin to kill him. *Lovely.* She's pretending to seduce him, and he's okay with that. She's smart and snarky—but she has no idea what she's walked into. And he's more than peeved that they only sent one person. They're going to need an army if they want him dead.

Morrigan Quill is one of Hell's bounty hunters. She sold her soul to keep her sister safe, and now she's working off her contract by catching bad guys and dragging them back to hell. When Lucifer makes her a new offer—that's definitely too good to be true—she can't say no. All she has to do is kill a powerful and crazy-hot fallen angel, who will totally kick her ass in battle.

Good thing he won't see what's coming next.

AMARA
an imprint of Entangled Publishing LLC

A modern-day Game of Thrones *meets JR Ward's*
Black Dagger Brother series.

THE
ROGUE
KING

by Abigail Owen

Kasia Amon is a master at hiding. Who—and what—she is makes her a mark for the entire supernatural world. *Especially* dragon shifters. To them, she's treasure to be taken and claimed. A golden ticket to their highest throne. But she can't stop bursting into flames, *and* there's a sexy dragon shifter in town hunting for her...

As a rogue dragon, Brand Astarot has spent his life in the dark, shunned by his own kind, concealing his true identity. Only his dangerous reputation ensures his survival. Delivering a phoenix to the feared Blood King will bring him one step closer to the revenge he's waited centuries to take. No way is he letting the feisty beauty get away.

But when Kasia sparks a white-hot need in him that's impossible to ignore, Brand begins to form a new plan: claim her for himself...and take back his birthright.